Acclaim for Adrian McKinty's

THE ISLAND
A Thriller

"Extraordinary." —T. J. Newman, *New York Times* bestselling author of *Falling*

"Unrelenting suspense. It reminded me a little of *Jaws*."
—Stephen King

"What a shock it was to discover how deeply invested I became in the fate of the characters of *The Island,* a propulsive, insane story about an all-out struggle for survival between an Australian family and a group of American interlopers...Heather, who starts as a clueless young bride who expects her older husband to take care of her and has no love for his children, becomes not just a Charlize Theron–worthy badass but also a great stepmother who helps two damaged kids come into their own."
—Sarah Lyall, *New York Times Book Review*

"Brilliant and relentless...You'll never go on vacation the same way again." —Don Winslow, *New York Times* bestselling author of *City on Fire*

"Adrian McKinty has created a perfect niche for himself: the high-concept domestic thriller...In *The Island,* he returns to the concerns of families, this time with a stepmother involved, and asks yet another question, often one that comes at midnight, on a darkened road: What would you do if you accidentally killed someone?...McKinty is a master, speeding up and slowing down the narrative at just the right time, turning this midnight morality play into a bonafide summer thrill ride."

—Tod Goldberg, *USA Today*

"One of this summer's best standalone thrillers."

—*Boston Globe*

"Thriller fans, think nothing can shock you anymore? Check out *The Island*. It's an adrenaline rush from beginning to end, with its terrifying chase scenes and truly disturbing plot bordering on horror."

—Sarah Jinee Park, *Reader's Digest*

"Wow, this book left me breathless and on the edge of my seat from the very first page—this is thriller writing of a high order. Gripping and unpredictable, prepare to be hooked and pumped full of adrenaline as McKinty deftly weaves a compulsively readable plot with characters that you are rooting for. No one does high-stakes tension like McKinty. Put *The Island* at the top of your TBR—you won't regret it."

—Sarah Pearse, *New York Times* bestselling author of *The Sanatorium*

"A tense, adrenaline-fueled thriller." —Angela Haupt, *Time*

"The locals aren't always friendly in vacation hot spots, but on the closed-to-the-public island Tom sneaks his family on to for fun, they're out to kill. Maybe Disney World next time?"

—*People*

Other Mysteries and Thrillers by Adrian McKinty

THE MICHAEL FORSYTHE TRILOGY
Dead I Well May Be

The Dead Yard

The Bloomsday Dead

THE SEAN DUFFY SERIES
The Cold Cold Ground

I Hear the Sirens in the Street

In the Morning I'll Be Gone

Gun Street Girl

Rain Dogs

Police at the Station and They Don't Look Friendly

STAND-ALONES
Hidden River

Fifty Grand

Falling Glass

The Sun Is God

The Chain

AS EDITOR (WITH STUART NEVILLE)
Belfast Noir

THE
ISLAND

ADRIAN McKINTY

BACK BAY BOOKS

Little, Brown and Company

New York   Boston   London

Back Bay Books / Little, Brown and Company
Hachette Book Group
1290 Avenue of the Americas, New York, NY 10104
littlebrown.com

Originally published in hardcover by Little, Brown and Company, May 2022
First Back Bay trade paperback edition, June 2023

Back Bay Books an imprint of Little, Brown and Company, is a division of Hachette Book Group, Inc. The Little, Brown name and logo are trademarks of Hachette Book Group, Inc.

The publisher is not responsible for websites (or their content) that are not owned by the publisher.

The Hachette Speakers Bureau provides a wide range of authors for speaking events. To find out more, go to hachettespeakersbureau.com or email hachettespeakers@hbgusa.com.

Little, Brown and Company books may be purchased in bulk for business, educational, or promotional use. For information, please contact your local bookseller or the Hachette Book Group Special Markets Department at special.markets@hbgusa.com.

Oodgeroo Noonuccal, "Not My Style," from *My People*. Copyright © 1992 by Oodgeroo. Reproduced with permission of John Wiley & Sons Ltd.

ISBN 9780316531283 (hardcover) / 9780316417020 (large print) / 9780316436199 (international) / 9780316540544 (Canadian) / 9780316531290 (paperback)
LCCN 2021939745

Printing 3, 2023

LSC-C

Printed in the United States of America

Be not afeard; the Isle is full of noises,
sounds and sweet airs, that give delight and hurt not.

William Shakespeare, *The Tempest,* 1611

Stuff myself
Of the bitter and the sweet,
Before,
that thing,
that thing,
outside
Comes.

Oodgeroo Noonuccal, "Not My Style," 1971

THE ISLAND

A crow with a skeptical yellow eye was watching her from the lightning-struck eucalyptus tree.

The crow was death.

If it called out, she was dead. If it flew toward Jacko and he turned to look, she was dead.

The crow observed her with a half-turned head.

She crawled through the brittle grass, reached the tree trunk, stopped, and caught her breath.

She wiped the sweat from her forehead with the bottom of the T-shirt. She sucked the moisture from the shirt as best she could.

She composed herself for a minute and then crept past the tree until she reached the edge of the heath. There was nothing now but beach between her and Jacko. No vegetation. No cover. There wasn't much point crawling anymore.

Slowly, ever so slowly, she got to her feet.

Carefully, she moved the machete from her left to her right hand. It was a heavy old thing, caked with rust. She gripped the split wooden handle and hoped it wouldn't fall to pieces when she swung it.

Steadying herself, she cautiously advanced.

She had killed before—salmon, trout, duck.

This was different, though, wasn't it? Very different.

This was a human being.

Jacko sat with his back to her, his legs astride the oil drum. The ancient rifle strapped over his shoulder looked lethal enough from here.

She walked closer, slowly, on bare feet over the stones and gravel.

In the bay something huge moved under the water not far from the shore. They had been right not to try to swim to safety. That was the scarred dorsal fin of a great white. Jacko had seen the shark too. He stood, slipped the rifle from his shoulder, and took a shot at it. The gun went off with an almighty bang that ripped through the stillness. Herons and gulls lifted from the mudflats.

She looked back at the crow.

It wasn't fazed. It was still perched on the highest blackened tree branch, gazing at her sideways. It had observed scenes like this play out before. No doubt it was expecting carrion soon.

Jacko had evidently missed. "Bugger!" he said to himself and stood there holding the rifle in both hands as the shark swam into the bay and was lost to view.

She waited for him to put the gun away, but he didn't.

He just stood there, staring at the water.

Olivia was still sprawled in front of him, unmoving.

The walkie-talkie hissed.

Jacko tugged the rifle bolt backward and a brass cartridge came flying out onto the sand. He pushed the bolt forward again and a new round slipped into the chamber.

If she made any sound now and he turned, she knew that he would shoot her point-blank in the chest. She knew guns and had pretended to like them to get time with her dad. She knew that the exit wound from a .303 at this range would be the size of a baseball.

She stood still, waiting for him to reshoulder the rifle, but Jacko just kept gazing at the sea, mumbling to himself.

The sun was behind her, and her shadow was inching into his field of view. She didn't like that. If there had been any other way of approaching him, she would have done it, but there was no other way. If he peered just to his left, he'd see the tip of her silhouette.

At least she was upwind.

The seagulls landed. The herons settled on the water.

The sun beat down on her exposed neck and arms.

Finally Jacko reslung the rifle over his shoulder and sat. He took out his lighter and cigarettes. He lit himself a smoke and put the lighter in his pocket.

She tried a step forward. The shadow moved too.

Jacko didn't flinch. She was fifteen feet away now. He leaned back and blew smoke at the sky. She took another step toward him. Toes, then sole, then heel. Placing her feet on the stony beach with the lightest of touches.

Toes, sole, heel.

Another step.

And another.

Until—

A short, sharp stab of perfect pain.

The jagged edge of an old bottle had pierced the skin of her heel.

She bit her lip to stop herself crying out. Her shadow was swaying from side to side, seemingly trying to attract Jacko's attention. Blinking away tears, she crossed her legs and sat. She was bleeding, but the bottle had not penetrated too deeply. She took hold of the glass fragment and eased it out of her foot. She licked her thumb and rubbed at the wound, and it began to feel better. She took a flat stone and held it against the cut. The bleeding slowed. It would have to do. She couldn't sit here all day.

She got to her feet again and took a few tentative steps.

Her treasonous shadow was well into Jacko's field of view now.

Closer.

She could read the writing on the back of his sweat-drenched yellow tank top. There was a red star above the words BINTANG BEER.

She could smell him. He reeked of body odor, cigarette smoke, engine oil.

It was quiet. The echoes of the rifle shot were gone and the only sound was the seawater rushing through the channel.

To her left the last hint of early-morning mist was evaporating in the sunlight. The air was expectant with the coming heat. It was going to be a scorcher. Easily over one hundred and ten degrees.

It was, she remembered, February 14. Funny how the seasons were reversed like that. Back home it would be in the forties or even colder.

Valentine's Day.

Exactly twelve months ago Tom had come in for his first massage-therapy appointment in the clinic in West Seattle. It had been snowing. When he'd lain down on the table, he still had snowflakes in his hair.

What a difference a year made.

She'd been childless then, on the verge of unemployment, living in that damp apartment near Alki Beach. Now she was married and responsible for two children and about to kill a man she barely knew on a different beach on the far side of the world.

She took three more careful steps and raised the machete.

1

The sign said ALICE SPRINGS 25, TENNANT CREEK 531, DARWIN 1,517.

She took that in for a second or two.

If they somehow missed Alice they would have to go another five hundred kilometers (over three hundred miles) before they could get food, water, or gas. She looked through the windows on either side of the empty highway and saw exactly nothing. The radio had been drifting in and out for the past twenty minutes but the signal, perhaps, was getting a little stronger. She could make out John Lennon singing about "old flat-top" who was "groovin' up slowly."

She could identify pretty much every Beatles song from just one or two bars or a snatch of lyrics. Her parents and almost everyone else on Goose Island had worshipped John Lennon, and with only intermittent TV and internet reception, music had been even more important. The song ended and a DJ began his patter. "That was 'Come Together,' the opening track of *Abbey Road*. And before that we had 'Hey Jude.' Can anyone tell me what album 'Hey Jude' was on?"

The DJ paused for his listeners to reply.

"It wasn't on any album, it was a seven-inch single," Heather whispered.

"Nah, don't call in. This isn't a competition. It's a trick question. 'Hey Jude' never got released on any of the original Beatles albums, just the compilations. Well, mates, I hope you enjoyed the balmy weather at midnight where we just hit the low temperature for the day—thirty-six degrees centigrade, which for you oldsters is ninety-six point eight degrees Fahrenheit."

Tom groaned in his sleep and she lowered the volume. He had a busy morning ahead, and every second of sleep he could get now would help him. She turned to look at the kids. They too were asleep. Although Owen had been on his phone until about a half an hour ago, hoping against hope that a Wi-Fi signal would materialize out of the desert. Olivia had conked out long before that. Heather checked that both their seat belts were still securely fastened and turned her attention back to the empty road.

She drove on.

Rattling transmission. Moths in the headlights. The drumming of the Toyota's wheels on the blacktop.

She reflected that the Mad Max movies had been skillfully edited to erase the actual tedium of driving through outback Australia. The landscape from Uluru had all been like this. It made one long for the comparative excitement of the morning traffic jam on the West Seattle Bridge. No other vehicles at all here; just the noise of the Toyota and the radio drifting in and out. There were no people around, but at a roadwork sign she could see big khaki machines covered in dust resting by the cutoff like slumbering mastodons.

She drove on and began to worry that she had taken a wrong

turn. There was no sign of a city or an airport. The GPS hadn't updated in a long time and according to it, she was lost in a vast blank nothingness somewhere in the Northern Territory.

Her uneasiness increased as the road surface got worse. She looked for signs of life ahead or out the side windows.

Nothing.

Damn it, back at the construction site she must have taken the wrong—

A big gray kangaroo suddenly appeared in the headlights.

"Shit!"

She slammed on the brakes, and the Toyota shuddered to a stop with an alarming amount of deceleration. Tom and the kids were flung forward, then pulled back again by their seat belts.

Tom groaned. Olivia whimpered. Owen grunted. But none of them woke.

"Wow," she said and stared at the kangaroo. It was still standing there, five feet in front of the car. Another second and they would have had a serious accident. Her hands were shaking. It was hard to breathe. She needed some air. She put the Toyota in park and, leaving the lights on, turned off the engine. She opened the door and got out. The night was warm.

"Scoot," she said to the big kangaroo. "I can't go on if you're in the middle of the road."

It didn't move. "Scoot!" she said and clapped her hands.

It was still staring at the car. How could it not understand the universal language of *scoot*?

"The headlights might have blinded it. Turn 'em off," a voice said from the darkness to her right.

Heather jumped and turned to see a man standing a few yards away from her in the desert. On learning that she was going to Australia, Carolyn had warned her about the "world's deadliest snakes and spiders," and when that hadn't worked she sent her a list of movies about hitchhikers murdered in the bush by maniacs. "It's an entire genre, Heather! It must be based on reality," Carolyn said.

Heather had watched only one of them, *Wolf Creek,* but that was scary enough for her.

"I didn't mean to startle you," the man said. Her heart was thumping, but the man's voice was so calm, gentle, and unthreatening that she was put immediately at ease.

"Um, sorry, what was that about the lights?" she asked.

"The headlights must have blinded it. Turn 'em off and give it a minute," the man said.

She reached into the Toyota and killed the lights. The man waited for a few moments and then walked onto the road. "Go on, big fella! Go on out of it!" he said and clapped his hands. The kangaroo turned its head, looked at both of them with seeming indifference, and then, at its own pace, hopped off into the night.

"Well, that was something. Thank you," Heather said and offered the man her hand. He shook it. He was about five foot six, around sixty years old, with dark, curly hair. He was wearing a red sweater with jean shorts and flip-flops. They had been in Australia now for nearly a week, but this was the first Aboriginal person Heather had come across. Out here in the middle of nowhere.

"You're not from around here, I reckon," the man said.

"No. Not at all. I'm Heather, from Seattle. Um, in America."

"I'm Ray. I'm not from around here either. We just come in for the show. Me mob, that is."

"Your mob?"

"Yeah, we just come in for the show. Come in every year."

As her eyes adjusted to the darkness she saw now that there were a lot of people with him in the desert. In fact, it was an entire camp, maybe twenty or thirty in all. Older people and young children. Most of them were sleeping but some were sitting around the embers of a fire.

"Where are you trying to get to? Alice?" Ray asked.

"I'm trying to reach the airport. If I keep going on this road—"

"Nah, they should have signed it better. This road'll take you on a big circle out into the bush. Just go back to where you saw the roadwork and go right. You'll be in Alice in fifteen minutes. There won't be any traffic."

"Thank you."

Ray nodded. They stood awkwardly for a moment. She found that she didn't quite want the conversation to end. "What's the show you're talking about?" she asked.

"The Alice Springs show. It's the big event of the year in these parts. The white fellas don't like us to be around town but they can't stop us coming in for the show."

"What is the show? A state fair?"

Ray nodded. "Something like that, I reckon. It's a livestock show but there's food and music. Rides for the kids. People come in from hundreds of miles away. It's usually in July. Having it earlier this year. Mobs from all over the territory, even some from Queensland. My mob's been walking in for three days."

She gazed at his "mob" again with wonder. These people—grandmothers, parents, young children—had been walking across this desert for three days?

"None of the nippers will have met an American before. Something for them to talk about. Mind if we say a quick hello?" Ray asked.

Heather spent a few minutes meeting Ray's family—the ones who were awake, anyway. His granddaughter Nikko, his wife, Chloe. Chloe admired her earrings and Heather begged her to take them as a thank-you gift for Ray's helping her back on the road again. The gift was accepted but not before Ray gave Heather a small penknife he'd made himself.

"I'm selling these at the show. Jarrah hardwood and meteor iron," he said.

"Meteor iron?"

"Yeah. From the one that came down at Wilkinkarra."

The penknife was carved with emus and kangaroos on one side and what she took to be the Milky Way on the other. It was beautiful. She shook her head. "I can't possibly take this! It must be worth hundreds of—"

"I'll be lucky to get twenty bucks each. Take it. It's fair dinkum. An exchange. The earrings for the knife. See the ring at the bottom of it? I've been told that if you put your keys on that and put it in the tray outside the metal detector with your phone, you can even fly with it. They just think it's a key-fob thing."

Ray was not to be talked out of the gift and she accepted it with good grace. She got in the Toyota, waved goodbye, and retraced her journey to the roadwork sign; this time she took the correct turn for Alice. As the town got closer, the road became more certain of itself. Houses and stores loomed out of the dark. She saw campfires with men and women gathered around them. More Indigenous people who, apparently, had all come in for the show.

The phone reacquired a GPS signal. The radio came back on. "At the next junction, take a left for Alice Springs airport," Google Maps suddenly announced in a perky Australian accent.

Heather was at the airport ten minutes later. She drove to the rental-car lot and turned the engine off. A sign said DO NOT FEED DINGOES, WILD DOGS, OR FERAL CATS above a drawing of a sad-looking dog and an indifferent cat. She made sure the doors were locked and let everyone sleep for a while longer.

"We're here," she said finally and gave Tom a gentle shake.

He stretched. "Oh, great. Thank you, honey. I would have driven some! You should have woken me. Any problems?"

"Not really, but there was a big kangaroo in the middle of the road," she said, attaching the penknife to her key chain.

"You saw a kangaroo and you didn't wake us? Come on, Heather!" Owen grumbled from the back seat before a yawn convulsed him.

They woke Olivia and got their bags and walked dazed and bleary-eyed into the terminal building. They were three hours early for the flight. Tom had never been late for a flight in his life and he wasn't going to start a bad habit now. The airport was deserted except for an overly made-up goth couple who apparently looked nothing like their passport photographs. When it was her turn at the X-ray machine, Heather smiled at an older female security officer.

"Goths these days, too much makeup and not nearly enough pillaging," she said. The woman thought about it for a second and then chuckled to herself. She waved the family through.

No one confiscated the penknife. Which was lucky for Heather. Because two days later it would save her life.

2

They walked a sleepy Owen and Olivia to the gate. The flight boarded early and they were the only passengers in the business section; in fact, they were practically the only passengers on the whole plane. Tom was a nervous flier. You wouldn't think from his professional persona that he ever got nervous, but he did. When he had first come into the massage clinic, Heather realized almost immediately that his back problems were not the result of "an old skiing injury" but tension that he was storing in his shoulders and lower back. Doctors were often the most skeptical about the benefits of a good massage, but all she had had to do was grind it out and he was 80 percent cured by the end of the first session. The fact that he kept returning for massage therapy had more to do with the connection that they had made than any "injury."

The flight attendants began making the safety announcements. She patted Tom's leg and he gave her a smile.

"I'm hungry," Owen said.

Heather fished in her backpack and offered him a granola bar. He shook his head. "Not those ones! Oh my God, Heather, you know I hate those ones!"

"We finished all the strawberry ones. This is all we have left," Heather said.

"Forget it, then!" Owen said. He put his headphones back on, pulled up his hood, plugged his phone into the charger, and restarted his driving game.

Heather did a little meditation while the plane taxied. *Everything is the path.* Her tiredness was the path, Owen's dirty look was the path, Tom's stress was the path, Olivia's beautiful, sleepy face was the path.

They took off just before the dawn, and the landscape from the left side of the aircraft was spectacular, the sun coming up over what seemed to be a vast red emptiness. Australia was almost as big as America but had less than a tenth of the population. A desert of ocher, red, and vermilion. Immense Saharas of iron-oxide nothingness interrupted by huge sandstone boulders that looked like grave markers for a long-extinct race of giants. She thought of Ray and his "mob" walking through that to get to the show. It beggared belief.

Her eyes were heavy. *I'll just close them for a minute,* she thought.

She woke when they touched down in Melbourne. She'd been dreaming about Seattle. Snow in the woods of Schmitz Park. "Where..." she began and then remembered.

The airport was like all airports, and the city from the back of a big SUV seemed like all cities. Tom was in the front chatting with Jenny, the conference rep. Heather sat in the back next to a still dozing Olivia. Owen was awake now, buried in his book about Australian snakes, his hood pulled up, not looking out the window. At dinner parties, one of the things Tom and his Generation X friends worried about were Millennials and Generation Zers not "engaging fully with the world," but Heather didn't blame Owen at all for not engaging. The world had taken his lovely mother from him just before his twelfth birthday. The world had shoved a skinny stranger who was supposed to be a "new mom" into his life. What a crock.

"As per your request, I've put you in an Airbnb on the beach," Jenny said, leaning around and looking at Heather. She was a young woman in her twenties, copper-haired, smiley.

"I didn't ask for—" Heather began.

"I asked for it, sweetie," Tom said. "So much better than the conference hotel. I checked it out online. It's great. A home away from home."

"Oh, sure, that's fine," Heather agreed, although secretly she had been looking forward to room service and a bit of pampering while Tom did his conference stuff.

They drove along the glittering Melbourne shoreline, past a lighthouse and a marina. There were palm trees and a beach and an indigo ocean.

Tom gently prodded Olivia. "This reminds me, why do you never see elephants hiding in palm trees?"

"Why?" Olivia asked sleepily.

"Because they're very good at it."

"No more dad jokes!" Olivia pleaded.

"I thought it was funny," Heather whispered.

Tom chuckled, took Heather's hand, and kissed it.

"But I wouldn't quit doctoring to go into stand-up," Heather added.

"Look at you, crushing my dreams," Tom said, slapping his hand to his forehead.

"Are you enjoying Australia, Heather?" Jenny asked.

"It's my first time ever outside of America! So, yes, it's all very exciting," Heather replied.

"Jet lag over?"

"Nearly, I think. We had two days in Sydney and two days in Uluru. So it's a little easier each morning."

"And what is it you do?" Jenny asked.

"I'm a massage therapist," Heather said. "I mostly look after the kids now, but I still have a couple of ornery clients who refuse to go to anyone else."

"Me mate Kath is a physiotherapist," Jenny said. "Kath's a riot. The stories she has. Strict, she is. Makes the old folks do their exercises. Kath says the difference between a physiotherapist and a terrorist is that you might have a chance of negotiating with a terrorist."

"I'm not quite a licensed physical therapist just yet," Heather said, although she knew Tom hated it when she mentioned that.

"Well, here's the bay," Jenny continued. "We're right on it. Weather will be perfect for the beach. You like the beach, eh, kids?"

Neither of the kids said anything. They turned down a quiet suburban road called Wordsworth Street and stopped at a large rectangular modernist house.

"There's a pool—you and the kids can swim while I work," Tom said with a big grin. He was very handsome when he smiled, Heather reflected. It made him look younger. Actually, he looked terrific for his age. Late thirties, you would have said, though he was forty-four. There was almost no gray in his hair, and his diet kept him lean. His hair was longer now than he normally let it grow and this morning it fell across his forehead like the wing of a young crow. According to the lengthy profile in the article on "Seattle's Best Doctors," his eyes were a "severe, chilly azure." But not to her. To her they were intelligent, playful blue eyes. Loving.

Jenny helped them carry their bags to the porch. "Anyone

need the toilet? Fab toilets in here. Heather? Looks like you gambled a little on a fart and lost, no?"

"Er, I'm fine."

"Great house. Nothing but the best for one of our key-note speakers. Guy who owns it is a wanker, but his place is a beaut."

They went inside a large open-plan living room furnished with leather sofas and cushions and expensive-looking rugs.

"Bedrooms are upstairs," Jenny said. "All with sea views."

"I have to do the meet and greet," Tom told Heather. "But I'll be back tonight. You just relax and have fun."

Heather kissed Tom on the cheek and wished him luck. "Take care, honey," she added, sitting down.

Jenny smiled. "I'll look after him. It's my job. Any questions?"

"Um, what's a wanker?" Heather asked.

"A compulsive masturbator," Jenny replied.

Heather sprang up from the sofa.

"It's not meant literally, sweetie," Tom said. "It's merely an expression."

And then, just like that, the rep and Tom were gone.

"Damn, look what Cardi B just posted!" Olivia said, showing Owen her phone.

"Oh my God. Why does she even bother? She's just a Walmart Nicki," Owen said.

Olivia laughed. "That thing about Drake? Drake wouldn't work with her."

"Are you guys talking about Drake...the rapper?" Heather attempted.

"Seriously, Heather. Don't even," Olivia said. "You don't know what we're talking about."

Owen was going to pile on but another big yawn took him

and then Olivia yawned too. Heather got them upstairs and ushered them each into a bedroom, which, mercifully, they did not fight over.

She picked out a room for herself and Tom. It overlooked the street and the lighthouse and was decorated in a kind of Aztec style. When she checked to see if the kids wanted anything to eat, she found both of them dozing on top of their beds.

Heather took off Owen's shoes and tucked him under the duvet. She did the same with Olivia and pulled the curtains closed and went back to the master bedroom. The conference organizers had provided them with what was presumably an expensive bottle of red wine. She opened it and poured herself a glass, kicked off her slip-ons, and stripped out of her T-shirt and jeans. She put on a robe and was about to slip into a shower when she noticed the door that led outside to a small but perfectly serviceable rooftop swimming pool.

Her bikini was packed away in one of the suitcases, but the rooftop was protected by a privacy wall. Heather carried the wineglass to the pool's edge, slipped out of the robe, and dropped into the cold blue water. She allowed herself to sink to the bottom of the pool and let the driving and the dust and her aches and pains ease slowly away.

This had all been so much more stressful than she'd been expecting, the kids 24/7 with no school or friends to play with. She opened her eyes and looked at the big indigo Australian sky through the lens of pool water. So like a Puget Sound sky but so strangely alien too.

She'd been holding her breath for thirty seconds.

She had known this was going to be a tough trip but she hadn't realized quite how tough. These past five days she'd barely had a moment to herself.

Children were fishing lines entangling you in their cruelties and wants and sticky fingers and dramas and disappointments. The mommy industrial complex made you think it was all going to be hugs and campfires and peewee soccer practices, and that was all bullshit.

She burst to the top of the water at thirty-five seconds. She gasped for air and found that she was on the verge of tears. She fought it and the tears went away. She shook her head and climbed out of the water.

Back inside, she went through the wrong door and found herself in a massive closet that was empty but for hundreds of coat hangers. The closet had a huge mirror at its rear. Heather hadn't seen a mirror in a few days. It sucked her in. Her mother, the painter, claimed that sadness always leaked through the eyes. Heather's green eyes looked more tired than sad. Her face had picked up a tan and her hair had bleached a little in the sun. She'd lost weight, which was not a good thing because it was all muscle mass. She hadn't been doing her exercises or yoga. She looked frail, like one of those Manson chicks, and when Tom told people she'd grown up on a sort of commune you could tell that they were thinking NXIVM sex cult or worse. Of course it was nothing like that.

She grabbed her phone, sat cross-legged on the floor, and dialed a number.

"Hello?" a female voice said.

"Hi, it's me."

"Whoa, girlfriend! I was wondering if I was ever going to hear from you again. Pretty sure the hitchhiker killers or the spiders were going to get you."

"Not yet. What time is it there, Carolyn?"

"It's five thirty. Five thirty in the evening."

"Here it's the morning. Tomorrow morning, I think."

"Man, that is freaky. Seriously, are you looking out for the spiders? And did I warn you about those blue-ringed octopuses that kill you in ten seconds?"

"You did. Funnily enough, very few blue-ringed octopuses in the desert," Heather said.

"Don't blame me when they get ya. How's the trophy husband?"

"He's good."

"I'll bet he is! He's a tall drink of water, that one. And how are the little monsters?" Carolyn asked.

"You shouldn't call them that."

"Ha! I knew you would get Stockholm syndrome sooner or later. Cough me an SOS in Morse code if he's in earshot."

"He's not and everything is OK."

"You'll come and see me when you get back? Show me your photos, tell me everything?"

"Of course."

"I haven't seen you for ages."

"The ferries—it's complicated."

"He doesn't like you coming back here, does he?"

"You're crazy."

"It's the drugs, isn't it? He thinks we're all degenerates. You should never have told him about our marijuana crops. And yet he gives his own kids so-called prescription drugs. They're hypocrites, these doctors, and—"

"Oh my God, Carolyn, can we change the subject? How's everyone at home? Tell me about the Sound. What's the weather like there?" Heather interrupted.

"Let me go to the window. You can't see shit. Fog and rain. Drizzle."

"I dreamed it was snowing," Heather said. "How's Scotty?"

"He's hanging in there. He came by to see me yesterday. Just nudged open the door and came in. I gave him a couple of pets and he fell asleep on the mat."

"Seen my dad?"

"Yup. He's good. Been out kayaking."

"And my mom?" Heather asked.

"On her good days she just flicks paint at you as you go past."

"And on her bad days?"

"She insists you come in and look at her art."

"Oh, boy, I miss you guys. But I'm seeing stuff in the world now, you know?"

"Tell me! What's Australia like?"

"It's beautiful. Stark and red and gorgeous. And the people are super-friendly."

"I've heard that. Look out for any random Hemsworths and pass on my number."

"I will," Heather said. "Are you OK?"

"Yeah, I'm great."

"Writing any songs?" Heather asked.

"No. You?"

"No."

Silence down the line. A little bit of tension creeping into the static.

"You know I'm real happy for you, honey . . ." Carolyn said.

"I'm sensing a *but* coming."

"But, man, when you left, you said you wanted to be a singer or an actress. You said you wanted to soar—"

"And now I'm just a boring housewife crashed to earth in a tangled mess of wax and feathers," Heather said.

"See? You had talent. That's a lyric right there. Who knows where you could have gone? New York? Hollywood?"

Heather yawned. "I better go, I gotta take the kids to the beach in a bit."

"God, he really has you where he wants you, doesn't he? Twenty-four-hour live-in nanny with benefits and he doesn't have to pay you a dime."

"That's not the way it is," Heather said.

"Isn't it? Be honest with me, girl. I won't report you to the Mommy Gestapo."

Heather sighed. "Well, it's been a tough week. A tough year, in fact . . . it's—"

"Spoiled rich kids, right?"

"No, look, it's me, I guess. I was never an aunt, and you know babysitting was never my thing. No one tells you how mean they can be. I love Tom and I'm so grateful for everything he's done for me, but it's just . . . exhausting sometimes."

"Of course it is. Even with good kids."

"They're not terrible and I feel bad for them . . . their mom—"

"You gotta protect *yourself*, honey! It's about you and your life. Don't end up like the first wife, drunk and dead at the bottom of the stairs."

"Carolyn! You know that's bullshit. Judith had MS, balance problems—"

"Just teasing. I'll swap lives for a bit, even with the shitty kids, if you think he'd go for a feisty redhead."

"He might." Heather laughed.

"Speaking of booze, are you still going to that winery tour you talked about?"

"I don't know. I hope so," Heather said and yawned again. "I need sleep. Later, babes."

"Take care, honey."

"You too. Pet Scotty for me."

She hung up, went to the bedroom, lay facedown on the bed, and was asleep in seconds.

Owen woke her an hour later by poking her in the neck. "You were supposed to take us for ice cream," he said.

"What? Where...oh, yeah, sure. Beach, then ice cream. Give me five minutes."

She went to the bathroom to freshen up and opened the door a little when she heard her name. "Don't tell Heather but I found a record player downstairs," Olivia was saying. "A shit-ton of vinyl."

"Don't tell Dad either! I'll bet there's classical."

"At least with Dad, it's kind of age-appropriate. With Heather, it's such Millennial hipster bullshit. I'm dreading the day when she confesses that she's a Hufflepuff and asks us what Harry Potter house we're in," Olivia said.

"Cringe city!" Owen agreed and both kids laughed.

Heather closed the bathroom door and allowed herself a "Little shits" under her breath. The kids were already accomplished child-soldiers in the war between generations. And really, if either of them had taken the trouble to look at her Spotify playlists, they would have found Porridge Radio, Chance the Rapper, Vampire Weekend, Post Malone, Big Thief, the Shaggs...she sighed and realized she was never going to win this one.

The house was well stocked with sunblock and beach towels. She gave Owen his Ritalin, Olivia her Lexapro, and the three of them went across the road and found themselves on St. Kilda Beach. Owen almost never took off his hoodie but it was so warm, Heather supposed that even he would eventually cave.

"Come on, let me take you both in the ocean," she said.

"No way," Owen grunted but Olivia followed her down to the water. Olivia was lean, like her dad, and she had her mother's blond hair and coloring. She'd been growing fast in the past year. Her mind may have been grieving and shutting down but her body didn't know that. The body was stretching out. Fourteen, but you would have guessed sixteen or older. Heather and Olivia tried the water but it was surprisingly cold. Owen dipped in a toe and gave them a you-tricked-me scowl.

They found a café selling fish and chips and ice cream at the St. Kilda Sea Baths. Heather was convinced she'd been short-changed by almost three dollars but she was too timid to kick up a fuss about it. She silently reproached herself as they ate and walked back across the road to the house. She made sure both kids showered and dried off. Olivia had finished all her home-work and offered to help Owen with the astronomy worksheet for his science and nature class. Olivia had gotten through the past year OK but poor Owen was having to repeat his science course. Owen refused the assistance and a fight ensued. Heather sat them both down in front of a Godzilla movie on the TV.

She was exhausted. But she knew this was the price she had to pay—to be with Tom, she had to be with the kids. And she wanted to be with Tom. She loved Tom, not despite all his little quirks and weirdnesses, but because of them—the whole pack-age. The smarts, the grief, the fastidiousness, the dad humor, the way he looked at her first thing in the morning, the way he was changing himself for her. When he told her the thing about the wanker, he hadn't rolled his eyes the way the Tom of three months ago might have. He hadn't quite conquered all of his condescension, but he was trying to be a better man.

She told the kids she was going for a walk; she went around the block and found a 7-Eleven. The clerk told her a pack of

Marlboros cost twenty bucks and after he showed her the price sticker, she believed him. She smoked two cigarettes and listened to Starcrawler's "Bet My Brains" on the way back home.

The kids were digging the movie.

Tom texted her several ice-breaking "jokes" for his big conference speech with the query Funny or not funny?

She didn't have the heart to text back Not funny but she made a mental note to tell him to do one joke, maximum.

When *Godzilla* finished, she opened a closet marked BOARD/BORED GAMES. Both kids moaned but she imposed her will and they decided on Risk. She found the record player and, ignoring the Beatles albums, put on Mozart.

When Tom came home at six p.m. looking beat, Olivia had almost taken over the world. He sat happily on the sofa and watched, enjoying the fact that the kids were doing something delightfully old-school and loving the hell out of it. She brought Tom a glass of wine and as they retreated to the kitchen, Olivia mopped up the last of the resistance in Asia.

"How was your day?" Tom asked her.

"We all had a nap and then I took the kids to the beach. How was your day?"

"Fun. I met the local bigwigs in orthopedic surgery. We swapped knee stories. Australian knees are as crappy as American knees. Thank goodness," Tom said, kissing her.

"Did you see I won? Oh, no kissing, please!" a triumphant Olivia said, coming into the kitchen with Owen trailing behind her.

Tom laughed. "Listen, I've got a number of recommendations for dinner places. And then tomorrow, while I work on my speech, you guys can chill."

"Forget chilling! We haven't seen a single cool animal since we got here," Owen said. "Jake said on my Instagram that he thinks I'm really in Utah."

"I'm sure Jake was only teasing."

"Dad, please! We can't stay here! We have to explore a bit before we go home. We have to at least see some koalas. Please, please, please!" Owen said, and even Olivia joined in with an only semi-sarcastic final "please."

"I think they make a fair point," Heather offered.

"Didn't you want to go to those wineries we talked about?" Tom asked.

Heather shook her head. "Let's do something for the kids."

Tom nodded wearily. "All right, I'll think about it," he said.

3

Tom woke just before the dawn. The inevitable adrenaline dump after a busy day meeting people had sent him straight to sleep. Heather was snoring softly as he slipped carefully out of the bed. He watched her for a moment or two and smiled broadly. She was the best. She was so funny, mellow, and sweet. The kids weren't quite sold on her yet, but they'd get there. Judith wouldn't have come to Australia in a million years, but for Heather, everything was an adventure.

He went to the roof, sat by the pool, and meditated for ten minutes, breathing deep and surfing the now. Then he did fifty push-ups followed by fifty sit-ups. This was a routine he'd been doing since his early days in medical school as a way of calming his mind and keeping himself focused. He could never have coped this past year without his morning rituals.

Next, Tom went downstairs, got a drink of water, and called the car-rental place. He was annoyed to discover that the Porsche Cayenne he had reserved was no longer available. He would have to take either the E-Hybrid or an older Turbo.

"I wanted the new Cayenne. I called about it last night," he said, trying to control his temper.

"I'm sorry, sir, we don't have any in the lot. The customer before you got the last one. We have the Turbo or the E-Hybrid. The hybrid is our top Porsche rental, it's—"

"No, thank you. It's a long drive. There is no way I would ever trust a hybrid!"

"We do have a BMW SUV for—"

"I'll take the Turbo. Can you get it over here by nine o'clock? I'd like to make an early start. We're at three Wordsworth Street in St. Kilda."

"Of course, sir."

Tom hung up, steaming. No one ever did their job. No one.

He changed into shorts and a T-shirt, pulled on his sneakers, and went for a run along the shore. Then it was upstairs to the swimming pool. He dove into the water and did a lap or two before coming back inside. He showered, and because the mirror was steamed, he shaved with the electric razor using his phone camera. He'd lost weight on this trip and it suited him. He looked like a young Ted Hughes.

"You did it, buddy. You survived the past year. I'm proud of you, partner," he said to Phone-Camera Tom. "A paper in the *Journal of Orthopedic Surgery*. International conferences. Keynote addresses. Success at forty-four. Who would have thought it? If Judith could see you now, she'd be happy for you."

Phone-Camera Tom thought about that for a second and slowly shook his head.

He wrapped himself in a towel and went into the bedroom. Heather appeared from a closet door he hadn't noticed before. She was wearing a robe and listening to that "212" song she loved and he hated.

"Where have you been?" Tom asked.

"Narnia," she said.

Tom grinned. "Do anything interesting?"

"Queen stuff...and, you know, I could slip out of my royal garb pretty quick," she whispered.

"The kids?"

"Are sound asleep."

She stripped and he stripped and they fell onto the bed. They made love for the first time since they'd left America, climaxing together as sunlight streamed through the shutters. Heather rested on Tom's chest.

She kissed him on the chin. "You missed a spot when you were shaving."

"I'll fix it."

"I like it. It gives you a hipster, Zappa-esque quality."

Tom shook his head. "People like their doctors to look boring. Boring and calm and competent."

"You're two of those things," Heather said, kissing him again.

Tom closed his eyes. "This has been a hard year for all of us. And I've been trying, haven't I?"

"You have," Heather said. "We all have."

"I really love you, babe," Tom said, kissing her back.

"I love you too...uh-oh. Everything OK?" she asked. "Now you've got a worry wrinkle in your forehead."

"I didn't get the car I wanted. I wanted the new Cayenne with the advanced GPS and the rear camera and the accident-avoidance system, but they only had the—"

The door opened and a sleepy Olivia came in.

"When are we leaving?" she asked as Heather covered herself.

"As soon as Owen gets up. And, look, if we really have to do this trip, we need to leave early and get back early. I've got to work on my speech. The conference is going to put it on YouTube," Tom said.

Olivia ran into the hallway. "Get up, Owen! You're late!" she screamed.

Owen growled a response and a fight began. Tom slithered out of bed, ran to the bedroom door, and closed it. The fighting was instantly muffled.

"I thought you were going to put a stop to that," Heather said.

"Parenting 101, honey: what you can't see or hear isn't happening," Tom said.

Despite the fighting, an hour later they were in a bright orange Porsche Cayenne heading southeast out of Melbourne on the highway. The road was big and new, carving mercilessly through Melbourne's drab eastern suburbs. The Porsche was as comfortable as you would expect, although it was an odd-looking thing with a large front "snorkel" for driving through flooded rivers.

No flooded rivers today. They were ten thousand miles away from America, but this, Tom reflected, could have been suburbs anywhere. Targets, Walmarts, strip malls. Interesting, though. This, he imagined, was the "real Australia," off the tourist trail, where people actually lived.

They drove down through the Mornington Peninsula, the suburbs gradually thinning out and a hilly country emerging. Heather pointed out kookaburras and big black ravens on the sagging telegraph wires. She took a picture of a lorikeet and sent it to Carolyn.

The kids, however, were not interested in birds and were getting increasingly frustrated. "Where are the kangaroos? Where are the frickin' koalas?" Owen demanded.

Tom looked at him in the rearview mirror and frowned. That kid was so unlike his sister. If Tom had gotten a trip to Australia when he was Owen's age, he would have appreciated every second of it. Now Owen would be huffy until they got back and he took his diazepam. Tom was about to give Owen a piece of his mind when Heather put her hand on his thigh. "Kids, here's one your dad told me yesterday," she said. "Koalas aren't technically bears—do you know why?"

"Please, Dad, don't let her say it! Yours are bad enough!" Olivia begged.

"Because they don't have the right koalifications," Heather said as both kids face-palmed.

The road got rougher and went to a single lane as they approached the coast. Wireless and Siri and Google Maps ceased working.

It was another hot day out there—106 degrees—but inside the car, everyone had a water bottle from the Airbnb and it was a cool 68.

It was noon now and they hadn't seen much of anything and Tom wanted to get back to Melbourne to work on his keynote speech on knee-replacement surgery. The kids were hungry, so they stopped at a little food stand. Smoke from a barbecue was fighting a rearguard action against a persistent swarm of mosquitoes. A scraggly-looking geezer in his fifties was selling beer and soft drinks and "sausage sizzles," which appeared to be sausages between pieces of Wonder bread.

Heather, Olivia, and Owen each got a sausage sizzle at a pricey five bucks a pop. Tom demurred and got a can of beer instead. They sat down at a picnic table in the shade.

With no phone signal, Tom grabbed his massive book of Chekhov stories and plays. Owen took out his astronomy worksheet from the back pages of his snake book. He stared at it angrily for a minute or two. "This is impossible," he muttered at last.

"I can help you with that," Olivia said.

"I don't need your help!" Owen snapped.

An ancient-looking Volkswagen camper van pulled up and a thin couple in their late fifties or early sixties exited. They got two cans of Victoria Bitter and sat down at the free table under the shade. The couples couldn't help but say hello.

"I'm Tom and this is my wife, Heather, and these are my kids, Owen and Olivia," Tom said.

"I'm Hans and this is Petra," Hans replied.

"We're Americans. From Seattle," Tom said.

"We are from Leiden in Holland," Hans said. "I'm an engineer. From a very long line of engineers. Auto engineers."

"Oh, yes?"

"Yes indeed. My great-grandfather invented the steering wheel."

Owen raised his head from his homework. "Your actual grandfather, like, invented the steering wheel?" he asked incredulously.

"My great-grandfather."

"He told you that?" Owen asked.

"Yes."

"I doubt it," Owen said, shaking his head.

"So what do you do, Petra?" Heather asked the woman.

"I am a sociologist," she replied.

Owen was still regarding Hans with deep twelve-year-old-boy skepticism. It was starting to get a little uncomfortable. "I think it is too hot here. We will eat in the car," Hans announced. The couple went back to the Volkswagen van.

"Owen, why did you give that guy a hard time?" Tom asked when they'd gone.

"I didn't give him a hard time. I totally believed him. After all, *my* great-great-grandmother invented the spoon. Before that, only forks," Owen said.

"And our great-great-great-grandfather invented fire," Olivia said.

Heather, Owen, and Olivia were all laughing now and Tom started laughing too.

A Toyota Hilux pulled in and two men got out. The bigger of the two was wearing a sort of cowboy hat, jeans, a red-checkered shirt, and boots. He was about thirty-five, with a neatly trimmed black beard, dark eyebrows, and blue eyes. Handsome, Tom supposed, if you liked the rugged, outdoorsy type. The second man was slightly shorter, maybe around six feet. He was older, about fifty, balding. He was lean and rangy and looked a bit menacing. His left cheek was scarred and there was an old tattoo on his neck that could possibly have been an anchor. He was wearing overalls with rubber boots and no undershirt.

Tom looked at his watch. It was noon. "Well, folks, time to head back," he said.

"We haven't seen a koala!" Olivia protested.

"We haven't seen anything!" Owen added.

"We gave it our best shot. But I have to get home to work," Tom said.

Owen went into a complete meltdown: He was the worst dad ever. This trip sucked. Why had they even bothered coming to Australia if they weren't going to see anything? Olivia crossed her arms, shook her head, and glowered with all her might.

Tom looked at Heather but she was helpless in the face of this.

"Excuse me, mates," a voice said. It was the taller of the two men. "Couldn't help overhearing—you kids wanna see a koala?"

"Yes!" Olivia said.

"Follow me," the man said.

The family followed him to the back of the Toyota, where, in a cage under a blanket, there was a sleeping koala.

"Oooh! Can we hold him?" Olivia asked.

"Nah, sorry, can't do that," the man said. "They're very vulnerable to disease, and you're Americans, I take it."

"Yes, from Seattle," Tom said. "I'm Tom and this is Heather, Olivia, and Owen."

"I'm Matt, and this experiment gone wrong is me brother Jacko," Matt said.

"Hey! Watch your mouth!" Jacko snarled.

"Where did this little guy come from?" Heather asked, gesturing to the koala.

"We're from across the bay there—private island—and there's koalas bloody everywhere. And wallabies, echidnas, wombats— it's like Jurassic bloody Park, mate," Jacko said.

The kids turned to their dad. "We have to go!" Olivia said.

Tom shook his head. "Did you say *private* island?"

"Yeah, sorry, no visitors," Matt said.

"Dad!" Owen protested and Olivia chimed in with a theatrical sigh of disbelief.

Tom looked at them. They had had a very tough year. And he'd been so strict on this trip. Maybe a little ugly-American grease would do the trick? "Is there a ferry? We'd be willing to pay," Tom said.

Matt shook his head. "There is a ferry but it's not about the money. Ma doesn't like visitors. Dutch Island is her place, you know?"

"How much money?" Jacko said.

Tom had taken out three hundred bucks at the Alice Springs airport and he'd received his conference per diem of seven hundred dollars. He had close to a thousand Aussie dollars on him. He opened his wallet. "Four...five hundred bucks? Just to see, maybe take some photos? For the kids," he said.

"You Yanks! You can't bloody buy everything, mate!" Matt said, shaking his head with disgust. But Jacko put his arm around Matt and led him away for a minute. The two men got into a furious discussion. The Dutch couple had come out of their van to see what was happening.

"*Dutch* Island, did he say?" Hans asked.

"If you can do nine hundred bucks, that will be three hundred each for me, Matt, and Ivan, who runs the ferry," Jacko said. "But you'd have to be bloody fast. Just some quick photos and then off again."

"Nine hundred bucks! That's crazy," Tom protested. That was—what? Five hundred American?

"Dad!" Owen wailed again.

"Maybe we should just go back to Melbourne," Heather said.

"You'll be missing out. It's a very special place," Jacko said. "Unique. Animals everywhere. We make our own electricity. Grow our own food. No phones. No taxes. No law enforcement. When was the last time we had a copper out here, Matty?"

"Before my time," Matt said. "But that's not the—"

"Koalas, birds, even some penguins," Jacko continued.

"Penguins, Dad!" Olivia said.

"Six hundred is my limit," Tom insisted.

"If we can come too, we can chip in the difference," Hans said.

Matt was shaking his head this entire time but Jacko's wolfish grin only widened. "I think we have a deal, then, mates."

4

The convoy of vehicles stopped at a decrepit wooden jetty poking a bony limb into the bay. The ferry was a flat-bottomed vessel with a diesel engine, a tiny little foul-weather cabin, and a ramp at each end. Very similar to the small ferries you saw on Puget Sound.

Ivan, the ferry pilot, was a tall, powerfully built man in his fifties with long graying blond hair and boozy green eyes. He was smoking and wearing heavy denim overalls despite the heat. He'd been surprised to see three cars but when Jacko gave him three hundred bucks, he tucked it into his pocket and nodded.

Tom drove on first, followed by the Dutch couple and the Toyota.

They got out of their cars while Ivan unhooked the two hawsers tying the ferry to the shore. He used a stick to fend the ferry away from a bunch of old tires protecting the dock and then he put the diesel engine into gear and they were away.

"If you want to see sharks, I'd go to the port side. That's the left side for you landlubbers," Ivan said as he stubbed out one cigarette and lit another and Jacko took the tiller.

They went to the port side and caught a glimpse of a tiger shark's fin, which made Owen favor everyone with a smile. "How big is the island?" Tom asked.

"Four kilometers lengthwise," Ivan said. "In old money, that's about three miles wide, and it's two from top to bottom."

"Where are the koalas?" Heather asked.

Matt came over from the leeward rail. He had taken his hat off. With his long chestnut hair, Heather thought he looked like one of those men a woman in a '90s Tampax commercial would be riding her horse to meet. "The koalas will be in the trees," Matt said. "Look, don't drive far from the dock. There's no internet or Wi-Fi and it's easy to get lost. Definitely stay away from the farm—that's in the middle of the island."

"I would like to see an Australian farm," Tom said.

"No!" Matt said. "You're not supposed to be on the island at all. Nothing to see, anyway. It's just a hobby farm now. Sheep, goats, generator, a well. Just for us. Just for the family."

"So how do you live?" Tom asked.

"The federal government had a prison just down the road here from the 1910s to the 1980s. They paid us rent and we sort of live off the remains of that cash. They tried to run it as a tourist attraction after it closed, but Ma put a stop to all that."

"She bloody did," Ivan grumbled.

"Over here! Another shark!" Owen said, taking Tom's arm and leading him to the front of the ferry with Olivia. Hans followed them, leaving Matt alone with the two women.

"How many people are there on the island?" Petra asked Matt after a time.

"Including the kids, about twenty-five, twenty-seven, I think."

"Do you have a school?" Heather asked.

"The older kids go to boarding school. The younger ones are homeschooled, if you know what that is."

Heather smiled. "I do. I was homeschooled."

"In Seattle? I thought that was a big city," Matt said, becoming, perhaps, slightly more friendly.

"I just moved to Seattle a few years ago. I grew up on a small island myself. Goose Island in Puget Sound."

"What was that like?" Petra asked, genuinely curious.

"We moved there when I was little. After my parents got out of the army. It's sort of an artists' colony," Heather said, digging the experience of telling perfect strangers some of her story. "It was founded in the 1970s but it attracted a lot of ex-servicemen, army veterans with PTSD, that kind of stuff. They have art therapy. And nature. And it's real quiet. It, um, got a bit too small for me, so I moved to Seattle."

"I did exactly the opposite," Matt said. "Like your folks. I moved here. I married in. I'm not one of Ma's sons. I'm a son-in-law."

"It's a bit, um, off the beaten track?" Petra suggested.

"That's the point," Matt said. "I grew up in a flat in Melbourne. Single mum. The trams, the cars, people yelling. Does my head in, the city. I came here with Tara, Ma's second youngest. But she and Ma fought like cats and cats. She buggered off and I stayed. I learned bushcraft out here and I can see a hundred different birds on a morning walk."

"Bushcraft? Birds? You and my dad would get on famously," Heather said.

"Sounds like we would. That's not your dad with you, is it?" Matt asked.

"No! Tom's my husband!" Heather said, coloring.

"You seem barely old enough to have children," Petra said.

Heather looked at Tom and the kids. "I'm his second wife. His first, Judith, died a year ago," she said quietly.

"Oh no, poor little things," Petra said. "But I am sure you are a comfort to them."

I try, Heather mouthed but did not say.

Matt tried and failed to light a cigarette. Heather lent him her Zippo, and the cigarette caught.

"Is there an Aboriginal heritage here?" Petra asked.

"No. Look, this is *not* a tourist destination," Matt insisted.

"We took care of them lot. We did a black line on the bastards," Jacko said as he and Ivan swapped places at the tiller.

"Black line?" Heather asked.

"You know about the Black Line of Tasmania, of course?" Jacko said.

Heather and Petra shook their heads.

"Two thousand men under Major Sholto Douglas marched across Tasmania to capture all the remaining Aboriginals. Killed the lot of them," Jacko said gleefully. "They did the same here on Dutch Island soon thereafter."

"And the dream lines?" Petra asked.

"We had one come here a few years ago spouting that nonsense. Remember that, Matt?" Jacko said.

"I remember," Matt said.

"He comes here and he tells us that because we have no natives, we're a land without a Dreaming. The nerve of him. What a bloody fraud. Ma saw right through him. All his talk about demons and bunyips. Ma had me and Ivan chase him off with our shotguns! Should have seen him run!" Jacko cackled.

"Oh, dear," Petra said and she looked at Heather, whose eyes widened with alarm. Heather's feeling of unease was growing as the ferry chugged inexorably closer to shore. To distract herself, she watched as Ivan steered the tiller with his foot and cast a fishing line into the water.

"What is he fishing for?" Heather found herself wondering out loud.

"If sharks are here, it's probably big fish like salmon and tuna," Petra said.

"Do you fish, Petra?" Heather asked.

"Oh, yes. Hans and I go fly-fishing in Germany," Petra said. "You?"

"Not anymore. My dad grew up fly-fishing in Kentucky, but, gosh, the real fisherfolk in my family are from my mom's side. Her mom—my grandmother—grew up on the Makah Reservation. Mom said they could fish anything out of the sea. Whales, even."

"He better stop fishing now. We're getting close," Matt said. "Last chance for the dunny, everyone."

Olivia tugged Heather's sleeve. Heather put up her hand like a kid in school. "Is *dunny* 'toilet,' by any chance?" she asked Matt.

Matt grinned at her. "Yeah, mate, just inside the little cabin there. Make sure you turn on the light and check for spiders before you sit down."

Olivia looked at Heather and shook her head.

"What spiders should we look out for?" Heather asked.

"Follow me, I'll check for you. Redbacks. Real nasty, they are. Hide under the toilet seat sometimes. Can kill you in some circumstances." Matt walked over to the tiny little toilet, opened the door, and had a look around. "You're safe," he said.

"What the hell is that?" Olivia asked, pointing at a massive spider on the far side of the wall. It was a brown hairy thing as big as her hand.

"Oh, those are harmless. It's a huntsman spider. Actually, they do us a big favor. Eat the flies. They won't hurt you," Matt said.

Olivia was not reassured in the least. "I'll hold it," she said.

"Are you sure, honey?" Heather asked.

"Yes!" Olivia said, embarrassed now. She folded her arms and stomped to the prow of the boat to be with Owen and her father.

"Is the bathroom OK?" Petra asked Heather.

"If you have a problem with spiders, it might not be a great idea," Heather said.

Matt took over steering duties while Ivan joined Jacko at the front of the boat. Jacko gave Heather the creeps and she couldn't help but notice both men ogling Olivia. She hadn't been sure at first but then she saw Jacko nudge Ivan in the ribs as Olivia bent over to pick something up off the deck. Heather could handle those looks with a contemptuous eye-roll or a cutting remark, but Olivia wasn't used to this kind of creepy attention from older men. Blue eyes, long legs, blond hair, pretty face—she would be a heartbreaker in three or four years. But not now. Heather was going to say something but fortunately they were getting very close to shore and both men got busy with fending the ferry off as Matt killed the engine and it glided toward a concrete slipway.

"All right, folks, in your vehicles! Be no more than half an hour, forty-five minutes tops, and I'll take you back," Ivan announced as he lowered the ferry's ramp.

"Yeah, get your koala pics and go before Ma rumbles ya," Jacko muttered.

"Be careful, and seriously, don't be long!" Matt added to Heather.

They got in the Porsche and set out to explore the island. Heather was relieved to be back in the air-conditioning; Australia was her first experience of a hot-weather climate and she had decided that she did not much care for it. The road wound east from the ferry pier. The landscape was not inspiring. There were no koalas anywhere, just a large grassy heathland that had been burned in a recent bushfire and the occasional eucalyptus tree with a crow in it. Heather looked at the dreary yellow-and-brown nothingness with the feeling that they had been royally conned.

"Well, this sucks!" Owen said, giving vent to what they were all feeling.

"Maybe if we go farther in?" Tom said.

"I think we're supposed to stay close to the shore," Heather said.

"We'll get what we paid for," Tom said, irritated, accelerating the Porsche.

They drove through a crossroads and came to what was presumably the remains of the old prison. A house and a few tumbledown buildings covered with lichen and moss. An emaciated gray-haired older man stepped out from the shade of one of the buildings and furiously flagged them down. Tom stopped the car and wound down his window. "What are you doing here?" the man asked, amazed.

"We, um, we're looking for koalas and—"

"You need to leave," the man said. "This is private land. It's not safe. You all need to go. Now!"

Heather grabbed Tom's knee. "I *really* don't like it here."

The man hit the Porsche with his walking stick. "Go!" he yelled.

Tom nodded and rolled the window back up. He was as spooked as the rest of them. They drove back to the crossroads.

"Which way?" Tom said, flustered.

"Left!" Owen said.

"Straight on," Heather said.

"I think we veer right," Tom said and took the right road, which soon became a dirt track with long grass on either side.

"Shit! Wrong way," Tom said. They turned and drove back to the crossroads again.

"The ferry guy said to be forty-five minutes tops," Olivia said, looking at the clock on her phone.

"Don't worry, we'll make that easily," Tom said, hitting the gas. The Porsche accelerated. The road curved. The sun almost directly ahead was sinking toward the horizon. Something blue caught Heather's eye. "Look out!" Heather screamed.

A woman in a blue dress riding a bike had come out from a side road, completely oblivious to the Porsche bearing down on her. Heather had a momentary feeling of weightlessness. It wasn't that the car had lifted off the ground or anything like that; the Porsche SUV was totally safe. This feeling was from another branch of physics entirely. This was the feeling that her life had gone into one of those multiverses Tom was always going on about. In one universe Tom had called the car-rental place five minutes earlier and they'd gotten the Porsche with the radar and the accident-avoidance system. In this universe Heather yelled "Tom!" as the front of the SUV completely enveloped the woman on the bicycle.

5

The disc brakes were powerful but the Porsche had been going too fast and it had too much momentum.

"Oh, sweet Jesus!" Tom cried as the Porsche plowed over the bicycle with a sickening thud. They scraped and slid along the ground for twenty yards before skidding into a drainage ditch. The airbags inflated and Heather was jolted back by her seat belt. They came to a stop as the wheels spun and the engine died.

Heather opened her eyes.

The world was tilted thirty degrees from the horizontal. Tall white grass on either side of the road. The woman and the bicycle were nowhere to be seen. The airbag was slowly deflating in front of her.

Heather's neck was wrenched and she had dug the nails of her left hand into her wrist. Her dad and mom had taught her about self-triage. She inventoried herself for bleeding or broken bones but she knew she was basically OK. She disengaged the seat belt and turned around to look at the kids.

The side airbags in the back seat had inflated and deflated.

Olivia was dazed but looked OK. Owen had cut his cheek on his seat belt.

"Are you OK, Owen?" she asked.

His eyes found hers and he nodded.

"Say it. Tell me if you're OK or not."

"I'm OK," he said.

"Good. Olivia, are you OK?"

Olivia nodded. "I think so. What happened?"

"Did we hit something?" Owen asked.

Heather looked at Tom. His airbag was wedging him into his seat. His side of the car had entered the ditch, and his body was angled away from her.

"Tom? Tom! Are you hurt?" she asked.

"What? No...not...hurt. Head...window." He groaned.

"Let me see."

He had banged his head against the window and had a scrape on his forehead; he was clearly stunned, perhaps concussed.

For the past six months Tom had done everything for her. Opened doors, paid bills, argued with waiters, cleared her credit card debt, done almost all of the driving, and certainly handled all the emergencies. But he would need a few minutes to recover and the kids couldn't—

She would have to—

"I'll get out," she said. "Kids, I want both of you to stay in the car for now. Both of you take your seat belts off. Olivia, help your brother."

Heather's shoulder ached where the seat belt had smacked into her. She pushed aside the deflated airbag and found the handle to open the door. Her fingers tingled and her arm felt like rubber. She pushed the door and nothing happened. She pushed harder and still nothing. She kicked the bastard and it opened.

The heat hit her like a wave.

She'd forgotten the heat. The AC must have really been cranking.

She got out of the car and fell onto the road. Her hands burned on the asphalt.

Getting up, she took a breath and then hobbled around to the front of the SUV. The woman was not there. A faint hope coursed through her. She scanned the grass on either side of the road. It was tempting to think that Tom had somehow avoided the woman but Heather knew that was not the case. She had felt the crump of the bike under the tires.

She got down on one knee and looked beneath the SUV, and there was the bicycle, under the back left wheel. She hurried back behind the car and saw the woman's body, horribly mangled, another ten feet down the road.

She ran and knelt beside her. "Are you...oh my God."

Both of her legs were twisted underneath her in an unnatural position that legs could not possibly go. She was bleeding through the blue dress. Heather lifted the dress and saw a massive scrape across her chest but no obvious penetrating wound. She did not appear to be breathing.

"Oh my God, I am so sorry! Oh no, I am so, so sorry. You poor...we didn't see...oh my God..."

Blood was oozing from her nose and mouth.

She needed a doctor. "Tom! Get out here!"

Heather put her hand on the woman's neck and counted off ten seconds, but there was no trace of a pulse. She gently tilted the woman's head back, put two fingers in her mouth, and cleared it of blood and broken teeth and a hunk of flesh.

"Come on, *please*..." Heather said and breathed.

She tried to blow air into the woman's lungs but it came back into her own mouth as an unholy reflection of lifegiving air: acrid, warm, stale, reeking of blood. Something was blocking the windpipe. She lifted the limp body. "It's going to be OK," she said.

She thumped the woman's back and another chunk of flesh fell from her lips.

"Tom! I need you! Get out here!"

Heather laid her on the ground again and gave her mouth-to-mouth resuscitation and this time the air did seem to reach what was left of the woman's lungs.

Heather began doing chest compressions.

She did this for a count of twenty and then checked the pulse. Nothing.

Blood was pouring from her ears, eyes, mouth, nostrils.

Flies were beginning to land on her.

"Shit." All Heather was doing was moving blood around a dead woman's body. She was not going to be able to save her. Only medical professionals with a trauma team and blood products and—

She took the phone out of her jeans and dialed 911.

No, not 911. What was the Australian—000.

She dialed 000. There was no signal. She held the phone up as high as it would go. No signal.

She ran to the front of the car and climbed across the scalding-hot hood, burning her hands as she scaled it.

Tom was staring at her through the windshield, dazed. The kids were stirring behind him.

"Check on the kids and get out here!" she said.

Tom looked at her, baffled for a moment, and then nodded.

Heather looked at the phone. No service, it said.

The farm Matt had talked about couldn't be too far away.

Would they have a phone? Didn't Matt say that they *didn't* have phones here, or was she misremembering that?

She jumped off the hood and ran back to the woman.

She tried pumping her chest again.

She tried and tried.

Blood poured from the woman's mouth by the cupful.

Heather stopped what she was doing.

The woman's entire chest cavity must be filled with blood. A major blood vessel had probably ruptured. There was nothing she could do. There was nothing anyone could do. The impact had killed her and she'd surely been brain-dead for minutes now.

There had never been a possibility of saving her.

Heather tugged the blue dress back down over the body. What a kind, lovely, gentle face the woman had. Someone's daughter, sister, wife. A young life wiped out by them.

"I'm so sorry. We didn't see you. Oh God, I'm so sorry," she said as tears filled her eyes.

Heather heard a noise behind her—Tom getting out of the car. He finally appeared next to her covered with dirt. He must have climbed out the window on his side of the car and scrambled to her along the ditch.

"Oh my God!" he said. "What have I done!"

"It wasn't your fault. She came out of nowhere."

"I honked the horn! Didn't I? My God. She didn't even look around!"

"There was nothing you could do, Tom." She stood and tried to take his hand but he brushed her off.

"Is she dead? Are you sure?" Tom asked.

"She's dead. She was killed instantly."

"CPR! I'm a trained...let me see...we can...shit, look at her!"

"I thought so too. But I've done that. It's too late. Tom, look, there's nothing you could have done. You braked as soon as—"

"If we'd had the new model. The one I asked for. The accident-avoidance radar would have braked the car for us. That's the one I wanted. I told you that!"

"I know."

"It was you and the kids. We weren't supposed to come here! I wanted to work on my damn speech!"

Tom's fists were clenched. His eyes were wild, staring; he looked almost unhinged.

He didn't get like this often but she'd seen it once or twice. His rage had taken her by surprise. She knew she had to snap him out of it quickly.

He had six inches on her. She stood on tiptoes and reached up and put her hands behind his neck and tilted his head down to look her in the eyes.

"Tom!" she said, snapping her fingers in front of his face.

"I had no idea there would be people on bicycles in this heat! Who rides a bicycle when it's a hundred degrees? I was looking for koalas in the trees. They should have told us. Did you see any speed-limit signs? I didn't see one."

"There were no signs, Tom. She came out of nowhere."

"I can save her! There's always hope. I did rotations in the ER during my residency!" Tom said and got down on his knees.

She knew there was no way he was going to believe she was dead until he saw it for himself.

She looked up and down the road. There were no cars. No one was coming.

Yet.

She examined the Porsche. Both wheels were in the ditch, but it was a narrow trench, less than a foot across and only two feet deep. They should be able to get going again pretty quickly. They would almost certainly have to push the car out, though. Important to lighten the weight. She would drive and Tom would have to push. The kids could help. Owen was strong, and Olivia, with those long legs, could add to the leverage.

Tom had begun CPR.

She let him try it for a minute.

"It's not working," he said.

"She's dead, Tom."

"I was driving too fast. That guy spooked me. And I was looking out the window and driving too fast. We have to call the police. An ambulance," he said.

"It's too late for all that now. There's nothing anyone can do."

Tom stood and tried to get a signal on his phone.

Heather walked to the Porsche, opened the hatchback, and rummaged for the beach blanket. She grabbed it and checked on the kids, who were still fumbling with the airbags and their seat belts. She walked back to Tom and draped the blanket over the woman.

Heather looked up and down the road again. Still empty.

She considered the situation.

What she was thinking now was the *wrong* thing to do.

Absolutely the wrong thing to do.

Legally.

Morally.

It was a crime called a hit-and-run.

Tom had killed the woman. And now she was going to compound the horror of this act. It felt plain wrong. But all her instincts told her that this was the only option.

She tried to think what her mom would tell her to do.

Her mom, she decided, would tell her to wait for the authorities.

Her dad would tell her to get the hell out of there.

She returned to the Porsche and opened the rear door. She leaned in and unbuckled Olivia's seat belt.

"Are you OK, honey?" she asked.

Olivia nodded and then shook her head. "My arm hurts."

"Let me see."

The seat belt had scraped her arm. It wasn't broken. "I'll get a Band-Aid on that in a minute. Let me help you out. Take your water bottle."

She took Olivia's hand and tugged her out of the car.

"Wait by the front of the car for a bit while I get your brother."

"What happened?"

"There's been an accident. I want you to wait by the front of the car. I know it's hot. Can you do that for me?"

"Yes," Olivia said, still dazed.

Getting Owen out was trickier. He was practically catatonic. He had retreated behind his "wall," which was a thing he'd been doing since his mother's death that Heather had never really got a grip on.

"Olivia, you need to help me with Owen."

"Owen! It's me! Come on," Olivia said and they bundled him out together.

Heather walked back to Tom. "I've got the kids out of the car. You three can push, and I'll drive us out of the ditch," she said.

"At that farm place, they might have a radio. We could call an air ambulance," Tom suggested.

"No, Tom. The impact killed her, and you . . . we ran her over. Her lungs and internal organs are crushed. I know you know that. There's nothing anyone can do now."

Tom still looked dazed, but he was nodding.

This was the moment.

Heather had to make the decision now. It was her call and she knew Tom would go along with it.

But what was the right course of action?

Her moral compass and survival instincts were swinging in wildly opposite directions.

"Look, honey, you met those people," she began. "It's all one family on this island. They control the ferry, which is our only way off. We have no phone service. We can't get help. We're entirely dependent on them."

"So?"

"You heard what Jacko said about the police. He told me they chased someone off the island with shotguns. It sounds like they're a law unto themselves here."

"What—what are you suggesting?" Tom asked.

Heather looked at him. Tom was older, yes; he had read more, yes; but he moved in very small circles. He came from money, and his experience of human nature was surprisingly limited. One night sleeping rough in the Tacoma bus station would have taught him more than a thousand books.

"We hide her in the long grass with her bike. We get the car out of the ditch and we drive down to the ferry and get off this island as soon as possible. When we're safely back on the mainland, we can tell the cops that we may have hit something when we were driving. We thought it was an animal but we're not sure."

"You want us—me—to leave the scene of an accident? An accident we caused?"

She looked into his eyes. The pupils were big. His hands were shaking. He was somewhere else again.

"What's h–happened?" Olivia asked. Her curiosity had gotten the better of her and she'd come to see what was going on. Owen was ten feet behind her. "Is that blood?"

Heather turned. "Go back to the front of the car, please, Olivia. Take your brother."

"Is someone dead?" Olivia said, her hand up against her mouth. She was pale, trembling, scared.

"Damn right someone's dead," Tom muttered.

Heather winced, took Olivia by the hand, grabbed Owen by the arm, and escorted them to the front of the Porsche.

"There's been an accident. You two will have to be brave, OK?" she said softly.

She noticed that there was blood and a dent on the Porsche's snorkel. They'd have to get that clean before they returned it to the car dealership. The big stainless-steel bumper at the front of the car was dented too; not badly, but it would still need to be explained.

Owen shook off her hand. "Dad killed her, didn't he? He killed her," he said strangely, distantly, as if from the bottom of a well. Owen, like Olivia, was both older and younger than his years. He was twelve, sometimes going on fifteen, sometimes a scared little boy.

Heather walked back to Tom.

"How are the kids?" he asked.

"The kids are going to be OK. Look, you did your best. You braked. You honked the horn."

"Yes," Tom exclaimed. "Yes, I honked the horn. And this wasn't the car that I wanted. I wanted the other one."

"You did everything you could. This wasn't our fault. I think we should go now. I think we should get in the car and get to the ferry as quickly as possible."

Tom nodded.

"We'll get the body off the road and drive to the ferry," Heather said.

"We really shouldn't do that. It's a crime," Tom said.

"I don't think we have a choice. They're scary people. They have guns. It's all one family. Do you trust them to call the cops?"

He thought about it. "I can see what you're... but this is a huge decision," Tom said. She noticed that the sweat was pouring off him. And the graze on his forehead was bleeding.

"You know what? It's my fault, Tom. I'm making the decision," Heather said. "You banged your head. This is my call, OK? You don't have to think about any of this right now. All you have to do is help me get the body off the road. We're going to put her in that long grass over there."

"You want us to actually *move* her?"

"We have to. You're going to take her by the ankles and we're going to put her in the grass. OK?"

Tom got down on his knees and bent back the woman's legs. They made a grotesque cracking noise that chilled the blood. Tom lifted the woman's ankles, and Heather picked her up by the shoulders. Sticky warm blood oozed between her fingers. And now the flies were beginning to congregate en masse. They landed on Heather's hands and arms and on the dead woman's face.

"Are you sure about this?" Tom asked. "You don't ever move a body. I remember when I found Judith... those stairs... I didn't want the kids to think she'd done it on purpose. I wanted to change things. Hide the glass, hide the whiskey bottle. But I had to leave everything the way I found it... we shouldn't be doing this."

"We've already moved her. It's too late now. Just go a few steps back. It's easy. Please, Tom, do it now, I can't hold her forever! Go!"

Tom began backing up toward the heath.

"That's it, over the ditch and into the grass."

Getting over the ditch was tricky but they managed it. They laid the woman down in the long, white dry grass. "Now the bike," Heather said.

They dragged the front wheel of the bike from under the back tire of the Porsche. They carried the wrecked bike into the grass and hid it too. Heather adjusted some of the kangaroo grass stems, making them vertical again to hide their trail.

She ran back to the road and threw the bigger fragments of the bicycle into the grass. There was blood and smaller bike parts, but they couldn't do anything about that. Heather closed her eyes for a few seconds and then opened them and tried to find where they had hidden the body in the heath. You couldn't see a thing. Especially from a moving car.

She wiped the blood from her hands onto the blanket as best as she could. She wiped Tom's hands and forehead. Their fingernails were filthy and they smelled putrid. Blackflies and mosquitoes were landing on them with impunity.

"OK, now we just have to get out of here," Heather said as calmly as she could while putting the blanket back in the trunk of the Porsche. "Kids, I need you to help your dad push the car out of the ditch," she said, leading them to the back of the car.

"What happened to that lady?" Olivia said.

"We're moving her out of the sun and then we're going to call the police," Heather said.

"Do you know what you're doing, Heather?" Olivia asked. "Shouldn't we get an ambulance or something?"

"Yes, we'll get an ambulance later, Olivia," Heather said. "We just need to get the car going. Tom, please come here and show the kids what to do. I'll drive."

"I should drive," Tom said.

"No, I'm lighter than you and you're stronger than me. You push and I'll drive."

"That makes sense," he said.

Heather walked along the ditch and got in the driver's side. She adjusted the rearview and caught a glimpse of her own face.

Where had this Heather come from? Had this Heather been lurking there the whole time? Was it just because Tom was concussed and she had to step up, or was this always part of her? Adrenaline was some of it. When that wore off, she'd probably become a wreck.

She engaged the traction control and switched it to low gear mode. Her old Honda was a manual and she was comfortable with clutch and stick. This wouldn't be difficult. She hit the ignition button and the Porsche started.

"Everyone ready?" she asked.

"Yes," Tom said.

"Push!" she yelled and applied pressure to the gas pedal.

The wheels spun in the ditch and the car didn't move.

"Did you switch on the traction control?" Tom shouted.

"Yes! Keep pushing," Heather replied.

They shoved, and the front wheel began to crawl its way out of the ditch. She kept the steering wheel steady, and ever so slowly the heavy vehicle climbed out onto the road.

They were perpendicular to any oncoming traffic. "Get in! Get the kids in!" Heather said. Tom jumped in the front passenger seat. The kids got in the back.

Now all she had to do was turn the—

Something in her field of view.

Another car was coming. A Toyota. One of the vehicles from the farm. She was never going to be able to turn in time. *Shit. Another thirty seconds and no one would have been the wiser...*

She turned the Porsche onto the left side of the road, and the Toyota pulled up next to them. A window wound down. It was Jacko and Matt.

"Hi," Heather said.

"What happened to you lot?" Matt asked.

"Nothing. Just turning," Heather said.

"Did you go in the sheugh?" Jacko asked.

"The what?"

"Ma calls it the sheugh. That ditch. Did you go in it?"

"Yes, but we're OK now," Heather said.

"Your airbags went off," Matt said.

"They did," Heather said. "Car is so sensitive—we weren't even going fast...anyway, we're fine, thank you for stopping. We better go if we're going to catch the ferry," Heather said.

"Is your husband OK? You OK, mate? You look like shit. You hit your head?" Matt asked.

"I'm fine," Tom said.

"What about the kiddies?"

"They're fine. Everyone is fine. We just better go get that ferry."

"Yeah, you should go," Matt agreed.

"We will. Thank you."

"You didn't see Ellen by any chance? A girl on a bike?" Jacko asked.

"No," Tom said quickly.

"We didn't see anyone," Heather added. "Well, I guess we better go. Bye."

She wound the window up and waved and began driving down the road.

In the rearview she saw Jacko and Matt sit in the car for a moment before Matt opened the door and got out.

She saw him get down on one knee and begin looking at the ground before she lost sight of him at the bend in the road.

"Shit," Heather muttered and hit the gas pedal hard. "Seat belts, everyone!" she called and drove the Porsche at seventy miles an hour in the direction of the ferry pier.

They reached the ferry terminal in two minutes, and fortunately the ferry was there.

She slowed the Porsche and fixed a smile on her face.

"No one say anything, OK?" she said, looking at Tom and then turning around to the kids. "No one say anything. We'll sort this out when we're over the water."

She waved to Ivan, pulled the car to a stop, and wound the window down as he came over.

"Hi there!" she said.

"You see a koala or two?" Ivan asked, leaning into the car window. It was then that Heather noticed he had a black-and-yellow object attached to his overalls. It was a walkie-talkie.

"Oh, yes," Heather assured him.

Ivan picked his nose and sighed. "So *you're* going to drive onto the ferry? Not your husband?"

"I'll drive. He's a bit tired."

"You know, I can do it if you want. Never driven a Porsche before," Ivan said.

Heather took a quick look at the blood all over the steering wheel. "No, I'm happy driving it on if you'll guide me," she said with a winning smile.

"Course I'll guide you, missy. No worries. Take a little spill, did you? I see the airbags went off."

"Not really—we just went into a ditch. The airbags are so sensitive. The rental guy warned us about it," Heather said.

"Modern cars! Drove me old Holden Sandman thirty years, never had a problem. Kids get pics near the koalas?"

"Um, yes," Heather said, hoping Ivan wouldn't ask to see them.

"Evil little bastards. They can give you a nasty scratch. The koalas, I mean, not your kids! All right, I'll put the ramp down and you just drive on slowly. Come to a full stop and put your hand brake on. What you Yanks call the emergency brake. It's right next to your seat."

Ivan lowered the ramp and she drove onto the ferry.

"That wasn't so bad, was it?" Ivan said.

"Not at all."

Heather turned the engine off. Ivan put his hands into his pockets and pulled out a pack of cigarettes. He lit one.

He didn't seem to be in any particular hurry to get going.

"Um, look, could we go over now?" Heather asked.

Ivan shook his head. "I'd just as soon wait. That Dutch couple should be along any minute. I told them to be sharpish."

"Matt said you'd take us over now," Heather said.

"Matt? He gets a bit big for his boots sometimes. He's not even an O'Neill. He's a Watson. This is my ferry and I decide when we bloody go."

"We're sort of rushing to get back to Melbourne. We have a dinner reservation."

Ivan grunted and put his hands on his pockets. "I'd have to make two trips..."

Heather reached into her jeans pocket, pulled out a fifty-dollar bill, and examined it to make sure there was no blood on it.

"That would be a big hassle for you. Perhaps if I made it worth your while?" she asked, holding the bill out the window.

Ivan grinned and snatched it. "Let's get going."

He raised the ramp and closed the gate at the back of the ferry.

Heather looked behind her to see if she could spot any other cars coming down the road.

So far, so good.

Ivan unhooked the ropes that attached the ferry to the shore and jumped back onto the boat. He started the diesel engine.

"Should we tell him about the woman?" Olivia asked.

"No one says anything until we're on the other side," Heather hissed.

"Mainland Australia, here we come!" Ivan announced. "You can get out of the car if you want."

"We're OK," Heather replied.

A white wake boiled behind the ferry, and Dutch Island slowly began to recede into the distance.

Heather found that she had been holding her breath.

Ivan walked up to the car window.

"Anyone tell you about the foxes? Me and Kate have been trapping the little bastards. Invasive species. Kate's got quite the collection of skulls. They pay us for them. The state."

"We didn't see any foxes," Heather said, putting her hand over the blood on the steering wheel.

"All right. Well, look, if I see any sharks I'll let you know and you can take a pic," Ivan said and went back to the tiller.

"I think we—" Tom began and stopped as Ivan snapped the walkie-talkie off his lapel.

"What?" Ivan was saying. "I can't hear you. I can't bloody hear you."

He put the diesel engine into idle. He banged the walkie-talkie and fiddled with its dial. "I can't hear you, mate," he said.

Heather's knuckles were white as she gripped the Porsche's steering wheel. Sweat drenched the back of her T-shirt. She knew she looked like shit. Police-lineup-guilty.

"Maybe we should—" Tom began.

"No," Heather said.

"I think I got you, mate!" Ivan said. "Speak up."

Ivan walked to the back of the ferry and had a conversation on the walkie-talkie that Heather couldn't hear.

She didn't like this at all. She took out her phone and thumb-typed Help to Carolyn, the last person she had texted.

Unable to send. No wireless signal, the report came back.

Ivan clipped the radio back onto his lapel.

He picked up a sports bag, unzipped it, and removed an object.

Heather leaned over the steering wheel to see what it was.

"What's he doing?" Olivia asked.

"I don't know."

Ivan walked slowly back to the driver's-side window. He pointed an ancient-looking revolver at Heather's face. "Hand me all your phones and then get out of the car nice and slow-like. If you do any monkey business, anything at all, I'll shoot one of the kiddies. Do you understand me?"

6

The Toyota Hilux was waiting for them at the Dutch Island dock. They were bundled into the back by a fierce blond woman with a pump-action shotgun.

This, they learned, was Kate, the youngest of Ma's children.

"No talking," Kate said.

The road from the ferry to the farm was bleak. Empty heathland punctuated by maybe a dozen abandoned burned-out vehicles dumped and left to rust. The farm itself was a motley collection of barns, sheds, frail Buster Keaton houses, two smaller homesteads, and a large farmhouse facing a yard. The buildings had corrugated-iron roofs in a state of disrepair. Children in dust-bowl overalls watched the car arrive.

They were marched into the farmhouse.

The kids, Heather saw, were wilting fast. Olivia was wearing her jeans and a Grimes T-shirt. Owen was wearing heavy green cargo shorts with his usual red hoodie and Adidas sneakers. She'd pulled on DL 1961 jeans and a black T-shirt. Tom was in thick chinos and a white long-sleeved button-down oxford shirt. All of it was sartorially appropriate for Washington State heat but not Australia heat.

"Over here!" Kate said and forced them onto a sofa.

The room began to fill up with people.

Matt, Ivan, Jacko, and another brother, Brian, squeezed onto an opposite sofa. Matt had taken off his cowboy hat. He and Jacko and Brian had all gotten rifles. Kate was standing by the window with her shotgun. No one was speaking. It was a large space diminished by the accumulation of generations of furniture and knickknacks. There was a fireplace with a fire actually burning in the grate, in this heat. On a mantel there were dozens of family photographs; more on the wall with ancient yellow wallpaper that was peeling in the corners. Pictures of the farm in better days. Pictures of Ireland. Postcards from Sydney and London. Years of baking summers had cracked the floorboards and filled the cracks with dead bugs and garbage. The sofas were leather, patched with duct tape, covered with blankets. Seemingly the whole O'Neill clan had come in here to gawk at them. Men and women with guns. Kids who had been giggling now hushed. A dog sitting between Matt's legs looked nervously up the stairs.

A grandfather clock was ticking impossibly slow seconds.

No one seemed to know what was going to happen next.

The temperature was unbearable.

Heather was squeezing Tom's hand on one side and Olivia's hand on the other. Normally Olivia didn't let Heather touch her. At least Tom seemed to be doing a little better. He had lost that terrible pallor, and his eyes were back to normal.

"What time does Danny get back?" Jacko asked Matt in a low voice.

"Won't be back until after six," Matt said.

"Right..." Jacko said.

The stairs creaked.

Creaked again.

Everyone looked up.

Heather saw a pair of feet at the top of the landing. The feet took a step down and became a pair of ankles and then calves. A powerful woman in pink slippers and a pink dress was making her way down the stairs with the assistance of a stick on one side and a little girl on the other. She was in her seventies, pale, with an eye patch over her left eye. She was wearing a bright copper-colored wig. There was something terrifying about her that had nothing to do with the way she looked. Heather had massaged plenty of older clients, many of whom were physically imposing. This was something different. This woman changed the gravity well of a room. Electrified it. Heather could tell that everyone in here was afraid of her, and that made Heather afraid of her too.

She came down the staircase slowly.

Very slowly.

Two kids scrambled up from a rocking chair near the fire. Matt turned the chair so it was facing the room, not the fireplace. When she reached the bottom of the stairs, the woman wheezed heavily and then continued her progress across the living room like an old pope arriving at an inquisition.

Matt helped the woman into the rocking chair and when he sat down again, the dog hid under his legs.

A noise like a broken lawn-mower engine escaped from the woman's mouth, and a child brought her a glass of a clear liquid that she knocked back with satisfaction.

This, evidently, was Ma.

"They're the Americans?" Ma said in a rattle that seemed to come from the wrong side of the grave.

"Yeah. Americans," Matt said.

"I've known a few Yanks. Terry said they were all right in Vietnam. Ones I met were OK. What does he do for a living?" Ma asked.

"He's a doctor. Dr. Thomas Baxter. He looks after people's knees. He's got ID. It checks out," Matt said.

"How much money in the wallet?"

"Four hundred bucks."

"And how much did you scumbags get already?" Ma said.

"Nine hundred," Matt replied sheepishly.

"That's not much. Not much for a life. What does she do?"

"Massage therapist, she says," Jacko said.

"Jesus. One step up from whore," Ma said. "When does Danny get back?"

"Not until after six, maybe seven," Matt said.

"Who else did you bastards let onto my island today?" Ma said, scowling at Ivan.

"It wasn't my fault, Ma. Jacko and Matt—" Ivan protested.

"Enough! I'm surprised at you, Matthew," Ma said, shaking her head.

"I'm sorry, Ma."

"You let another vehicle on, didn't you?" Ma said.

"Yes, Ma, couple of Krauts," Ivan said.

"And where are they now?"

"Probably waiting at the ferry," Ivan said.

"Well, somebody bloody find them and bring them here!" Ma growled.

Jacko nodded at a kid, who ran outside.

"Look, I'm very sorry about this," Tom said. "She came right out of nowhere. I honked the horn and the woman didn't hear me—"

"She's deaf!" one of the children said.

"Deaf?" Tom said.

"Yeah, Ellen was deaf," Ma said.

"I couldn't help it. I went straight into the back of her. It all happened so fast. I mean, obviously we will cooperate fully with the authorities."

"What will you do, *Dr. Baxter?*" Jacko asked, sneering through Tom's title.

"It's, um, Tom. Um, look, I'll admit full responsibility. And— and I'm sure my insurance company will pay out accordingly," Tom said.

"Insurance companies don't always pay out, do they?" Ma said.

"They will. I'm admitting fault."

"Where are you going to do this admitting of fault?" Ma asked.

"Here, and of course back in Melbourne. I'll make sure I cooperate fully with the police investigation and even postpone our flight back if necessary."

"Nah," Ma said. "No Melbourne. No flight back."

Murmurs in the room and then silence again.

The melancholy ticking clock. The fire crackling. Mosquitoes buzzing. Dog whining. At the back of the room, Heather saw the man who had sold them the sausage sizzles. When the Dutch couple were rounded up, everyone who knew about them coming over here would be in this house under Ma's control.

"You tried to hide the body. You did a hit-and-run. That's a crime. That's a crime on Dutch Island and in Victoria and in America," Ma said.

"That, um, that was my fault. Tom had hit his head. That was my idea," Heather said. "I don't know what I was thinking. I was scared. I wanted us to get over to the mainland first before we called the police."

"Scared. Aye," Ma said. "We don't want anyone to be scared, do we?" Ma shook her head and closed her eye. She seemed to be thinking things over. A log in the fire cracked and split.

"Look, uh, maybe Ivan and me should get the ferry over to Stamford Bridge and call the coppers, let them handle it—what do you think, Ma?" Matt asked.

Heather looked at him and mouthed, *Thank you.*

Ivan and Jacko shook their heads.

"Too much history with Vic police. You know what'll happen," Jacko muttered. "One of us will get bloody blamed for it and for other shit, making our own grog or something, and this bastard will get off scot-bloody-free."

There was a murmuring of agreement from most of the adults in the room.

"Nah, no cops. Terry never needed no cops," Ma said.

A long silence. Kids whispering. Sweat pouring down Heather's back. It had to be 115 degrees in here. Even the big blackflies looked defeated and lethargic.

"Perhaps I could agree to some sort of down payment. Now. As, um, proof of my sincerity and culpability," Tom suggested.

Heather gave his hand a little squeeze. This was maybe the way to go.

Ma coughed and someone got her another drink.

Tom got to his feet. "Look, I'm very sorry, I understand your—"

"Who said he could stand up? Sit him down, Ivan!"

Ivan thumped Tom in the stomach with the butt of his rifle.

"Jesus! Not with the gun, mate!" Matt groaned but it was too late; Tom was doubled over on the floor.

Heather found herself getting up and lunging at Ivan. He slapped her hard on the face. Harder than she'd ever been hit in her life. She turned almost completely around and went down too.

The children screamed. The dog began to bark.

"Christ, Matt, I can't think with this racket. Why did you bring 'em in here? Get them out of my bloody house while I decide what we're going to do!" Ma said.

Heather dry-heaved in panic.

No one knew they had come here. Their phones were gone. The conference organizers wouldn't start to get worried about Tom until Monday night or even Tuesday morning before his keynote. And by then it would be too late.

7

Ma pointed her stick at Jacko and Matt. "It didn't used to be that I'd have to say something twice around here. Get them out of my house! Get 'em out, search 'em good, put them in the old shearing shed until Danny gets back."

Heather was facedown on the wooden floor. Her left arm was underneath her body. She reached into her pocket, took out the miniature penknife she'd gotten in Alice Springs, and shoved it down the front of her jeans. Not a moment too soon. Jacko grabbed her painfully by the hair and tugged her to her feet. His brother Ivan pushed her to the front door, where Kate grabbed her by the back of the neck and gave her an extra shove. She tripped down the porch steps and put her hands out to save her face as she fell again into the dirt.

It was dusk and the red disk of the sun had sunk into the mainland, leaving great throbbing waves of heat in its wake. Olivia was crying. Heather got to her feet and tried to take Olivia's hand but Jacko shoved them apart.

They were marched to the old shearing shed, which was a wooden structure about thirty feet long by ten feet wide. The door had a padlock on it. There was straw on the floor and it stank inside. It clearly hadn't been used for shearing for many years. The family was pushed in.

"Sit!" Jacko said.

Heather sat on the floor.

"We should tie them up to be on the safe side," Jacko said.

"Yeah," Kate said.

"Ma didn't say anything about tying anybody up," Matt said.

"Use your head, mate. Yeah, easy, we'll tie their hands," Ivan suggested.

"Nah, you lot are as thick as pig shit. They can still just untie themselves," Kate said. "We have to tie them *to* something. Tell Freddie to go get us some number three cord, I've got this. Meanwhile, let's do what Ma told us to do and search the bastards."

"My specialty," Jacko growled. "Bloody cops frisked me so many times, I know all their tricks. Did we get their phones?"

"Yeah," Ivan said. "No signal here, of course."

"Grab that lad for me, will ya?"

Heather saw them push Owen against one of the walls of the shed. Jacko searched his pockets and ran his hands up his legs and back. They took Owen's money and the twenty-sided die he always kept with him. They'd already gotten Tom's wallet and phone. They took his keys and a pen and didn't find anything else when they searched him.

"You next, missy," Jacko said to Olivia.

"Could you please get one of the women to search her?" Heather asked. "She's just a frightened little girl."

Jacko made a fist and shoved it into Heather's cheek. "You're getting on me nerves. You better shut up or I'm going to break your bloody jaw," he said.

"You better not!" Tom said.

"Or you'll do what?" Jacko growled.

"I'm sorry, I—" Heather began.

"Didn't I say *shut up*?" Jacko screamed.

Heather nodded. She was trembling all over.

"Just go easy on the girl, mate," Matt said to Jacko.

"I know what I'm doing," Jacko said and patted down Olivia. He turned to Heather. "You last, princess," Jacko said.

"She's the troublemaker," someone muttered from the doorway.

"Yeah, I know," Jacko said and pushed her face against the shed wall. Heather felt his rough hand move up and down her legs. He reached in her jeans pockets, took her money and the cigarette pack from yesterday, slapped her ass pockets, and ran his hands up over her back and under her arms. "Marlboro," Jacko said, pocketing them.

"Cigarettes?" Tom blurted out. As if Heather's secret smoking habit from that lost world mattered now.

"Is she clean?" Ivan asked.

"She's clean," Jacko said. "Now, what about tying 'em?"

"Yeah, I've been thinking about this," Kate said. "What do you reckon, lads? Tie their hands, space them well apart, and then—see those ewe hooks on the ceiling?"

"Yeah?"

"A rope from each of those hooks to a rope around their necks. Take the slack out of it, and that way they can't move around in here to help untie each other. What do you think?"

"Who knew it? Kate's a bloody genius!" Jacko said and all the men laughed.

"This is madness! You can't do that to children!" Heather begged them.

Jacko turned to Tom. "She really is a troublemaker. She is

going to get you and your family seriously hurt, mate, if she doesn't shut up."

Heather shook her head at Tom.

"I think my wife is worried something might happen to the kids," Tom protested. "You can't possibly think about putting nooses around the necks of small children."

"Eye for an eye, then," Ivan said with an unpleasant laugh.

"If you tie the rope around their waists, you can secure them to the side of the hut that way. I think that will be safer for everyone," Tom suggested.

"Secure them to what? Those planks? Nah, mate. The hooks are the only way," Kate said. "Just tell your bloody kids not to move around too much and they won't choke themselves to death."

"Hang about! What if they stand up?" Matt said. "Your plan is rubbish, Kate."

Kate glared at Matt. "Tie their hands, rope around the neck going to the ewe hook, and another rope from the neck to the plank behind their head. That satisfy you?"

"They won't be able to move a bloody inch." Jacko laughed.

"That's the idea, mate," Kate said.

Heather watched helplessly as the children were sat down on the floor, their hands tied in front of them, and a noose run from each one's neck to a hook in the ceiling. Another rope around the neck tied them to the wall of the shearing shed. Tom was next. She was last. Jacko pushed her down, tied her wrists together tight, and put two ropes around her neck.

"Make sure it's good and tight on her," Ivan said. They took almost all the slack off the noose and she could barely move a muscle without the ropes starting to choke her.

"Maybe we should tie their hands *behind* their backs?" Jacko asked.

"Oh my God, how have we made this so bloody complicated? Just leave it!" Ivan said.

"All right, mate. Everyone cozy? Right, just hold on to your knickers until Danny gets back," Jacko said and closed the door on them, plunging the shed into darkness.

8

Matt took Kate by the arm and led her away from the shearing shed.

She shook him off. "What?" she demanded.

"We can't do this. We can't keep these people. One of us is going to have to go over to the mainland and get a cop," Matt said.

Kate took a step away from him.

"Are you crazy? You want me to tell Jacko you just said that? Or Ivan? Or Ma?"

"We have to think about the future, Kate. You know as well as I do that the trust fund is running out. How long can we keep this all going? Two more years? Three?"

"What's your point?"

"That eco-lodge idea Terry had. It's a *good idea*. Tourists coming over legit. Staying the night, spending money. We all benefit. But if we do this, it's all over, isn't it? Forget it."

"Terry's dead."

"Yeah, but the idea isn't. You agreed with it. You, me, Janey, maybe some of the others. We talk to Ma before Ivan and Jacko and that lot get her worked up."

Kate was shaking her head. "Ma thinks you're the golden boy, Matt. She trusts you."

"I'm *thinking* of Ma. I'm thinking about what's best for all of us. You want Jacko to run this thing? With half a jug of grog in him? Bloody Jacko?"

"They came over here. They killed Ellen. They'll get what's coming to them!" Kate insisted.

"This is going to end up with more people dying. Ivan told me what happened to that girl Jacko picked up in the early 2000s. Jesus! It doesn't have to be that way. We can talk to Ma, you and me! Our whole future is at stake here. Look, when the trust's done and the money's gone, what will we have to fall back on? Nothing. The eco-lodge, tourism—that kind of thing could save us."

"I don't like this sort of talk, Matt. We're family—we're united," Kate said.

"Of course we are. But we have to do what's best for the family in the long run. Not just tonight."

Kate considered it and then shook her head and slowly raised her shotgun. It came to rest pointing at Matt's chest. "You have to make a decision, Matty," she said. "Are you from over there or are you from here? Are you one of them or one of us? Which is it?"

"You wouldn't," Matt said, staring at the gleaming double barrels of her shotgun. A gun that had killed hundreds of rabbits, cats, foxes, and God knew what else.

"Them or us, Matthew?"

Matt took off his hat and shook his head. The hatband was drenched with sweat. He mopped his brow and nodded. "Ma took me in. Treated me like a son. It's always going to be family first."

Kate lowered the gun. "That's what I had to hear, Matt. Jacko and Ivan never need to know we had this conversation. But I'll be watching you. Just remember where your loyalties lie."

9

The kids were crying. Heather was trying to breathe. Dozens of flies were circling in slow spirals about him. Tom's head was throbbing. They'd done this all wrong. If they'd come clean in the first place, perhaps the O'Neills wouldn't have reacted with such hostility. He should have followed his first instincts: Confessed all. Gotten the police involved. Why had he listened to Heather? She was a Millennial. She didn't know anything.

He shook his head.

It was too late for recriminations.

This didn't necessarily have to be a fatal mistake. This wasn't some hick county in America. This wasn't the third world. This was Australia, one of the most civilized countries on Earth. They would threaten them and try to bully them, but an arrangement *would* be made. This very situation had happened to Thomas Edison in Germany. Edison had run over a peasant woman in his car and he had simply opened his wallet and paid off the entire—

"What's going to happen to us?" Olivia asked softly.

"Nothing's going to happen, sweetie. They're just trying to intimidate us. That's what bullies do," Tom said.

"You killed the woman," Owen said.

"It was an accident, Owen. I didn't kill her. She swerved onto the road with her bike. It was an accident. It's the sort of tragic thing that happens all the time."

"That's a lie. You are both liars. That's not what happened," Owen said, leaning forward but stopping abruptly as the ropes choked him.

Tom looked at Heather for support but she was writhing around in her jeans trying to get comfortable or doing God knew what.

"This is your fault, Heather," Olivia cried. "We should have called the police. You don't run away when you have an accident! Didn't you ever learn that where you came from?"

"There was no phone signal," Heather said.

"Now they're going to take revenge on us," Olivia said.

"That's not how things work. Not in Australia. Not anywhere. They're angry now but they'll see reason. This is a police matter. Sooner or later they'll call the police," Tom insisted.

"They said there aren't any phones here either," Owen said.

"They'll take the ferry over to the mainland and call from there." Tom could see Heather still wriggling in the dirt. "What are you doing over there?" he asked.

Heather was drenched with sweat. She looked up at him. "I shoved my key chain down the front of my jeans. I think I can get it out."

"What good will that do?"

"There's a penknife on it," Heather whispered. "I picked it up in Alice Springs. I thought they'd make us turn out our pockets, so I hid it."

"Jesus!" Tom said. "You're amazing."

"Amazing if I can get it out," she said as she tried to manipulate the penknife down her pant leg.

Tom's senses heightened. Here was a plan B in the making. He looked through the cracks in the timbers. It was dark. Presumably the O'Neills would debate what to do overnight and in the morning they'd probably be more rational. But why take that risk? If they could cut through their bonds, it wouldn't be difficult to dig under the dirt at the back of the hut. It was, what, two miles across country to the ferry? If the boat was still there and he could get its diesel engine working, they'd be across the little strait to the mainland in fifteen minutes. They were in a semi-enclosed bay—surely the currents were bound to take them ashore. If he couldn't get the diesel engine working, they could maybe launch it anyway and drift over on the tide.

Heather had now maneuvered the penknife down her leg and out the bottom of her jeans. She grabbed it in her tied hands and opened the blade. It was a tiny little thing.

"Is it sharp?" Tom asked.

"Yes," Heather said, testing it with her thumb. "Shall I try to throw it to you?"

"No! Don't do that. It might land in the middle between us, and then where would we be? Cut yourself free first and then bring it over," Tom said in a loud whisper.

Heather began sawing at the binds on her hands.

"Is it working?" Tom asked.

"I don't know. I think so, yes," Heather said.

"I can't breathe, Dad," Olivia complained.

"I'm sorry, honey. Try to put a finger between the ropes and your neck," Tom said.

"OK," Olivia replied, as if this were somehow a normal question and answer.

"What'll we do if we can cut the ropes?" Owen asked.

"We'll get ourselves free and then dig under the planks at the back of the shed. We'll make a run for it into the undergrowth. The ferry dock is only two miles away across country. We can easily get there," Tom said.

"And then what?" Owen asked.

"We'll take it to the other side."

"What if the ferry is tied up on the other side of the channel?" Owen said.

Tom winced. He hadn't thought of that. "We'll hide out on the island."

"They'll find us," Olivia whimpered.

Tom shook his head. "No, they won't find us."

Tom could see that Heather had the penknife between the thumb and forefinger of her right hand. The rope was very thick hemp and she looked so awkward trying to cut it. "Is it definitely working?" he asked.

"I think so," she said.

"Good, keep at it."

"Can you really do this, Tom?" Heather asked him. "Hide us from them?"

"Of course I can," he assured her.

Owen was getting excited now. "We could get rabbits. We could make spears and hunt them."

"Don't be dumb, Owen," Olivia said.

"Did you tell anyone about us coming here?" Heather asked.

"No, but the GPS on our phones was working all the way through most of the peninsula, so the police will be able to track our movements and figure out where we went."

"They won't know we've come over here, though. The GPS wasn't working on the ferry," Heather said.

Tom didn't need her negativity now and she had that young person's thing of saying everything that came into her head. "Honey!" he said with mild reproach. "The police will figure it out, won't they?"

Heather picked up on his signals. "Yes, yes, you're right, of course. The cops will be looking for us by now and they'll get us tomorrow."

Tom nodded. If they stayed calm, looked around them, tried to be present, it would be OK.

"That's right. All three of you have to trust—"

Voices, people moving toward them...

"Shit, they're coming back, hide the knife in the dirt," Tom said.

Heather fumbled the penknife into the floor as best she could just as the shed door opened.

"We need to talk to both of you again," Matt said.

"We need water for the children," Tom said.

"I'll get you water. We decided we'd better talk to you and your wife before Danny gets here," Matt said and began undoing the rope that tied Heather's neck to the timber frame. Tom had an anxious moment as Matt looked at the floor near where Heather was sitting, but he didn't see the penknife. Matt undid the rope around Tom's neck and pulled them both to their feet.

"This is utterly disgraceful. You should be ashamed of yourself. You can't keep us like this. These are little kids! What are you thinking?" Heather said to Matt.

Even in the gloomy light of the hut, Tom could see that Matt was embarrassed.

"Look, yeah, I'm sorry about all this. But I did bloody tell you not to come here," Matt said.

"If you insist on keeping me and Tom so we can sort out some form of compensation, then so be it," Heather said. "But you need to take the children to the mainland on the ferry."

Tom gave her an *I've got this* look. He wanted to deescalate the situation. Heather was getting herself worked up. There was no way Ma would ever allow such a thing. "No, we don't need you to do that. But our kids need water," Tom said.

"I'll bring them water. Come on," he said. "Danny's on the ferry. He's nearly here."

"I'm not leaving these children in here by themselves," Heather said.

"I give you my word nothing's going to happen to them. Trust me," Matt said. He said it so sincerely that Tom believed him, and Heather found herself nodding.

"Come on, Heather," Tom said. "Let's be calm and we'll go fix this."

Kate was waiting outside the shearing shed with her shotgun. "She's in the farmyard," she said to Matt. "We brought Ma's chair out."

They trudged between the farm buildings and odd bits of machinery that resembled sinister modern-art installations.

They reached the farmyard, where the Porsche was still parked, and Tom noticed the Dutch couple's camper van. Where were they in all this?

Ma was sitting in her rocking chair with about fifteen or twenty people gathered around her in the twilight. The flies had not dispersed when the sun set, and there was a smell of decaying kelp blowing in from the sea. Most of the adults were armed, Tom noted. Heather had better not try anything foolish.

"Danny's coming. We better settle this now," Ma said. "You two stand in front of me. We're gonna sort this out like grown-ups. Fair dinkum and shake on it. Agreed?"

Tom nodded. "Of course. Once again, I am so sorry about Ellen. I apologize profusely on behalf of myself and my family."

"Good," Ma said. "You'll have to apologize to Danny too. Make it a real bloody good one. He loved that girl."

"I will. Yes. And, look, before Danny gets here, maybe we could come to an arrangement and present it to him as a *fait accompli*," Tom suggested. "A *fait accompli* is a—"

"I know what it is!" Ma said. "I went to Mount Lourdes Grammar, didn't I? Let's see if we can get this sorted."

Tom began to relax. Admittedly, Ma looked terrifying, but this was a note of compromise. The word *sorted* was a good sign. Also, there was a strong hint of Ireland in Ma's voice. She must have come over here as a little girl. The matriarch of Dutch Island was not the descendant of some isolated inbred cult of pagan idol worshippers. She was just another immigrant trying to make good in a big country.

Tom gave Heather a reassuring smile. He walked closer to Ma, head bowed, hands bound in front of him like a defeated enemy. "Obviously, what happened here is a terrible tragedy. It was my fault and I'm sorry and my heart goes out to Ellen's family and Danny."

"Danny will be gutted," a man said from the crowd. There was a general murmuring of agreement.

Tom bit his lip. Yes, the entire island was one large family, but Ma ran the roost. Her word would be law. All he had to do was persuade her.

"I'm very sorry about the accident, but there was nothing malicious in it. It was no one's fault. It was just one of those things that happen," Tom said.

"You were going too fast on that road," Kate said, and again there was grumbling from the crowd.

Tom knew a heated dispute would be fatal to his cause. He just had to agree and appear contrite. "Perhaps you're right. Perhaps we were going too fast," he continued. "I did try to save her. I tried hard. I'm a doctor and I did my best. And afterward, when we saw it was no good, we just panicked. We did completely the wrong thing. Look, there's no way we can bring back Ellen. But we can offer you, um, compensation."

"Do you mean money?" Jacko asked.

"Yes."

"You're a doc. How much is in that? Me niece Maya is a nurse and she gets paid shit," Ma said.

"I've been doing well lately. I made Seattle's Best Doctors this year and, um, well, to be honest, I married into quite a bit of money," Tom said.

"How much money?" Kate asked.

"My late wife, Judith, came from a wealthy Seattle family. Have you heard of Microsoft?"

Matt and Kate and Ivan all nodded. "We know it," Matt said.

"Judith's father was an early investor. We have shares and—"

"Shares! How much do you have in cash?" Ma demanded. "Here in Australia?"

"Just a few hundred dollars in Australia," Tom admitted.

"But we can get more here tomorrow by wire transfer from America," Heather added.

"I was coming to that. We can get money transferred here from America quite easily. A lot of money."

"How much?" Ma asked.

Tom leaned back on his heels. Everyone was looking at him. Moths were flying into the arc lamps. The stars were coming out. The air was freshening. Temperatures were cooling— both literally and metaphorically. He had won them over with common sense and calm persuasion. The thing they didn't teach you in medical school, bedside manner, was one of the most important skills to learn.

He had this.

Money was the key. They had moved on from revenge to money. Tom knew he had to pick the right Goldilocks amount. Not too much to seem preposterous but not too little either. "Five hundred thousand dollars. U.S. dollars," he said.

A few *ooh*s went through the crowd.

"Half a million bucks?" Kate said skeptically.

"I have that in my account, yes," Tom insisted.

"How does the transfer work?" an older woman in filthy blue jeans and a ripped tank top asked. She also had a gun, an ancient-looking rifle that she was using as a walking stick.

"Yeah, how—how is that supposed to work?" Ivan demanded.

"It's in a checking account in America. I have more in a savings account but I can transfer everything from the checking account without raising any suspicions," he said.

"It's a load of bollocks," Kate said.

"How is it bollocks?" Matt asked.

"If we let them go to Melbourne to get the money, we'll never hear from any of them again," Kate said.

More murmuring.

"We keep the nippers here. He goes and gets the half a million in cash and brings it back. And we swap the dough for the kids. A hundred thousand to Danny in compensation for his loss, the rest split between us," Matt said and looked at Ma for her approval.

"A hundred thousand for a dead wife!" Kate said.

"Well, like me, she wasn't blood, was she?" Matt said.

There was some laughter from the crowd. Tom saw that the mood was changing. They were becoming more reasonable. "I think that's fair," Tom said.

"It might be. Ellen's only been here a year," Ma conceded.

"No! The kids can't stay here as hostages. They'll be terrified. Tom takes the kids with him and I stay here and he—" Heather began but Tom interrupted.

"For God's sake, Heather! I've got this, *honey*. It'll be OK. Maybe I could take Olivia with me to help sort things out. You'll be here to look after Owen. I'll get the cash from the bank and be back this time tomorrow. Everything will be fine. Then we can all go home. We can get this done," Tom said.

Her brow furrowed and then she nodded. "OK."

Ma also gave him a nod.

He began to relax a tiny bit. *This might actually work.*

"How do we know he's good for the money? That's a lot of money," Kate said.

"Americans are rich!" someone else said.

"Look at his bloody car, you idiot. It's a bloody Porsche, ain't it?"

"I'm good for the money," Tom insisted over the rising hubbub.

Ma nudged Ivan next to her. He lifted the pistol and fired it into the air.

Everyone immediately shut up. In the silence Tom could hear Heather whimpering.

"Right! Now that I have everybody's attention," Ma said. "First off, Dr. Thomas Baxter, if you come back with coppers, you will never see your wife or little boy again. Do you understand?"

"I completely understand," Tom replied.

"We will have taken them to another location."

"I understand."

"Second off, if you come with one dollar less than five hundred thousand, the deal's off."

"I won't. I'll bring exactly that amount."

"Third off, if, after you've all gone back to America, the coppers come up here asking questions about missing money, you better watch your back, matey boy. 'Cause we will tell the coppers about what you done and that will only be the start of it. We're a big family. One of us will get to America and find you."

"I won't renege on the deal. This is what I wanted to do from the very beginning. I know I did something wrong. I know there's nothing I can do to reset that. But I would have done this even if you weren't keeping my wife and son...as..." His voice trailed off. He didn't want to say the word *hostages*. This was an extraordinarily delicate situation and he didn't want to further screw everything up with the use of inflammatory language. "As your guests," he said.

Heather was agitated. She was normally so levelheaded; that was part of the reason he'd been attracted to her in the first place. She was the opposite of Judith in many, many ways. In the year he'd known her, she hadn't often lost her cool, but these were extraordinary circumstances. He could not afford to let her blow it now.

"It'll be OK, Heather, trust me," he said softly. "Look at me, honey. Look at me. Trust me. This will work. Take a deep breath. Come on."

She took a breath and nodded. "You'll come back with the money?"

"Of course."

"And you'll make them give us food and water?"

"Yes."

"All right."

In the distance Tom could hear the sound of a motorbike.

"That'll be Danny coming," Matt said. "Do we have a deal?"

"We do from me," Tom said.

"From us too," Ma said. "We're reasonable people, Dr. Baxter. We live here by ourselves. We don't do harm to anybody. We don't invite people to our island, but if they come, coppers or government, we expect them to be respectful."

"Of course. We made the mistake and I'm very sorry about it."

"We didn't want any of this—" Ma said.

"Sorry to interrupt, Ma, but we have another issue," Jacko said.

"What is it?" Ma asked.

"We found the Krauts and we're keeping them up at the house, but they really want to go," Jacko said.

"Tell them the ferry needs fixing," Ma said.

"Gotcha," Jacko said.

"Any other problems I have to solve?" Ma said and took a long drag of her cigarette.

"The children can't possibly stay in that room overnight. You'll have to move them," Heather said.

Oh, shit. We've won this. Don't cause any trouble, Tom was screaming at her telepathically.

Heather amazingly seemed to pick up on his thought. "Well, at the very least, we'll need some bedding and something to eat and drink, and you'll have to let us visit the bathroom, otherwise it's going to be very unpleasant in there," Heather said.

The motorbike was very close now. It was driving up to the farm. Everything was hushed, waiting.

A line of clouds.

The silent stars.

The silent yellow sickle moon.

"Danny's gonna lose his shit," Jacko muttered.

"We've done our parley and we made a deal," Matt said. "Danny's gonna have to like it or lump it."

"Yup," Ivan agreed. "Like Matt said, she wasn't blood."

The motorbike pulled to a stop in front of the farmhouse.

The eerie quiet grew deeper.

Flies.

Moths.

Vacuum.

Void.

Everyone waiting.

Suddenly there was a scream. "I reckon they told him," Kate said.

"You might be onto something there, Katie," Jacko said with a chuckle.

There was the sound of a scuffle, and the door to the farmhouse burst open with a gift of silver light.

There was a terrible wail, like a dog dying.

The sound of arguing.

Then silence.

A silhouette in the doorway.

Danny was carrying Ellen's body in his arms.

"Oh, shit," Matt whispered. "Jacko, be ready for him to do something dumb."

Danny carried Ellen into the farmyard. Like all the O'Neills, he was tall and skinny. He had thinning red hair and dark eyes.

He looked at Tom. "Is he the one?" he asked Ma, spitting the words out.

"Take it easy there, mate, we've fixed this," Jacko said.

"Yeah, they told me what you fixed," Danny said. "You think I'm going to take your dirty money? You think I'm gonna take one cent of that? For her?"

Danny set Ellen gently on the ground. She was a rag doll, broken in a dozen places. Danny caressed her face, shaking. "She was everything. She was better than all of you lot put together and you bloody know it!" Danny said.

"I'm so sorry. I really am," Tom said. He meant it. That poor woman. It was awful. But... but that wasn't the issue now. The issue was what to do next.

Danny stood. His eyes were red and vacant. He pointed a finger at Tom. "You killed her!"

Tom nodded. "It was an accident. And I'm sorry. But I—I take full responsibility."

"That's not enough!" Danny yelled.

"Steady on, mate. We've agreed. You missed the meeting. We all agreed and Ma decided," Matt said.

"Did you decide, Ma? Without me?" Danny said in a faraway monotone.

"I did. We decided. It's for the best," Ma replied firmly.

Danny walked over to Tom and poked him in the chest.

"I'm very sorry," Tom said softly.

"Sorry, are you? Sorry!" Danny's face was contorted with rage and grief. His eyes were slits of dark fury. Spittle ran down his chin. "And you've agreed, have you?" Danny said, still prodding Tom in the chest. "This rich bastard runs over my Ellen, an innocent who wouldn't harm a fly. All I have in the world. And you've agreed that we don't do anything about it?"

"I'm really devastated by what's happened. She just came out of nowhere, I—" Tom began. Danny shoved him hard in the chest. Tom tripped over his own feet and fell. Danny attempted to kick him but Matt wrapped Danny up in his big arms and lifted him off the ground.

"Ma made the call, mate!" Matt said.

Tom warily got to his feet.

"You can't decide nothing without me!" Danny screamed. "Look at her! Look what he done to her! She was beautiful. She was all I had. What am I going to do?"

"Mate, calm down, it's going to be all right," Matt insisted.

"How! How is it?" Danny yelled. "What about *his* wife? What if I do something to her?"

"No. This has nothing to do with my wife. This has nothing to do with my family. I was driving the car. This is on me," Tom said.

"On you?"

"On me," Tom said.

"Right, OK, OK, I understand," Danny said, calmer now. "Put me down, Matt. It's OK, put me down, mate."

Matt cautiously released his grip and Danny dropped to the ground.

"Nothing can bring back Ellen. Nothing. This is what's for the best," Matt said.

"I understand," Danny said. "I went out and got a job and got a wife. And you lot do nothing but sit here smoking and bitching and knocking back the grog in your trackies. And you scumbags are deciding for me?"

He went back to Ellen's body and kissed her and held her. He took something out of his pocket. A crucifix, Tom thought, as he saw it glint in the moonlight.

No, it wasn't a crucifix, it was a . . .

"Look out!" Heather yelled as Danny turned, ran at Tom, and stabbed the knife into him with such force that it nearly knocked him off his feet.

Heather screamed.

"Huhh," Tom said as the knife penetrated deep into his right side.

"Jesus! What have you done!" Tom heard Matt yelling.

"He got what was coming to him," Danny yelled back.

Danny pulled back the knife to stab Tom again. Before he could do it, Heather was on his back, scrambling to get her tied hands around his throat.

She has fight in her, that one, Tom thought as his legs gave way and he fell to the ground like a destringed marionette.

The ground was warm. Comforting.

The view from here was of feet and sideways farm buildings.

Heather was a tiny little thing, and Danny was, by comparison, a big man. It wasn't a fair fight, but Ivan and Matt were stepping in.

"You bloody arsehole!" Ivan was saying.

Danny was yelling something back.

The voices were fading. Everything was fading.

The fields.

The falling stars.

The sickle moon dissolving into vapor above the Earth.

His eyes were heavy.

Four thoughts went through his failing consciousness. Four thoughts that were four words:

Judith.

Heather.

Olivia.

Owen.

He tried to surf the now but it was so hard; the now kept slipping between his fingers.

He felt a spasm of worry, anxiety, fear.

Regrets.

Mistakes.

The day was cooling.

The earth was warm.

When he closed his eyes, the world disappeared completely.

He couldn't feel his fingertips.

He couldn't feel his legs.

And then there was no "he" to feel anything at all.

10

Heather had the hemp rope around Danny's neck and she just kept tightening it until Danny collapsed to his knees, dropping the knife.

"Stop this, Ivan!" Ma said.

Ivan grabbed Heather by the hair and tossed her into the dirt like she was nothing.

"I'll have her," Danny snarled, recovering himself.

"You've done enough mischief tonight, mate," Jacko said, putting a boot on Danny's back and flattening him. Matt took the rifle off his shoulder and pointed it at Danny. "That's enough, Dan!" he yelled.

Danny laughed bitterly. "Oh, it's come to this, has it? Who are you, anyway? You don't give orders to anybody here. Least of all me."

"I'm as much an O'Neill as anyone. And I am not going to have you tell me any different," Matt said.

Heather wasn't interested in any of this now. She crawled toward Tom.

He was lying on his side in a pool of blood.

"We have to call an ambulance!" she wailed hysterically.

"We've no phones here," Kate said.

"You have to help him!" Heather yelled.

"That's enough," Ma said.

"No! We can still save him," Heather said. "Please! We can help him!"

Heather grabbed Danny's fallen knife in her tied hands and struggled to her feet. There were half a dozen guns pointed at her now.

"You have to help," Heather pleaded, brandishing the knife.

"You should drop it, sweetheart," Kate said.

Ivan smacked Heather on the side of the head and snatched the knife out of her hands as she fell.

And then Kate fired a barrel of her shotgun into the air and everyone froze.

"Thank you, my dear," Ma said. "This is a bloody shambles, this is! Takes me to sort it as usual, eh? Never a moment's peace. First things first—get the bodies up to the house. Take 'em to the old meat locker."

"Krauts are up in the house. What about them?" Ivan said.

"Jesus wept! Don't let them see anything. And don't let them go. Keep them here until we figure out what we're going to bloody do," Ma said.

"We know what we're going to do," Jacko said. "We're not letting the cops have Danny."

With difficulty, Ma got out of her rocking chair. "Does anybody listen to me around here anymore?"

"Yes, Ma," half a dozen men said.

"Get these bodies up to the house!"

Two men picked up Tom, one taking his ankles and the other his shoulders, and carried him away. Heather was sobbing now. Tom was dead. Tom, who was so calm and centered. Tom, who knew everything. What the hell was she going to do?

Another two men took Ellen up to the house. Killer and victim united. What were their ghosts talking about?

Tom, oh my God, Tom.

Heather squeezed her eyes tight.

Tried to erase the last few hours.

That lifeless face. That lifeless crow's-wing fringe.

This can't be happening.

I'm in Melbourne. Tom's gonna wake me up and we're going to go see penguins and koalas.

She attempted to open her eyes but had to wipe blood from her eyelids first.

Mosquitoes.

Upside-down moon.

Crowd of people with guns.

Black blood in the dead-Tom dirt under the dead-Tom stars.

A little kid pointing a toy gun at her.

Real men with real guns.

She sat up.

People talking in low voices.

Heather knew she wasn't going to get many more chances to make them see reason.

"You have to let us go now. This has gone too far," she said.

"Shut this bitch up, Matthew. If she talks again without my permission, break her jaw," Ma said.

"You hear that?" Matt said to Heather.

She nodded.

"So what *are* we going to do?" Ivan asked.

"Get rid of them, sharpish!" someone said.

"Hold on," Danny said, wiping the dust off his clothes. "You have to ask me what to do. They belong to me. All of them."

"You stupid bastard," Kate said. "You cost us five hundred grand. You always were a dumb arsehole. Thick as shit, you. Thick as shit."

"Cut him some slack, Katie. Ellen's dead," Matt said.

"She is. She was all I had. You know that. No amount of money . . ." Danny's voice trailed away.

People came over to pat Danny on the back and touch him and hug him. Some took the opportunity to spit at, pinch, or poke Heather.

She could feel herself sinking. She was so thirsty. Everything ached. She was sitting cross-legged on the ground. A blood trail was making its way toward her through the dust. She tried to breathe. Breathing hurt. Her ribs hurt. The air was thick. Her grandmother said the dead could see us through mirrors. Maybe Tom could see her somehow. What would he advise her to do?

"If I have to be out here, can someone do something about the bloody mozzies?" Ma said.

Someone lit a fire in a brazier. Cans of beer started getting passed around.

"The question remains: What do we do with the three of them?" Matt said.

"Top 'em. No choice," Jacko said.

"No," Matt said. "That will stir things up."

"Who's going to miss them? They're not even Aussies, none of them," Ivan said.

"Let's find out who's going to miss 'em, Kate," Ma said.

Kate grabbed Heather by the hair and pulled her to her feet.

"Where are you from?" she asked Heather.

"What?"

Kate slapped Heather across the face. "Where are you from, bitch?"

"Seattle, Washington."

"And what *exactly* were you doing down here?" Kate asked.

"Tom's here for a conference and we came along for some sightseeing. We went to Sydney and Uluru and Melbourne, and the kids wanted to see some koalas in the countryside..."

Kate dropped her and she fell back into the dirt.

"Yank tourists, Ma, that's about the size of it," Kate said.

"Tourists. So who will miss them, do you think?" Ma wondered out loud.

"Somebody will," Matt said.

"Yes! Tom's the keynote speaker," Heather said. "At the, um, at the International Conference of Orthopedic Medicine. You can't just disappear us. The car-rental company knows too. We had to sign forms. The best thing to do is let us go and—"

"That's enough!" Ma said.

"No, wait, listen to me, things don't have to—" Heather began but Kate leaned down and with one big white paw squeezed Heather's cheeks *hard*.

"The only witnesses are the Krauts, is that right?" Ma asked.

"Our Ned was running the food stand. No one saw them follow us to the ferry except for the Krauts," Jacko said.

Ma lit a cigarette and waved for people to clear a space around her chair. The murmuring gradually ended and the crowd grew quiet. Heather's head had stopped pounding and in the silence she could hear birds roosting in the distant eucalyptus trees. A jet was high above her, its vapor trail just visible in the moonlight.

Everything was moving into the future. She was too. Tom, poor Tom, would be dead forever. She had to consider herself and the kids now.

"Please. I know what you're thinking and it's not going to work," Heather pleaded.

"You forced us into this. You killed Ellen and tried to cover it up. This is on you," Ma said.

"Don't make things worse. You—"

"Matt! I told you to shut that bitch up," Ma said coldly and calmly. "This is your final warning, girl. If you speak again without my permission, I'm going to have Lenny, our blacksmith, cut your tongue out with his leather-cutting scissors. Nod your bloody head if you understand. Not one bloody word from you. Do you understand?"

Heather nodded.

"Just the Krauts, eh? Matt, what if we dumped the car somewhere on the mainland?"

Matt nodded. "The car's GPS will have stopped well before Stamford Bridge."

"Jamie, could you smash the car up bad?" Ma asked someone whom Heather couldn't see.

"Oh, yeah. Easy. Lotta drop-offs on the Red Hill Road. Some as deep as twenty-five meters. Car goes over one of those, little tampering with the fuel lines...boom."

"What do you think, Ivan?"

He thought for a long time before finally clearing his throat. "I like the plan, Ma. Cops will find the car in a few days and just think, *Ah, too bad, dumb Americans forgot which side of the road to drive on,*" Ivan said.

"The Melbourne cops are smart, though—what if they come over here?" Kate asked.

"We don't know nothing about any Americans; we keep ourselves to ourselves."

"Oi, look, this is my decision, innit? Mine," Danny said. "Under the old laws. They done *me* wrong, not any of you."

"You cost us half a million bucks, Danny! You can shut your mouth!" Ivan said.

"What is it you want, Daniel?" Ma asked.

Danny strode into the center of the circle. Someone had passed him an earthen drinking jug and he took an enormous sip of liquor that was so strong, Heather could smell it from where she was sprawled on the ground.

"What do I want?" Danny said after a pause.

"There's nothing they can give you now, mate," Matt said.

"Yeah, no, look...I lost a wife and I heard there's a girl. I want to see the girl. Bring her to me," Danny said, wiping his mouth.

"Ivan?" Ma asked.

"Maybe not a good idea, Ma. If we're going to go down this route, there can't be any survivors," Jacko said.

"I want my rights," Danny insisted.

"You lost a wife, not a kid," Matt said.

"I can't take this violent bloody bitch. We can't trust her," Danny said, pointing at Heather.

Kate laughed. "You're right. She'd cut all our throats, this one."

"It's my right, innit?" Danny said.

"What would the cops think, Ivan, if there were only three bodies?" Ma asked.

"I suppose the girl might have survived the crash, gone wandering for help, got lost, and her body was never found," Ivan said.

"It might even help us," Jacko said. "The cops will be focused on finding the missing girl over on the mainland. We won't be part of the story."

"Kill them all!" someone yelled.

Ma put her hands up for silence. "I've listened and I am going to sleep on my decision," she said. "We don't need to do anything tonight, do we, Matt?"

"No. And we don't want to be running the ferry at night anyway. Nothing unusual," Matt said.

"Tomorrow, if I decide that way, we can take the car over to the mainland and have Jamie crash it up the Red Hill Road. The rest of us can get to bed now. My legs hurt. I forgot me good ciggies," Ma continued.

"What about me?" Danny said.

"Bugger you, Danny!" Jacko snarled.

"All right, we'll let Danny take a look at the girl. Someone go get her!" Ma said.

"So the plan is we kill this one and the boy?" Kate asked, gesturing toward Heather.

Heather shook her head no. This was unreal. They couldn't mean that. This was all some kind of mistake. A nightmare. A—

"Maybe," Ma said. "Where's those ciggies?"

A little girl handed Ma a pack of cigarettes. She lit one up and passed the box around.

"Where are the Krauts now?"

"They're still up at the house," Jacko said. "I told them we were getting the ferry repaired and they bought it, but then the geezer said something stupid."

"What did he say?" Matt groaned.

"He noticed the snorkel on the Porsche was bent and asked if someone had had an accident."

"Shite!" Ma said. "You've really screwed things up for us, haven't you, Daniel?"

"Ellen's dead. I want me rights."

"You're getting your rights, Danny," Kate said. "But, mate, because of you we're going to have to kill two more people to be on the safe side."

Heather got to her feet. "You cannot be serious about this! Have you all lost your minds?" she cried.

"I warned you! I bloody warned you. Didn't I warn her? Take out her tongue, Lenny," Ma said.

A large, tanned, lean bald man began moving through the crowd. He was wearing a leather apron and a singlet coated with filth. His eyes were black; his expression was dull. He reeked of dried blood and offal.

He grabbed Heather violently by the head and locked his arm around her neck.

She punched and scraped at his arm as he shoved two enormous fingers into her mouth. She bit the fingers, but it was like biting into blocks of wood.

"Yeah, I can do this. Jodie, go get me scissors, I'll take care of her," he said. Heather tried to scream but she couldn't breathe or make a sound.

11

Olivia was listening to the yelling. She was very scared. She didn't know what was happening out there. She didn't know what she was supposed to do next. They had taken her phone, but the phone wasn't her go-to source. Most kids her age asked Google or Siri or Alexa when they wanted to know stuff, but she had always gone to her dad. Her dad knew everything. Her dad knew everything about the world, and her mom had known the answers to any problem she'd ever had at school with friends or teachers or body image. Her mom had been as smart as her dad but she hadn't liked to show off about it so much. One of her parents had always known what was going on and what she should do next.

But her mom was dead and her father had been taken away from her.

She was left entirely to her own devices, without her dad or her comfy blanket or her Lexapro.

Owen was no help.

Owen was buried deep in his hood, saying nothing. Not even sniffling. In the rush to get out Heather had forgotten to give them their medications today. She was always doing stuff like that. Heather was too young to be a real mom. Moms made lists and checked them and didn't forget things. Moms looked after you. The transition between ADHD Owen and OCD-panicky Owen was always tricky to navigate. She could handle things but Owen hadn't had any of his medicines for a day and a half, so he was going to be a pretty big mess soon. It was probably better to leave him alone.

It was so hot.

Olivia's throat ached.

She was terribly thirsty.

She let the flies land on her. She was too exhausted to fight them now. They crawled up and down her arm.

Dad had killed that woman.

But it was Heather's fault.

He was driving fast to impress her.

Heather was easily impressed. She wasn't very smart. She hadn't even graduated high school. Olivia's mom, her *real* mom, had a PhD. Her real mom was a biologist.

Olivia managed to put two fingers between the ropes and her throat. It made breathing a little easier.

They had put ropes around her neck like they were going to hang her. They probably were going to hang her. They were probably going to kill all of them. Eye for an eye—all that stuff from Sunday school.

The ropes were scratchy and it hurt to move. The ropes around Owen's neck were over his hoodie. He'd been smart to do it that way. They weren't scratching his neck. He was just sitting there like he was dead. He wasn't even crying. She was crying. And no one was helping. No one was going to help. Her mom was dead, her dad—

"Hello," a voice said.

A voice right next to her.

Olivia turned, startled. A little face was staring at her through a gap in the planking. A seven- or eight-year-old girl with blond hair and big dark eyes.

"Hello," Olivia said. "What's your name?"

"Niamh," the girl said. "What's your name?"

"Olivia."

"Is that your brother?" Niamh asked.

"Yes. He's called Owen."

"Hello, Owen," the little girl said.

Owen said nothing.

"He's not much of a talker," Olivia explained.

"You shouldn't be in there," Niamh said. "This is for sheep. The sheep use it as a dunny sometimes. It's not a place to live."

"A dunny is a bathroom, right?" Olivia asked.

"A dunny is a dunny!" Niamh said, amazed by this question. "Where are you from?"

"We're from America," Olivia said.

"I know America. It's somewhere near Sydney, I think. Me da went to Sydney. Are you sad?"

"Sad? Yes, I suppose so. I want to go home."

"Are you sad about your dad?"

"What do you mean?"

"Are you sad that he's dead?"

"He's not dead," Olivia said, a jolt of terror hitting her.

"He is dead. What do you think happens when you die? The schoolie says we go to heaven and become angels but me da says there's no such place. Me da says when we die, we don't do anything."

"Why do you think my dad is dead?" Olivia asked.

"'Cause Danny chopped him with his knife. Chopped him real solid-like. All the blood and guts come out and then he lies down and he just stays there doing nothing."

"That's not true!" Olivia said.

"It is true. They did stuff to your mum."

"Heather's not my mom."

"Lenny's going to cut your mum's tongue out. Lenny is going to put his big scissors in her mouth and cut out her tongue so she can't talk back to Ma no more. Ma didn't like that."

"No! None of that happened."

"It's true. Ma told them to take your da and Ellen up to the old meat locker. Two dead people together. If you look through the window, you can see them on the big table. Come out and see for yourself," Niamh said.

"Can you let me out?" Olivia asked.

"What?"

"Can you let me out?"

The girl walked around the front of the shearing shed and then came back. "They put a thingy on the door. What do you call those metal things?"

"A padlock?"

"Yeah."

"Is there any other way out of here?" Olivia asked.

"I don't know. There used to be a big hole in the roof where you could see out, but they fixed that."

"The roof is too high anyway."

"One of the ewes butted her way out last winter," Niamh said.

"Where?"

"Do you see where the wall's a different color?"

"No, it's too dark in here to see anything."

"Next to me, where I am. Jacko repaired it. He used drift-wood. I don't think it's very strong. And it's not painted or anything. Ivan is a better carp...someone coming," Niamh said and slipped off into the shadows.

Olivia heard the key turn in the padlock. The door opened. Owen peeked out from his hood.

"All right, you're coming with me," a man said. He was a giant of a man with a mustache and jet-black hair. He stank of sweat and alcohol. He squatted in front of Olivia and untied the rope that ran from her throat to the hook above her head. He untied the other rope attaching her to the wall. He pulled her to her feet by the back of her shirt.

"Where are you taking her?" Owen said.

"You shut up, little fella, if you know what's good for you," the man said.

He led Olivia outside and locked the shearing-shed door.

"What's happening?" Olivia asked.

"You'll see soon enough," the man said.

He walked her to the farmyard, where a large number of people had gathered. There was a fire burning. Music.

"Wait a minute," the man said. He fumbled at something tied to his belt. It was a clay bottle. He uncorked it and gave it to Olivia. She took it in her tied hands. It smelled bad.

"What is this?" she asked.

"It's grog. You're going to need it."

"I—I don't want it."

"Let me help get it down your throat," the man said. He opened her mouth by squeezing her face, then tilted the liquor in. She had no choice but to swallow as it burned. Her eyes were watering and her throat was on fire.

She stumbled and the man lifted her by the waist and carried her into the center of the circle. Another man was holding Heather by the neck and shoving a big pair of pliers into her mouth.

Olivia screamed, broke free of the man dragging her, and ran to Heather. She kicked the man with the pliers, and he was so surprised he let Heather go. Olivia fell into Heather's arms.

"They killed Dad! They killed him, didn't they?" Olivia said, sobbing.

"I'm so sorry. I'm so sorry, baby girl," Heather said, pulling Olivia close, wrapping her tied hands around her, and hugging her as hard as she could.

Olivia buried herself in Heather's chest. She'd never really hugged her before except that one time at the wedding, before Christmas. And that was only out of politeness.

Heather rocked her back and forth and began crying too.

"What do I do now?" the blacksmith asked.

"Leave it be," Matt said.

"Is he really dead?" Olivia whispered.

"I'm so sorry, honey. I am so, so sorry," Heather whispered back.

"There's the girl! I want a look at her," Danny said.

"Let him look at her," Jacko said.

Olivia felt an arm wrap around her and pull her away from Heather. Heather tried to reach for her but the man in the leather apron pushed her down.

"What do you think, Danny?" Jacko said.

The one called Danny was staring at her. He was skinny and red and repulsive. His tongue was lolling, and spittle was dropping from his lips. He seemed very drunk. He reached out and touched her hair. Olivia flinched.

Some of the men started to laugh and someone shouted, "Go on, Danny, son!"

"How old are you?" Danny asked. His breath reeked of that same grog the other man had given her.

"Fourteen," she said.

The old woman with the cane was coming over now, the one they called Ma. She tilted Olivia's head back and looked at her. Her hands were cold and clammy.

"Well, Danny?" she asked.

"No one will ever replace Ellen, but it's better than nothing," he said.

"Life's a balance. Nature treated you harshly today. This restores the balance. You can take her," Ma said.

There were a few laughs from the assembled men.

Olivia saw that Heather was on her feet now. The man with the pliers moved in front of her. She went around him and took a step toward Ma. "You've done nothing wrong so far," Heather said.

"What do you mean?" Matt asked.

"You haven't done anything wrong. Not a thing. Everything bad that's happened has been either Tom's fault or his fault," she said, gesturing toward Danny. "If you put us back on the mainland—"

"You'll go to the police. Of course you will!" Ma said angrily.

"So we go to the police. But none of this comes back to any of you except him. You haven't done anything," Heather said.

"We kidnapped you," Matt said. "We held you against your will."

"No, you kept us in protective custody while you tried to reach the police on the mainland. If you let him take her now, then it's all over," Heather insisted. "You're going to have to kill all of us. And the Dutch couple. Are you sure you're going to get away with that? That's a hell of a big decision."

"I made my call," Ma said.

"You said you were going to sleep on it. We're not going anywhere. We're locked in that hut. You can decide in the morning," Heather said.

Matt looked at Ma. "There is something in what she says."

Ma leaned on her stick and shook her head. "Where does it stop? Terry's word was the law and that *was* the end of it in his day," Ma said.

"Excuse me, but you won't be going back on any decision. You'll just be thinking about it overnight. What difference will that make? We're not leaving," Heather said.

"What difference will it make to you?" Matt asked her.

Heather looked at Danny and then at Matt. "It's my job to protect these kids," she said quietly.

"And what about the other two?" Ma wondered. "I suppose we'll have to keep them as well. What are we going to do with them, Matt?"

"We can decide that in the morning too," Matt said.

Ma took a handkerchief from a pocket in her skirt. She blew her nose into it and examined its contents. She looked at Matt and finished her cigarette. "I said I would sleep on it, didn't I?" Ma said.

Matt nodded. "I think that's a very good idea."

"No! You said I could have her!" Danny wailed.

"And maybe I'll say it again, but you shut your mouth for now, Daniel."

"I just want me rights!" Danny said.

"And you'll get your rights. But you'll have to wait. All right, Jacko. Put them back in the shearing shed and lock them in. And put the Krauts in there too. We'll fix all this in the morning. If Danny gives you any trouble, have someone throw him down the bloody well."

12

Heather had won this battle. There would be many more. But she had bought herself some time.

Danny started howling and protesting behind them as Jacko led them back to prison. With her hands still tied, Heather put her arms around Olivia, but Olivia ducked under them. Heather knew the girl was still trying to take everything in.

Tom would have to talk to her about—

Wait. What was happening? Tom. How could Tom be...

She swallowed.

Tom, oh no. Oh God. Not Tom. It hadn't been love at first sight, but it was pretty damn close. He was so funny and charming and smart. All the books he'd read. All the stuff he knew. And that old-world East Coast courtesy. It sure didn't hurt that he was so easy on the eyes. So 1950s handsome. So 1950s calm and with his shit together. He couldn't fix a gearbox like the Goose Island men, but he could make you a cup of hot chocolate and read you poetry on a rainy afternoon or put the kids to bed early on a Saturday night and lock the bedroom door and bang your brains out.

And now he was dead. And she was in a nightmare. In the middle of nowhere surrounded by crazy people. She was so thirsty. Her head was light.

How easy it would be to fall, to let that warm red dirt consume her too...

She was reeling. But she couldn't reel. She had to keep *her* shit together, for herself and now for Owen and Olivia.

They reached the shearing shed. Jacko unlocked the door and shoved them both inside.

"We haven't had food or water for hours," Heather said.

Jacko leaned into her face. "I thought you would have learned your lesson, you mouthy bitch. Now you shut it or I'll shut it for you."

"We need water," Heather said.

Jacko separated Heather from Olivia and sat her down. He put the noose around her neck and tied it tight to the roof beam. He tied a second rope around her neck to the back wall so she couldn't move. Then he began the same process with Olivia.

"Not tight," Heather said. "Matt agreed to that."

"Matt's soft," Jacko said, and, looking deliberately at her, he slowly tightened the noose around Olivia's neck so that she began to choke. Olivia tried to get a finger between the rope and her throat but it was already taut.

"Please!" Heather said. "Don't!"

"Ma said make sure you're all secure," Jacko said.

"She didn't say kill us!" Heather protested.

"She's not dead. She's as snug as a bug in a rug. Aren't you, darling?"

"It hurts," Olivia said, gasping.

"Please," Heather said.

"I like it when you say *please* like that. Say it again," Jacko said.

"Please, she's just a little girl."

Jacko shook his head. "Nah, she's a woman now. Will be when Danny's done with her, anyway," he muttered.

"*I'm* a woman," Heather said. "Please, leave her."

Jacko nodded. "You are a woman, aren't you?" he said, loosening the noose around Olivia's neck. Olivia gasped for air in big gulps. Jacko padded across the shearing shed. He brushed the remaining strands of hair back on his head and grinned a yellow jackal smile.

He crouched down in front of Heather and looked at her. "A young one too—how old are you? Younger than him by a country mile."

"I'm twenty-four," Heather said.

"Twenty-four, eh? Well, twenty-four, it's either you or her. What's it gonna be?"

"Those aren't your orders," Heather said desperately.

"Orders? Nobody gives me orders. I don't have any orders!" He laughed. "You're already dead, sweetheart. All of you. Or haven't you been paying attention?"

"I'm sorry, I didn't mean *orders*. Ma just asked you to lock us in here. You heard her. She's going to sleep on what to do with us."

"She can sleep for a thousand years for all I care. Now, sweetie, as lovely as this little chat has been, your job now is making a choice. Who's it going to be? You or your little blond daughter over there?"

Heather's throat was dry. Her head was swimming. "Please, you don't have to do this," Heather said.

"Yeah, I like it when you say *please,* all American-like, but the time for talk is done. You or her? Ten seconds."

"Matt said—"

"Ten, nine, eight, seven, six, five, four, three—"

"Me," she said.

"That's what I thought," Jacko said. "Now, be a good girl and take it out."

Owen was staring at her. Both kids looked horrified, terrified. Owen didn't even know about his dad yet.

"Owen, Olivia, I want you both to close your eyes. Owen, pull that hood back over your head too. Eyes shut tight both of you."

Owen pulled the hood over his head. Olivia shut her eyes tight. Neither of them, she hoped, knew what was about to happen next. Jacko's jeans were originally blue but they were so encrusted with filth they had turned a reddish black. He was grinning. The rifle was strapped over his back.

She looked at him.

He mind-read her. "Now, don't you do nothing silly, Heather," he said. "'Cause you know what'll happen to you and you know what will happen to her."

She was tempted to smash him in the balls with her tied hands. She could probably give him a pretty painful whack, but then what? He would break her face and then he would rape Olivia.

She reached up to his fly and tugged at it. It was so coated with grime and rust that she couldn't get it down.

"You can do better than that, Heather," Jacko said. She tried harder but the fly would not come down.

"I don't think it's had much practice," she said.

"I hope for your sake you're not trying to smart-mouth me, little girl," Jacko said. He took a step back, undid his belt and zipper, and pulled his pants down. Just then the door opened and Matt was standing there with the Dutch couple.

"What in the name of living shit is this?" Matt said.

"None of your bloody business, mate," Jacko replied. "Come back in ten minutes!"

"Like hell I will. Get out of here."

"Says who?"

Matt slung the rifle off his shoulder and pointed it at Jacko. "Says me, arsehole."

"You do that and you'll be in here with them," Jacko snarled.

"And your head will be all over the bloody ceiling."

The two men stared at each other.

The air crackled.

Heather held her breath.

Maybe she could try to—

Jacko took a step back and pulled up his jeans. He looked at Heather and then at Matt and spit. "Tight bitch anyway, you can tell," he said and stormed out of the shed, muttering to himself.

Heather's heart was pounding in her ears. Her hands were shaking.

"All right, you two, sit on the ground," Matt said to the Dutch couple. "I can't have either of you walking around in here, so I'm going to put these ropes around your necks and attach them to the shed."

"Are you mad?" Hans said. "You can't do this!"

"Look at the kids. If I'm doing it to them, I'm bloody doing it to you," Matt replied. "Now sit!"

The Dutch couple sat on the dirt floor of the shearing shed. Their hands had already been tied and they'd been stripped of their possessions. Heather could tell that Hans wasn't absorbing what was happening but Petra understood now. She began to cry as Matt put the rope around her neck.

"Really, this is absurd!" Hans said. He still wasn't getting it. In his head, he was writing a stern letter to the Australian tourism board.

When the Dutch couple were secured, Matt checked the knots on the kids and Heather. They could pick at those bonds all night and wouldn't get out of them.

"We need water if we're going to survive until morning in here. Food too. But water most of all. You won't be making *any* decisions about what to do with us if we don't get water," Heather said in a quiet but insistent whisper.

Matt nodded. "Hold on," he said.

He closed the shed door and locked it.

"What is happening? I cannot believe this!" Hans exclaimed.

"Ze houden ons gevangen. Ze gaan ons morgenochtend vermoorden," Petra said dispassionately.

The only word Heather thought she understood was *vermoorden.*

Yes, they are *going to murder us.*

The shed door was unlocked and opened. Matt came in with a liter bottle of water. "That's the best I can do," he said, putting it in front of Heather.

"Thank you," she replied. "How are we going to pass it to one another?"

"Um..."

"Can you get the children to take a drink each? Please," she said.

Matt was clearly embarrassed. "What?"

"I can't. Could you do it for me, please? Just hold it to their mouths and get them to drink."

Best way of getting an adult to bond with a child is having the adult feed them. It's primal, one of the parenting books Tom had made her read said.

Matt sighed. "OK, then," he said.

"Kids, I want you to take a big drink each," Heather said.

They were so thirsty both kids drank greedily from the bottle.

"What about us?" Petra inquired.

"You can share with her," Matt said, plonking the bottle down in front of Heather.

"How are we supposed to go to the toilet?" Hans asked.

"You're going to have to figure that one out for yourselves," Matt said.

"Where's my dad?" Owen said.

Matt looked at Heather. "I'll let your mum explain that."

"She's not my mother," Owen said.

"Well, she'll tell you," Matt said. "I'm leaving but we'll be keeping an eye on you, so no funny business. If you sit still, you won't get strangled. If you mess around, I'm not to blame for what happens. And no noise if you know what's good for you. Ma likes her sleep. Good night," he said.

"You're really going to leave us like this?" Heather asked.

"What can I do?" he said. He exited the shed and locked it.

"Where *is* your husband?" Hans asked when he had gone.

Heather knew there was no way around this now. But someone needed to be holding that boy tight while she said it.

Poor Owen. Poor Olivia. Oh my God, those poor kids.

Heather took a big drink of water.

"Tell me," Owen said.

Owen was too smart for Heather to sugarcoat it or fob him off with an *I don't know . . .*

"Owen, I want you to look at me," Heather said. "Look at me, Owen. Please."

"They killed him, didn't they?" he said from the depths of his hood.

"Owen, I—"

"They killed him because he killed that woman," Owen said mechanically.

"No," Hans said. "They killed him?"

"Owen, I'm really sorry. I tried to stop them. We had sort of worked everything out but then the woman's husband showed up. I'm so sorry, honey. I really am sorry, I wish I could come over there right now and hug you, baby."

Hans and Petra began talking heatedly in Dutch.

"Is he definitely dead?" Owen asked quietly.

"I'm sorry," Heather said.

Owen looked at her furiously and then buried his head back in the hoodie again. His whole body began to shake.

"I'm so sorry, Owen."

"Shut up, Heather!" Owen said. "Just shut up, OK? Shut your stupid mouth!"

Heather nodded. It was OK for him to let this out. Olivia too. They would be dealing with this for years. If they weren't all murdered in the morning. Her pulse was racing. Where in the name of God was that penknife? Had she lost it? How could she have lost it? She had buried it here just as they were leaving. She needed to find it—

Was it by the iron hoop or—

Over to the—

There it was. *Thank you, God.*

She grabbed the knife and despite having almost no leverage began sawing at the bonds on her wrist. The rope was thick but the knife was incredibly sharp, and once she had a good angle, it began slicing through the hemp.

Olivia was looking at her. She had stopped crying now. Owen was making little beeping noises from inside his hood. The Dutch couple continued their heated talk.

She sawed. Felt the friction. Sawed more. She ignored the flies, the mosquitoes, the oven heat, the fact that Tom, her rock, her savior, was dead.

She looked outside through a gap in the plank walls. It was quieter. The crowd seemed to be dispersing now and returning to the big main farmhouse or the smaller satellite houses.

Heather sawed at the rope as the sweat poured down her forehead. Her fingers were burning from the friction, and little whiffs of smoke were coming from the fibers. She took a break and put down the knife and unscrewed the cap on the water bottle—not an easy thing to do with tied hands. The water was lukewarm but good. Only half a bottle left. Save the rest.

Another check outside. No obvious movement. Couple of voices from the main yard. Lights still on at the house. Smart thing to do might be to wait until the wee hours. When everyone was quiet, they could make a clean break without pursuit. Or maybe it would be better just to friggin' go as soon as they could in case someone decided to separate them or put a guard on the shed or Jacko or Danny came for Olivia...

Cross that bridge when they—

She picked up the knife. She held it between finger and thumb. She sawed, sweated, sawed.

Suddenly the blade went through one of the main strands.

She sawed harder, and another strand popped almost with a twang.

She cut the final strand and she was through!

She shook her wrists and the rope fell off her. She slackened the noose at her neck. In another thirty seconds, she was completely free. If she stood, she might be visible from outside. Best to keep low. She crawled to Olivia and removed the ropes around her neck, then did the same for Owen. "Dad didn't want to come here. We made him! It's our fault!" Owen said.

"No, it's their fault. They killed him."

She tried to hug Owen but he wouldn't let her. "Don't friggin' touch me, Heather!" he wailed, pushing her away.

She attempted to untie the rope at Hans's neck. "Do not do that! We do not want any trouble," Hans said.

"We're all in trouble," Heather replied.

"*You* are in trouble. If we associate ourselves with you, we also will be in trouble."

Heather turned to Petra. "What about you?"

"I—I don't know," she said.

"Just let me loosen the rope at your neck. I can see it's choking you."

Petra looked at Hans, who said something to her fast in Dutch.

"It is better if we are not helped by you," she said.

"OK," Heather said. She knelt in front of Owen, unscrewed the top from the water bottle. "You're going to take another drink of this if I have to force it down your throat, OK?"

He didn't answer.

"OK?"

"He's behind his wall," Olivia said.

"His what? Oh, yes, that," Heather said.

"You don't really understand about his *wall,* do you? You don't know anything about us," Olivia said. "Owen! Owen! It's me, Olivia. Come out and take a drink."

Owen stirred and grabbed the bottle. He took a little drink and then a bigger one.

"Well done," Heather said and crawled back to Olivia. She began sawing at the ropes around Olivia's wrists but Olivia stopped her.

"What are you doing?" Olivia asked.

"I'm cutting you loose and then we're going to get out of here," Heather said.

"No," Olivia said. "I—I don't think so. You'll just get us in more trouble."

Owen nodded. "She doesn't know what she's doing. Dad might know what to do, but she doesn't."

"Come on, guys!"

"No! Don't touch me!" Olivia said and began to hyper-ventilate.

Owen and Olivia were looking at her the way they often looked at her: with contempt. This time, of course, through a veil of grief, terror, tears.

Heather closed her eyes. She hadn't wanted to be their step-mother. What she'd wanted was to have a roof over her head and be comfortable and have nice things and maybe see a bit of the world. What she'd wanted was Tom. She was far too young for motherhood. She had literally never thought about it. She was exactly the wrong age to be Olivia and Owen's mom. When she attempted to play with them, she wasn't like one of those cool mothers who goof around and make everyone feel at ease. No, she was like one of those older kids on the periphery of the playground who are too lame to make friends with people their own age.

You couldn't say she hadn't tried.

She had tried.

If the kids didn't want to come, well, she could escape by herself.

Easily.

Yes.

That acknowledged, Heather nodded, opened her eyes, and

squatted down in front of Olivia, who was still in a panic. "Take deep breaths, honey. That's it. In through the nose, out through the mouth. Big breaths. Good. Doing better?"

"Uh-huh."

"Now, listen to me, Olivia. If we stay here, they are going to kill us," she said, enunciating every word.

Olivia took thirty seconds to think about it. A little sob went through her like a wave. She nodded and held up her hands. Heather sawed through the rope until Olivia was free. "They hurt," Olivia said.

"Rub them until you get the circulation going again. They'll start to feel better soon," Heather assured her. She looked back up at the house. The lights were off now. The only light on in the whole farm was the arc light directly in front of the shed. Not good.

She forced a determined look onto her face, crawled to Owen, and began sawing at his bonds.

"How are we going to escape?" Owen asked her.

"I don't know . . . yet. But we'll think of something."

"What are you thinking of doing?" Petra asked.

"Getting out of here and running away," Heather said as she continued to saw.

"I think there might be a way out," Olivia said quietly.

"What?"

"There was a little girl here earlier. She said she could come in to see us. She said there was a loose board on this side of the shed. I'll check it out," Olivia said.

"But what will you do if you get away?" Petra asked. "What will you do after?"

"Phones don't work here, so we'll have to get off the island to call the police."

"You are going to swim to the mainland?" Hans scoffed.

"No. We're not going to swim. We'll think of something."

"You are making a mountain of a molehill, I think," Hans said and then added something to Petra in Dutch.

Heather nodded to herself and sawed through the final bit of hemp, freeing Owen. "Rub your wrists, get the blood back into them," she said softly.

Keeping low, Heather scurried across the shed to where Olivia was pulling at the wall.

"Look at this," Olivia said, tugging at a loosely fitting plank near the floor. "The little girl said it was a different wood. It's coming out as I pull it."

"It's not only the wood; these are just one-inch nails. We can do this if we pull together," Heather said.

She and Olivia tugged and out the plank came with a loud tearing sound.

They froze for a minute to see if there was any reaction outside.

A dog barked in the distance but no one came.

"We did it!" Olivia whispered.

Heather looked through the hole. There, outside, just fifty feet away in the deep darkness, was what they had called the heathland.

They had created a big enough gap in the shed wall for a child to crawl through, and perhaps if they dug underneath it, an adult could squeeze through too.

"It's good," Heather said.

"Are you quite sure your husband was killed?" Hans asked. "Perhaps there was an altercation and you did not see what happened to him? Perhaps he has been taken to a hospital?"

Heather crawled back over to Owen. "Get yourself together. We're leaving," she whispered.

"Is that what we're doing, Olivia?" Owen asked his sister.

"Yes, it is," she said.

"We're going to take the water bottle, if that's OK," Heather said to Petra. "We're going to need it more than you."

"It is not your water. It is for all of us!" Hans protested.

"They will need it more," Petra said.

Heather crawled back to the hole and began digging into the earth with first the penknife and then her hands. The dirt was thicker and heavier than it looked and it did not give easily. It had been baked hard by the sun for any number of summers. She dug deeper and made a little furrow. "What do you think?" she said to Olivia.

"I can get through," Olivia said.

Heather nodded.

"Do you want me to go?"

"No, not yet. Let's get it deep enough for all of us."

"Are you saying that because I'm fat?" Owen asked. Heather couldn't tell if this was a mordant attempt at one of his snarky jokes or not.

"I'm the problem. You're not the problem," Heather said. "I just wish we had a better tool to dig through this ground."

"What about one of those hooks in the ceiling? Couple of them look loose," Owen suggested.

"Perfect. You dig with the knife and I'll see if I can reach one. Don't hurt yourself."

"I've used a knife before!"

Heather stood up cautiously and touched one of the hooks in the ceiling. Many years ago this place must have been used for hanging game birds or something of the kind. The hooks were rusted but firmly nailed into the crossbeams. The first one she touched was solid, as was the second. The third, however…she wiggled it and it started to move. Hans was very tall and she was on tiptoes. He could do this easily. She looked at him.

"No," he said.

"Why not?"

"We are not getting involved in your trouble," he explained.

"No, you just want to wait here all night, tied up by the neck, until the morning comes, when they are almost certainly going to kill you," Heather said.

"Why would they do that?"

"Because they are going to make up some bullshit story about what happened to me and Tom and the kids, and you would be able to contradict that story. Therefore, the smart thing to do—the only thing to do—is kill you."

"This is Australia, not America," Hans said.

Heather nodded. Well, at least she'd tried.

"They are not evil," Hans added.

"Perhaps they are worse than evil—they are bored," Petra said.

Hans said something dismissive-sounding in Dutch.

All the hooks in the ceiling were too solid for her to remove. She was just going to have to dig with her knife and her bare hands. She dropped to the floor and helped Owen carve a furrow in the dirt big enough for both of them to wriggle under the wall. She dug with her nails and fingers. She would have used her teeth if she'd had to.

"OK," Heather said. "Do we have everything?"

Olivia nodded. Owen grunted.

"I'll go first," Olivia said and she got down on her belly and began wriggling through the gap in the timbers. She was half-way through when there was the sound of a door slamming up at the house.

"Hey!" they heard someone yell. "What are those bloody Yanks up to now? Turn that bloody light off!"

Everyone froze.

"Turn that light off, someone! It's coming right in me window!"

"Back inside, Olivia! They mean the light in front of the shed," Heather whispered.

Olivia slithered back inside.

"Quick! Back to where you were, and put the ropes over your hands," Heather said. The kids scrambled back to where they'd been sitting, and she put the nooses around their necks.

She heard a door open and someone come out of the farmhouse.

She put the ropes around her own neck and sat down. She was still fumbling with the rope around her wrists when she heard a key turn in the shed's padlock. The door opened and Matt was standing there with a rifle in one hand.

"Everything all right in here?" he asked.

"Yes," Heather said, panting.

"They want me to turn the outside light off. It's filtering into the house."

"That's fine. Maybe we'll sleep a bit."

"We get up early round here. With the sun. I'll make sure you get some food in the morning," Matt said.

"Thank you," Heather said.

"No probs," he said.

"You're very kind," she said, just to keep him looking at her and not at the ropes the kids had hastily draped around their wrists. Not to mention the hole behind Olivia.

"I don't know about that. All this . . . it's Ma's decision . . . well, like I say, I have to turn the light off, but, as you say, maybe you can get some kip, you know?" he said.

"When does the sun come up?"

"This time of year, around five o'clock."

"Thank you. We will try to sleep until then."

"Before you go, I would like to say something," Hans said.

"Oh?"

Heather's heart was in her mouth. She looked at Petra, but she didn't appear to know what Hans was going to say.

"I want to ask about this lady's husband. She seems to think that something happened to him. Is he, um, is he dead?"

"Yeah. He's dead. Danny killed him. I couldn't have prevented it. I didn't see the blade on him. Fast bugger."

"You understand that this has nothing to do with my wife or me?"

Matt nodded. "Duly noted. Get some sleep if you can," he said, then exited and locked the door.

He turned off the light and Heather waited until he had gone back to the farmhouse before moving. She took the ropes from around her neck and removed the ropes from the kids' necks.

"All right, Olivia, you go first," Heather said.

"I think...perhaps...we should come with you," Hans said.

"You both want to come?" Heather asked.

He and Petra had a brief conversation in Dutch.

"Yes," Petra said.

"All right, then," Heather agreed. "But you do what I say. The kids are the priority. OK?"

"Yes."

Heather took the penknife from her pocket, cut the ropes on their wrists, and unhooked the ropes from their necks.

"Olivia, you and Owen go first. Keep low and wait for us in the long grass over by the edge of the farm."

"What if someone sees us?" Owen asked.

"In that case, don't wait for us, just run and keep running," Heather said. "Try to hide somewhere until you see a police car."

"OK," Owen said.

Olivia crawled through the hole and vanished into the darkness.

"What's it like out there?" Owen asked.

"It's all clear, come on!" Olivia said.

Owen went next. He had a little trouble getting through the hole but he made it. Heather turned to Petra and Hans. "You have to come immediately."

"We will come," Petra said.

Heather lay down on the dirt floor and pushed the water bottle out ahead of her. She crawled through the dirt, and in just a few seconds she was outside. Most of the stars were obscured by clouds, and the air was still. She could hear someone playing music in one of the distant farm buildings.

She pushed herself up to a crouch.

"Over here!" Owen whispered. He was hiding behind an ancient steamroller a few yards away. She ran to him. "I told you to go to the grass!"

"The grass is too far away," Olivia said. "We would have gotten lost over there. We would have had to shout to find each other."

Heather nodded. Petra's head appeared in the hole, and she pulled her long lean frame through quite easily. Hans came immediately after. "Over here!" Heather said. They came over and crouched behind the steamroller.

"Now what?" Hans asked.

"Now we run like hell," Heather said.

13

Matt woke with a start. Something was wrong. He could feel it. Something was wrong beyond the bigger wrong of what they were about to do to the Baxter family.

Blue was awake. Looking out the window. Nose up against the screen.

Matt pulled back the curtains. The sun was starting to come up. His watch claimed it was 4:50, and he could believe it. Jesus. Owen and Heather and the Krauts—or, more accurately, the Dutchies—would all be dead by 9:00.

Killing that little boy, bloody hell. That was going to be rough. But what choice did they have now? Ma would never let the cops take Danny away. He was the youngest boy, and for Ma it was love/hate. Unlike most of the family, Danny didn't sit around all arvo drinking grog. Danny had gone over to the mainland and got himself a job and a girl. Poor bastard. Nah, Ma would never let them take him. It would be the bloody Alamo out here before she allowed that.

There was nothing else for it—die they must. It was going to be horrible.

Blue was growling about something. Matt slid up the screen and helped Blue out. His room was on the ground floor but Blue still managed to land on the other side with a loud thump. He recovered and his fat little body and arthritic legs hobbled over to the old steamroller. Blue didn't like something about the steamroller. That's what had woken him. That's what was wrong. Something over there. "Oi, Blue, what is it?"

The dog looked at him and barked.

"Is it a fox?" Matt asked, but he knew it was no fox.

He knew what it was.

"Shit," Matt said, pulling on pants and a T-shirt. He grabbed his rifle and climbed out the window.

He ignored the steamroller and ran straight for the old shearing shed. "How's everyone doing in there?" he asked.

Silence.

Yeah, of course.

He unlocked the door and kicked it open. He looked inside, nodded. Light was pouring in from a hole at the back of the shed.

How had they done it? He examined the hole.

They'd kicked out the timber somehow and then dug through the dirt. Most of the tracks in the dirt floor focused on where Heather had been sitting. Tracks from her to the kids and the door. The lightest tracks were from the Dutch couple. This was Heather's plan. The Dutchies hadn't wanted to come but had changed their minds at the last minute. They hadn't seen Tom get killed, but Heather had convinced them that they were going to be next if they stayed. So she was clever and persuasive.

Cleverer than she bloody looked. Danny was right about her.

But it wouldn't make any difference. She would have to stay with the kids. The Dutch couple would stay together, and more than likely they'd tag along with the Americans. Perhaps one person could evade capture for a day or two, but five of them together? Two of them kids? And that Dutch bloke was in his late fifties or early sixties. Easily two meters tall. Stick out like a sore thumb, he would. And the fat American boy might not get a mile without passing out.

They'd catch them.

Matt went back outside and around the back of the shed. He patted Blue, who was waiting by the steamroller. "Good boy. Yeah, I see it. They escaped from the shed and came here. Good boy. If you had your puppy legs, I'm sure you would have run them down by now," Matt said and Blue wagged his tail in agreement. Matt bent down and examined the tracks.

She'd sent the kids out first and they'd waited here. Then she'd come, then the Dutch couple. Where had they gone next? He followed the trail into the long grass with Blue limping along beside him. The trail was fresh, only about two or three hours old. They must have been sawing the ropes when he came by to bring them water. He wouldn't tell Ma that part.

They had run east straight toward the old snow gum plantation about five hundred meters out from the farm. They were making for the larger clump of woods on the far side of the island. They might get cover over there. It was one of the few places on Dutch Island that wasn't heathland. It wasn't a bad plan, but . . . Matt bent down and examined the ground.

No, that wasn't right, was it?

"Come on, Blue," he said. He followed the trail for another three hundred meters into the heath where it spread out and then, yes—

Stopped abruptly.

"That's what she wants us to think. She wants us to think

they're trying to hide out in the wood. But that's not what they're doing at all, is it?"

Blue barked in agreement.

"They're all headed south toward the ferry, aren't they? They don't know that I had Brian take the ferry and tie it up on the other side of the channel last night, Brian grumbling and moaning about having to kip over there. But it's a bloody good job, isn't it, Blue?"

Blue wagged his tail.

It was a bloody good job because otherwise she might have been able to steal the ferry and escape. She looked like a light breeze could blow her over, but she was a shrewd one, this one.

Matt shook his head. He wished he'd asked her a few more questions about her background. Massage therapist, she'd said she was. From the city. But there were clues he should have picked up on. What was it she'd said? *Goose Island community . . . homeschooling . . . Indian reservation . . . bushcraft*. She'd said something about her parents being in the army. They might have taught her some survival skills. And there were other things about her too. She had attempted to take sole responsibility for the hit-and-run. She hadn't hesitated to go after Danny. Yeah, all of that could amount to a nasty little combo.

In retrospect, he should have gotten one of the older boys to watch the shearing shed all night.

Lock-the-barn-door-after-the-horse-is-gone thoughts. He patted Blue on the head again. "With all due respect, mate, we might need to get some dogs from the mainland to help us out here," he said.

He walked back toward the farm. Kate was standing on the veranda, all chill, with a cup of coffee. Nobody knew yet.

"Kate! Sound the alarm! The Yanks have escaped!"

"What?"

"The Yanks have escaped! Wake Ma! Never mind, I'll do it."

He raised his rifle in the air and fired it three times.

By the time he got back to the house, everyone was up.

14

Deadfall and dry grass. Furrows, bulging roots, ravines, gullies. Bladygrass. Blowfly grass. Prickly Moses bushes. Hard, red, ancient dirt. Spinifex.

Something flying overhead through the ebbing darkness.

Owls? Bats?

The air warm, pungent, metallic.

The terrain was harsher than it looked from the window of a car. What had seemed like pleasant fields of yellow-white grass from the road was actually tough country. The little hills were covered with divots and sudden drop-offs, the undulating effect of the landscape making for an exhausting trek. In the grass there were tall thistles covered with needlelike spines. They all knew that silence was important, but every few minutes or so Heather would hear a sharp gasp of pain as someone brushed against one of these thistles. She, Olivia, and Petra were in jeans, which afforded them some protection. Owen and Hans, however, were wearing shorts.

The hills and the thistles had nixed her plan of *running* to the far side of the island, and they didn't actually get close to the ferry terminal until the sun was starting to come up.

When they were almost there, Heather had them stop and take a break. She handed around the water bottle, making sure Owen and Olivia drank first.

After Owen drank, he fell on his back and gulped air.

Olivia sank to her knees.

The ferry pier was over the small range of low hills to the west. Only about a quarter mile now as the crow flew.

"I'll go ahead. You stay here," Heather said.

"No, I am coming with you," Hans insisted.

As soon as the two of them reached the brow of the last hill, it was obvious that the ferry was not there. Heather scanned the coast, but nope, it wasn't tied up anywhere here. It must have been docked on the other side of the channel.

"Now what? The boat is gone," Hans said.

"It's not gone, it's just tied up over there," Heather said.

"But we cannot get it," Hans said.

Heather walked cautiously down to the dock. The O'Neills weren't here yet but they would be soon enough.

There was no way to summon the ferry. There was no phone or walkie-talkie or even a bell. And what would happen if they successfully signaled it? If anyone was sleeping on it over there, it was bound to be one of the O'Neill family.

The mainland was just a mile and a half away. So close. Heather could see cars over there. Lights from houses farther down the coast.

"Let's get back," she said to Hans and they solemnly trudged back to the others, who were waiting up on the mesa.

"The ferry is not there," Hans announced.

"Now what do we do?" Petra asked.

"I don't know," Heather said and sat down in the grass. She looked at the kids. Olivia seemed to be doing OK, given the extraordinary circumstances, although she had gotten very good at concealing how she felt.

Owen was a wreck. All the water was gone now and he was clearly dehydrated. He was not in good physical shape to begin with. His mother's death had hit him very hard, and he'd retreated into video games and overeating and hiding in his room. He'd been excused from gym and he'd given up riding his bicycle and skateboard. He wore only a shapeless hoodie and shorts, and clearly this night jog up and down hills had brought him to the limits of his physical capacity. Furthermore, he hadn't had his ADHD or antianxiety medication for two days now, and Tom said that he needed those pills every day.

"Hey, Owen," Heather said, coming over to him.

He shrugged her away. "Don't touch me, Heather!"

She nodded and gave him space.

"Now what will we do?" Hans asked.

Heather turned to look at him. The Dutch couple seemed OK after their exertions. They both appeared to be in their late fifties or early sixties, but they were lean, fit, and strong, like a lot of Europeans.

"What do you suggest?" Hans asked her.

"I don't know. But we should get away from here. We're exposed. When they find out we're missing, they're going to come to the ferry and check around here first."

"The trail you made leads them to the woods," Hans said.

"That's not going to fool them for very long. They know our best chance of getting off the island is to come to the ferry, so they'll show up pretty soon."

Petra hoisted a finger into the air. "Listen," she said.

Heather listened, and sure enough, over the sea and the

morning chorus, they could hear two vehicles coming toward them from the farm.

"They know," Hans said.

"They're in a big hurry," Olivia said.

"We have to hide! Up there, farther back in the grass. Come on!" Heather said.

She grabbed Owen by the arm and they scrambled up the slope into the long grass. A Toyota Hilux and a Land Rover appeared on the brow of a hill five hundred yards away.

"Everyone, get down! Don't move!" Heather said.

The two vehicles drove to the ferry terminal and stopped with a squeal of brakes and a spiral of dust.

Four men and Kate got out of the cars. They were all armed with long rifles. Jacko, Matt, Danny, and Ivan. Matt examined the ground.

"They were here," Matt said, his voice carrying easily in the morning air. "They were here in the last hour but they've gone now."

"Did they swim for it?" Kate asked him.

"I don't know."

"The sharks will have took 'em," Jacko said.

Matt walked down to the water and looked at the little beach next to the ferry dock.

"No one's been on this beach," he said.

Hans and Petra crawled next to Heather, who had the best view.

"What's happening?" Hans asked in a whisper.

"It's Matt and some of the others," Heather whispered back.

Hans peeked over the lip of the grass. "Five of them," he said. "And they have guns."

"Yeah. We have to get to cover somewhere. We're exposed on this hillside and it's going to be very hot in an hour or two."

"You want us to keep going now?" Hans said.

"We have to, don't we?"

"But your plan was to take the ferry. They control the ferry. We have no other way of getting off the island."

"Maybe we could get some branches and make a raft or try to swim it," Olivia suggested.

"You saw the tiger sharks?" Hans said.

Olivia nodded.

"We'll think of something else," Heather said. Neither of the kids was a great swimmer, and the current looked strong. "But we have to get away from here."

Hans shook his head. "No. This is not an American Rambo game. This is foolishness."

"What's *your* plan, then?" Heather asked.

"We should announce ourselves clearly and distinctly with our hands over our heads and then we should walk down there and demand to be taken over on the ferry."

Heather stared at him. "Are you insane? You know what's going to happen if you go down there."

"What?"

"They'll kill you."

"No, they won't. I haven't done anything."

"That doesn't matter."

"We have no water. No food. In this heat, we will be dead by nightfall," Hans said.

"We'll find water," Heather said.

"There's no fresh water here. The only spring is at the farm in their aquifer. How could we last one day without water in these temperatures?"

Heather had no answer to that.

Both kids were paying attention and looking frightened.

"What are the men doing now?" Olivia asked.

"Matt's down on the sand trying to figure out if we swam for it," Heather said.

"We should have put some tracks on the beach," Olivia whispered.

"We should have. I didn't think of it," Heather admitted.

"We tried it your way. It did not work," Hans said. "We have no alternative but to give ourselves up and make them see reason."

Heather turned to Petra, who nodded. Petra appeared to be on the side of her husband now. Heather had lost the argument. She looked east. The massive yellow sun was already several degrees above the horizon and beginning to torch the island. It was indeed going to be another searing day. Concealed by the long grass, Heather reached into her pocket and pulled out the penknife. She slid out the short blade.

"I have decided. We are going to go down there and surrender," Hans said, getting up.

Heather dived on him and pushed the penknife against his throat. "No!" she said.

"You're going to kill me?" Hans said, apparently unfazed.

"You know how sharp this thing is. You saw what it could do."

"You're going to cut my throat?" Hans said.

"Yes. We have to look after the kids."

But Hans was big and very strong and surprisingly fast. Before Heather had time to react, he grabbed her right wrist and dragged it away from his face. He twisted her arm behind her back and rolled her off him. "Drop it," he said as he tugged her hand backward. She thought her elbow was going to pop out of its socket. "Drop the knife!" Hans said.

The pain was unbearable. She dropped the knife.

Hans dragged her away from the blade and flopped her onto her back. "I have been very patient with you," he said. "I thought you were different from the other Americans I have come across, but you are exactly the same. Come, Petra. Let us end this foolishness."

"No, wait, *please*," Heather said. "If you go down there now, they'll take us too. At least give us fifteen minutes to get away from here."

Hans shook his head. "You must do what you want. Petra and I have had enough of this."

"Dat is een vergissing, Hans. Er is niets veranderd sinds gisteravond," Petra said.

"Everything has changed! We have no water, there is no ferry, there is nothing more we can do," he insisted.

"They will kill us. You know they will," Petra said.

"This is a civilized country. We are living in the twenty-first century. This silliness is over," Hans said.

"Please just let us get away. Five minutes—what difference will it make?" Heather said.

"I have listened to your madness for long enough," he said and got to his feet.

He walked to the brow of the hill and waved at the O'Neills. "Up here!" he cried.

Heather picked up her penknife, grabbed Owen and Olivia by the hands, and pulled them to their feet, and, not knowing where they were going, they began to run again.

15

The blowfly grass. The bladygrass. The kangaroo grass. The
spinifex.

Thistles, divots, clay.

A hawk.

Sun.

Heat.

A rifle shot.

Owen: "I can't..."

Olivia: "You can."

Eyes front. That's the entire world. The one hundred yards in
front. Don't look back.

A little valley sloping down. Another hill going up.

A wail behind them. Yelling. Another rifle shot.

Running through the bladygrass.

Running through your own breath.

Through your own fear.

Thistle spines tearing at their legs. Divots in the red dirt
tripping them.

Indigo sky. Cirrus clouds. Crows watching them through two
hundred feet of heavy air.

Someone behind them. Hard breathing. Close. Closer. Someone gaining on them.

Don't look back.

Don't look back.

Don't look—

Heather looked.

Petra, red-faced, panting.

No one else on the hill yet.

"Hans?" Heather gasped.

"He went down to them."

"Why didn't you go?"

"They'll kill us. I tried to tell him—"

"Did he tell them we were up here?"

"I don't know. Where are we going?"

"I don't know."

Yet another gunshot and the sound of a car revving its engine. Heather tried to listen as she ran. She'd grown up with vets and their cars on Goose Island. Men who didn't talk about war or pain or loss talked about cars. She drove a stick. She knew engines. She knew gearboxes. That whining noise was the Toyota Hilux's 3.0-liter V-6 straining hard as it drove up the slope in first gear.

Hans had told Matt that they were up here, and the O'Neills were coming to find them.

She scanned the terrain for any conceivable bit of cover.

There was nothing.

They were half a mile from what seemed to be mangrove trees to the west and farther than that from a clump of eucalyptus trees to the north. There was nothing around them but featureless heath. No hiding places.

Shit.

That slope had been pretty steep. Maybe the Toyota wasn't

going to make it. She strained to hear. Nope, it was still coming. If they could—

Owen tripped and went down face-first into the red dirt. He pulled down Olivia, and Heather fell too.

"Ow!" Owen yelled.

"Are you OK?" Heather asked, trying to get a look at his face.

"Don't touch me!" he said, batting away her hand.

"She was just asking if you were OK," Olivia said.

"Jesus Christ! I'm OK, I just fell!" he said, panting.

Petra crouched next to him. "You're OK," she said.

The engine was really screaming now. Heather peeked over the grass and saw the big black snorkel air intake of the Toyota creeping over the brow of the hill.

She hit the deck. "Crap."

"What is it?" Petra asked.

"We have to keep low. Flat as we can. They've gotten the pickup truck up here. They're going to be looking for us."

She peeked up over the grass. They had stopped the truck and were gathered around the front of the vehicle.

"Maybe it broke down?" Heather asked hopefully.

"Are we going to keep running?" Olivia asked.

"We can't," Heather said. "I don't think we can make it to those trees without being seen."

"There's a kind of, like, old streambed or something over there. Could we lie down in that?" Olivia asked.

"Where?"

"Over there, just where I'm pointing."

There was indeed a very narrow fissure, possibly a dry creek bed, about thirty feet away.

"If they have dogs, the dogs will sniff us out and we will be trapped down there," Petra said, looking at the creek.

"If they have dogs, we're finished anyway. Olivia, you and Owen slither over to the dried creek and lie down in it. I mean slither—don't crawl. Petra and I are going to stay here for a bit and keep an eye on these guys to see what they're doing. Owen, did you hear me?"

"I heard you."

"Go, then, both of you."

Both kids wriggled on their bellies toward the streambed. Heather peeked back over the grass. The men were still gathered around the cowcatcher at the front of the Toyota.

"What's happening?" Petra asked, peeking over the grass too.

"I dunno. Could they have cracked the crankshaft on the way up the slope?"

The men cheered and fired rifles in the air. They stepped away from the vehicle and got back in the cab. The Toyota drove toward them. Now Heather saw what the men had been doing. They had tied Hans horizontally to the cowcatcher and were driving with him on it. They gunned the car up to forty miles per hour, smashing into the divots of the terrain and becoming airborne on the small hills.

Hans was still alive, but if they kept this up, he wouldn't be for long.

"No!" he began yelling. "No! No!"

Petra opened her mouth to scream. Heather covered Petra's lips and pulled her down. "There's nothing you can do for him."

"But he cooperated! He was trying to help them. Matt would have seen that."

"Matt's not in charge anymore. Jacko and Kate are running things."

Jacko had had that look in his eyes. Months, maybe years,

of boredom and frustration. Now he was going to have some fun.

If this was what they did to Hans, who had tried to surrender peacefully, God knew what they were going to do to them.

"I have to help him!" Petra said, struggling to get to her feet.

16

As Petra tried to get up, Heather tackled her, pulled her to the dirt, and climbed on top of her.

"Listen to me! We have to hide or they'll kill us too. They'll rape you and me and Olivia, and they'll kill us all. Do you understand?"

Petra was shaking her head no.

"They will kill us! Do you understand?"

Petra was sobbing now.

"We can't surrender! We can't," Heather said and finally Petra nodded.

"If I let you go, will you stay down?"

Petra nodded again and Heather cautiously released her.

Now the Toyota was driving away from them. The men hadn't seen them yet. Two of them were leaning out the windows of the cab, whooping and shouting. They did not appear to be doing any kind of rigorous search. They were driving this way and that, hammering the car for all it was worth.

The car did a slow 180 turn, and now they *were* coming toward them.

Heather ducked back under the lip of the grass.

Hans was yelling now. A horrible noise that Heather knew she would remember her whole life, however long that was. His voice pierced the general cries and the sounds of the engine. He was terrified and Petra could hardly bear it.

"Come on, let's get down to the hollow," Heather said softly.

Petra nodded, tears streaming down her face. She was gasping for air. Not knowing what else to do, Heather rubbed her back.

They slithered through the grainy red dirt and the sharp grass and reached the little dried-up creek where the kids had taken shelter.

"What's going on?" Owen asked.

"They're looking for us. Best we stay here," Heather replied.

The two women lay down next to the kids while the Toyota careened this way and that over the scrub. The sound was more muffled down here, but occasionally Heather could hear a war whoop or a rifle shot.

Heather lay there and kept the kids' heads down.

The flies. The heat. Sluggish, cigar-shaped clouds moving through the sapphire sky like evil alien ships.

"It's coming closer now," Owen said.

He was right; the Toyota was heading straight toward them. Could they have been seen? Of course they could have.

"Nobody move," Heather whispered.

The engine revved, and the Toyota bumped over the terrain.

Closer.

Closer.

It leaped the dried-up stream about twenty yards ahead of them, stopped, turned in a big circle, and headed away again.

Heather was lying next to Olivia. Her eyes were closed and

her lips were moving. She was praying. Heather had never really learned how to do that properly. Tom had taken the kids to church most Sundays. She'd gone once and told Tom that she didn't want to go back, and he'd been OK with that. As churches went, it had seemed pretty inoffensive. Just plain wooden benches and a harmless old man up at the front telling people to be good, not the terrible hypocrisy-ridden place her father had said church was, but she supposed it all had to do with the denomination. She watched Olivia, fascinated. Her message was going straight from her to God. Heather found that she was holding her breath, waiting for an answer or a bolt of lightning or something, but the only sound was the whooping from the Toyota.

It was coming back their way again.

Men's voices:

"Where are they, Hans? Tell us!"

"Faster, you drongo!"

"We'll learn that Kraut!"

"Come on, Kate, step on it!"

"Whoo-hoo! It's like the movies, ain't it?"

"In spades, mate!"

"Hans! Tell us where they are!"

"Come out, come out, wherever you are!"

"Where are you going to hide, kiddies?"

"They hide in the grass and we'll huff and we'll puff and we'll blow their bloody house down, won't we?"

Olivia was shaking all over. Heather stroked her hair. "It's going to be OK, baby," she found herself whispering.

"We can't stay here forever. They will bring all the other cars. The whole farm will come. They know we are here," Petra protested.

"Just stay down. We don't have any choice!" Heather said.

The Toyota was roaring toward them again, across the parallels and meridians in another intersecting curve. Olivia put her hands over her ears as the engine revved like a monster and the pickup jumped the ravine just five yards behind them.

Surely they had been spotted?

Heather waited for a screech of brakes or a gunshot.

But the Toyota kept going.

It headed out onto the scrub, and then—

A crash followed by silence.

Men began yelling. The Toyota had stopped. Engine turning over. Wheels spinning.

"Wait here, kids. I'm going to take a look."

"I'll come with you," Petra said.

Heather climbed out of the hollow and scrambled up the dirt embankment. The Toyota was in a gully three hundred yards to the south, its front wheels in the air. They'd tried to jump the gap but hadn't made it. The truck had hit the side of the gully in the middle of the front axle and was stuck.

It wouldn't be too difficult to get the Toyota out. Another vehicle could pull it, that one down at the ferry or the ones back at the farm. But they hadn't seen that yet and hadn't realized they were going to need more than manpower. They were trying to rock the Toyota out of the ditch, which would never work.

Matt went around to the front of the car and began untying Hans. If he was still alive, they were going to make him push too.

Heather stared at Matt. She had thought he was going to be the voice of sanity, that he was going to help, but he had made his choice.

"This is our chance to get out of here," Heather whispered to

Petra. "This will keep them busy for half an hour. They'll need a winch. We should go."

"Where will we go?"

"It's going to get hot. I think we should head for the mangrove trees by the water," Heather said.

The shore was half a mile to the northeast.

"And then what?"

"We'll worry about the 'then what' when we get there."

"I shouldn't leave Hans, I—"

"I'm sorry."

Petra shuddered and sobbed and finally whispered, "Yes."

They climbed back down into the hollow and explained what was happening. "We'll head for the trees by the shore," Heather said.

The dry streambed was going in the direction they wanted. They crawled along it for a hundred yards before it became too narrow, and then, gingerly, they climbed out onto the heath. The men were swearing loudly and kicking at the car.

"This way," Heather said. "Be sure to keep low."

The grass more or less covered the kids but Heather and Petra had to run in a crouch, Groucho-fashion.

It took them half an hour to make it to the mangrove trees, which ran along the narrow beach for several hundred yards.

When they got into the shade, both kids flopped onto the sand. Owen had taken off his hoodie and tied it around his waist. His T-shirt was drenched with sweat. Olivia sank down next to him.

Heather sat on a rock and tried to gather her wits.

The heat was unbearable. They had no water. Horseflies and mosquitoes were landing on them and sucking their sweat and blood with impunity.

"Can we drink that water, Heather?" Olivia asked, pointing at the sea.

"No, it's seawater. We can't drink it unless there's a river pouring into it," Heather said. She took off her shoes, rolled up her jeans, waded into the sea, and cupped a little bit to her mouth. She drank and spit it out.

"It's not good to drink, but I want you kids to bathe in the shallows and cool off a bit. I'll keep watch," Heather said, wading back to shore. She would watch for sharks. Tiger sharks, bull sharks, great whites—these waters were thick with predators.

It was not yet noon and it was well into the nineties. At least it was slightly cooler here than on the heathland because of a hint of a breeze blowing through the channel.

"Perhaps we could make a raft, like Olivia said?" Petra suggested.

"That might be a possibility," Heather agreed. The children were panting in the heat. "Kids, please, I want you to cool off in the shallows. But no deeper than your ankles."

The kids bathed, and while they dried off, Heather and Petra walked up and down the beach looking for suitable mangrove branches or driftwood, but the trees were stunted and the branches narrow and twisted. They were more mangrove bushes than actual trees. They broke off a branch and put it in the water, where it partially submerged.

"I don't know why it's doing that," Heather said. "Wood should float better than that."

"I don't know either," Petra said. "We would need hundreds of branches to make anything that could support even Olivia's weight. And how would we tie them together?"

"We could cut our clothes into strips and use those," Heather suggested, but she was skeptical—what they were thinking of would require days of work, perhaps a week. They were already exhausted just from this morning's exertions, and none of them had had any water since before dawn.

Owen was excitedly digging in the sand.

"What are you doing there, Owen?" Heather asked.

"Either of you ever watch Bear Grylls? His early shows, not the new shit ones."

Heather and Petra shook their heads.

"I found a couple of plastic bottles on the beach," he said.

"With fresh water?" Heather asked excitedly.

"No, they're empty, but look," Owen said, becoming animated for the first time in days. "I think we can make some kind of...yeah, hold on."

He took one bottle and half filled it with seawater, then he took an empty bottle and held it next to it. "What's the idea?" Heather asked.

"We make a still. Water evaporates from the full bottle into the empty one, leaving the salt behind."

"Will it be clean water in the other bottle?" Olivia asked.

"Completely."

"We don't really have time for this now, Owen," Heather said.

Ignoring her, Owen took the seawater-filled bottle and placed it on the sand in the sun. He buried the empty bottle under the sand on a downward incline so it was cooler and the water wouldn't leak out. He carefully placed the two bottlenecks together. "What's supposed to happen is that the sun will evaporate the water from the hot bottle and it'll condense into the cooler one," Owen said.

"Wow, it's actually really work—" Olivia began, but Heather put her hand up to silence her. She'd heard something. Was that a dog barking?

"Wait here," she said.

She scrambled through the mangrove bushes and climbed a little rise so she could see out to the heathland.

The sight chilled her.

Twenty people from the farm had formed a line and were making their way methodically along the edge of the plain. They were standing about fifty feet apart so they could cover three hundred yards of territory easily. The line included women and children, and most of them were armed. Someone was driving an ATV at one end of the line and there was a motorcycle at the other. Matt was there in his checkered shirt carrying his rifle; she heard him call out, "Blue," and his lame old dog came over and eagerly began limping beside him.

They were about two hundred yards away, but they were moving slowly and systematically in their direction.

Heather watched one boy with a gun climb through the mangrove bushes and presumably begin walking along the shore.

It was a replication of that thing Jacko had talked about, the black line. They were going to hunt the four of them down the way their antecedents had hunted down the original Dutch Islanders and the Tasman people.

Heather ran back to the others. "They're coming for us! We have to go!"

"How far are they?" Petra asked.

"Too close! Get up, Owen."

"The bottle's working!" Owen said.

"I'm sorry! We have to go."

"We're dying of thirst here!" Owen protested.

Heather pulled him up and Petra got Olivia to her feet, and they began running along the shore with the O'Neills in close pursuit.

17

The jaunty *Star Trek: Voyager* theme music began as the end credits rolled. The music was an ironic commentary on the previous forty-two minutes. Somehow Carolyn had missed this episode when it originally aired and had caught it only now on her Netflix binge rewatch. She was crying. In fact, she was quietly devastated. The only person who would understand was Heather. It was dark out. It was tomorrow in Australia. Heather might be up.

Carolyn's phone was dead. She really needed to get a new one. It was barely able to keep a charge now. She plugged it in, and, yup, a text came through from Heather herself. It was a photo of a bird. A parrot. Heather sure liked birds. There were no other texts. But would Heather want to hear her wee-hour ramblings about *Star Trek*?

Carolyn had been so worried about her going overseas. Heather had never even had a passport before, and she had gotten way skinny lately. Probably wasn't eating right. Still, she was a grown-up and married, and Tom was Mr. Rich Capable Doctor Guy.

Carolyn lifted her electric guitar off the floor and noodled with a tune. She hadn't written anything in a year or two. She and Heather had written dozens of songs when they'd been teenagers. Music and Star Trek series, they had shared.

She put the guitar back on the floor.

She typed, Have you seen the Voyager episode "Course: Oblivion"? and pressed Send.

Heather would reply as soon as she woke up or sobered up from her winery tour.

18

Heather now realized her mistake. Every few yards they had to duck under or climb over or go around or climb through the scrubby little mangrove trees. You couldn't easily escape up this beach. Progress was nightmarishly slow.

Going around the bushes meant they were up to their knees in water, and the tide was coming in. She looked to her right to see where the high-water mark was and found a line of scum and seaweed two-thirds of the way up the bank.

We're going to have to cut inland, she thought. But if they cut inland, they would be seen. It was afternoon now; the sun was heavy, huge, and orange in the northern part of the sky. Eventually it would sink into the mainland on the left, but that wouldn't be for hours yet. Seven or eight hours, possibly.

She could hear the pursuers yelling to one another up on the mesa. They were getting closer.

At this rate of progress, they'd get caught in seven or eight minutes.

"Keep going," Heather said as they fought their way through

the bushes. The bark and the leaves weren't particularly sharp, but still, they scratched at their skin. Skin that was already raw from thistle cuts and sunburn.

Headway was slow.

So stupidly slow.

Heather looked behind them. The tide was their enemy and their friend. It chased them and helped them. It hid their footprints, but in an hour this coastline would be underwater and they would have to move inland or swim.

Owen was fading fast. Even that sip of water left in the bottle would have helped. Should she run back and get it?

No. She'd be caught and then they'd all be caught.

She put one hand under his arm and helped him walk. "Any thoughts, anyone?" Heather asked.

"We could just stop," Owen said.

"We can't give ourselves up. Not now," Petra said.

Heather's throat was burning. She felt light-headed. The sun felt like it was draped just a mile or two above them. A watchful, proud, cruel sun. It was enjoying this. It was like the death ray from *The War of the Worlds*.

She'd never experienced anything like this heat. This was like her father's description of Fallujah.

Her dad would know what to do now.

Tom would know what to do now.

She had no idea.

She looked at the ocean, but there were no answers there.

She brushed the flies from Owen's face.

On the heath, Matt's dog was barking.

People were yelling to one another like it was a scavenger hunt or a picnic.

When Jacko had mentioned the original Black Line of

Tasmania, she hadn't given it much thought. Jacko's story was a historical curiosity. But now she understood what it meant. It meant massacre and murder and genocide.

This was how most creatures lived, had always lived, on Earth. The soothing nature posters in the waiting rooms of doctors and dentists were all a lie. In the bush, all the happy stories were written with white ink on a white page.

Owen slipped and fell. She pulled at his arm but he was unresponsive. Heather bent down next to him. He had passed out from dehydration or heat exhaustion.

Petra and Olivia turned to look.

"Run!" Heather said.

"We can't leave you," Olivia replied.

"Go! Just go, I'll carry him," Heather said.

Petra shook her head. "I'll help. We'll carry him between us."

Heather nodded. "Olivia, you go on ahead."

"I'll wait for you."

"No! You go ahead!" Heather insisted. "Just go."

"No."

She propped Owen up under his left arm. Petra supported him on the right. He was groggy and groaning. Heather wondered if he was going to die. People did die from heat exhaustion. To save them, you needed IV fluids and rest and proper medical care.

"Have you got him?" Petra asked.

"Yes."

"Let's go, then," Petra said.

The boy was deadweight between them. And the tide was coming in fast now. They were dragging him through wet sand, making hardly any progress at all.

That kid with the rifle on the beach would be able to see them soon. If the shoreline had been a flat bay or a curve, he would have already spotted them. As it was, the little Mandelbrot inlets and headlands protected them.

For now.

But not for much longer. They maneuvered Owen over a low-hanging tree branch. His ankles got stuck and they had to stop and lift his feet over one by one.

It took forever.

Heather looked over her shoulder. No sign of the teenager following them, but they could hear the O'Neill clan coming toward them across the heath.

"What do we do?" Petra asked.

Heather knew she couldn't reason with them. Not after what they'd done to Hans. They were capable of anything. They could do anything they wanted on their island. Eventually the police would come looking for the four of them. She had to pin all her hopes on that.

"Hide and stay alive as long as possible," she said.

They got Owen through the trees, and there was Olivia, standing there, hands on hips, refusing to move. "I told you to keep going, didn't I?" Heather snapped.

"I don't want to go by myself!" Olivia wailed.

"Just go!"

"And leave my brother? I can't."

"They're probably going to catch the three of us," Heather said. "You can run ahead by yourself. You have a chance."

Olivia shook her head.

"Just frigging go!" Heather insisted.

"You can't tell me what to do! You're not my mom," Olivia said.

"That's Owen's line, Olivia. You need some of your own

goddamn material. Come on, now, be a good girl and get the hell out of here!"

"And then what?"

"Just keep going as long as you can until dark. They'll go back to the farm then. Especially if they have us."

"Then what? If I do get away today, what am I supposed to do by myself?" Olivia said, sounding lost and bereft like the fourteen-year-old girl she was.

Heather forced her brain to function. Everything between her ears was like wet cement. What was Olivia supposed to do? What could she do by herself?

They carried Owen over another low tree branch. Heather looked behind her. Still no sign of the kid with the gun, but it wouldn't be long now at the rate they were moving.

"Hide until you see police," she told Olivia.

"What am I supposed to do about water?"

"Owen's bottle trick. Please, honey, just go," Heather said. "They're coming. Just go!" Heather looked in Olivia's eyes, pleading with her. *You still have a chance—please.*

"If that's what you want!" Olivia said and ran off down the beach.

The two women carried Owen for another few minutes until Petra called a halt. "I have to stop," she said.

"We can't take a break."

"I have to, I'm sorry," Petra said. She unhooked herself from Owen and flopped on the sand between two mangrove bushes. Heather could not continue without her, so she laid Owen down on the sand and then propped him up on her lap, out of the surf. She touched Owen's forehead. He was probably running a fever now and his lips were chapped. Dehydration, without a doubt. He couldn't take much more of this. He would die soon.

"I'm sorry, Owen," she said, and she started to cry.

The narrow strip of beach had been reduced to a few yards now, and the water was swilling about their legs. Heather took the penknife out of her pocket and pulled out the blade.

Petra looked at her and nodded. She picked up a sharp stone from the beach.

These wouldn't do much good against a rifle, but they weren't going to go down without a fight.

19

DUTCH ISLAND, AUSTRALIA

Olivia knew it was all her fault.

She was the one who had planted the seed.

Her.

ALKI BEACH, SEATTLE

Dad, we need a vacation. We need to get away. From this place. From the staircase. From this house. We need to get away.

I don't think so.

We'll make a trade. I'll start softball again in the spring.

You should do that anyway. You're a talented pitcher.

Dad! Come on, we need this. For Owen's sake. And mine too.

Owen? You think a trip to Australia is going to fix him?

We need to get away. I've been thinking about it. Your conference in Australia. Could we come? Me and Owen and Heather too if she wants. I've always wanted to see the outback. A kangaroo. A koala. Dad. Dad?

DUTCH ISLAND

Seawater lapping. Gulls. Heat. The sun cooking her brain.

Dad gone, the Dutch guy gone, Heather and Owen and the woman gone. Only her left. Running.

She didn't want to be by herself.

The sun.

The sea.

What choice did she have?

ALKI BEACH

It is good to have the ocean at one's back.

Why is it good, Dad?

It gives you heft, sweetie. It gives balance to a mind adrift on change and harassed by the irrepressible new.

What?

Doesn't matter. Listen. Listen to me, now. Your mother. Don't let them say things about your mother. She loved you. She would never do that to herself. It was an accident.

Was she drunk?

No. It had nothing to do with that. It was an accident. An accident. Yes...

Dad, are you OK?

Sorry. Of course. This is about your mom. Let's think about her.

DUTCH ISLAND

The heat was everything. The heat was incredible. The heat was destroying her cell by cell, killing her, as it would kill all of them.

This was all her fault.

Dad had been reluctant. Please, she'd said. Everything we've been through. With Mom. Good for Owen. You know how much he loves animals. Please. Let us come with you for once on one of these things. It's Australia. Like Disney World but better. Everything magic. The animals. The people. The landscape. The accents. A complete escape.

It had worked. Then they just had to convince Heather. Heather hadn't wanted to come. She was worried about bushfires. She didn't like snakes. She didn't have a passport. But Dad wasn't going to take two kids to Australia by himself.

And it had been awesome.

The desert.

Uluru.

Everyone had been so nice.

This island, too, had been her idea. Hers and Owen's. Dad hadn't wanted to come.

But Dad had come here because of the koalas for *them*. It all led back to her.

ALKI BEACH

A boat called a Zodiac.

The moon was part of the real zodiac.

The word *moon* came from the word for "mother." Mrs. Taggart said a lot of languages shared the same root. Even in Latin, where the actual word for "moon" was *luna,* they had the related word *mensis.*

Zodiac, moon, mother.

DUTCH ISLAND

Ocean at her back, sun overhead, the sound of *them* over there on the spinifex, as they'd called it.

She wasn't stupid.

She was fourteen.

When her dad was fourteen, fourteen was fourteen. When her mom was fourteen, fourteen was fourteen. But not now. Now fourteen was older. There were things you could see anytime anywhere on your phone. Could never unsee.

She knew the word *rape.* She'd known what it meant last night.

She wasn't dumb. No. She knew what was going to happen.

Sand.

Heat.

Sea.

She looked behind her. She was moving quicker now. The boy with the rifle would catch the others soon. She imagined Heather would try to fight him with the penknife. It wouldn't work. She didn't know anything. Her mom would have run rings around Heather. Who did she think she was? Owen said she hadn't even graduated high school. Best to leave her. Only problem was leaving Owen. Owen, a kid. She shouldn't have done that.

ALKI BEACH

The cold air.
   The snowflakes.
   The bobbing little Zodiac boat.
   I don't want to go.
   Olivia.
   I don't want to. It's not good for the ocean.
   Get in the boat.
   Owen doesn't want to do it either.
   You're being silly, both of you! Get in!
   OK, Dad.

DUTCH ISLAND

We're going to get caught.
   And I am going to die from thirst.
   At home Dad has those bottles of Evian in the fridge.
   At home.
   None of us are going home.
   None of us.

ALKI BEACH

Owen folding his arms.

Dad yelling at him. Dad losing his shit the way he used to.

Dad taking Owen by the shoulders and getting real close to his face: It was your mom's last wish. Don't you want to honor your mom, you little shit?

Owen crying.

Owen getting in the boat.

Dad pulling the starter on the outboard motor.

The Zodiac leaving the dock.

Dad saying nothing.

Owen still crying.

Dad dumping the urn.

Mom saying nothing.

Mom splintering into a million pieces in the black water of Puget Sound.

A single seagull.

Owen crying.

Dad not crying.

Dad mad as all hell.

DUTCH ISLAND

Water up to her knees.

Birds on those rocks would have to find somewhere else to rest soon.

The rocks would be underwater in an hour and all those weird birds would have to—

Olivia stopped and rubbed her eyes and stared at the line of rocks about twenty feet offshore. They were jagged and funny-looking, and if you imagined a little you could pretend they were the spines of a dinosaur's back.

A stegosaurus.

She looked at them and nodded and knew what she had to do next.

She turned and ran back the way she'd come as fast as she could.

20

Through the bushes. Through the water. Hard to breathe. Hard to think.

"Look behind us," Petra whispered.

Heather turned.

Less than a hundred yards back, coming around the bend, a man and a boy, both with guns. With them was a very little girl tagging along like they were going to a birthday party. The pursuers couldn't see them in this vegetation, but they were certainly going to catch them soon.

Heather had been cooking up a little Hail Mary plan in her head: Hide. Wait. Ambush the kid as he pushed through the bushes. She'd get one go at him with the penknife, but one go was better than none.

But she had no chance against two of them, armed. The man looked like Ivan, the big brute from the ferry.

Shit.

Her against the two of them?

Damn it.

So this was it, was it?

The giving-up place?

She'd always wondered where that would be.

Not after a twenty-hour waitressing shift. Not when that truck rear-ended her and totaled her Honda. Not when she got appendicitis and had to drive five hours to the VA hospital in Tacoma because she knew she couldn't pay the bill at the Bellevue Clinic.

It was here, on a slip of a beach on an island off the coast of Australia.

What the hell was up with that?

She saw Olivia coming around the bend in the bay as if someone was chasing her. Oh, shit, this really was—

Caught between—

But Olivia had an expression of grim satisfaction.

Something was—

Olivia reached them, breathless.

"What?"

"Around the next corner, there's a line of rocks just offshore, about fifteen yards offshore. We can wade or swim out there and hide and let them get past us," Olivia said, panting.

Mouth almost too dry to speak, Heather nodded.

Petra nodded too. They would have to move fast. Ivan and the kids were coming up the beach.

"Owen, we're going to be OK," Heather said. "Just a little bit farther."

With renewed vigor, Petra and Heather carried Owen through the mangroves and around the bend. And, yes, just off the coast, there was indeed a line of rocks.

"How will we do this?" Petra asked.

Heather tried to answer but she couldn't form words. It had to be over a hundred degrees away from the shade of the mangrove trees. They'd be exposed to the full glare of the sun out there on the rocks, but what choice did they have?

She swallowed a few times to get saliva in her mouth. "You go with Olivia. I'll swim Owen out. Just help me get him into the surf."

Petra nodded and they manhandled Owen down to the water.

"Go," Heather said. Petra and Olivia began swimming out to the rocks. Heather flipped Owen onto his back.

"Just relax, Owen. It's gonna be OK," Heather whispered into his ear. She crooked one arm around his neck, and, keeping his head raised, she swam into the bay.

The water was cold, but swimming with Owen was easier than she'd expected. She swam on her side, kicking with both her legs and pulling back hard with her right arm. In ten brisk strokes she reached the rocks, big black jagged boulders sticking out of the water.

She swam behind them.

"There's a little ledge on this rock here, see if you can put him on that," Olivia said from somewhere.

The ledge was only the size of a bookshelf and it sloped downward at thirty degrees, but the sea had worn it smooth and between the three of them, they managed to get Owen onto it. His eyelids were fluttering and there were white flecks on his lips. Where he wasn't sunburned, he was pale and his skin was cold to the touch.

Heatstroke, exhaustion, dehydration...

He needed water and food and rest and shade very soon or he was going to die. The rest of them would be dead soon after.

Heather checked his pulse. It felt weak.

"There," Petra whispered.

Three people were coming around the bend of the beach—

Ivan and the teenage boy and the little girl. As they got closer, their conversation drifted across the water.

"Nah, mate, St. Kilda have no chance, they have no depth," Ivan was saying. "Now, you look at the Bulldogs, that's a team that's going places. That's a team that can get through the ups and downs of a season. You wait and see."

"What are they talking about?" Olivia whispered.

"I don't know. The important thing is they're not talking about us. Their attention has wandered. That's good," Heather whispered.

Something nudged her leg.

She peered down into the water but couldn't see anything.

Dolphins?

No, not dolphins. She knew that for a fact.

Something happened when there was an orca in the water off Goose Island. Some change in the vibe. You could feel the danger through your skin.

She floated there, moving as little as possible.

She tried to see, but the water here was deep and opaque.

Ten feet to her right, a fin rose out of the water for a moment and then slipped beneath the surface again. That was no dolphin. It was an immature blue shark. It was only about four feet long, and blue sharks mostly fed on squid, but they could give you a nasty bite whatever age they were. It was circling to her right.

She wasn't sure if it had noticed them or not. One way to make a shark notice you was to start thrashing about and panicking.

She looked back at the shore.

Ivan and the children were almost parallel with them.

"I don't want to go to school," the boy said.

"It's up to you, mate," Ivan said. "Ma can't force you to go.

At least, I don't think she can. But it's school, it's not jail, mate. I did it and I'm OK. Bunch of poofs, but I reckon you can handle yourself. And Geelong isn't a million miles away."

"You went to the same school as me dad, Uncle Ivan?" the little girl asked.

"I did, Niamh. Three years. Geelong Grammar. Like I say, they were all a bunch of bloody wankers, but I got used to it."

"When Uncle Matty gets the drone working, can I fly it?" the boy asked.

"That's a big if. Matt's had that thing out of the box twice since he got it!"

Olivia was breathing hard. Owen's breathing was shallow. Petra was holding her breath.

The blue shark was over to her right.

It abruptly changed direction and headed lazily toward her.

Shit.

They were all bleeding. That's what had got its attention.

The fin went down. It was going for Olivia.

Heather couldn't even warn her.

She leaned all the way over and pulled back her leg.

If she timed this right . . .

She looked into the blue shark's right eye and kicked it in the gills just as it was opening its jaws to take an exploratory bite.

Olivia saw and gasped and put her hand over her mouth.

The immature blue splashed away, annoyed.

The little girl, Niamh, turned and looked straight at the rocks but didn't see anything. Or perhaps pretended not to see anything.

The boy and Ivan and Niamh continued to talk until they reached a thick clump of mangrove at the end of the little bay.

They disappeared into the trees and were gone.

"Let's get to shore," Heather said.

"Shouldn't we wait a little bit longer?" Petra said.

"There's a blue shark circling us. Let's get ashore. Come on."

They swam to the shore and dragged Owen into the shade of one of the mangrove trees.

"Do you think they will double back when they don't find us?" Petra asked.

Heather shrugged. "I don't know. I can only hope they'll keep going until it begins to get dark. It doesn't matter if they double back or not. We won't be moving Owen again."

21

Heather and Petra carried Owen to the shade of a mangrove tree and left him to recover. The seawater had cooled him down, but heatstroke wasn't the issue now. It was dehydration. She fanned Owen with mangrove leaves, keeping him cool as best she could.

One hour.

Two.

Three.

The O'Neills didn't return to the beach.

Olivia wrote *SOS* with stones and seaweed that they all knew the tide would take away.

The sun began to set.

Owen, amazingly, was still alive.

Water. If she didn't get water tonight, the boy was going to die.

Petra knew it. Olivia knew it.

Heather went up onto the mesa and climbed an immature eucalyptus tree.

The heathland was empty. There were lights on at the farmhouse two miles from here. Birds were roosting. Night was coming.

"Anything?" Petra asked.

"I think they've all gone."

Heather began climbing down. She missed her footing on the branch beneath her and grabbed for a handhold on the branch next to her. The dry eucalyptus limb could not take her weight; it snapped and she fell eight feet into the hard dirt. Her back took most of the impact.

"Are you OK?" Petra asked, running to her, alarmed.

"Uh, I think so," she said and lay for a while with one leg stuck on a lower branch.

Petra disentangled her.

"I didn't sign up for this," Heather said.

"What did you sign up for?"

Heather thought about it. "I don't know. I don't just mean *this*. I mean the kids, all of it."

Petra smiled sadly. "We never had children. Hans didn't want any, and I didn't protest too much. How...how did you end up with your husband? He was older, yes?"

"Some of my friends said I was crazy to marry a man in his forties. But I was poor. Lonely. Tom is...was fun. We hit it off immediately. It was an instant family with a yard and a picket fence—just microwave for one minute and you can have everything you want."

"Hans and I had very little in common at first," Petra said. "He hated my music. I was a punker, if you can believe it."

"I can believe it. I've always sort of been out of step with my contemporaries. I didn't realize how much until I left home and came to Seattle."

Petra nodded and they sat in silence.

When the sun had finally gone down in all its gaudy beauty, Heather stood. "I'm going to look for water. If I'm not back by morning, I guess it means they got me."

"I understand," Petra said.

Heather hesitated. "You'll take care of the kids as best as you can?"

"Of course."

The two women hugged.

"Good luck," Petra said.

Heather nodded and waved and headed east.

East under the upside-down moon.

Under the sky full of southern stars.

Under the Southern Cross and the Milky Way.

She walked through the spinifex and thistles and blowfly grass. She knew the Northern Hemisphere's sky like the back of her hand; there was no light pollution that far west on the Sound. The Big Dipper. Orion. The Dog Star. Night-fishing with her dad, she could see from one side of the heavens to the other, the stars rotating around Polaris. She smiled at the memory. None of that would help her here in the Southern Hemisphere, where even the moon was wrong.

She had a headache. She didn't know the biology of it, but she guessed that her brain cells, like everything else, were affected by dehydration. Her muscles ached and she was cramping, and she suspected that this was because of dehydration too.

Not much she could do about that.

A bat crossed the moon.

She heard nightjars.

Someone was driving an ATV a mile to the south.

The island was an approximate rectangle, three miles by two, with the farm in the middle. She approached the farm from the north, where the spinifex was tallest, but she quickly realized the farm's well was a no-go. They had turned the spotlights on around the farmstead, and on the roof of the barn she could see the silhouette of a man with a rifle.

She squatted in the grass and considered the situation.

Matt was clever, but he wasn't as clever as he thought he was. She wouldn't have played it like that. She would have turned the lights off and made everything seem like normal. Just have a few guys waiting in the darkness for her to approach the well.

The man on the roof of the barn did not look particularly concerned. He must have figured it would be a miracle if anyone had survived the day on the island in hundred-degree heat without water.

Heather backed away from the spotlight beams and gave the farm a wide berth. If she could help it, she wouldn't go anywhere near there.

Far too dangerous.

But she had a plan B.

She turned south and kept going until she hit the road.

She listened for the ATV, and when she didn't hear anything, she headed east again.

Her mouth was so dry, it was as if her tongue were made of sandpaper.

Her brain was operating in slow motion.

East.

Across this tundra.

Across this nothingness.

Over this land without a Dreaming.

The road was warm.

The night was warm. The sea breeze had decided not to come.

Little animals were scuffling about in the undergrowth. She fantasized about catching one and sticking her knife into its belly and drinking its blood.

What she wouldn't give for a glass of water. Didn't have to be cold water. Muddy ditchwater would do. Anything. She looked at the sky. Was there any chance of a rain cloud?

No. She could see in every direction all the way into space. There was nothing between her and the vacuum.

She marched on.

On.

She was so light now, she could feel the stars tugging her. The other worlds. The other civilizations.

How easy it was to drift upward.

You just let yourself go.

Go.

Up, up she went on a thermal until she could see all of the island. All of the bay. All of the state of Victoria. The rest of the great sleeping continent.

Higher. Deeper.

Now she could see all of Australia and New Zealand.

That looming presence in the south was Antarctica. So close to all that frozen water.

Farther up she went until she could see all of the Earth spinning on its axis through the darkness. Goose Island had its share of crackpots. She knew at least two people who were flat-earthers. If she ever came back, she would tell them that they were mistaken. She had seen the round Earth rotating herself.

If she ever came back.

So lonely out here.

Lights coming toward her.

The space station?

A UFO.

No. Shit. A car.

Back to Earth like an incoming V-2. She dived off the road and flattened herself in the grass.

A Land Rover speeding along. Music blaring from the vehicle. Music Dopplering in her eardrums.

All we are saying is...

All we are saying...

All...

She buried her face in the grass as the headlights swept across the blackness.

She sat up and watched the taillights barrel down the road.

It was going to the farm but she didn't care where it was going or what it was doing.

It was gone.

It had fallen into the past with yesterday and Tom and George Washington and Jesus and the painters of Lascaux and the dinosaurs and the dead stars that made the iron and nickel at the center of the Earth.

All gone.

She got to her feet and continued down the road.

In fifteen minutes, the old prison loomed out of the night. She slowed her pace and grew cautious but there was no real reason for caution.

All was dead here.

Rectangular pitch-black buildings. Silhouettes of abandoned farm machinery. She explored the equipment for a few minutes but there was nothing she could break off and use as a weapon.

She got down into a crouch and approached the nearest of the structures.

Most of the prison had been demolished, but a cellblock had been left standing: a long concrete-and-iron-bar building exposed to the elements. That little house on the rise must be the old guardhouse.

There were no lights on anywhere. She walked into the courtyard between the prison and the house and listened.

Nothing. In the far distance, she could hear surf breaking on the shore of the island.

The house was a two-story job with a balcony on the upper floor that went all the way around. She walked to the front door and examined it. A heavy wooden door with a keyhole. She tried the handle and then put her shoulder against it and shoved, but it didn't move.

Heather took a few steps back and examined the building with a more clinical eye. She shook her head to try to get her brain working better.

Two floors. Brick construction. Corrugated-iron roof. There were large windows on the ground floor with bars over them. She did a circuit of the structure looking for any points of entry but couldn't see any obvious ones.

Heather tugged at the metal bars covering the windows. Although they appeared rusty and very old, none of them seemed loose. She tried every metal bar on every window on the ground floor and then shoved her shoulder against the door again.

Sighing, she tried to figure out what to do.

There was no guarantee that the house would have water. Maybe this whole thing was a fool's errand.

She walked back to the old cellblock and looked inside the

individual cells. Cobwebs hung from all the doorways and the building stank of urine. Watching out for venomous spiders, she examined each cell for anything she could possibly use.

There was a lot of garbage on the floor but the paper waste was mildewed and fit for nothing. There were a few crushed beer cans with liquid inside. She was so desperate she was tempted to pour the contents into her mouth. She decided that if she couldn't get into the house, she'd risk being poisoned and do just that so she could have at least some liquid in her system for the journey to the beach.

Back into the courtyard.

The waning sickle moon slipped out from behind a solitary cloud and for a moment she got a really good view of the old guardhouse. There were no bars on the floors of the upper windows. If she could find a way up there to that second floor...

She wondered what time it was. How long she had been away? One hour? Two?

On the north side of the guardhouse there was a narrow veranda with a rocking chair and a wicker chair. The rocking chair was useless, but perhaps she could stand on the wicker chair and climb up one of the columns to the second-floor balcony. From there it would be comparatively easy to get to one of the windows, break it, open it, and enter the guardhouse.

Heather picked up the wicker chair. It was not as light as she'd been expecting and she had some trouble carrying it around to the side of the veranda. She pushed it down *hard* into the sandy soil and leaned it against the wooden pillar holding up the balcony.

She estimated the distance from the top of the seat to the

iron railing on the second floor balcony as about six feet. If she stretched her arms and didn't fall off the chair and was strong enough, she could pull herself up.

Standing on the seat, she tentatively put one foot on one armrest and then the other foot on the other, and when she was certain that the chair was not going to slip from underneath her, she placed one foot on the back of the—

The chair slipped and she tumbled backward into the sand with a mild *whump*. "Ow," she said and put her hand over her mouth.

It wasn't as bad as falling off the tree into the red dirt.

She lay there in the sandy grass and looked at the stars. She stared at the starless space called the Coalsack. You couldn't see that in the Northern Hemisphere. At Uluru, a guide had explained that it was a nebula, a vast dust cloud many light-years across. To the Aboriginal peoples, it had looked like the head of an emu. She closed her eyes. She was alone here in the nothing, but it was OK. Solitude was an old friend that welcomed her after all these months with kids and their friends and their mommies. It would be so easy just to keep her eyes closed. Just to lie here on the sand all night. Eventually, without water, all her systems would begin to shut down. Her kidneys would stop working and her heart would slow, and maybe, if she was lucky, it would just stop completely.

None of this was her responsibility.

She was just a kid herself.

She was twenty-four, but really, she was younger than that. She'd left home only a few years ago. She hadn't really wanted to come to this island. The kids wanted koalas and she'd been trying once again to get them on her side.

The kids were not her kids.

They didn't like her very much. In fact, they barely tolerated her. They weren't her problem.

What was the difference anyway between dying here and dying in some trailer in the woods decades from now. It was all the same groove. The universe wouldn't even blink.

Just lie here.

Drift.

Dream.

Fade away on the current.

She thought of Seattle. She thought of Goose Island and the Sound. Of her father and looking west through the yellow of seven p.m. She thought of "Into Dust," that song by Mazzy Star that her mom liked.

The moments ticked slowly past.

So easy...

Too easy.

Your body is a longbow carved from hickory, her father said.

Your body is a blade sharpened by tears, her mother said.

Heather sat up.

She stood and brushed the sand off her jeans.

She righted the chair and steadied it in the sand and, after achieving equipoise, she put her left foot on the right arm. So far, so good. She put her right foot on the back of the chair. The chair began to list, so she jumped and grabbed one of the iron railings of the second-floor balcony. The chair fell from under her. She pulled hard on the railing. Her arms felt impossibly weak. This wasn't going to work. If she could hook a leg up, take some weight off her—

She swung her torso to the left and right; on a final leftward swing, she managed to lift and land her foot on the lip of the balcony. She hung there precariously for a second or two.

"Come on," she growled and pushed off on her foot. She rose almost vertically, like the vampire in *Nosferatu,* and somehow found herself standing on the narrow part of the veranda on the other side of the railing. She stepped over the rail, and there she was on the second-floor balcony. Just like that.

"Oh God," she said and caught her breath.

She walked to the door and pulled the handle, but it was locked. There were no windows open.

Heather had no idea if this building had a caretaker or not. There was definitely space for a couple of bedrooms up here but there were no signs of occupation. No hum of an air conditioner, no creaking boards, no snoring, no noises of any kind.

She stood there considering for a moment and then shoved her elbow into the glass panel above the door handle. It broke and fell out in two big pieces that shattered inside the house.

She went back to the rail, ready to jump and run.

She waited.

And waited.

Nothing stirred.

She put her hands gingerly through the broken glass and turned the handle.

The door opened and she went inside what was clearly a bedroom. There was a bed and a closet and a dresser. Everything covered with dust.

She hesitated for a moment and wondered if she could perhaps lie down on the bed.

She shook her head. Maybe up here there might be a...

She walked into the hall and—yes! There at the end of the landing was a bathroom. She ran to the sink and turned on the tap. Without any fuss at all, water came pouring out of the faucet. She looked at it in amazement.

All that water just pouring down the drain.

She touched it with her finger and then she cupped her hands, filled them with water, brought it to her lips, and drank.

It was like drinking the waters of heaven.

She cupped her hands and drank again and again.

Heather held her mouth under the faucet and let the water gush down her throat.

"Oh my God," she said. "Oh, dear God."

She splashed the water on her face and let it drip down. She put in the drain plug, filled the sink, and shoved her head under the fresh water. She blinked her eyes a couple of times to clear them of dust and dirt. After thirty seconds, Heather pulled her head out and sat on the toilet.

She unplugged the drain and let the water run out, fascinated by it, as if it were some exotic substance she had never seen before.

Heather didn't want to stop drinking. She turned the faucet back on again and let it run directly into her mouth.

As her brain started to revive, from somewhere in its deep recesses, she remembered that drinking too much water too quickly could kill you, so, reluctantly, she removed her face from the sink and took a couple of final big sips.

Oh God, that was good.

She edged out of the bathroom and found a rickety wooden staircase that led down into a kind of parlor. A table, a sofa, an ancient-looking television set, a mantelpiece covered with framed photographs. She picked one of them up. It appeared to be a police officer—or, more likely, given the surroundings, a corrections officer.

She put the photograph back and went through a door into a hall that had been converted into a kind of reception area and ticket booth. Everything was covered in a thick layer of dust. Pamphlets about the old prison were piled up on a table next to an old-fashioned till. She put a couple of them in her back pocket to maybe use for kindling. In a fridge that wasn't plugged in, there were a dozen small bottles of water.

Holy shit.

She found a cloth carrier bag and began loading the bottles in. She took all of them. This would help. This would help a lot. This would save them. And when they'd drunk their fill of water, they could come back here and refill the bottles from the sink upstairs. Perhaps they could even hide out here until the police came?

Perhaps.

Would Matt and the others notice the broken window upstairs?

Worry about that later.

She wondered if there was any food around.

There was a sign that said TEA/COFFEE 2 DOLLARS, which meant there had to be a kitchen somewhere down here, and if there was a kitchen there might be a cupboard full of food. She walked back into the parlor and looked for a door leading to a dining room or kitchen.

Something didn't feel right.

Had she missed something?

Maybe there was food in the other room in a drawer or something.

No, that wasn't it.

The floorboards.

A pressure change.

She held her breath.

The sound of breathing.

There was someone in the house.

How could there be? The place was deserted. There was dust over everything.

It was her imagination.

Or a possum, perhaps.

The hairs on her neck were standing up. Her body knew, even if she didn't. The ancient alarm bells were ringing in her limbic system.

Then the light came on.

22

She froze.

"Drop the bag and put your hands up or I'll blow your bloody head off," a voice said.

She dropped the bag of water bottles and put her hands in the air.

"Have a seat on the sofa over there. Nice and slow-like."

Heather's eyes adjusted to the light. The man was skinny, rangy, medium height, about sixty-five. She recognized him. He was the man who had warned them to leave yesterday morning. He was wearing shorts and a Hawaiian shirt with flip-flops. The shirt was encrusted with stains and hadn't been washed for a long time. He had a stringy white-and-gray beard that dangled down to a point about eighteen inches beneath his chin. The shotgun was an old-fashioned, long double-barreled thing. It was impossible to tell if it was loaded or not. If someone was pointing a gun at you, you had to assume it was loaded.

She wasn't sure if she could remember everyone who had been at the farm that day, but she didn't think she would have

forgotten that beard. Was it possible that he didn't know what
was going on?

"Sorry, I didn't know this place was occupied. I was looking
for some water," Heather said.

"I'll bet you were looking for water. This island is dry as a
bloody bone."

"Yes, it is. You're probably wondering what I'm doing here.
We broke down and—"

"Save it. I know who you are. Do you know who I am?"

"No," Heather said, deflated.

"I am Trouble with a capital *T*. I'm Death with a capital *D*.
If you give me any problems at all, I won't hesitate to kill you.
Do you understand?"

"I understand."

"Now, you just sit there and do nothing while I call Matt on
the walkie."

She wasn't going to panic.

She had rehydrated and her systems were all beginning to tick
back online.

He'd spoken long enough for her to realize that his accent
was not Australian. Or not entirely Australian. He was originally
from Britain or Ireland. What he was doing here was anyone's
guess, but crucially, he was an outsider unrelated to the people
down at the farm. He was not family.

"I said sit down!"

She sat on a sofa that sagged in the middle, sucking her into
it, trapping her. It would take her two or three seconds to get
out of this thing. More than enough time for the man with the
shotgun to blow her head off.

"My name is Heather," she said.

"I know who you are. Sit there and shut up."

The man began rummaging one-handed in a drawer next to the TV. He couldn't find what he was looking for, so he turned on another light.

There was a hole in the window screen, and the room was full of moths and insects that began flying into the light bulbs.

The man found the walkie-talkie and sat in a chair a good nine or ten feet from Heather. "So you probably know there's no phone lines out here. Not since the prison closed, anyway. But we keep in touch pretty good through these," the man said, waggling the black-and-yellow walkie-talkie at her. Mocking her with it, it seemed. "Got these at Woolies. Ten bucks. Do the job. We all have 'em. Good range, too, unless you're over one of the hills or something. Good enough to call Matt. We'll have the boys down here in a jiffy."

"Please don't do that. I'm looking after two children. I just came to take some water," she said.

"Steal some water, more like. You didn't ask anyone, did you? Broke in here and took what you wanted, didn't you? I told you people to leave. You should never have come here in the first place!" the man said and began fiddling with the radio.

"Please don't call Matt. Please just let me go. I can tell you're not part of the family."

"Oh? How can you tell that?"

"You have a different accent than them."

The man found the on switch to the walkie-talkie. He adjusted the volume and the room filled with the ominous sound of static. If he called Matt, she was dead and the kids were dead.

"You're Irish, are you?" she guessed.

"Yeah, I'm Irish, what of it?"

"Where are you from? Are you from the same place as Ma?"

"Ma was a ten-pound Pom. You probably don't know what that is."

"No."

"She come over on the boat all the way from Liverpool but she's as Irish as me. That's why I was allowed to stay here. I'm the only outsider that didn't marry in. Have you heard of a place called Ballymena?"

Heather shook her head.

"That's where I'm from."

"How did you end up here?"

"I come over to work in the prison. Help close it down, really. Sort of stayed after that."

"I saw your photograph on the mantel. You were a corrections officer in Ireland."

"No, I wasn't. I was a police officer."

Heather's heart started beating faster. "A police officer?"

"Yeah, something called the RUC. You heard of that?"

Heather shook her head again. "What's your name?" she asked.

"Rory."

"Nice to meet you, Rory," she said.

He grunted a response and continued to fiddle with the walkie-talkie.

She leaned forward on the sofa. "I'm looking after two children. Owen is twelve. Olivia is fourteen. Owen is badly dehydrated. He's going to die tonight if I don't get back with water. And the rest of us—you know what they're going to do to us, don't you? They're going to kill us all. They're going to rape me and Olivia and then kill us."

"That's none of my business," he said.

"Back in Ballymena would it have been your business?"

"I suppose," Rory said and smiled. "You think you're smart, don't you?"

"No. I've screwed everything up."

"Matt told me about you. He said you were crafty. That I was to watch out for you."

"You have to help us! Against them."

Rory shook his head. "I can't afford to do that, can I? If they find out I helped you, they'll be after me next, won't they?"

"Tom's . . . my . . . the kids need water."

"It's not my problem, love. I didn't ask you to come here, did I? This was your choice. None of this is anything to do with me. You hit Ellen with your car. You can't involve me in it. I've nothing to do with it and if they find out I was even talking to you, I'll be for the bloody chop, won't I?"

"You can't just let us have a little bit of water?"

"And then what?"

"If we can get to a boat—"

"There's no boat. They have the only boat. The ferry. We're on this island with them. It's theirs. They grew up here. Old Terry used to say that Dutch Island was never legally incorporated into the State of Victoria. They consider Australia to be a foreign country. They're a law unto themselves. They know it like the back of their bloody hand. They know every nook and cranny and everything that goes on."

"How come they haven't caught me and the kids yet?"

"That is a bloody miracle. You are living on borrowed time. They'll find you. This is their backyard. They're only toying with you."

She shook her head. "They're scared now. I—"

"Are you having a laugh? You have no idea. You seriously think you're outwitting them? They're letting you live. They're just having a wee bit of fun. They don't tell me everything, but they told me to watch out for you and they told me they're bringing dogs over from the mainland tomorrow. Bloodhounds. If I let you go, they might track you to here and they'll ask me questions, and if they see that broken window I'll have to make up some bullshit about it. You've already got me in the crapper. Now, you just sit there and I'll call Matt, and if you move an inch I'll blow you in half, so I will!"

"I don't think you'll shoot me. You're a policeman. You know what's right."

"I do know what's right. You killed Ellen and you're going to pay for that."

"We've already paid for that. They killed my husband, Tom. They killed him in front of me. And now there's only me to look after those two little children."

He nodded. "Yes, I heard what Danny did."

She looked in his eyes. Tried to find answers there.

She had to risk it.

He was terrified of them. But he was an ex-cop.

Ever so slowly, she got out of the sofa and got down on her knees. She clasped her hands together in a pleading gesture. "Please, for the kids."

"You must be deaf, lady. Deaf like poor Ellen. I can't help you."

"You're really going to let them murder me? And a little boy and a little girl?"

"What can I do? Me against twenty-five of them?"

Heather tried another tack. "My dad was in the army. He, um, talked about soldiers who had lost their moral compass."

"Is that what I've done?"

"Yes. And I think you know it," she said.

He shook his head. "Everything happens for a reason. Me

coming here thirty years ago. You coming here yesterday. Us having this conversation now."

"Maybe the reason is that you're supposed to let me go. They'll never find out about this conversation. They'll never know you helped me."

"They'll know. They'll find out. They know a lot more than you know and see a lot more than you think. It's a game to them. They're letting you run around in their backyard. I'm lucky. They accept me. I've done OK by them. And I don't bother them and they don't bother me. They pump water to me from their aquifer, let me live in peace."

"Please."

"No more *please*s. You shouldn't have tried to escape. Ivan and Jacko are pissed off. Look, I'm not privy to everything they're up to, but Jacko was telling me what they're going to do to that Kraut if he doesn't talk. I don't want that happening to me."

Heather swallowed. "What are they going to do to Hans?" she asked.

"Jacko says he still hasn't told them where you're hiding out."

"He doesn't know. What will they do to him?"

"There's a big red-ant colony over behind the barn. You must have seen the mound when youse come in?"

"No."

"Millions of the wee skitters. Old Terry learned that trick in Vietnam," he said with a shudder.

Heather felt cold all over. "They're crazy, you can see that," she said, putting her hands together and leaning forward to beg some more.

"Listen, love, if you move one inch closer, I'm going to shoot you." He put down the walkie-talkie and cradled the gun in both hands.

"No, you won't. You're not the type. I'm not threatening you or doing anything to hurt you. I've learned my lesson. I'm getting the water and I'm going to go."

He was looking at her down the barrel of the shotgun. His finger was on the trigger. She had no doubt now that the weapon was loaded. His knuckles were white; there was sweat on his upper lip, and even in the yellow light she could see that his pupils were dilated. This was not a bluff. One slip of that trigger finger, and he would blow her in half.

She thought of Olivia and Owen.

She swallowed hard and blinked the tears out of her eyes.

So much tension in her shoulders that she felt like she was going to snap.

She knew if he pulled the trigger, she wouldn't feel a thing. She wouldn't hear anything. Her life would instantly cut to black. The blackness would last until the end of the universe, when everything would be black.

She swallowed again. "I'm going to back away from you, Rory. I'm going to do it real slow. I'm going to reach over to the bag with my left hand. I'm going to lift it up and gently put it over my shoulder. Then I'm going to walk away and you are never going to see me again. And no one from the farm will know that I was here, and we both come out of this alive."

"If you touch that bloody bag, I'm going to blow your bloody head off. Do you hear me?"

"I hear you. You're *not* going to shoot me, Rory."

"Believe me, I will."

She took a deep breath. She had to make him see that letting her go was the win-win solution.

"The cops are going to show up here eventually," she said. "And when they do, they are going to be asking lots of questions.

My husband was a well-known man. There are going to be cops all over this island looking for evidence of what happened to us. They're going to take you in for questioning."

"I can handle cops."

She looked at him. "Why do you stay here? What's here, Rory?"

"Peace, quiet, birds. Lots of birds."

"My dad likes birds too."

"Shearwaters are my favorite. Burrows all over the southern dunes. They fly here from Alaska, if you can believe it."

She smiled. "You're not a murderer, Rory. You're not like them. You're not part of this yet. You've done nothing wrong. You're police."

"Maybe you're right about all of that," Rory said after a long pause. "Maybe I don't want to kill you. But I don't have to. I can shoot this thing at your legs. You'll be singing a different tune when I blow your kneecaps off. Is that what you want? I'll bloody do it. Now, sit back down again."

She felt the sights settle on her lower body.

Shit, he was really going to do it.

His bluff had beaten her bluff.

She wasn't good at this.

"I'm sitting down," she said.

Rory rested the shotgun on his lap, picked up the walkie-talkie, and found the right channel. "Oi, Matt are you around?" Static. "Matt?"

"Yes, this is Matt. Who's this?"

"Rory. You'll never believe who just walked into my house."

"Who?"

"The American."

"You're kidding! She with the kids?"

"Just her."

"Are you pulling me leg?" Matt asked.

"Nope. I got her here."

"Well done, mate! Hold the fort! Me and Kate will be right there. Over and out!"

Rory put down the walkie-talkie, picked up the gun, and grinned at Heather. "Out of my hands now, love. Out of my hands," he said. "I'm done talking. If you make one more sound I'll give you both barrels. Let's just sit here in peace and wait for the others."

23

Sweat under her ass. Shotgun pointing at her knees. Two 30-watt bulbs eking out a ration of rancid-butter-yellow light. Dust. Three moths. Four flies. Rory's cracked lips and grim razor-blade smile.

Seconds counting down.

Five-minute drive from the farm to the prison.

Three hundred seconds.

As soon as Matt and Kate arrived, it was the end of days.

Owen would die in the wee hours.

The others wouldn't last much longer.

Ticktock.

Ticktock.

Shotgun.

Iron sight.

Three moths.

Four flies.

Sweat.

Lunge at him. Just go for it. Jump.

No. He'll shoot you.

He won't; he was a policeman.

That was a lifetime ago.

Yellow light.

Moths.

Flies.

Sweat on Rory's upper lip.

Ticktock.

Ticktock.

Was that a car engine?

It was.

Shit.

She was dead. Kids were dead. Go, Heather. Go. Now.

"I'm going to get up now. I'm going to get my bagful of water bottles and I'm going to walk out the front door and I'm going to go, OK?"

"Don't you bloody move!"

Keeping her hands above her head, she slowly got to her feet. She swayed there for a moment.

"Don't do it!"

She walked across the living room and picked up the bag of water bottles. She walked to the front door and fumbled with the lock.

"Don't! I'll shoot."

She opened the door and pushed on the screen door.

"Come back here!"

The hairs were standing up on the back of her neck.

Her legs were rubber.

The screen door opened.

"This is your last warning!"

She stepped into the night. Onto the veranda.

Just a few . . .

Fire. Light. Noise.

Something struck her arm and shoulder.

Pain. Heat. A hot scarlet flame.

She fell to the ground, dropped the bag, got up, and ran as hard as she could into the darkness.

There was another shotgun blast, this one nowhere near her.

She ran and ran over the dry grass and red dirt.

At a hundred and fifty yards, she turned and looked back.

A Jeep arrived. Matt, Kate, Ivan, and Jacko got out.

Rory was reloading the shotgun, pointing into the darkness. Pointing in the wrong direction.

It was then she realized that he had deliberately missed.

There was heated conversation before Jacko walked off the veranda. "Yeah, run, you bloody mingy bitch! See how far you get! I'm enjoying this!" he yelled.

Kate aimed her shotgun into the darkness and fired both barrels.

Heather ducked down and, trembling, watched the white-hot buckshot rip the air.

"When I catch you, I am going to skin you alive like one of me foxes!" Kate screamed.

Heather crouched in the darkness trying to ignore the burning sensation in her shoulder and upper arm. It was like trying to ignore a hot iron rod being pressed into your flesh.

The O'Neills were talking to Rory. Heather crawled a little closer so she could hear.

"Yeah, mate, she's crafty, all right, sleekit wee skitter, so she is. And fast—she just ran out of here like a mad thing. I shot at her twice," Rory said, his voice carrying in the still night air.

"Did you hit her?" Matt asked.

"I'm not sure."

Matt climbed down off the porch and looked at the ground

for a minute or two. He dipped his fingers into the soil and examined them. He stared into the dark and rubbed his chin.

"I think you did hit her, mate. With a couple of pellets, at least," Matt said.

"Good on you, Rory!" Jacko said.

"Yeah, she's fast as Shergar, the, uh, Derby winner, but I gave her a good go," Rory said.

"She won't stand a chance tomorrow," Jacko said.

"With the dogs?" Rory asked.

"Yeah, Davey Schooner's dogs. Trains 'em for the cops. Kelpie-hound crosses. They'll find them all in a couple of hours. They don't smell like anything else on this island," Jacko said.

"Bloody bitch. I knew she was bad news," Kate muttered.

"Nah, no worries, Kate. Bit of fun and games. She'll be right in the end," Ivan said.

"Well, we should go. Lock your windows and doors, Rory. Board up that top window. I doubt she'll be back, but you never know. I'll tell Ma you did OK. She'll be proud of you, mate," Matt said.

"Thanks, Matt."

"If you see so much as a bloody shadow, shoot first, ask questions later," Kate said.

"I will do. She'll not get the drop on me twice."

Kate, Ivan, Matt, and Jacko got back in the Jeep.

Rory waved to them and then sat down on the rocking chair on the veranda. The shotgun was across his lap.

He sat there rocking himself back and forth until the taillights of the Jeep were long gone.

When it was quiet, he stood.

"I know you're out there," he said.

Heather flattened herself in the dirt.

"I'm going to leave this bag of water bottles here. I'm going to bring it in in the morning. So if you want it, you're going to have to take it tonight. Do you hear me?"

Heather said nothing.

"Smart. Keep being smart. If you ever come back here again, you're a dead woman. I will blow your bloody brains all over the place. This is your one Get Out of Jail Free card. Everybody is entitled to one and this is yours. Just one, mind. I will shoot you. I can't afford to miss again. Not with them lot. Not with Ma." Rory put the shotgun over his shoulder, opened the front door, and went inside.

A few moments later the house lights went off.

Heather waited.

And waited.

Then she began crawling, fast, through the long grass. The red soil was dry and rough, and she had to be careful not to kick up too much dust.

She crawled as carefully and as quickly as she could, circling the house. Checking the windows, checking the lights. In ten minutes, she was facing the front porch again. The grass was lower and the cover was sparser.

With scraped knees and hands, with her left shoulder hurting and bleeding and her left arm on fire, she inched her way back to the house.

The bag was sitting there with all that precious water.

Dust trail ghosting her.

Twenty-five feet between her and the porch.

He could be waiting at some darkened window with a rifle. There was no guarantee he was not.

"Hell with it," she said. She got up, ran to the porch, grabbed the bag, and sprinted back into the wee hours.

24

Heather walked through the night with the bottles. She walked under the stars and moon in the same filthy skin of fear, but at least now she walked with hope. Northwest toward the shore. She heard the sea. It was so unfair for Tom and the kids. After the year they'd had. But if she could keep it together and make it back, the children at least might have a—

Oh my God, what now?

Something to her left.

A biped. Walking. *Loping* through the grass.

Tall and dark in the spilled moonlight, a white snout sniffing the air, like a bear that smells you before it sees you in your yard.

Heather fell to her knees. It must have seen her. How could it not?

It was close.

Forty yards to her—

And then, to her right, she saw that there were two of them.

That same white skull. Hollows for eyes.

Even without making any noise, she was giving everything away.

Her arm throbbed. Her shoulder hurt. Blood rolled down her fingers into the parched grass. She was trembling all over. It was as if a spotlight were on her.

They were hunting in pairs. Hunting her.

One looked at the other and they nodded and kept going. She was trapped between them. The one on the left was on a path that would take it within feet of her.

All she could do was kneel in the dirt and keep still. They were both carrying something. Something she recognized. Something blacker than the dark around them.

In the bright southern starlight the unmistakable shape of a Remington 870 long-barreled pump-action shotgun.

As they got closer, she saw that they were wearing denim overalls and had animal skulls on their heads. Wolf skulls. Or, more likely, dingo skulls.

There was a moment when all three of them were on the same line of longitude and then they walked past her and kept on going until they reached an ATV parked on the grass.

"Fee-fi-fo-fum, I smell the blood of an American!" Kate yelled into the spinifex. She sat on the ATV and lit a cigarette. "You're all cowards! Skulking there in the dark! Well, the dark's your only friend. Get a good night's sleep, 'cause ready or not, tomorrow morning, here we come! You're gonna work tomorrow. You hear me, Heather? Work. And this is one massage that ain't gonna have a bloody happy ending!"

Kate and her partner laughed, flipped on the lights on the ATV, and began driving back to the farm.

Well, if they'd been trying to terrify her, they had succeeded. And this was only the start of it. Civilization meant nothing here. Perhaps it had always meant nothing. There were no monsters on Dutch Island, but the beast was man, had always been man.

She was shaking. Goddamn, she could do with a cigarette. She gulped down the air and tried to calm her nerves. But it was hard. The day had tossed her about like a deerskin kayak on the Sound.

"Come on, Heather, just get up and walk, one foot in front of the other."

She got up, and the grass and the Milky Way brought her to the eastern shore.

Petra was waiting by the big eucalyptus tree.

"You made it!" she said, hugging her.

"The kids?"

"Hanging on."

"Owen?"

"Yes."

"I got the water."

"I'll give it to him. I've done first aid; I'll rehydrate him carefully."

Heather followed Petra to the beach.

Petra gave them the water.

Heather watched them drink.

It was one of the most beautiful things she'd ever seen in her life.

Petra drank and then, finally, Heather drank.

The kids started to revive. Within minutes, they were alert and chatting to each other. Amazing how resilient they could be.

Amazing.

She asked Petra to come and talk to her.

"What is it?" Petra asked when they were out of earshot.

"I got hit by two shotgun pellets. You're going to have to dig them out with the penknife. One's in the back of my arm, one's in my shoulder. I can show you exactly where, and there's good starlight."

Petra looked skeptically at the stars and waning sliver of moon and shook her head. "Show me," she said.

Heather took off her T-shirt and bra and lay down on the beach. "Can you see?"

"Perhaps we should wait until morning."

"No. Now, please. I don't know how it works but...I think... the danger of infection."

"I can try, if you want. Are you sure?"

"Yes."

"I'll...OK. I'll get something for you to bite on."

"Talk to me about something."

"What?" Petra asked.

"Holland...no, that thing you were talking about. The dream lines." Heather put a twig between her teeth.

"Yes. I've been reading a lot about that since I got here. It's quite interesting. The Aboriginal people were often nomadic, following what they thought of as dream lines through an actual geography that was also a mythological landscape. By following these ancient routes, they believe that they sang the Earth into being..."

The pellet in the arm wasn't hard to find. It was embedded in the fat just above the elbow. Petra rummaged with her finger and got it out easily. "One gone," she said.

The shoulder pellet, however, would have to be dug out with the penknife.

For some reason, Petra was talking about the Sex Pistols now. "And that is why Johnny Rotten talks about England's

Dreaming. England has to reimagine its own mythological future and..."

Heather took the twig out of her mouth and panted like a dog.

Petra continued talking to distract her. "What do you do, Heather?"

"I was a massage therapist. I was pretty good at that."

"And how did you end up here?"

"My husband was in Melbourne for a conference. About knees."

Petra began to laugh. "My husband was here for a conference too! About old cars. He's writing a book. He thought we might find some interesting specimens on the island."

"Husbands."

"Husbands."

"I only really came here for the three-hour tour," Heather added, weakly singing the three words of the *Gilligan's Island* theme, which, of course, Petra had never heard.

"Are you sure you want me to keep going?" Petra asked.

"Yes."

Heather bit down on the twig again. She bit down hard. The pain was everything. The pain was the path.

The ball in the shoulder was lodged in the muscle. Petra worked on it with her fingers and then the penknife for fifteen minutes.

Heather was drenched with sweat. She had bitten two sticks in half.

"I got it!" Petra said.

Heather gasped for breath in the sand.

She was weak. So weak.

She went down to the sea to bathe the wound.

She was her mother's favorite saying come to life. *The cure for everything is salt water: tears, sweat, or the sea.*

The water was warm. It cleansed her. Floated her. Helped her. She wished she could stay in the ocean, but most sharks were night feeders.

She waded out of the water and sat on the beach with her knees tucked under her chin. Petra placed a poultice of wet sand and eucalyptus leaves over the wounds.

"Are you OK?" Petra asked.

"How are the kids?"

"Fine. Sleeping," Petra said.

"Sleeping? Really?"

"Sleeping."

Heather nodded and found that she wanted to cry some more, but crying was a luxury and there were no tears left.

25

A black iron nothingness. An ellipsis of time. Perhaps a minute; perhaps ten thousand million years.

A nimbus of yellow goblin light.

And from the nothingness, a poker stirring the cold gray ash of sentience.

Pain, diffuse and weird. A surrender to a more urgent, primal logic. The rawness of now.

"He's awake."

"I see that. Will he live?"

"I doubt it. Who knows? I'll put a couple more milligrams of morphine in his drip."

"Are you sure you know what you're doing?"

"Do *you* want to take over?"

"No."

Diminishing pain.

More darkness.

Another ellipsis.

26

The sun, never tiring of the human comedy, was coming up on the eastern side of the island.

Blue-dirt sky. Red-dirt sky. Yellow-dirt sky.

Heather was up on the mesa, sitting in the long grass, keeping watch.

No vehicles yet.

No movement from the ferry.

Clouds under the fading final stars.

The sea shape-shifted from rough to smooth, from black to dark green to a brilliant magenta.

It was Valentine's Day. Tom would have remembered to get her something. He never forgot anything. He remembered big chunks of every book he'd ever read. Could recite fifty lines of poetry at a time. He had helped so many people with his knowledge of knees and ankles and everything in between. And those scumbags had killed him like he was nothing.

She looked out across the water. It was amazing to think that less than ten miles away were the outer suburbs of Melbourne. Police, lawyers, doctors, churches, hospitals, and everything you needed for civilization to work. Just across that little strip of water and over those fields. Help.

But it was no good thinking about that. The ferry was on the other shore, waiting. Waiting for the men with dogs. Trying to raft it or swim the channel with the kids would be suicidal.

She watched a plane fly toward the city. How long until someone realized that they weren't coming home? How long until someone figured out where they'd gone? The O'Neills wouldn't deny that they'd come over to Dutch Island; there were witnesses who would corroborate that. But that wouldn't bother them.

Heather could just see Matt standing there, grinning and being all cooperative, a couple of days from now when they were dead and buried. *Yeah, that's right, your witness was correct, Detective. They did come over here on the ferry. They took a few photos and went right back. Just ask Ivan, he took them over. I expect you'll find their car stuck in some ditch over there somewhere.*

And that would be that; the cops would find the car stuck in some ditch over there, and what had happened to the family would be one of those unsolved mysteries TV shows loved to talk about.

Flies and wasps flew about her head. Her belly rumbled. Her belly ached. No food for anyone for over a day and a half now.

But at least they had water.

She walked back to the beach and checked on everyone. Olivia and Owen were sleeping together under Owen's big hoodie, which he had draped over them like a blanket. Petra was lying beside them with a protective arm over the boy.

Heather smiled. *Thank you, Petra.*

She tapped Petra on the shoulder. "It's OK, it's only me," Heather whispered.

Petra stirred, shivered. "Is everything all right?"

"So far. I'm going back to the mesa to see what's happening."

"OK," Petra said, reluctant to move and wake the kids. "I'll look after them," Petra added.

Heather nodded and walked to an old gnarled gum tree that had been burned to charcoal. A bird with blue feathers and a long beak was sitting on the upper branches gazing at her.

The bird squawked.

"Same to you," she said.

She sat at the base of the tree.

The dogs were coming today. Dutch Island was not big. There were no forests, no mountains, no places to hide. The dogs would find them.

If they gave themselves up, she knew exactly what would happen. Probably only Olivia would survive. And that wouldn't be much of a survival.

Better to risk it with the sharks.

"What would you do?" she asked the bird.

It was looking south.

She followed its gaze and saw movement by the ferry terminal. She watched for a while and saw vehicles on the far shore.

She heard the sound of motorcycles and that distinctive Toyota Hilux engine.

She leaned against the tree and waited.

Eventually she heard the ferry's big diesel engines kick in and she watched the vessel churn up a wake. There was a pickup truck on it and some kind of cage in the back of the pickup.

The dogs were coming.

She ran back to the beach. The kids were already awake. Petra was pointing at the water. "The ferry is coming back," Petra said.

Heather nodded. "They are going to be hunting us with dogs today. We've got to move. We've got to keep one step ahead of them."

"Where will we go?" Olivia asked.

"As far away from here as we can get. Our scent is all over this beach."

They watched the ferry cross the water. They could hear a couple of the dogs barking excitedly. She was angry at herself. The trail from the prison would take them directly here. She should have thought of that last night, tried a diversion or a—

"We should go," Petra said.

And it was on. Olivia, Owen, and Petra got to their feet and brushed themselves off. Olivia knocked sand out of her sneakers. Owen tightened the belt on his shorts.

South was the ferry terminal, east was the heath, west was the water—their business now was north.

North along the beach.

Through the rock pools.

Through the mangrove bushes, mosquitoes, flies, land crabs. The kelp was stinking; the day was hot and it had only just begun.

The tide was out, exposing those friendly rocks from yesterday. They'd be seen easily if they tried that trick again. The rocks wouldn't save them today.

Heather could hear another motorcycle and an ATV. At least two cars. A lot of people. Three or four dogs.

She didn't know if they were doing that line thing again, but they weren't fooling around today.

"What's the water situation?" she asked Petra as they waded around a large clump of trees that was blocking the beach.

Petra looked in the bag. "One and a half bottles."

"That's it?"

"Yes."

Heather nodded.

"We will save them for the children," Petra said.

"Yes," Heather agreed.

Up the beach.

Through the flies.

In the sun.

In the red Southern Hemisphere sun.

Sunburn on sunburn.

Up the beach.

Running.

Moving.

Wading.

Swimming.

Resting.

Moving again.

North along the curvy shore.

No geographer or Google Earther knew this bit of shore as well as them. The rocks, the little bushes, the tide pools, the dried-up river estuaries. The bays that curved in, the headlands that jutted out. The swamp, the drowned mangrove trees, each gully, each rock, each—

"Look! Over there—what's that in the sand?" Owen said.

"What do you see?" Heather asked.

"It's something. What is that?" he said, running to a bit of the beach she couldn't see. He picked up the object and showed it to her. "What do you think? This will come in handy, yeah?"

He gave it to her. It was a knife. A big knife. No—a machete, with a cracked wooden handle and a rusted blade about nine inches long.

"Yes, well done, Owen, this will help."

She balanced it in her left hand and then her right. It was a rusty old thing that looked like it had been lying on the beach for a hundred years.

At least I'll go down swinging, Heather thought. "Let's take a water break," she said. She handed their penultimate bottle to Owen and Olivia. "Ration it, just one sip each," she said.

After that, she held it out to Petra, who shook her head.

The ferry had landed. They could hear the dogs and the motorcycles but it was hard to tell where exactly they were. Olivia climbed a tree to look.

"They have motorbikes and a horse and cars. It's all of them. There are two groups. They seem to know that we were over there on the beach. They're coming from there." She pointed.

"The north?" Heather asked, alarmed.

"Yes. And up from the ferry dock."

"From the south too?"

"If that's the south, yes."

"How far away are they?" Heather asked.

"I don't know. Not far."

The dogs must have tracked her scent from the prison. And that made sense because they had spent the night not too far from the dock or where they had picked up Hans. The O'Neills would figure out that, realistically, they couldn't have traveled very far in the heat.

"They must have realized now that they just missed us yesterday," Petra said.

"They'll find us today. They'll make sure. They'll search this whole beach until they find us," Heather said.

Petra shook her head and smiled. "Not necessarily," she said.

"There are no rocks to hide behind today, and we can't—"

"Do you see that gully ahead of us? It is a dried-up river. It must have dried up a long time ago."

Heather looked where Petra was pointing. It was what on Goose Island they called a hollow way—a portion of land, an old pathway or a river, that was lower than the rest of the terrain. "What about it?"

"It leads deep into the heathland. Perhaps a kilometer. If we're lucky," Petra said.

"That won't fool the dogs," Heather said. "They'll sniff us right out."

Petra nodded. "That is what I am counting on," she began. "Listen to me. This is what we must do. I will run down the gully and keep going until I reach the end. And I will make a lot of noise so that I will attract their attention. The dogs will hear, and both groups will converge on me. I will go east as far as I can before they catch me. And you will go north along the shore as far as you can. At the very least, I will buy you some time. Perhaps a few hours."

"Are you crazy? They'll kill you. Forget it. Come on, let's go!" Heather said.

Petra shook her head. "No. I am not coming with you. You are going to go north along the beach. I am going this way. You will look after the children and I will draw them away as best I can."

"Why?"

"Because, Heather, this is the only way. It's simple mathematics. Four of us or one of us."

Heather opened her mouth and closed it.

She could see the look in Petra's dark brown eyes. Steadfast. Determined. "Are you sure?"

"Yes."

Heather nodded and the two women hugged.

"We should swap T-shirts," Petra said. "If the dogs are tracking you, it might help."

Heather put on Petra's gray Leiden University T-shirt and Petra put on her plain black Target one.

"Thank you," Heather said.

"Good luck," Petra said.

And each woman knew she wouldn't see the other alive again.

27

Petra ran down the gully *fast*. Certainly faster than she'd been going with the Americans. She'd always been fast. Even in Holland, where everyone biked, everyone was skinny, everyone ran. She'd been a sprinter and she was good—although not quite good enough to make a career of it.

She finished high school with no real ambitions in either athletics or academics. It was 1977 and she was the perfect age. She moved to London. She signed on the dole. She found a squat in Hackney. She listened to the Damned. She listened to the Clash. She listened to the Pistols. John Lydon was talking directly to her. She wanted to hear more about England's Dreaming.

She followed the Pistols all over England and back to Europe. She met a Dutch boy at a Pistols gig at Club Zebra in Kristinehamn, Sweden.

"This is the worst music I have ever heard," he said to her in his peasant accent.

"That's the stupidest thing I have ever heard," she replied.

And thus their lifelong relationship had begun.

Hans had encouraged her to enroll in college. She hadn't been

interested in further study before, but now she read everything.
Hans was a competitive bicycle racer, and at first she'd gone to
watch him and then she too became a racer.

She was better than him. She won trophies.

She was fast.

And more important than being fast, she was determined.

She read Tim Krabbé's *The Rider*. She read it and, for a while,
it became her bible. She was one of Krabbé's "true alpinists."
The true alpinist does not climb mountains because "they are
there"; the true alpinist's will is not so weak that it is bent by a
mere mountain.

It was all about will.

The ravine was only a meter wide and a meter deep.

She ran on.

Stones, red dirt, red clay under her feet—definitely a river-
bed. A winter phenomenon, and not every winter.

She could hear Hans's voice in her head, see his face. *They are
going to catch you. They are coming in a pincer movement. Go faster
and keep your head down and then when they are behind you, you can
slip out of the hollow and double back to the beach.*

"I'm not going anywhere near the beach. I will go this way
as far as I can. I will make noise and keep going and going,"
she said.

You alone on the flat land? They will get you.

"Yes. Eventually," Petra said with a smile.

Why are you doing this?

"Because of the children, Hans."

You and the children. You won't forgive me for that, will you?

"Of course I will, my darling Hans. It was *our* decision."

Petra, is there any other way? The dogs . . .

"I will contrive to get myself shot before the dogs get me."

Hans said nothing and then he too smiled.

The sun was almost directly overhead and the T-shirt was drenched with sweat. Hans had been correct about black. Heather's black T-shirt absorbed the heat. Her gray one was a few degrees cooler. A long-sleeved cotton shirt would have worked even better.

She kept running as the gully narrowed.

A mosquito had settled on her left arm. Only the female mosquitoes bit you, because they needed blood to make eggs. There was, Petra noted, no female solidarity between them. Petra didn't mind. "Live, little mosquito, make your eggs," she said and it flew away from her, satiated.

She had gone about four hundred meters.

It was time to make some noise.

She stopped and caught her breath and looked back.

The two teams were converging on the beach where they had been.

"Where are you going, you bastards!" she yelled in her best Johnny Rotten voice and ducked back into the gully.

That will do the trick, poor dead Hans said in her head.

"I think it will," she replied.

She could hear the dogs. Four of them. Four dog voices. Twenty human voices. Kids with them. What kind of sick people were they to bring their children with them?

She ran on as the gully got narrower and narrower.

Surprisingly, she found that she wasn't so much scared as sad.

What a waste. All the things she knew. All the stuff about humans and their mores. All her travels. All her languages. She had English, French, Dutch, and German.

All the experiences. Working in the university. That year in Mali. That terrible year where she'd studied the effects of tragedy on nurses in the children's cancer ward in Amsterdam. Those were the real heroes, the nurses who worked there. She'd written a book about it. It had been translated into German and Danish.

The dogs.

Coming up fast.

Faster than her.

She wasn't that old. Hans wasn't that old either.

They'd almost never argued. Not even about having kids. *We'll buy a house and ride our bikes and we'll travel,* Hans said. *We'll see the world. We don't need kids dragging us down. Too many kids on the planet anyway.*

The gully was at an end now. She'd thought it might come to an end in a little spring or a pool of water she could drink from, but there was nothing.

She stopped and looked behind her. Dogs and men coming her way.

Good.

She picked up a flat rock and climbed out of the ditch.

"There they are!" someone yelled.

Here I am. Watch what a retired Dutch woman in her sixties can do.

She ran east. She didn't look back. She kept running. She was surprised that one of the motorcycles didn't draw level with her but all the fissures in the ground might be impeding their progress.

It was no problem for her. She jumped the little trenches and ditches and ran up the gentle slopes.

They had let the dogs off the leashes.

She didn't look back.

The dogs weren't barking. This was all business now. The motorcycles had ceased their whining.

She was too fast for the flies.

All she could hear was the pounding of her own feet.

The pounding of sixteen doggy legs behind her.

They were getting closer.

Closer.

Paws on dirt.

Big breaths.

Snarling.

One of the dogs leaped at her and bit into her left leg. She fell and tumbled down hard and got up and clubbed the dog in the face with the rock. It collapsed onto its belly. She hit it again in the eye. She hit it a third time, killing it. The other dogs had reached her now. They were bloodhound crosses, simple-looking things. She went for them with the rock and they backed away. They sniffed around their fallen comrade and then looked at her, aghast. This wasn't part of the game, was it?

She got back on her feet and ran on.

The dogs did not pursue her now.

She began to think of the slim possibility of escape.

And then the world detonated between her shoulders and there was the cracking sound of a single rifle shot.

28

Heather, Olivia, and Owen went along the beach until they were sure the dogs were heading east.

Then, tentatively, they got up onto the heath and ran easier and faster parallel to the shore. They kept close to the sea. They kept low.

They heard a rifle shot and Heather shuddered and they kept going.

They made good progress until they reached a graveyard for rusted old cars and vans. Heather and the children had sprinted into the middle of it before they saw a hand-painted sign that said DANGER: LIVE AND UNEXPLODED ORDNANCE. AND OTHER SCARY SHIT. DO NOT ENTER.

"Stop!" Heather said.

"What does *ordnance* mean?" Owen asked.

Heather looked around them. She saw now that the cars were riddled with bullet holes and between them there were craters where explosives had been set off. The O'Neills must have used this as a target range. Some of the craters were enormous and some of the cars had been blown apart. There could be unexploded grenades or homemade booby traps or anything.

They were more than halfway through the range; was it better to keep going or retrace their steps?

"Kids, I want you to get behind me and follow in my footsteps. But far back. We've walked into some kind of weapons-testing range. Don't touch anything or pick anything up. Do you understand?"

She turned to look at Olivia. "Get Owen behind you, and you stay far behind me. If I step on something or something happens to me, you know what to do."

"What?"

"Keep going and look after your brother."

"What if you're hurt?"

"Leave me. Look after Owen, OK?"

Olivia nodded.

"Don't move until I say so."

Heather walked slowly between the wrecked cars, placing one foot carefully in front of the other. In the dirt she saw shell casings and fragments of Molotov cocktails and what looked like the ring off an M67 grenade.

When she had gone twenty feet, she turned to Olivia and nodded. Olivia began walking in her footsteps and Owen followed his sister.

Paper targets riddled with buckshot lay on the ground. Broken glass was everywhere.

Their progress was slow.

Dogs in the distance.

"I stepped in something," Owen said.

"What kind of something?"

"Something metal."

Oh God.

"Owen, I want you to—"

"I'm lifting my foot."

"No, wait!"

"It's OK. Crushed soda can."

Heather breathed again. "Be careful. I know they're coming but we have to go slow."

Slow.

In case...

In case...

And there it was. Not unexploded ordnance but an iron animal trap, its ragged jaws rusted but still terrifying-looking. She imagined it was there to catch dingoes or foxes or something.

If she hadn't seen the sign, she or one of the kids could have run right into it. She picked up a stick and shoved it in the ground next to it as a marker. "Owen? Olivia? Do you see this thing to the left? It's a bear trap or something. Stay clear of it! Keep in my footsteps."

The kids followed Heather. She made sure they gave the trap a wide berth.

And eventually they were past the makeshift range.

It had slowed them down. Fifty yards in twenty minutes. They had to really hoof it now.

"This way!" she said and on they went, parallel to the shore.

All the old tunes:

Thirst.

Sun.

Dogs.

They had gone another quarter of a mile before Heather realized that she had miscalculated again. The shoreline had sunk gradually to their left and on their right a ravine had widened and deepened. For the past ten minutes they had been running on a peninsula that came to an abrupt end at a cliff.

Heather, in the lead, almost ran straight over the edge before catching herself.

She appraised the situation and swore. They could try and get down the cliff, which looked steep and dangerous, or they could retrace their steps back to the range, with its ordnance and mantraps.

The cliff was the apex of the triangle. There was a vertical drop to sand on one side and rocks on the other.

"Do you think we could climb down here?" Heather asked Olivia and Owen.

Owen shook his head. "Look at it. It's limestone, isn't it?"

"What does that mean?" Heather asked.

"It'll crumble in our hands and we'll fall."

"How far do you think that drop is?" Heather asked.

"Three stories," Olivia said.

"No. Two, two and a half," Owen said.

"Twenty feet, I think. A twenty-foot drop into sand," Heather said. "Do you think we could do that? It's either that or go back the way we came."

"We'll break our legs," Owen said.

"It's sand. From the top of the jungle gym on Alki Beach to the sand, that's about ten feet, isn't it?" Olivia said.

"It's not that high. And even if it were, this is twice that! And there might be rocks here we don't know about," Owen said.

Heather lay down flat on the ground and looked over the edge at the cliff's face. Owen was right—it was nearly vertical, and the rock looked powdery, treacherous. She examined the sand down there on the beach. There didn't seem to be any rocks. "Shh," Heather said.

From deep in the sky's silence, there was something coming. Something ringing that alarm bell in the fight-or-flight mechanism of her animal brain.

A vibration, like the twang of a longbow string, like the hum of an arrow.

She stood and listened.

"What—" Olivia began but stopped when Heather raised a finger.

Yes.

Over the barking dogs.

Over the sea.

The hunter was always finding new ways to hunt.

The prey needed to adapt quickly to survive.

What was that? What—

"Hit the deck, guys! Get cover. It's a drone."

They rolled into the spinifex just as the drone flew parallel to the shore, its tiny helicopter blades buzzing, its fish-eye-lens camera scanning 360 degrees around it.

It looked for them. Like a hawk looking, a hawk that knows only boredom and hostility and implacability in its tiny light-filled brain.

The drone flew lazily along the coast and looped back over the heath.

It hovered and buzzed and mocked.

Heather held her breath.

The drone did a figure eight in the sky over their position.

Had they been seen?

Perhaps.

Perhaps not.

It hung in the sky and then tilted its body toward the sun and headed east.

"Did they see us?" Olivia asked.

"I don't know."

Bloodhounds and a drone and an entire extended family after them on a small island—Petra's sacrifice would buy them at most only a few hours, Heather thought wretchedly.

"We can't go back. We've got to get down here," Heather said. "There are two ways to do this. One, I lower you as far as I can and then drop you the rest of the way into the sand. Two, I jump down there first and try to catch you guys when you jump."

"If you lower us, you won't drop us until we say OK, right?" Olivia asked.

"I'll hold you until you tell me to let go."

"Then I vote for the first way," Olivia said.

"Owen?" Heather asked.

"I guess."

"Good. Remember to land like a paratrooper—bend your knees and roll to the side. Olivia, you first?"

Olivia walked to the cliff edge, turned around, lay on the ground, and carefully dangled her legs over. Heather held on to her arms and gradually lowered her down. Heather's arms and Olivia's body length took about six feet out of the drop, but it still looked like a long, long way for a child to fall.

Her mind reeled for a second or two. How the hell had it come to this? That this was the least bad choice—forcing a little girl off the edge of a goddamn cliff.

Olivia was a skinny thing but Heather's arms were aching already. "Are you ready to drop?" she asked.

"Yes!"

Heather opened her hands and Olivia slipped and fell into the sand with a disconcerting *clump*.

She bent her legs but sort of splatted instead of rolling.

She lay there and didn't speak.

"Olivia? Olivia!" *Oh my God.*

"Are you OK?" Owen asked.

Olivia got up and waved. "It's OK. Come on...no! Wait! Go back! There's someone coming. Hide! Go back!"

29

Heather didn't know what to do. She froze on the edge of the cliff until Owen grabbed her hand.

"She said to hide!"

They dived into the long grass.

The drone appeared again in the southern sky.

The sound of dogs was getting closer.

She heard what sounded like a muffled scream.

Oh my God.

The drone zoomed out to sea and headed south.

What was happening?

She crawled to the edge of the cliff again. No sign of Olivia or anyone else.

"We have to get down there, Owen. I'm going to lower you and I'll be right after."

Owen shook his head. "No, Heather! You don't know what you're doing! You have no plan. You never did! All you're doing is running. I'm going back the other way. Maybe in that ordnance place I can find a grenade or something and fight those people!"

"You can't do that, Owen."

"Watch me. I've had it with you ignoring all my ideas. I'm leaving! I'll get a weapon and I'll get Olivia and we'll get out of here by ourselves."

"No, please don't," she said, trying to grab his arm.

He snatched his hand away from her and began heading south, back the way they'd come. "You're weak and you have no plan. You don't...you...I can do better on my own. You're shit! I'll find a grenade or dynamite, and I'll take them all on instead of us taking it."

She watched him go, muttering to himself.

It would, of course, be easier with just her and Olivia.

Easier to hide, easier to run.

Owen had always been the more difficult of the two children. There was something unspoken between him and his dad, some unresolved anger. She was often the target of Owen's rage and frequently got caught in the cross fire between him and Tom. She had tried to make things better but clearly had only made things worse. Part of this was her fault. She had underestimated how much the kids would dislike her. She had thought she would win them over. But it didn't work like that. Not at the ages they were. Carolyn had warned her. Carolyn had an older sister and cousins. *They are going to hate you,* Carolyn had said. It was too soon after their mom...

She should have said no to Tom. But the big new house, the car, Tom's reassurances...

And really, if you looked at it, she had done her best by all of them. She had tried her damnedest.

Without either of the kids, she would have a much better chance of survival. Perhaps she could swim over to the mainland by herself or negotiate a way out.

The distance lengthened between her and the boy.

She closed her eyes.

He would be dead by nightfall.

Oh, yes, if she were alone, her chances would increase exponentially.

She imagined it for one beat, two, three, four, five, six, seven...

She sighed, opened her eyes, and sprinted after him.

She skidded to a halt in front of him and said, "I was wrong, Owen. Wrong about the seawater distilling. I should have listened to you. We need you. Me and Olivia. Stay with us, *please,* OK?"

He was crying. He'd been terrified she was going to let him go. He wiped his cheeks. Sniffed.

"Will you stay with us, Owen? Will you help us?"

"OK. I guess I can't leave my sister."

"Thank you," she said and put her arm around him and they went back to the edge of the cliff. Heather lowered him slowly, her left shoulder aching. Owen was heavier than his sister. The shoulder with the shotgun wound began oozing blood.

She tried to release him but Owen did not want her to let go.

"I'm going to break my legs," he whispered.

"Bend your knees and tuck yourself in and roll and you'll be OK." Heather grunted as her arms began to ache.

"How do you know I'll be OK?"

"My dad has jump wings."

"I don't know what that means!" Owen said and wriggled free of Heather's grip and dropped into the sand. He did not bend his legs or roll. He hit the sand feetfirst and fell back hard.

"Are you OK?" Heather asked.

"Yes!"

Heather tossed down the machete and penknife, turned, and began lowering herself down the cliff. She was about to tuck in her knees and let go when her shoulder gave and her hand slipped and she just fell.

One second of drop.

A long second.

The force of the sand shocked her, and her ankle turned as she rolled.

When she got up, she could see the figure of a man a little ways down the beach beyond the mangrove trees.

"Get down," Heather whispered to Owen as she gathered the knife and machete.

"What's he doing?" Owen asked.

Heather shook her head. "I don't know."

"Where's Olivia?"

Heather looked at Owen.

"He must have seen her! He must have her!" Owen said.

"We'll see. We'll have to get close," Heather said. "He'll be wary. Don't make a sound."

"What are you going to do?"

She put her finger over her lips.

They slunk into the bush and crawled as close to the man as they dared.

He was on the walkie-talkie, breathing hard, laughing. It was Jacko. The man who had tried to rape her.

"Right into my lap, mate. If I don't win the bloody prize, no one should win any bloody prizes. The little girl said they separated but I don't know about that. I reckon they must be close. Send Kate in the four-wheeler and then bring the dogs... Yeah, mate, see ya, over and out."

He sat down on an old oil drum. He had a rifle strapped

across his back, and there, sprawled in front of him—that splash of golden hair—was Olivia.

"He found her," Heather whispered, wondering if she was alive or dead.

"We have to save her!" Owen said.

Heather nodded. "You stay here," she said.

The breeze was coming in off the water. She would be upwind of him, and Jacko was looking very relaxed. Very pleased with himself. That would help. But he was big and strong and dangerous.

Beyond the mangroves where they were hiding, there was a strip of grass about fifteen yards wide. At the edge of the grass there was a eucalyptus tree she could get behind.

From the tree to where Jacko was sitting on the drum was only twenty feet of beach.

"You should take your sneakers off. They've been squeaking a bit," Owen said.

She slipped out of her shoes and slithered through the grass with the machete, watching Jacko, watching for the drone, listening for the dogs.

A red-tailed cockatoo landed in front of her and began clawing at the sandy soil with its talons.

It caught sight of her, squawked loudly, and flew off over the sea.

Jacko watched the cockatoo, utterly uninterested.

Heather continued on.

Jacko was smoking a cigarette. He was wearing raggedy denim jeans and a Bintang Beer tank top. He'd attached a piece of rope to a rifle and slung it across his back. It looked like an antique weapon, something from World War II or maybe even before.

The wind was blowing toward her, carrying his cigarette smoke and BO, and bringing no smell from her to him.

Jacko was looking at the water. She crawled toward him on her belly. The ground was thick with sand fleas. Flies were landing on her hair and arms and the back of her neck.

She had to go real slow now or else she would make a splashing noise. She looked back at Owen to make sure he was well hidden.

She couldn't see him at all. Good.

With the machete in her left hand and pulling herself forward with the right, she sidled closer.

She got within ten feet of the eucalyptus tree.

Too late, she discovered it had a crow in it. A crow that might sound an alarm.

But it merely looked at her with an eye that had a peculiar yellow tint to it.

She breathed deeply, crawled to the tree trunk, and stopped for a moment to compose herself. Then she crept past the tree to the edge of the heath.

She was on the beach now. He was close.

She got to her feet, switched the machete from her left hand to her right, and moved slowly toward him.

Jacko stood and took a shot at a shark in the water but evidently missed. He reloaded the rifle and, after a few moments, slung the rifle over his back, sat down on the oil drum, and lit a cigarette.

She was being careful but she accidentally stepped on the edge of a broken bottle. She swallowed down a yell, sat, removed a piece of glass from her heel, stood, and advanced again.

She remembered again that it was Valentine's Day. Exactly twelve months ago Tom had come in for his first massage-therapy appointment in the clinic in West Seattle. It had been snowing. When he'd lain down on the table, he still had snowflakes in his hair.

What a difference a year made.

She'd been childless then, on the verge of unemployment, living in that damp apartment near Alki Beach. Now she was married and responsible for two children and about to kill a man she barely knew on a different beach on the far side of the world.

She took three more careful steps.

30

Her shadow threw itself in front of Jacko.

He saw it, flinched, turned. "I was bloody right!" he said.

The machete was high in the air. She swung it hard toward his neck but some animal instinct make him swerve to the right just as the heavy blade would have connected with his shoulder.

The machete sailed through the nothingness. Unbalanced, she slipped and almost fell.

She righted herself.

She and Jacko were three feet apart now. He'd been drinking but he didn't look drunk. She could smell his fury. He, no doubt, could smell her terror.

He tried to get the gun off his back but she was too close so he changed his mind and punched her in the face. A fast, little bony rabbit punch that connected with her cheek and hurt like hell.

She staggered backward and scraped her ankle on a piece of rock.

Jacko swung at her again with a right hook, but this one missed and overbalanced him now. Jacko, however, had been fighting with his brothers and cousins since he could walk, and he recovered quickly. He kicked Heather in the left kneecap.

She'd been watching his hands and hadn't expected a kick.

It caught her unawares, sending a shooting pain up her entire left side. It was like his feet were made of iron. Her left foot gave way; she went down and she knew she wouldn't get up in time to prevent him kicking her again.

He didn't do that.

Instead, he took three steps away from her and then, carefully, he took the rifle off his back and pointed it at her.

"Now, you just sit right there, sweetheart," he said. "Drop that blade you got."

She shook her head and tried to get up.

The pain in her knee was horrific.

She had to save Olivia, she had to keep going, this was the only—

"I said stay still! Don't you bloody move a muscle. This is a Lee-Enfield Number Four. Me granddad killed three men with this at Tobruk. At this range it'll split your head in half. You get me?"

She nodded.

"Drop the blade!"

She dropped the machete.

"Take three steps back."

"I don't think I can get up."

"On your arse, then, backward, away from the blade."

She did as she was told.

"Now, you just sit there on the ground and don't do nothing."

Olivia groaned behind him and tried to move. She'd been hit hard and her mouth was bleeding. Jacko stepped on her back, shoving her into the sand. He took a little yellow walkie-talkie out of his pocket. "Ivan, are you there?"

Static.

"These things are terrible," Jacko told Heather. "No range. Toys, really." He pressed Talk again. "Oi! Ivan! Are you there?"

Static.

He gave the walkie-talkie a shake. "Oi, Ivan, are you bloody there?"

"We're here...we were just checking the body of the Kraut woman," Ivan said through a blizzard of hiss.

"You won't believe what I done now," Jacko said.

"What?"

"I've only gone and caught the Yank woman too, haven't I."

"No, you haven't!" Ivan said.

"I have. She come running at me with a bloody great knife and I knocked her on her arse," Jacko said, licking his lips and leering at her triumphantly.

"Serious?"

"Fair dinkum, mate. She tried to get the drop on me and I got the drop on her!"

"Well done, mate! And you got both kids too?" Ivan asked.

"Her and the girl."

"Ask her where the boy is," Ivan said.

"Where's the lad?" Jacko said.

"We separated. I told them to hide somewhere. I don't know where he is," Heather replied.

"Bollocks! Where is he?"

"We separated. I thought we'd have more of a chance."

"Balls you did. You wouldn't leave the bloody kids."

"They're not really my kids. They're Tom's. We've been married less than a year. I told them to hide and I'd get help. I didn't mind separating. The kids hate me," Heather said.

She said this with such passion that Jacko went for it for a few beats but then smiled a horrible graveyard smile and shook his head.

"Nah. It's not you. Is he in the bush over there?"

"I don't know where he is."

Jacko put the walkie-talkie to his mouth. "Listen, mate, she says the boy isn't with her. If you send a couple of lads over in the Toyota and bring one of the dogs, we'll soon flush him out. We'll have all of them in one bloody swoop."

"Did you really get them or are you pissing us about?" Ivan asked.

"I got them! I saw the girl and ran her down, clobbered her, and this one comes at me with a knife. I got 'em both!"

"Well done, mate. We'll be there. Over and out."

Jacko put the walkie-talkie in his pocket and lifted the rifle and looked down the sight at her. "Tell the boy to come out or I'll blow your bloody tits off."

The Lee-Enfield was pressed against his shoulder. He was squinting at her with one eye closed, his finger on the trigger.

She shook her head.

"Big mistake. You know what we're going to do with you? We're going to rut you. Every man and boy on this island. Me first. And then it's Terry's anthill."

Heather caught her breath as she saw Owen stand up from the undergrowth. He was holding a long tree branch in his hands, one of those brittle, dry eucalyptus branches that looked as if they would snap in half if you gripped them too hard. He was going to try to use it as a club or spear.

She tried to catch Owen's eye. She didn't want to shake her head, because if she did, Jacko would almost certainly spot the gesture and spin around, and, startled, he might pull the trigger.

"Your life is worth nothing out here, Heather. Not after what you done to Ellen. I could bloody kill you right now and nothing would happen. No cops. No nothing. Do you understand?"

She nodded. "I completely understand."

Owen was walking closer. It was madness. That spindly branch would barely irritate Jacko if Owen got near enough to swing it.

She tried telepathy. *Go back, go back, go back! Go back to the bush and run!*

Owen's chin was jutting out and he was biting his lower lip the way he did when he was set on doing something. Olivia was sitting up now. She was going to try to do something too.

Oh my God.

"OK, OK. Look, I'm sorry," Heather said. "Please don't shoot. I'll get up. I'll get up slowly and I'll call Owen, OK? You were right. He's in the bush waiting for me. I'll get up now, OK? And I'll yell for him to come."

Jacko nodded and took a step back from her while keeping the gun pointed at her head. "Yeah, that's what I thought. You're quite the bullshit artist, aren't you? But I saw through you," he said in a snarl of triumph.

She stood up awkwardly, blinking in the sunlight, and stumbled two steps toward the machete lying in the sand. Jacko didn't seem to notice, or if he did, he didn't care. What could she do with death only a hair-trigger-pull away?

She cupped her hands to her mouth. "Get away, Owen! Run! I have a plan! Run!" she screamed.

Owen hesitated.

"Get away from here! Run!" she yelled.

Jacko turned and saw Owen vanish into the undergrowth. "You really are one stupid bitch, aren't you?" he said. He deftly flipped the rifle, took half a stride forward, and clubbed her in the face with the butt. The brass cover on the wooden stock caught her on her left cheek and left eye.

She staggered backward, tripped over her feet, and collapsed.

Her forehead was bleeding. Blood was pouring out of her nose. The cut on her foot reopened.

"Come back, you fat little shit!" Jacko yelled and ran after Owen.

Heather tried to get to her feet. Her left leg responded but her right had a mind of its own. The landscape was swimming. Her head throbbed. She spit blood.

Swayed.

Two horizons. Two suns.

The day seemed to pulse its wings. The wind picked up.

Thick wool carpets of heat.

Unappeasable sunlight.

Olivia had risen and was scrambling after Jacko.

"No! Wait!" Heather said. She rubbed her eyes.

There was the sound of a gunshot.

Her heart missed a beat. She couldn't breathe.

She stood on the machete handle. She picked it up and hobbled after Jacko.

The crow was still watching her from the lightning-struck eucalyptus tree. Still waiting for the body.

She reached the mangrove bushes.

"Little bastard. Won't get far, I tell you that," Jacko was saying into the walkie-talkie.

He was walking back toward the beach.

Walking through the trees.

The wind freshened even more.

Didn't he hear that roaring?

What was all that noise?

Why couldn't he see her?

She could see him.

He was holding the rifle vertically in his right hand, the walkie-talkie in his left. There was no sign of either Owen or Olivia.

Suddenly Jacko froze. "What's that?" he said.

He spun around. His eyes were wild. He was spooked.

He fired the rifle into the bushes.

His back was to her. He was only ten feet away.

The air was full of sand and blowing leaves. Grit in her eyes and mouth.

There were two of him, phasing in and out.

She waited for the two to merge and when they did, she ran at him and swung the machete at his right shoulder. The blade went in two inches and hit bone. Jacko screamed, dropped the rifle. She tugged out the machete for another go.

"Bitch!" Jacko yelled and turned fast and kicked her in the gut.

The air was knocked out of her.

Legs liquefying.

But it wasn't as good a kick as he thought.

She steadied herself.

Jacko bent to pick up the Lee-Enfield and didn't see her next blow coming. The machete tore open his cheek and pulled right through to his lips.

He screamed again, fell to one knee, and scrabbled around in the dirt until he found the rifle.

He aimed it at her and pulled the trigger.

At point-blank range.

He couldn't miss.

But he hadn't ejected the spent cartridge or chambered a new round. He looked at the Lee-Enfield in bafflement.

Heather swung the machete a third time. He was a stationary target.

She couldn't miss.

With a clang and a sickening thud, the machete hit him between the shoulder and the neck. He was knocked back onto his haunches.

The blood was pouring from his mouth now. She tugged the rifle from his hands. She pulled back the bolt and chambered another .303 cartridge. Jacko made a last desperate lunge at her.

She shot him in the gut.

Their eyes met.

He was confused.

"Do you smell that?" he muttered.

The smell was cordite and saltwater marsh and red blood cells.

"I smell it," she said.

"The bunyip," Jacko said, then keeled over and died.

31

Owen and Olivia had watched the whole thing. They hadn't run. They should have, but they hadn't.

They ran to her now.

She hugged them and kissed them and hugged them again.

They hugged her back.

"Is he dead?" Owen asked, pointing at Jacko.

"He's dead," Heather said, gasping.

She had killed a human being. A living man. He had been trying to kill her, but that didn't matter. He had been a person with a brain and ideas and experiences and it was all gone now and she had taken it. It was a terrible thing to do when you thought about it.

She sank to her knees. *I'm sorry it had to be this way. I'm sorry we came. I'm sorry for all of this.*

"Can I touch him?" Owen asked.

Heather got to her feet. "No. We have to move fast. You guys wait over there while I see what he's got," Heather said.

"Here's your shoes," Owen said, handing them to her.

"Thank you."

She searched Jacko and found a tin canteen a third full of water, some money, cigarettes—*her* cigarettes—a cigarette lighter, 8x50 binoculars, a plastic shopping bag with loose .303 ammunition, and the walkie-talkie. She took everything, including Jacko's belt, shoelaces, socks, and hat, which she put backward on Owen's head.

She put her sneakers on and examined Olivia's face. Her lip was still bleeding a little. "Where did he hit you?" she asked.

"It was just a slap. He saw me and I tried to run, but he was too fast."

"I'm sorry, baby," Heather said.

"Forget it. It doesn't hurt. What do we do now?" Olivia asked.

"We have to get away from here. North, I think. Take a drink," she said, handing them Jacko's canteen. They both gulped the water.

"You drink something," Owen said, handing her the canteen.

"I'm OK."

"You haven't drunk anything," Olivia said. She was standing with her hands on her hips, feet apart, blocking Heather's path.

"Get out of my way. We have to get moving," Heather said.

"We're not going anywhere until you drink something," Owen said.

Owen's serious, resolute brown eyes again. Olivia's equally strong-minded blue eyes.

Heather reflected on how much they'd changed since...

Yesterday.

"We all drink again, then," she said.

They drank and they were so thirsty they finished the last of the precious water.

"I'm sorry for saying that you were weak and shit back there," Owen said. "You're not."

"It's OK, honey, everything's OK," Heather said. She screwed the canteen cap back on and strapped the rifle over her back.

They hid Jacko's body in the undergrowth and covered it with dirt and branches. The others might not find it for a day or two, which would give them an information edge.

Heather bathed her wounds and they set out north.

They saw the drone again hovering around where Jacko had been.

Then they heard the ATV and the dogs and the Toyota.

They cut inland through hilly terrain and stopped at a grove of four gum trees, big old trees that had somehow survived dozens of fires and droughts and blights and efforts to turn them into useful things. It was a spooky place. A long time ago, someone had crashed an old bus up here, and over the decades it had rusted and fallen apart and become part of the landscape. An exposed rock face near the trees was covered with handprints that looked as though they were thousands of years old.

The flies were fewer here, and there was a hint of a breeze and the heady smell of eucalyptus.

They stopped to rest in the shade of the trees. Heather applied a leaf poultice to the cut on her foot, and Olivia cleaned the wound on her face.

They were on a hill and they had a view south over the heath. It seemed to be the highest point on the island.

Heather took out Jacko's walkie-talkie.

"Do you think we can risk an SOS?" she asked the children.

They both nodded.

She pressed Talk.

"Hello? Hello? Can anyone hear me? My name is Heather

Baxter. I'm on Dutch Island. We need the police!" She tried every channel but all she heard was static and, on one channel, Matt's voice drifting in and out.

"Not enough range," Owen said.

Heather looked west over the sea at the landmass over there—a continent the color of sand and pine needles that was not answering her call.

They sat under the shade of the biggest tree, catching their breath, recovering. Waiting for the drone or the dogs or the men with guns.

"What do you think a bunyip is?" Owen asked.

"You heard him say that?" Heather asked.

"In the book I was reading, they said it was a mythical Australian monster," Olivia said.

Heather nodded. If it was a monster they were afraid of, she'd become that monster now that she had a rifle.

"So frickin' lit. What type of gun is that?" Owen asked.

"It's a Lee-Enfield Number Four. I shot one once when I was a girl. It belonged to a friend of my dad, a Canadian guy. This is an old one—see all the scoring on the stock and how the sight's worn down? It's from World War Two, I think."

"Cool! Can you show me how to use it?"

She thought about that. Tom would have said no. But if she got hurt or killed and they had the rifle, they'd need to know what to do.

"Both of you, come here," she said. "Like I say, I've only ever had an afternoon with a Lee-Enfield, but most bolt-action rifles operate on the same principles. It's actually pretty easy. Let me show you guys how it works."

She took off the bolt and removed the magazine. It looked

like it hadn't been serviced in years. It needed gun oil, and the walnut was cracked, but she cleaned it the best she could.

She showed them how to load the weapon, how to eject the cartridge, how to aim, how to brace it against their shoulders, and how to shoot.

"There's going to be a kick, so be ready for that when you pull the trigger, but don't be scared of it, and don't tug the trigger—pull it, *gently*."

"Who taught you all this?" Owen wondered.

"My mom and dad were both in the military," Heather said, without elaborating about her father's breakdown and eventual medical discharge.

"Were they in the war and everything?" Owen asked.

"Yes."

"Did either of them kill anybody?"

"Yes."

"If we have a rifle, could we go down to the ferry and sort of hijack it?" Owen asked.

"Maybe. I think they tie it up on the far shore, but I'll check tonight."

"I'm hungry," Olivia said.

"I'm thirsty," Owen said.

"I know," Heather said.

There was nothing else to say.

She took out the pack of cigarettes, her own cigarettes back again. She lit one with his lighter.

"Can I have a puff?" Owen said.

"No."

"Why not? You're smoking."

"It's like parents always tell kids: Do as I say, not as I do."

Silence.

A lagoon of blue sky. A green sea. And that sun pouring down countless photons into the dreary, withered yellow valley on the very northern tip of Dutch Island.

Owen was staring at the trees. "Do you remember what they told us at Uluru? A single gum tree standing by itself might be evidence of an underground water source. And here there's four of them."

They stared at the eucalyptus trees.

"They're drinking from somewhere," Olivia said after a while.

"You two wait here in the shade and I'll see what I can find," Heather said.

"I'm coming with you. Two eyes are, like, totally better than one—I mean, four eyes are better than two," Owen said.

"I'll help too!" Olivia announced.

They walked to the base of the biggest tree. It was old, blackened, and weather-beaten; all the bark had gone from the trunk, and the lower branches crumbled to the touch. It wasn't dead, though—there were leaves on the upper branches.

The soil around the tree was dry red dirt filled with large rocks and smaller white stones. Little spiky tufts of grass were growing up through the browner bits.

Heather bent down, dug two fingers into the soil, took out a clump of earth, and examined it. It fell apart in her hand.

Olivia was watching her. She grabbed a handful of soil and held it up to the light. "What does a spring look like?" Olivia asked.

"A little bubbling thing of water," Heather said. "But I don't see anything like that. More likely it's beneath the ground. Maybe very deep."

In the book Olivia had been reading, *Dark Emu,* there was something about the Aboriginals digging deep wells into the aquifers in the desert. Although Australia was a dry continent, rain had fallen on it for hundreds of thousands of years and accumulated underground in layers of rock. Perhaps there was such an aquifer here.

"We'll keep looking," Heather said. "Those handprints on the rock mean that people did come here in olden times."

Owen was walking around the tree in widening circles looking for any signs of water.

"What was that?" Olivia said.

"What do you hear?" Heather asked.

"The dogs are coming this way."

"We may have to move soon," Heather said.

Olivia dug her hand deep into the soil and took out a handful of dirt. Six inches down, it was even drier than on the surface.

Heather took the rifle off her back and helped move the earth as Olivia dug into the soil with two hands, burrowing into it like a Labrador.

Owen joined in, scooping a handful of dirt into his palm and running it through his fingers.

For two kids whose father had been killed and who were scared, hungry, and thirsty, they were doing very well.

"Does it feel moist to you?" Heather asked.

"It's like the graham-cracker base of a cheesecake."

Heather smiled. "Yeah, it is like that, isn't it?"

While Heather kept watch, they dug farther into the soil, but it just seemed to get drier and drier the deeper they got.

"How deep do these roots go down?" Olivia asked.

"I don't know. Many hundreds of feet? I'm not sure," she said, looking at the mesa. Now Heather could hear the dogs.

She took out the binoculars and saw a red motorcycle.

A mile away.

"OK, forget the water, guys. We're going to have to move."

"I don't think I can go much farther. My legs are cramping," Owen said.

"I know, sweetie, but we've got to go."

There wasn't much fight left in any of them. They'd had no food for two days. Hardly any water. The sun still had four or five hours to go before it sank into the mainland.

Or maybe this was the place for a last stand? On a hill with a 360-degree view and a rifle?

"Could we hold them off here?" Owen asked, eerily echoing her thoughts.

"Not for long."

"What is it like to kill someone?" he asked.

"I don't know. Not good, I guess," Heather replied.

"Dad's a killer too," Owen said. "A liar and a killer."

"That was an accident. It's a different thing," Heather said. She looked at the terrain and shook her head. No—no last stand here. They could flank the three of them easily with vehicles, and there was no real cover, just four big trees. They would have to move.

She watched the little scrambler motorcycle move through the drab white grasses, coming inevitably on a vector that would bring Kate and her shotgun and all the O'Neills up here.

"Remember what the guide told us at Uluru? Isn't this the sign for 'water hole'?" Owen asked. He was pointing at a drawing of a circle within a circle on the rock wall that jutted between the trees.

"You're right!" Olivia said.

"And what's this?" Owen asked.

Near the handprints there was a layer of moss growing over the bare rock.

"It's moss," Heather said.

"It's moving," Owen said.

"What do you mean, it's moving? It can't be moving."

"It's moving in the wind."

"Is there something behind it?"

Owen dug at it with his fingers. "I think there's like a hole or something behind it," he said.

Heather walked to where he was pointing, and sure enough, under the moss there was a hole about two feet wide packed with rocks and dirt.

She tore through it and found what appeared to be a narrow entrance.

"What is it?" Olivia asked.

"I think it's a mine or a cave or something. Hold on."

She removed more dirt and crawled into a narrow tunnel. It was barely an opening, just wide enough to squeeze through. Once it had been larger, but cave-ins and rockfalls had closed the passage.

She struggled through the opening and it began to get a bit wider. She flicked on Jacko's lighter and saw that it was a natural cave, not a mine.

She went a little farther. She could breathe the air, so there was some kind of ventilation.

The tunnel was thirty feet long and she could stand now on the sandy dirt. It was much cooler in here than the world outside, and the acoustic properties were unusual. When she went around a dogleg in the passage, she saw the ground sloping down dramatically to what appeared to be a pool of water. That would explain the coolness and the acoustics.

She ran back and crawled out through the cave mouth. "It's a spring! There's water! A great big pool of it!"

"Is it drinkable?" Olivia asked.

"One way to find out. Follow me," she said.

She flicked Jacko's lighter on again and they trailed her along the passage. This time she noticed many more handprints on the wall and drawings of animals. They went around the dogleg and down the slope. There was enough space for them to stand quite easily around the pool.

"It looks dirty," Owen said.

"That's only the light, I think," Heather said.

There was moss floating on the water and a few dead insects. She cupped her hands and took a drink.

It was saline and minerally, but it was definitely fresh water. Cool, too, coming from a deep source in the bedrock. She drank and felt energy rushing through her. She drank again, and her muscles began to loosen. She felt the sinews unclench in the back of her thighs. She felt her toes and thighs and fingertips.

Her brain began to unfog.

"I think it's good, kids. It's not going to taste like the bottled water you're used to, but it's fine to drink. Drink up. Slowly."

Olivia hesitantly leaned forward and scooped a little of the water into her hands. She poured it into her mouth and looked at Heather and smiled.

"It's good!" she said. "I like it."

She began scooping handfuls into her mouth.

"Careful, not too much, you don't want to overload your system," Heather said. "That's it, slowly, take a little break now."

Olivia nodded and leaned back on the cave floor with a big happy smile on her face.

Heather had thought that Olivia would never smile again.

"That was awesome," Olivia murmured.

Heather turned to Owen. "OK, kid," she said. "Now you."

"What if there's poo in it?"

"It's good, drink it," Olivia said.

He dipped his finger in and licked it. "It'll do," he said.

Heather smiled.

"It's cold down here. I'm actually cold," Owen said.

"Are you ever happy?" Olivia said.

"I'll get our stuff," Heather said. "We're going to hide here. I'll start a small fire and then I'll go try to lay a scent trail for the dogs. I'll be back in an hour."

Heather got a quick fire of moss and eucalypt going for the kids and went back outside. She got the rifle and the canteen and put them in the cave mouth. She rearranged the moss over the hole and ran down into the heath away from the hill. She rolled around in the grass, trying to get as much scent on the ground as possible, and then she ran to the beach. She left a ton of prints on the sand and was about to wade into the surf when the drone came zipping in from the sea and found her.

It hovered ten feet above her head.

She threw a pebble at it, but it just moved out of the way.

She wasn't going to lead it back to the cave, and she couldn't lose it on this damned beach.

It buzzed and zipped above her.

She could imagine Matt looking at her through his laptop or phone or whatever it was he used to control it.

She sat down on the sand and looked at it.

She wasn't going to panic.

She was going to think.

Those four little rotor blades must use a lot of energy keeping that thing in the air. And the battery couldn't be very big. How long could one of those things stay up there without needing to recharge?

She had no idea. An hour? Twenty minutes?

More likely closer to the latter.

The drone looked at her.

She looked at the drone.

It had to be at least a ten-minute flight back to where Matt was with the dogs. It had been hovering here for five. If he wanted to keep it, surely he would have to fly it back soon.

He'd made a mistake, showing himself. He should have hovered a couple of hundred feet up. Trailed her from the sky as long as he was able.

She smiled at the drone's camera.

"What do you call a boomerang that doesn't come back?" she said.

The drone bobbed in the wind.

"A stick," she said.

The drone dived toward her; she ducked, and it soared into the air and headed south.

"Must have heard that one before," she muttered as she waded into the surf. She swam nervously north for two hundred yards and carefully walked onto the shore via rocks. The sharks had spared her.

She circled back to the heath the long way and took an even longer way back to the cave entrance.

The dogs were definitely coming. They would spend a lot of time on the beach.

That little diversion might buy her and the kids a few hours. Perhaps enough to get them through to nightfall. She hoped so.

She entered the cave. "Kids?" she said.

No answer.

"Kids!"

"We're here. Is that you, Heather?" Olivia said, coming around the cave dogleg and holding the rifle.

"It's me."

They sat together by the pool and waited and watched the fire's embers, and time continued on its silver arrow toward the end of the universe.

They couldn't hear dogs or people or anything.

The O'Neills could be just overhead, or they could be a mile away.

They waited. And waited some more. Waiting in the sand by the pool in silence.

It was like one of those submarine movies. The men in the tin can bracing for the ship to drop a depth charge...

Finally, when she thought perhaps three hours had gone by, she crawled back to the cave mouth with the rifle.

The sun was going down.

No sign of anyone.

She listened.

No yelling.

No dogs.

She scanned the horizon with the binoculars. No one. She went back to the underground spring and told the kids that they were safe for the night. They would be back tomorrow. The dogs would not be so easily fooled by her swimming and would certainly find them tomorrow.

But that meant they had tonight.

32

The sun was setting on their third day, going down in a gaudy blaze of red and gold. Sinking on the people in their cars and in their houses and in restaurants and bars; on the rich and the poor, on the runaways and the forsaken and the nameless and the lost.

Above them, the first stars were coming out.

"We need food, Heather," Owen said in a quiet voice.

"I know."

She took off her shoes and handed them to Olivia.

"What are you doing?" Olivia asked.

"I'm going to climb this tree as high as I can and I'm going to try really hard this time to get help on the radio."

"This tree?" Owen asked.

"Yeah."

"I'm not sure that's how radios work. I just covered that in my science homework. You don't need to climb a tree. I think radio signals bounce off the atmosphere," Owen said. "Did you do physics, Heather?"

On Goose Island, Heather *had* done physics with her mom

for a few days in the trailer-park classroom whose big windows looked across Puget Sound to the snowcapped mountains of Olympic National Park. She'd taken in nothing. Her mind had been over there walking through the snow, through the rain, learning the tracks of cougar, black bear, elk, and black-tailed deer.

She'd never learned about radio waves or how radios worked. In fact, she had failed the science section of the GED exam. A classmate at South Seattle Community College had called her "simple" once. She knew she wasn't simple. She did well in stuff she liked. She'd gotten all the biology and botany questions right. Even here, ten thousand miles from home in a landscape utterly unlike her own, she could identify lyrebirds and bowerbirds. A short-tailed shearwater was flying over the hill to her left, the same type of shearwater she had seen many times on the Sound.

The little shearwater gave her comfort.

"I'm going to climb it anyway. It won't hurt to try this again," she said.

"I think it's a good idea," Olivia agreed.

Heather looked at her. Olivia returned her gaze. Olivia's mouth creaked up into an encouraging smile. Their relationship had changed between sundown yesterday and sundown today.

Heather climbed halfway up the big eucalyptus tree and turned on the walkie-talkie. "This is an SOS. This is an SOS. My name is Heather Baxter, I'm on Dutch Island in Victoria, Australia, and I need help as quickly as possible!" she said into the device.

She listened for a reply but all she got back was static.

"What did they say, Heather?" Owen yelled.

"Nothing yet."

Wind was blowing through the leaves. Black bark crumbled under her toes. It was good to be in a tree in this little wood. Trees were older brothers; trees turned sunlight into food; trees were gateways to other places.

She pressed the Talk button again. "If you can hear this, please contact the police. My name is Heather Baxter, I am on Dutch Island in Victoria, Australia. My husband, Tom, has been murdered here by members of the O'Neill family. I have escaped from them and am hiding out on the island with two children, Owen Baxter and Olivia Baxter. We are in great danger. Please send help."

She repeated this message several more times and listened for a response but there was nothing but white noise.

She tried all nine channels.

The battery life on the walkie-talkie showed only two bars out of four. She'd better conserve it. "Kids, do either of you know what the emergency channel is on a radio?"

"In America, channel nine is what truckers use for emergencies," Owen said.

She turned back to channel 9. "My name is Heather Baxter, I'm on Dutch Island. I need help. I need someone to call the police and help me. Please. My life is in danger. Please. My name is Heather Baxter, I'm an American on Dutch Island near the city of Melbourne."

A voice crackled through the static. "Heather, is that you?"

She grabbed hold of the tree trunk to stop herself from falling. "Matt?"

"It's Matt...that you, Heather?"

She didn't know whether to answer now or not.

"Heather...still there?"

She let the static be her reply.

"Heather...must have found one of our walkie...don't know if you can hear me...only a half-watt rechargeable from Bunnings...range is on the back," Matt said, his voice fragmentary in the blizzard of static.

"So?" she said.

"...bad news for you is that a half-watt radio transmitter only...range of a kilometer at most in the...no one coming to help you."

"I'll try anyway," she said.

"...need to talk...serious conversation about Tom," Matt said before his voice disappeared into the static.

She pressed Talk. "What about Tom?" she asked. Static. "Matt?" Static. "Matt?"

No answer.

She listened and listened but it was only hiss now on every channel.

The battery light began to waver, so she turned off the walkie-talkie and climbed down out of the tree. They must realize now that she had killed Jacko. How else could she have gotten his walkie-talkie and why hadn't he shown up at the farm?

"I've broadcast our message and hopefully someone heard it," she told the kids.

"I'm not feeling so good," Owen said.

They were both starving. The kids had water but they hadn't eaten anything for nearly three days. *Food.* She had to get them food. She looked west. Black clouds were heading in their direction.

She handed Owen the pamphlet she'd taken from the prison, which had been squashed in her back pocket. "This can help with our kindling. Let's get leaves and wood to rebuild the fire," she said. "I think a storm's coming."

33

The rain was hammering on the corrugated-iron roof so hard, it woke her. Carolyn shivered. She had fallen asleep in the recliner under the blanket. The big-screen TV was frozen in front of her. She forgot what episode she'd been watching. Janeway was taking the mood of the senior officers of the *Voyager* about some problem they had encountered. Heather would probably know which episode it was just from the pause screen. Her knowledge of Trek lore was encyclopedic.

Carolyn wondered if Heather's new husband knew about that side of her. The geeky, fun, sci-fi side. Heather had not responded to Carolyn's previous text about *Voyager*. Maybe she was trying to downplay that part of herself and become the perfect doctor's wife. Perhaps all the Goose Island bits of her would start drifting away until the old Heather was gone forever.

Carolyn fumbled on the carpet until she found her coffee and vape pen. She pushed the button and the light blinked, and she sucked organic marijuana oil grown right here by her own fair hands on Goose Island. She sold it to medical-marijuana dispensaries for two hundred dollars an ounce. It had a very high

THC content. She coughed for a few seconds and then sipped the cold coffee.

She noticed that there was a new voice message on her iPhone. She played it.

"Hi, this is a message for Carolyn Moore," an Australian woman said. "Carolyn, this is Jenny Brook, I'm one of the ICOM reps here in Melbourne. One of our speakers is Dr. Thomas Baxter. He's got his wife down as his emergency contact and she's got you down as her emergency contact. The Baxters aren't answering their phones and I wondered if they'd gone to country Victoria or somewhere where there's no Wi-Fi. We've got a couple of things we need Dr. Baxter to do and we'd like him to give us a call. Thank you."

No doubt they were still at that fancy winery.

She dialed Heather's number and it went straight to voice mail.

Could Heather be in any kind of trouble?

She didn't think so.

But still...

It was dark outside. Melbourne was seventeen hours ahead of Seattle, if you could wrap your head around that idea.

Carolyn decided that she would sleep on it, maybe try to reach her in the morning.

If she couldn't get through, she'd call that rep woman on Monday or Tuesday. Heather and Tom should be able to spend the weekend eating gourmet food and drinking expensive wine without anyone having to get the cops involved.

34

Her belly rumbled.

Heather strapped the rifle over her back. She threaded a shoelace through the hole in the machete handle and attached it to her belt.

Heading south, she walked across the heath.

The cut in her foot didn't feel so bad. Her nose hurt. Jaw hurt. Shoulder ached like all hell. Everything else would do.

The temperature had dropped. She saw lightning stab at a spire on the mainland.

Silhouette of church, town, civilization, hope.

She did the count in her head.

One, two, three, four, five, six, seven, eight, nine, ten, eleven, twelve, thirteen, fourteen, fifteen—

There was a low rumble of thunder, which meant the storm was three miles away to the west.

The black clouds stretched to an infinity in the south. For all she knew, the tail of this low front might go all the way to Antarctica. It might be bringing hail and snow—if it snowed in Australia. She had no idea. Tom would have known. He'd read so many books; there must be one about exactly this situation.

But the bastards had killed him.

She gave the farm a wide berth and walked over the scrub to the dunes where the shearwaters were nesting. There was no moon. Venus was up. The Earth had turned on its axis, and the great sea of southern stars were coming out. The Emu. The Kangaroo's tail.

Lights to her right. Five hundred yards away. Probably Kate riding her ATV, looking for her.

Skull on.

Headlights on.

You can find me now, Heather thought. *I'm ready.*

I will make a hole in the night just for you.

Cold air was rising from the ground. Critters sang in the grass. Big moths flitted through the narrow columns of starlight.

Starlight from another time.

If only she could ride it backward to two days ago.

I will take us back and I will drive the car.

Or further back and Tom could do the Australia trip by himself.

Or further back and she could warn the world about 9/11 in crayon and there would be no war and her dad wouldn't have had to go to Iraq.

Kate drove on. Heather let her go.

She walked through the nightscape, making evanescent art in the grass, like those artists her mother loved, Andy Goldsworthy and Liza Lou, her feet following her mother's feet through the woods, carving ley lines in the pine needles of Goose Island and the bladygrass of Dutch Island, under the moon, under the dark moon who was always there, cherishing the votives and watching over the humans far, far down below.

Heather reached the southern shore of the island in an hour. She recognized the call of the shearwaters and found their burrows and reached into the holes and gathered a dozen eggs, which she wrapped in the shopping bag that Jacko had kept his .303 ammo in.

As she crossed one of the island roads, she saw something, something dead, just down the tarmac on the edge of the sheugh. It was a koala. It didn't smell yet and the flies weren't a black horde. She dragged it off the blacktop and cut off its head with the machete and disemboweled it and skinned it. She saved the liver and the heart and lungs. She made a bag with her T-shirt and transferred the eggs and ammo to that and put the koala parts in the shopping bag.

She walked home in her bra and jeans. The dirt had more give. It knew the rain was coming. It dreamed of becoming soil.

A single raindrop hit her arm.

She examined the sky.

It was a deep purple-black that soon was going to baptize and cleanse the earth.

Of course it would rain after they had gotten themselves a water source.

She approached the cave looking for signs of life but saw nothing. She had rehung moss over the cave entrance, and if you got real close you could see blue smoke from the fire making its way out of the mouth. But you'd need to get within twenty feet or so.

The cave would hide them from the humans, but she knew it wouldn't fool the dogs. The dogs were only getting started. They'd begin at dawn on the beach and eventually they'd follow the trail all the way here.

She moved aside the moss and went inside the cave.

"I got food," she said.

"What did you get?" Olivia asked.

She knew Olivia would never eat koala. "I don't know—it had been hit by a car. Wombat, maybe? And eggs."

The fire was going good. The eucalyptus twigs and leaves were so full of oil they were giving off a bright yellow flame that illuminated the entire cave. She added more branches, and within minutes they had a respectable blaze. They warmed themselves and enjoyed the light. It was better to cook on charcoal than flame but she couldn't wait all night.

She cut up the koala meat and internal organs and kebabbed them with eucalypt sticks. She made a tripod out of other sticks and set the meat next to the fire. The eggs she cooked on the machete blade, one at a time, so as not to waste any of them. They'd been lucky with the timing. In a couple of weeks, the shearwater eggs would contain more than embryos, but for now, they looked and tasted just like chicken eggs. Olivia stacked the fried eggs on a thin flat stone while Owen turned the meat.

They ate with their hands.

The meat was oily and tough and gamy and sour. Every bite was unpleasant. But they were starving and they wolfed it down. The eggs were good. And they drank their fill of the water.

"This is the best water I've ever tasted," Owen said.

Heather had a sudden comforting flash of memory of her brief time on the reservation with her grandmother. *Ča'ak* was the Makah word for "water." Her grandmother pronounced it *"wa'ak,"* which was the way the Indigenous people said the word on Vancouver Island too. It was the only word in Makah she could remember. *"Wa'ak,"* she whispered to herself to see if it would bring magic.

She closed her eyes and whispered it again. *"Wa'ak."*

No magic, but the fact that they had food and were still alive was wizardry enough.

Owen waved the pamphlet she'd taken from the prison. "You can have this back again. We didn't need to burn it. It's mostly photos of a really crappy-looking prison, but there is some info about the island."

"Really? Read it, will ya?" Heather said.

"OK. 'The former McLeod Federal Prison, established in 1911, was closed in 1989 because of growing costs,'" Owen read aloud. "'This facility is now being turned into a museum. It was Australia's last island prison, although there is some controversy as to whether Dutch Island can be considered a true island. At spring tide, the eastern coast reveals a dangerous causeway, the site of many fascinating shipwrecks.'"

"Ooh, sunken treasure," Olivia said.

"'Dutch Island was considered to be one of Australia's toughest prisons for hardened criminals,'" Owen continued. "'No prisoner ever escaped from Dutch Island, unlike Devil's Island in French Guiana and Alcatraz in California.'"

"Did you say *nobody* has ever escaped from Dutch Island?" Olivia said.

"Maybe we'll be the first," Heather said.

"We went to Alcatraz when we visited San Francisco, remember, Olivia? Do you know how many people escaped from Alcatraz, Heather?" Owen asked.

"Nope."

"Three. Or maybe none, depending on whether they drowned or not."

"Dad said they drowned," Olivia remembered.

"They totally escaped. And so will we. And speaking of spring tides, you wanna help me with my astronomy worksheet?"

Owen said, grinning and fishing a rumpled piece of paper from his cargo pocket.

Olivia laughed. "Wow, you still have that? Mr. Cutler will be impressed."

"You think I'll get an extension?" Owen said, laughing with her.

"Let me help you with it," Olivia said.

And the kids sat together and began reciting the planets and the phases of the moon.

Heather yawned and lay back on the cave floor.

She listened to the fire crackle and the kids talking and she closed her eyes and sleep came the way it never came in Seattle but the way it had come in the mountains of Olympic National Park when she was a girl.

35

Snow falling like tea leaves spilled from an old tin chest. Falling on the mountain and the wood and the newborn ferns. Falling on the doe tracks by the river that only she had seen.

The smell of kerosene lingered on the backpacks. She liked it. She was half high off it. That and the bacon and the lard, and the sugar in the breakfast coffee.

They were half a mile from the ridge that they had scouted last night.

Deep in the forest now. Through these big dinosaur trees with fairy-tale names: Sitka, Douglas fir, western hemlock, big-leaf maple, black cottonwood.

A cardinal chirped a warning. A raven watched them with indifference.

They reached the ridge and settled down to wait. They were well concealed behind ferns and a massive fallen oak lying in the understory like a dead god. Lichen wrapped the oak like an emerald bridesmaid's dress, and as the snow blew sideways from the mountain, it transmuted it slowly into the gown of the bride herself.

Her dad took off her backpack and helped her into a bivy bag. He set down the Mossberg and the Winchester.

They didn't talk. They communicated in signs. They were, she thought, like escaped prisoners of war in an enemy country not wishing to give themselves away.

She was warm enough in the bivy and her old coat, her dad's army beanie, and the fox-fur mittens that her mother had made for her last winter.

She lay on her belly and watched the elk herd gradually work its way up the valley toward them. Her father offered her the binoculars, but she shook her head.

A hawk circled above, his wings the color of the red wagon she'd had when she was a very little girl.

Her father checked the weapons.

The Mossberg shotgun was for a bear attack. It was loaded with birdshot and buckshot and slugs in an ascending sequence of lethality.

The single-shot Winchester Model 70 had been in the family since before the Korean War.

The elk were close now. She took off the mittens and cradled the rifle.

She looked through the sight, and the animals became startlingly close.

She loaded the .257 round.

She leveled the weapon and waited. And waited.

They were upwind and so effectively hidden that the elk had no awareness of any danger. The animals smelled earthy and nutty and she could hear them snorting and snuffling as they tore at the ferns and mosses. They were talking to one another in low-frequency moans like elephants.

Her father and she were not talking.

There was nothing to say.

They understood each other perfectly.

They both knew that all this was theater. That she was not going to go through with it. This was the second time he had taken her after big game. She was as stubborn as he was.

When the big bull elk was only twenty-five yards away, she sighted him in the heart and lungs just to the right of his dark brown mane. She moved her finger to the trigger.

She held it there for a moment.

"Pow," she whispered.

She safetied the Winchester and laid it on the snow.

Her dad picked it up and looked through the sight. "The bull?" he whispered.

"Yes."

He swung back the bolt, removed the .257 round, and returned it to the Ziploc ammo bag.

The elks still had no clue that humans were fifty feet away.

Her father put a sleeve on the Winchester.

He looked like he was finally going to say something but in the end he didn't quite know how.

He had been a staff sergeant. She assumed that that had entailed giving orders and barking commands, sometimes in extremis. But she had never even seen him yell at the dog. Her mother had also been a sergeant and she could certainly imagine her giving orders. But not him. He had left his articulation *over there*.

She had to be the one to speak. "I'm sorry if I let you down."

"No!" he replied. "Lord, no. It's OK. You're a good girl. You did the right thing."

On the walk back down she saw that the doe tracks by the river had been so effectively erased, it was as if they had never existed at all. Life, she supposed, was like that—a fleeting impression by a little stream in a big wood that was soon gone.

On the drive home they listened to Neil Young and Dolly and Willie.

It was dusk when they drove off the ferry.

Blue woodsmoke was coming from the cabins. All those little chimney tops in secret communication with the sky.

It was dark when they made it to the house.

The Sound was black. Seattle twinkled in the far distance.

Her dad had been thinking. Her mom had known she would pull this again. She'd said, "Leave the girl."

"I'll talk to your mother," he said. "We can probably get meat just as cheap at Costco."

"As cheap as free?"

"Nothing's free."

They went inside. Her mom had made chili from chuck meat. She already knew. She didn't even say anything. She just smiled and gave Heather a hug. Moms.

Heather helped her father with the dishes.

He cleared his throat. "There are times when you have to take the fight to the enemy. But he wasn't our enemy. It wasn't his time."

"No," she agreed.

He ruffled her hair. She felt the hand.

She shivered.

Woke.

The fire was dying. It was cold.

She sat up.

Breathed deep.

"Heather, do you think Dad is in heaven?" Olivia asked.

"Yes," she replied.

Heather's dad said there was no one looking out for you—no God, no dead ancestors, no angels. Just medics and corpsmen. Her mother said she never thought about it, but her mother's mother, Heather's grandmother, had told her stories about the Great Spirit, about the mountain gods, about the old religion.

She'd try a prayer to all of them.

She grabbed the rifle and got to her feet.

"Where are you going?" Olivia asked.

"The dogs will find us tomorrow unless I take care of them," she said.

Olivia took a second to process what that meant and then nodded. "Be careful," she said.

Heather handed her the cigarette lighter. "Keep the fire going. That eucalyptus wood burns well."

"Can you see if you can get more food?" Owen asked. "But no more wombat. I don't think humans are supposed to eat that."

"I'll look for something else. Keep the mouth of the cave covered."

"What if you don't come back?" Owen asked.

"I'll come back."

"But if you don't?"

"You and your sister hide until the police get here. The police will come. I promise you."

Owen left it there. If the police didn't come, they were dead. If they surrendered to the O'Neills, they were dead.

Heather ruffled his dirty hair and hugged Olivia. "Look after your little brother, OK?"

"OK."

The charcoal of the eucalypt skewers had coated the palms of her hands. She raised them to her face and ran a line of charcoal down her left cheek.

"Why are you doing that?" Owen asked.

"So I'll be harder to see," she said. She walked to the cave mouth. "Don't worry. I'll be back soon," she said.

She stepped outside.

The first priority was to kill the dogs.

Then she'd see what she could do to make the O'Neills hurt. Maybe if she could make them hurt enough, they'd give her the ferry.

That seemed unlikely.

Regardless, it was time to take the fight to the enemy.

36

She was composed. Calm. As calm as the sea, the grass, these old trees. She floated in the nowness of everything.

She scanned the hill and the heathland with Jacko's binoculars.

It was dark. Almost nothing stirred. Not a rabbit, not a wombat, not a sleepy koala. Just the shape of the yellow-white spinifex grass swaying in the breeze. She looked toward the mainland and the outskirts of the city. The sun had set long ago. The lights no longer held much interest for her. She watched dispassionately as a large passenger jet took a big turn over Mornington Peninsula and vectored north toward the airport.

There were other starlit vapor trails above heading away from Melbourne to Sydney or Perth.

That was another universe, that world of airplanes and cars and malls and police officers.

Thunder rumbled from the west.

Heather fixed the rifle on her back and the full canteen and machete at her belt.

She strode across the wasteland.

Under the Milky Way. Under the Southern Cross.

She had food and water in her belly.

A storm *was* coming.

She was the storm.

The O'Neills lived in a land without a Dreaming.

They didn't even know their own island.

Yes, Tom had killed that poor woman.

Yes, she had lied and tried to cover it up.

But that was only trespass upon trespass.

The original trespass was against the people who had lived here for a thousand generations.

She walked.

And as she walked, she played music in her head. All her mom's old albums: the Beatles, the Stones, the Who, the Kinks.

The wind picked up.

The temperature fell.

She was close now.

The farm was lit up by spotlights and house lights. She heard music. Were they celebrating? They were certainly winning the war of attrition. Did they know about Jacko yet?

She lay down in the grass and took out the binoculars. She scanned the farm for the dogs and found them chained near the porch. Three of them together, gnawing at their dinner.

She put down the binocs and checked the wind.

The wind was blowing from the west, from the sea.

Good.

She headed east around the farm, giving the dogs a wide berth. They wouldn't smell her but they were smart and they might hear her. Not many other big mammals out here on Dutch Island tonight.

Heather approached the old steamroller, took the rifle off her shoulder, and waited in the long grass. With the binoculars, she carefully scanned the roof. No one up there this windy night. She scanned the farmyard and that was empty too. She turned on the walkie-talkie and listened. Nothing on any channel. The lights were on at the main farmhouse but there wasn't much activity anywhere else.

She remembered what Rory had said about the anthills behind the steamroller. About what they were going to do with Hans.

Maybe she should...

Yes, she should.

She crawled toward the anthill.

A few pathfinder ants began biting her ankles. She tucked the bottoms of her jeans into her socks.

She had to know.

Creeping forward, she soon found both of them.

They were both dead.

Petra had been shot in the back and dumped naked on top of the ant mound. She was a moving sea of red bodies. Hans was just beyond her on a smaller mound.

A steady breeze was blowing from the southwest and it was rocking the arc light hanging on a wire in the middle of the farmyard. Hans's and Petra's bodies were swinging in and out of chiaroscuro like some insane video-art installation.

The ants had eaten Petra's face and were pouring into her bony white eye sockets to consume her brain.

The perfect horror of it made her catch her breath.

She began to cry. She sobbed and hugged herself and sobbed some more.

She wiped her cheeks.

"I got the kids to a cave! I found a cave," she told Petra. "It was worth it, what you did. It worked. Thank you."

Ants began biting at her elbows.

She slid backward from the anthill and rubbed at her arms.

She was about to slip back into the darkness when something horrifying happened.

Hans moved.

37

She fought the urge to run and scream.

She crawled past Petra to the smaller anthill, where Hans had been staked to the ground.

The ants were seething through his hair. His eyes were tightly closed and he had rolled his lips inward and was shaking his head from side to side puffing down his nostrils in an attempt to keep the ants out of his throat. The stench was appalling. He'd soiled himself, and the O'Neills had beaten him. She looked at him in horror and then quickly crawled to him. She took her canteen and poured water over his head and brushed the ants from his face. She dug the ants out of his ears and killed them and flung them off. She cleared his mouth and poured water down his throat.

The ants immediately began biting her. Their pincers were sharp and incredibly painful. Hans had to be in agony.

"Hans, it's me, Heather," she said.

"Heather?"

"Don't try to speak. I'm going to get you out of here," she said, giving him more water, wiping his face and neck.

"The children?"

"Are alive too. We found a cave and water. Don't speak. Just hold on."

"No. Heather. Get away."

They had wrapped wire around his wrists and attached the wire to tent pegs and hammered the pegs into the ground. Same with his ankles.

"Heather...you must go."

"Save your strength. Don't say anything. You're coming with me, Hans," she said.

"No."

"I'm going to get you out of here. We've got food and water. You're coming with us."

"You must go."

"If I can just get these pegs out."

"I am a dead man, Heather. A matter of hours...they cut a hole in my belly. I can feel them inside me."

"I can save you. Don't try to say anything more! I can do this," Heather said, gagging as she pulled desperately at the pegs.

"I wouldn't get...ten meters."

"I can get you free!"

"And then what?" He looked at her. "Poor Petra is dead...I am dead, but—but you can do two things for me."

"Tell me."

"Did you bring your penknife?"

"Yes."

"First...I need you to...cut my throat."

"What?"

"You must help me...I am too weak to do it myself."

She shook her head. "No, please, anything else."

"I can't do it, Heather. You...the carotid artery...is on the side of the neck. With your little knife, you can cut it and it will be over for me."

"I—I—I can't do that."

"I need your help. Will you do it?"

"No."

"I will hold your hand...I will guide you. Can you do it?"

She shook her head. But she knew he was right. Her mouth opened and a tiny "Yes" came out of it.

Hans told her the second thing he wanted her to do. It felt worse than the first. She agreed to do that too.

She took out her knife and opened the blade. She freed his right wrist from the wire. He held her hand and guided it to the carotid artery pulsing weakly on the left side of his neck.

"Here," he said.

"I'm scared," she said.

"What are you...afraid of?"

"Killing someone in cold blood."

"Heather, please remember...that it is not you...who is killing me. They have killed me. They are the killers."

She tried not to look directly at him. But she couldn't help it. His face was a mess of bite marks, scabs, wounds.

"Please," Hans said and she pushed in with the blade and together they cut his throat.

She scooted away quickly from the arterial spray, almost bumping into poor Petra.

The ants had eaten the skin off Petra's face, and parts of her skull were glinting in the arc lights.

Hans bled out in under a minute. They were together again in death.

She shivered and allowed herself tears.

She took a deep breath and nodded at him.

A thought occurred to her. If Petra was here and Hans was here, why wasn't Tom here too? What had they done with Tom's body?

She looked frantically for him for a minute or two but it was obvious that they'd done something else with Tom.

Why?

Because they needed Tom.

Because they were going to put Tom in the car with her and the dead kids over on the mainland. They were going to try to make it look like a bad car accident. Over there, well away from here.

They were going to disappear the Dutch couple, but Tom must be in storage somewhere. A freezer in the house, no doubt.

She shook her head. "It's not going to fly, is it, Petra?"

The intelligent Dutch woman's dead skull grinned at her.

The Australian coroner would not be fooled, right? Sooner or later he or she would look under a microscope and notice that Tom's cells had been distorted by ice. Ice in the heart of an Aussie summer? That didn't make sense. The coroner would call the cops; the cops would trace the last movements of the doomed family...

She nodded grimly to herself.

That would do as a plan B. Screw them over from beyond the grave. Plan A was to screw them now. It was time to carry out the second part of Hans's request. Enough hesitation.

She pulled on the nearest peg chaining Hans to the ground, the one at his left foot. Tugging it and wiggling it was the way to get it out. Heather hauled on the one next to it, and after some effort, it came out too. She heaved on the final peg at his left wrist. Hans was ready now to get his portion of vengeance.

38

Owen looked at the snake from behind his wall. He had built the wall inside his head, a wall with bricks just like in Minecraft. He hid behind the wall when he didn't want to deal with things. There had been a lot of not dealing with things over the past year. He had not dealt with his mom's death. He had not dealt with his dad meeting Heather. He had not dealt with his dad marrying Heather. He had not dealt with Heather moving in. He had not dealt with coming to Australia and his dad being murdered. He had not dealt with the three of them going on the run from actual Mad Max psycho-killers. Most important of all, he hadn't dealt with the fact that all of it was his fault for hiding behind his wall and saying nothing...

The wall's bricks were made of cinder blocks. Big gray cinder blocks that in Minecraft you could move around easily but that were harder to move in real life. He peeked over the top of the wall into the real world, into real life.

It was definitely a snake. The fire must have awakened it.

Snakes didn't bother you unless you bothered them—if you stepped on one by accident or something like that. Snakes, everyone said, left you alone. Australian snakes were no different. He knew a lot about Australian snakes. He had researched Australian snakes on his phone and his computer for days before the flight. He hadn't just read Wikipedia. He'd read e-books and gotten an actual book from Amazon. Owen knew he wasn't good at sports. Everyone said he had "learning difficulties." Some of the kids called him dumb when the teachers weren't in earshot. His mom and dad had fought hard for the schools to accept his diagnosis of ADHD, and now he took his medicine and got more time on tests. He hadn't had his medicine for three days now. Normally when he took a break from Ritalin and his anxiety meds, he got jittery and stressed, but he wasn't feeling stressed now.

He felt OK watching the snake uncurl itself and crawl in the direction of sleeping Olivia. It was about six feet long and brownish yellow. In this part of Victoria, it could only be an Australian copperhead.

The Australian copperhead had hollow fangs filled with venom at the front of its jaw. He remembered completely verbatim what Wallace's *Snakes of Australia* said about the copperhead: "Their venom is, by Australian standards, only moderately toxic, nevertheless a bite left untreated can easily kill an adult human. There is no copperhead antivenom."

Copperheads had killed children in the past. They ate small prey such as possums and rabbits. Occasionally they went for bigger targets like wombats and wallabies.

Did a sleeping girl look like a sleeping wombat?

Maybe.

She was a good sister. Most of the time.

The snake had curled into a figure-eight shape. It raised its head. "They are shy and retiring by nature, and prefer to escape rather than fight where escape is possible," the book had said.

Escape was definitely possible for this snake. There was plenty of room between the fire and the cave wall. No one was bothering it.

It must have gotten very hungry down here.

He supposed that if it did bite Olivia, that would be his fault too.

Owen went back behind his wall and built it a little higher.

39

If there's one thing the Dutch know about, it's water.

Hans had understood that the O'Neill farm was built over a sandstone aquifer. There were no rivers or lakes on Dutch Island, nowhere for rainwater to go but back into the ocean or down into those layers between the rocks. The O'Neills had been drawing water from the aquifer for decades, and the well had had to be drilled deeper, as the original water was not replenished. The actual wellhead itself was no longer necessary, as the water was pumped to a cistern, but they'd kept it.

Hans had seen all of this and knew it was a mistake.

Heather checked that the coast was clear. As the ants continued to bite, she pulled Hans by his feet to the well thirty feet away at the north of the compound. She dragged him slowly and carefully for fear of the dogs hearing or taking an interest. A few curious barks were all she heard. The dogs perhaps knew something was up but they weren't overly concerned about it yet.

The well was covered with an iron grating to keep out birds and possums. She set down Hans and lifted the grating. It wasn't heavy and she laid it carefully in the dirt. She felt another big raindrop on her neck.

There was a rope and a bucket hanging above the wellhead for anyone who wanted to drink water the old-fashioned way.

The knot was a double granny—nothing shipshape or finessed—and she had it untied in a minute. Her dad had taught her half a dozen knots he'd learned in the military. A bowline would do the job here. It was an easy one to do in the dark. You make a six, the rabbit comes out of the hole, runs behind the tree, and goes back down into the hole.

She looped the rope around Hans's feet and hoisted him up onto the edge of the well. Using the side of the well as a partial lever, she lowered him down. Her shoulders were straining and she was sweating, but this improvised pulley was dividing the weight in half by mechanics, which, she thought, was a branch of physics. *Take that, Owen.*

She lowered and lowered until the pressure began to ease and she knew he was floating in the well water. She let go of the rope and dropped it down into the well after him. Hans had wounds all over his body, and the longer his body floated in the well, the better chance it had to contaminate the O'Neills' water supply.

Another thought occurred to her.

The farm's generator was also upwind of the dogs.

Hmmm.

She crawled to the generator on the edge of the compound. It was a big beast, more than enough for the farm and the outlying houses. An 800 kW Caterpillar diesel. The fuel supply would be nearby.

Yup. The diesel was stored in two big plastic drums. They were far too heavy to tip over, and the plastic covering was weathered but thick and designed to resist the attentions of vermin. A determined woman with a knife might take all night to make a dent.

She walked around the drums looking for a safety-release valve or anything like that, and sure enough, someone had connected a faucet to one of the drums for filling up portable diesel cans. She gave the tap two hard turns, and the diesel began to pour out onto the dirt. The night was still warm and some of the diesel began to evaporate. It was hard to ignite diesel in its liquid form, but diesel vapor was very flammable. She should have brought the cigarette lighter with her. Would a bullet do the trick? She would have to see. The gasoline was stored next to the diesel in a similar drum. She turned the valve and let the gasoline pour out too.

No diesel to make electricity meant no way to recharge the drone.

No gasoline meant no ATV or motorcycle or pickups when their tanks ran dry.

She knew that so far, she had been very lucky. This was not the place to push that luck.

She disappeared back into the grass and worked her way around to the north of the compound.

It began to rain in big, slow drops.

The dogs were chained just under the front porch veranda. Three of them. Not bloodhounds exactly, but there was definitely hound in them. They were exhausted, lying there under the porch light, looking up occasionally as mozzies flew into the bug zapper, whining as the rain got heavier and colder. They were good dogs. They'd had an enjoyable final day on planet Earth.

She lay down in the dirt and got comfortable.

She took the rifle off her back.

Her father had grown up hunting possums and squirrels in the red maple and dogwoods of McCreary County, Kentucky, right on the Tennessee line. Heather was her dad's only child, so he had wanted to show her the gun lore that his dad had shown him. Although she had never really been that interested, she couldn't help but absorb a lot of it. And of course, now it came back. It had been coming back for days.

Always upwind. Always low. Always quiet.

Once inducted into the brotherhood of the gun, you could not forget. She made a little mound of dirt under the barrel just the way her dad had taught her to do it. She firmed the mound and made sure the barrel was horizontal.

It was.

She got comfortable and analyzed her target.

A west-to-east breeze, but not enough to make a difference over this distance, which was about one hundred yards. Maybe a little more; maybe four hundred feet. She looked through the binoculars and figured out where each of the dogs was lying. She flipped up the Lee-Enfield's iron sight and flipped it back down again. A long-range sight was not necessary.

There was something glinting in her sight line five yards ahead to her left. She tried to ignore it but couldn't. She laid down the rifle and crawled to the glinting object with the intention of covering it with dirt, but when she reached the spot, she found that it was a half-buried, ancient, unopened can of peaches. She put it in her bag and went back to her position.

She picked up the rifle and waited until she was still and the sight was motionless.

"I'm sorry," she whispered and took aim at the dog with the white patch on its brown face. The obvious alpha. She aimed at its heavy flank. It was sleeping. She squeezed the trigger and the rifle cracked and kicked, and the dog rolled over in the dust. So much dust. The second dog stood up and began to bark. She pulled back the bolt, and the brass cartridge exited with a *chiiing*. She loaded the next .303 round and aimed through the dust at the second dog, which had a pleasing dingo quality to its face. She shot it dead through the neck.

She ejected the casing and loaded another .303 round.

All the house lights had come on now, and windows were opening.

She tried to get a bead on the third dog but the dust was rising in thick orange columns into the darkness, like a Hubble photograph of star-birth clouds.

A head appeared at a window on a lower floor. It looked like Ivan's. He was yelling at someone in the farmyard.

His torso was an easier shot than the dogs—a big stationary target in a white T-shirt. But that wasn't the plan and she let him be.

Growing consternation around the house now. Shouting, yells, even sporadic gunfire.

Someone began ringing a bell.

The rain started to pour down.

She looked back at the porch. The dust finally cleared and she aimed at the third dog. It was barking like crazy. She shot it in the chest, killing it instantly.

It had been a nasty business but a necessary one.

She ejected the round and loaded another. She slung the rifle over her shoulder and crawled twenty yards into the heath.

The rain was cold and heavy and good.

They might possibly have night-vision or thermal-imaging scopes, so this was not the time to stand and triumphantly survey what she had done. She prepared to move, but then Matt came out of the farmhouse with his dog, Blue. The dog began sniffing the air.

The wind had changed. She was between the bay and the farm, and her scent would be carried on the freshening breeze.

Blue started barking.

Matt let the dog off the leash and screamed at everyone to shut up.

Blue was coming straight for her.

He was a clever dog.

She liked that.

She wondered how many bullets she had left. She should have checked. A soldier always knows, her dad would have said.

She sighted the dog along the length of his body and put her finger on the trigger.

The dog was limping toward her as fast as he could.

"Go on, Blue!" someone yelled.

"Go on, boy, find the bitch!" Ivan yelled.

This was a much smaller target, a slobbering profile trying to sprint through the dust.

Every second the distance between them shortened, making the shot easier but also giving them a bead on her.

She pulled the trigger and missed.

The dog bore down.

She pulled back the bolt, reloaded, aimed, fired, and Blue's head exploded. He ran on for half a second before tumbling over in a heap of arterial blood and dust.

She heard screaming back at the compound: "She shot Blue! The bitch shot Blue! Get her!"

"Where is she?"

"She's over there beyond the tire!"

"Over where?"

"You mob of bloody morons, just shoot everywhere!"

The entire compound was galvanized. Gunfire erupted from half a dozen shotguns.

Heather was already moving. Rifle over back, facedown in the dirt. Crawling over the cracked red soil and the sharp stones and the seashells that the glaciers had torn from the mountains and released here on Dutch Island in a great melting, millennia ago. She crawled with her body barely touching the ground to throw up no dust trails and leave no red djinn in the air.

They weren't giving up.

It was night, and the barbarians *were* coming.

The only question was whether the barbarians were them or her.

She crawled until she was fifty yards from where she had fired her last shot.

Half a dozen men were in the yard screaming bloody murder. Three more were shooting into the bush roughly in the direction of where she had just been.

Two of them were presenting stationary targets as they stood stupidly together.

Heather laid the rifle gently in the dirt and flipped the bolt back, and the empty brass cartridge sailed across the ground without catching the starlight and giving away her position. She pushed the bolt forward again and placed one of her precious final rounds in the chamber.

She heard a woman screaming in the farmyard. She looked through the binoculars and saw that the screamer was Ma; she was standing behind the screen door, half in and half out of the farmhouse. Heather cradled the rifle and looked at Ma through the iron sight. Half in darkness, half in light, but perhaps she was worth a try? Cut the head off the snake…except this wasn't a snake, this was a hydra. Ma opened the screen door and came out onto the porch. "Ma! Get inside! I'm taking the Hilux!" Matt yelled.

"Don't you bloody tell me what to do!"

"Oi, Matt, I think I see her! Over there!"

A bullet pinged off a rock three yards to Heather's right.

"Shit!" She'd been spotted.

Heather crawled for her life now, south, away from the compound, away, away, away.

She didn't try to avoid the little thornbushes or the jagged rocks. She crawled on her hands, elbows, knees, feet as fast as she could. Sand, rock, stone, red dirt, thorns…gunfire near her. Sporadic at first but then more concentrated. A dozen or more men and women shooting into the bush to the south of the house. Shotguns and rifles and then, cutting through the other sounds, the disheartening, terrifying *chug-chug-chug* of an AK-47.

She flattened her body in the dirt.

The AK tore up the field twenty-five feet to her left, the shells hammering into an old cast-iron water tank, ricocheting off in all directions. A ricochet could kill her just as easily as a straight shot.

"Do it, Ma!" someone yelled behind her.

"Get going!" Ma said.

Going where?

A shotgun blast screamed through the air.

Heather stole a look behind her. She could see Ma in the cab of the Toyota Hilux, which was driving in roughly her direction. She was leaning out the window with a weapon. Ma erupted in light as she fired a shotgun.

Heather flattened herself as the white-hot buckshot scraped the air above her head.

I thought that old bitch couldn't walk!

Heather had no choice now. She got up and ran toward the darkness of the mesa. The Toyota's headlights found her. Ma reloaded the shotgun. Heather hit the deck as Ma fired. The shotgun pellets were so close this time, she could hear them *whinnnn* above her.

She got up on one knee and aimed the Lee-Enfield at the Hilux driver. Matt. He saw her aim at him. He desperately turned the wheel. She squeezed the trigger and nothing happened. She ejected the spent cartridge. She rummaged in the bag, found a .303 round, loaded it, aimed, pulled the trigger.

A bullet punched through the windshield. She heard a screech of brakes, and this time the Toyota did not follow.

Either she'd killed Matt or he'd thought better about pursuit.

She ran and ran and ran.

Motorcycles came out looking for her, one going south, another east. The ATV came out and even the drone.

When she was nearly a thousand yards away, she stopped and caught her breath and drank water from the canteen.

Suddenly all the farm lights went out.

The generator had been bled dry of diesel.

She checked the ammo situation. She had three bullets left in the bag.

Was it worth risking a thousand-yard shot? Was it worth wasting one of her final three rounds in an attempt to ignite diesel and gasoline fumes?

Why not?

She lay down in the dirt and flipped the long-range sight and aimed slightly above the black mass that was the fuel tank for the generator.

The music in her head was "Day of the Lords" by Joy Division.

Careful, now.

Slow.

She pulled the trigger.

The .303 slug went straight through the diesel tank without igniting anything.

Damn it.

Worth another?

Hell with it. She danced the bolt. Aimed. She squeezed the trigger, and the rifle thumped comfortingly into her right shoulder. The explosive in the cartridge threw out a lead ogive that the barrel spiraled into the air with the faintest rush of smoke and the sweet smell of gunpowder. The bullet had been on a collision course with its target since it was manufactured in North London in 1941. It traveled across the heath at two thousand feet per second.

There was a yellow explosion that was so big, it might possibly draw attention on the mainland. She heard the roar a full two seconds after she saw the flame.

"That's for Tom. He was a doctor! And it's for Hans and Petra. And it's for scaring the shit out of *my kids*!" she said and stood and raised her middle finger.

40

She jogged for a half a mile before stopping and taking a sip from her canteen.

The rain intensified. Sheet lightning silhouetting her against the horizon. It smelled like Seattle rain. Like fir. It didn't smell like this parched continent. She wondered if all rain smelled the same.

Poor dead Tom would have known.

It took her forty-five minutes to make it back to the cave.

The O'Neills could get more dogs, but for now the dogs were dead and the three of them were safe.

Owen was sitting by the fire waiting for her.

"Hey, Owen," she said.

"Hey," he said. "You're wet."

"It's raining. I couldn't get any more meat. Everything OK here?"

"Yeah...I killed a snake."

"You what?"

"Over there, against the wall. I didn't know if it was going to bother us or not but it was crawling toward Olivia, so I had to kill it."

Heather was aghast. "What? A snake? Are you joking?"

"It's over there by the wall."

Heather took the rifle off her shoulder. There was indeed a dead snake by the wall. A brown snake about six feet long.

"I thought it was just going to mind its own business. They mostly do, you know. But then it started crawling toward Olivia. I was watching behind my wall. I have this wall thing."

"I know."

"I was behind my wall but I kept peeking over and it was coming closer, so I had to try to kill it."

"Oh, Owen! Oh my God!" she said, putting her arms around him and hugging him. "Didn't you even wake Olivia?"

"What was the point? I killed it."

Olivia was still sleeping, curled on her side by the fire.

"How did you kill it?"

"I picked up a big rock and threw it at it. I missed completely. The rock hit the cave wall but then dropped on the snake's back, kind of pinning it. I grabbed another rock and got close and dropped it on the snake's head."

"Jesus, Owen! What if it had bitten you? Or spit venom at you?"

"They don't do that."

Heather went over to look at the snake. "Where did you learn how to do that?"

"My snake book and the Primitive Technology channel on YouTube. That guy does a million things with rocks. You should watch it. I don't think it was completely awake. They're cold-blooded. They need to warm up. So not really a fair fight."

Olivia stirred. "You're back," she said.

"Owen, tell her what you did while I search the rest of the cave for any other guests."

"I don't, um, like . . . I don't want to brag or anything."

"For once in your life, brag."

Owen told Olivia about the snake. Olivia didn't believe it until he showed her. She hugged him and Owen didn't believe that. Heather didn't find any other snakes in the cave.

"I forgot to tell you guys, I found a can of peaches," she said, removing it from her bag.

"Wow, those must be fifty years old," Owen said.

"Do you think they're safe to eat?" Olivia asked.

"One way to find out."

Heather stabbed the machete into the lid and carefully opened the tin.

They ate the peaches.

They were the best-tasting peaches in the history of Earth.

The kids drank the peach juice and talked and even laughed.

They sat around the fire and Heather glanced at Owen's science homework. It was beyond her, but Olivia and Owen explained it.

"We need some music," Olivia said.

"Go on, then," Heather said.

At first shyly but then with more confidence, Olivia sang and rapped all of *Pink Friday* by Nicki Minaj with Owen joining in on the choruses.

"What about your stuff?" Olivia said.

"You wouldn't like it. I'm a woman out of time. Mostly."

But they insisted as she stoked the fire. They wanted a story or a song. She offered to sing them Greta Van Fleet or Tame Impala or Lana, but now Olivia actually wanted the retro-hipster stuff, so she ended up singing them the whole of the *White Album,* including the shit songs.

"You can really sing," Olivia said and meant it.

"Yeah," Owen agreed.

"Thank you."

They yawned and stretched and talked and fell asleep next to each other. Kids have the gift of sleep. They were so peaceful, they were part of a tomorrow when all of this was over.

Heather cleaned her rifle and put it within easy reach.

She had one bullet left.

She closed her eyes and lay down on the sandy cave floor, and within minutes she too fell through the dark blue midnight into a deep sleep.

She dreamed. The kids dreamed. The dreams syncopated.

On the land above all was chaos, storm, and lightning, but down here in the underworld all was quiet.

41

The sun was old iron, then blood, then faded yellow play-ground plastic. She sat on the tree limb and looked through the binoculars at the water and the mainland. You could possibly try a shot over there but that was a two-miler without a guarantee of hitting anything or attracting attention. Ammunition was precious. She watched a dorsal fin rise and sink beneath the waves.

The tree began to shake. She looked down. Owen was climbing up. He cleared the first level of branches and the second and the third. The old Heather would have told him to watch himself but he didn't need to be told much now. "Hey," she said.

"Whatcha doing?" he asked.

"Keeping an eye out."

"What's that bird?"

"Which one?"

"The one next to the crow on the other tree."

"Oh, that one. I dunno. Some kind of raptor. An Aussie peregrine? Here, look at it through the binoculars." She passed him the binoculars and resumed her rumination.

Olivia was at the bottom of the tree now. "Can I come up?" she asked.

"Sure."

Olivia climbed the eucalyptus tree and sat on the branch next to Owen.

Heather adjusted her position and looked in the direction of the farm. She couldn't actually see it from here, but she could make out an inky line of smoke coming from that direction.

"The bird has red on its front—what would that be?" Owen asked, handing her the binoculars back.

"Gosh, I dunno, Owen. Big mistake not bringing an Australian-bird guidebook here. Don't know why I didn't think of it," she said and adjusted the focus. "Some kind of kite, maybe?"

"Would Dad know?"

"He knew everything."

"He didn't know about birds," Olivia said.

"I need to go to the bathroom. It's a number two," Owen said.

Heather knew what the problem was. "Use grass. That, I guess, is what humans used for the two hundred thousand years before the invention of toilet paper."

He went off for two minutes. When he came back up the tree, he gave her a nod. "It worked OK. But now I'm hungry," he said.

"We can't get the eggs in daylight. What about that snake? Do you think we could eat that?" Heather asked.

"It's poisonous!" Olivia said.

"No, it's venomous, not poisonous! Dummy!" Owen said.

"Don't call your sister names."

"He's the dummy!" Olivia said.

"Apologize, Olivia."

"Make him apologize first."

Normally this could go for fifteen or twenty minutes, but today Owen said simply, "Sorry, I didn't mean that," and Olivia said, "I'm sorry, I didn't mean it either," like two goddamn kids on the Hallmark Channel.

"It seems cruel that they fly all this way and then we eat their eggs," Owen said.

"We'll get something else, then."

Heather scanned the horizon. She knew the O'Neills would start looking for them again eventually. But without the dogs and with fuel low in their vehicles, they might not be moving that fast. And maybe this morning, they would start feeling sick from the poisoned well.

"You learned all about birds on that place you grew up?" Olivia asked.

"Goose Island. Yeah, I guess I did."

"Why did you leave?" Olivia asked.

"Um, I think I just got to that stage when your parents suddenly flip from being always right to always wrong."

Olivia nodded and dropped out of the tree and went wandering by the old ruined bus.

"That's never going to happen to me 'cause I don't have any parents," Owen said.

Heather swallowed, hard. "Owen—"

"Hey, look what I got," Olivia said. It was a side mirror from the bus. "It's useful, right?"

"Of course it is! We can signal for help from passing planes. You catch the sun like this," Owen said, climbing down out of the tree and grabbing it.

"Hey, I found it!" Olivia said, grabbing it back.

"Can I see?" Heather asked.

Olivia brought it over, stood on tiptoes, and handed it to her. Heather caught a glimpse of herself. Her tanned face was caked with blood and dirt. Her hair was matted and wild. Her eyes were deep set, and her right eyelid was swollen. She had a yellow bruise on her forehead, a cut across her left eyebrow, and another cut on her cheek she didn't even remember getting.

"Wow, I look terrible," she said with a laugh as she handed it back to Olivia.

"Oh my God, look at me," Olivia said. She was sunburned with matted hair and red eyes.

"Let me see me," Owen said.

The sunburn did nothing for his appearance either.

"How did all this happen? How did we get so...lost?" Olivia said quietly, sitting down on the ground.

"We're not lost. We know where we are," Owen said.

"You know what I mean."

Heather climbed out of the tree. "We came to another world and we were driving too fast and we hit a woman. That's all," she said softly.

"Yes," Olivia said.

Heather sat down and put her arms around Olivia's waist. Owen sat down, and Heather put her arms around him too.

"We're not really lost, are we?" Olivia asked.

"No," Heather said. They were before, maybe, but not now. They knew this place. This strange continent in February without any snow. In all this orange. In all this red.

"Did you live your whole life on Puget Sound?" Olivia asked.

"I was actually born in Kansas," Heather replied.

"Where?"

"A place called Fort Riley. I don't remember much about it. We moved when I was little."

"What kind of a fort was it?" Owen asked.

"It was a big army fort. Both my parents were in the army."

"Were you in the army?" Owen asked.

"No."

"What jobs did you do?" Olivia asked.

"After I left Goose Island, I did a few things. I was a waitress. I worked reception at the VA hospital. I tried to be a singer. I told fortunes using the *I Ching* at the Pike Place Market. I was homeless for a while. And through a friend, I trained as a massage therapist. That's how I met your dad."

"How come you ended up on Goose Island in the first place?"

"After my father got back from the war, he had a lot of problems and a lot of issues. The whole VA mental-health system is a labyrinth . . . anyway, my mom knew the Sound pretty well. She's originally from Neah Bay. Do you know where that is?"

"No," Olivia said.

"You know the mountains that we can see from our house?"

"Back in Seattle?" she asked, as if that were an imaginary place.

"Yes. Well, that's Olympic National Park and beyond there, right at the edge of America, there's a place called Neah Bay, where my mom's mom is from originally. It's a reservation for the Makah people. After her parents divorced, my mom lived there for a while. When she turned eighteen she left to join the army and that's where she met my dad. After the war a lot of veterans were coming out of the army and moving to the Pacific Northwest, and a lot of them had problems and my mom knew about the community on Goose Island where they could sort of heal together. And it sounded good to my dad, so we moved there and that's where I mostly grew up."

"Did you like it?"

"Yeah. I didn't know any different. But like I say, when I

was a teenager, I knew I had to leave; I had to see the world. I couldn't stay there forever."

"And now you've seen the world. You know the world, like, totally sucks," Owen said.

Heather laughed. And then Olivia laughed. And then even Owen laughed.

The sun continued to rise over the bay, over the island, over the other islands, over the continent. It had had practice. It had been doing this here for millions of years.

"Can you take a look at my arm?" Olivia said.

"It's a mosquito bite. Don't scratch it," Heather said.

It looked worse than a mosquito bite. It looked like some kind of botfly bite. There might be larvae in a day or two, but there was no point in worrying Olivia about that now.

She cleaned the wound with the Leiden University T-shirt, patted Olivia's head, and said in the voice mothers have been using for ten thousand generations, "Shh, baby, it's going to be OK."

"Where are we going to live when we get back to America?" Owen asked.

"We could go live with Grandpa John and Grandma Bess. You don't have to look after us if you don't want to," Olivia said to Heather.

"Do you want me to still look after you?" Heather asked.

"Do you want to do it?"

"I really do," Heather said.

Olivia smiled and then Owen smiled. "I want to visit Grandpa John but I don't want to live with them," he said.

"We can do whatever we want," Heather said.

"Let's go check this thing out," Owen said, and the kids went over to play by the ruined bus.

Heather watched them.

The day was beautiful. The swaying grass. A blue-silk sky. Pink herons over the mirror sea.

"Uh-oh!" Owen said.

"Uh-oh what?" Heather yelled.

"I found another one of those fox-trap things at the back of the bus."

"Don't go near it!" Heather went over to see it. It was another vicious-looking animal trap like the one they'd nearly stepped in at the range, all red rusted teeth and black iron jaws. She was tempted to spring it with a stick but then reconsidered. If they were stuck out here another night, maybe it would catch them a sheep or a rabbit. She hadn't seen any rabbits or sheep outside the farm, but you never knew.

She told the kids her plan and then she marked the trap with sticks with little pieces of fabric ripped from her T-shirt.

"No one's allowed anywhere near the back of the bus!" she said, and she did a thorough scout of the hill to see if there were any more traps.

When that was done, Heather turned on the walkie-talkie again. Battery life was down to one bar.

"My name is Heather Baxter. We need the police. We are stranded on Dutch Island off the coast of Victoria..."

She repeated the message on every channel as the battery light faded.

Suddenly, on channel 2, a voice cut through the static.

"Heather, is that you?"

"It's me. Who's this?"

"Heather, it's Matt. What the hell have you done?"

"What do you mean, Matt?"

"We are all sick, Heather. Diarrhea, and some people have been vomiting! Hans! My God, Heather! You poisoned the well!"

"I guess you won't be chasing us today, then, will you?"

"You shot Blue! He was a good dog. Jesus. And the other dogs! And the bloody generator!"

"Tell you what, you just bring the ferry over and let us go back to the mainland, and your problems will be over."

"Funny. Our problems won't be over—you'll go to the cops!"

"I'll keep my mouth shut."

"Shit, you don't even know, do you?" Matt said.

"Know what?"

"We were trying to make a deal with bloody Tom when all hell broke loose last night."

"What are you talking about?"

"What do you mean, what am I talking about?"

"You said you were trying to make a deal with Tom."

"Jesus, you really *don't* know, do you? Gillian's a nurse, she... Christ Almighty. Hold on."

Heather eyes closed. She swayed, then righted herself.

What was he... he must be...

She was cold all over. Deathly cold.

"Heather...I don't understand this. You attacked the farm when I was trying to sort out a deal. What have you been doing?"

The voice on the radio. Holy shit. It was Tom.

42

Her old friend the crow with the yellow eye was staring at her as the world rotated back into view.

She must have fainted.

She had never fainted in her life.

Didn't people only faint in novels with characters named Darcy and Rochester? Nobody fainted in the real world.

"Heather!"

What was happ—Oh. My. God. She picked up the walkie-talkie. "Tom? Is that you?"

"Heather?"

"I'm here."

"I'm here too."

"How?"

"They saved me. Gillian saved me..."

"How are you—"

"Gillian. She's a nurse. Listen, Heather, it's hard to talk. I think I've made a deal."

"A deal? What? Tom...how can you trust them after all this?"

"We have to, Heather...only chance to get out alive...can't talk...I'm giving the walkie-talkie back to Matt."

"No!"

Static.

"Tom? Tom!"

"It's Matt again. Heather, can you hear me?"

"I can hear you."

"Tom's in terrible shape. He can't speak for long. He has a collapsed lung."

"He's alive? It's impossible! I saw him stabbed!"

"You saw him take a knife to the side. But Gillian saved him. Every remote station in Australia has emergency medical supplies. Little Niamh found him still breathing. Gillian used to be a nurse. We patched him up as best we could. Real meatball surgery, Gillian called it. He has a collapsed lung and probably liver damage. He needs to be in a hospital, Heather. He's in a bad way."

Heather burst into tears. "The kids don't know he's alive. Let me go get them."

"Let me talk to you first, Heather. We've made a deal. Despite everything you've done. Actually, I'll let Tom explain," Matt said.

More static before a weak-sounding Tom came back on. "Are the kids OK?"

"Yes."

"Are you OK?"

"Yes, Tom, I'm fine!"

"Good...I think we have to...trust them. We can do this," Tom said and broke off into a coughing fit.

Matt came back on. "He lost a lot of blood. He needs surgery and a blood transfusion. We need to get this done fast, Heather. You guys are going to have to come to the farm. You can go with me to a bank and we'll get the cash, and then when we get back, we'll let you all go. That's the new deal. It's sorted. Tom agreed."

It sounded so reasonable.

But these people were crazy.

The things they'd done. Insane, horrible, terrible, sadistic things.

"You were hunting us down. You were going to kill us!" Heather said.

"We were trying to find you! Why do you think we brought in the dogs?" Matt said.

"You killed Petra!"

"No, she attacked the dogs and they started tearing her apart," Matt said. "We tried to shoot them, and Ivan hit her in the back. Think about it, Heather. Who is the bad guy here? You came to our home. You killed Ellen. You attacked our farm. You shot our dogs. No one can find Jacko, and you've got his bloody rifle. You want to explain that?"

"No."

"You're the bad guy! We were minding our own business, living our own lives, and you came. My family has done nothing to your family. And you've wreaked havoc on us."

"Jacko was going to rape me."

"Well, Jacko's bloody gone now, isn't he? So, Heather, what do you think? You wanna get out of this alive?"

It sounded almost plausible. Tom had killed Ellen. She had tried to cover it up.

But that didn't make any—no. "Hans, what you did to Hans…"

"Yeah, I know," Matt said. "Shit. That was all crazy Jacko. Ivan and Jacko tried to get him to talk. It's mad, I know. Look, there's a couple of different factions here, Heather. It's complicated. I'm trying to steer the best course for us and your family...Tom wants to talk to the children. Can you get them?"

Heather was really crying now. Owen and Olivia were sitting in the cab of the ruined bus looking at her.

"Get over here! Both of you!"

They ran over. She had to stop herself from dry-heaving. She had to keep her voice steady. "It's your dad. He's alive," Heather said and handed Olivia the walkie-talkie.

The children listened while Tom spoke.

Heather walked far away from them. To give them space. This was family time. Private. It had nothing to do with her.

She sat under the shade of the farthest eucalyptus tree on a gnarled root so blackened and polished by successive waves of fire that she could almost see her reflection in it.

Last night's rain had changed the hill.

Flowers were peeking up through the grass. Red, blue, and yellow flowers—of what genus, she did not know. Insects were hovering over the flowers, and little birds were swooping everywhere, eating their fill.

"Heather! Heather!"

Olivia was calling her. She walked back to the brother and sister. "I'm here," she said.

"Matt wants to speak to you," Olivia said.

She nodded and took the walkie-talkie. "Matt?"

"We need to get this sorted today. Now. Where are you, Heather?"

"We're north of...we're somewhere."

"Can you walk to the farm?"

"Yes."

"Are the kids healthy enough to walk or should we get a car for them?"

"The kids are healthy."

"OK, so just walk to the farm. Come in with your hands up. We'll see you soon."

Her head was throbbing.

"No," she said.

"No, what?"

"I'm not going to do that. You killed Petra, you tortured Hans. You've got Tom over a barrel, and I don't trust you, Matt."

"You're going to screw everything up *again,* Heather," Matt said.

"I want...I want..."

"What do you want?"

"I want to talk to Tom in person. I want him to tell me it's OK to trust you."

"Nah, mate, a deal is a deal. It's done. You come to the farm."

"I won't do *that* deal. Tom is under duress; I don't know what you're threatening him with. I have two conditions. First, I want to talk to Tom in person, *alone,* with none of you around, before I agree to give us all up. Second, I stay here as your hostage, not the kids. Me. Tom takes the kids with him when he goes to get the money. The kids leave this island with Tom and they never come back. When you get back here with the money, you let me go."

Matt took a long while before coming back on the walkie-talkie.

"We agree to the second condition," he said. "Tom can take the kids to Melbourne as long as you stay as a hostage. But we can't agree to the first condition. Tom can't be moved."

"I've got to meet with him, I have to talk to him, I need to know it's safe. I need him to convince me to trust you after everything I've seen," Heather insisted.

There was another long pause before Matt came back on. "OK. Tell you what—northeast of the farm there's an area of burned heathland. The grass has been completely torched. No places for anybody to hide there. There's a black, dead eucalyptus tree."

"I know it," Heather said.

"You can meet Tom there. We can get everything prepared for later today. Six p.m."

"I'll be there," Heather said.

43

After strapping the Lee-Enfield over her shoulder, Heather gave Owen the binoculars and Olivia the canteen.

She held Olivia's and Owen's hands and they walked south through the blowfly grass and the spinifex and the kangaroo grass and the bladygrass.

She didn't feel the blades or thistles anymore.

She didn't feel anything.

Not the flies.

Not the heat.

No one spoke.

They were going to make a deal. It was the best deal possible. She wanted the kids off the island.

She would stay here.

Danny and maybe some of the others would try to rape her. Matt might try to stop them, but he was a brother-in-law, not a brother.

Tom would know this. He was a good man, a moral man, but he was a desperate man too.

Each footstep brought her closer to the horror.

She racked her brain for alternatives.

But there were none.

A miracle had happened. Tom, whom she had seen killed, was alive!

He was the smartest man she'd ever met. And if he trusted them, she would have to trust them too.

They continued walking in silence.

The sun would set in an hour or so.

They were close now.

The farm itself wasn't really visible, since it lay in the gully between two hills, but she could see a plume of white smoke from a cooking fire. They must be boiling the well water to drink it.

She smiled at that.

Despite what Matt had said, she was glad she and Hans had inconvenienced them. They deserved it. And her plan might have worked. She had made them sick, killed their dogs, destroyed their fuel. If she had gone on to do a series of raids and make their life hell, perhaps they would have given her the ferry just to get rid of her.

Perhaps.

They reached the brow of the hill and now on the other hill they could see the dead eucalyptus tree surrounded by scorched earth.

"So this is it," she said, smiling at the children. "You'll get to see your dad and you'll get to go home."

"What will happen to you?" Olivia asked.

"We're going to do a swap. I'm going to stay with them as a sort of, well, a sort of hostage, I suppose. When you're back in the city, Tom's going to give them money and they'll let me out."

"We're going to trust them?" Olivia said.

"Yes. Your dad thinks it's OK. They saved his life."

Owen shook his head and sat down in the grass.

"Come on, Owen."

"Sit, please," he said.

He was looking at her seriously. His gaze was determined. She'd never seen him with such a steady look in the year she'd known him.

"What's up, Owen?"

"Please sit—if we stand here for a long time, they'll see us," he said.

"OK."

She and Olivia both sat down in the long grass.

"I don't want you to make this deal," Owen said.

"I don't want to make it either, but it's the only way we can get your dad back."

He was struggling with his words.

She waited.

"I—I want to stay with you. I don't want Dad back," Owen said.

"What are you talking about?" Heather asked.

"You know I build this wall in my head out of Minecraft bricks. And I hide stuff behind it that I don't want to think about or see ever again," Owen said.

"I know."

"Sometimes I hide behind the wall, and sometimes I hide things back there that I don't want to see again."

"Sure."

"And if you build the wall thick enough and high enough, you forget what's back there."

"It's fine, Owen, it's a coping mechanism. You and your sister have been through so much in the past year. Lord knows—"

"No. You don't get what I'm saying. Neither of you do. You don't know what's behind the wall. Neither did I, really. Or anyway, I didn't want to think about it. But my head's been clear lately. At least since we got the water."

"Well, that's good, Owen, it—"

"Please just listen. What did Dad tell you about what happened to Mom?" Owen asked.

"That it was just an accident, that's all. Your mom was a very brave woman. All those years with MS. And then when she began to deteriorate...looking after you guys, doing her work. She sounds like she was an amazing person."

"What did Dad tell you *exactly* about the accident?" Owen asked.

Heather began to feel cold again.

"What he told everyone. He found her. She fell down the stairs. She'd been unsteady on her feet."

"He left out the bit about the drinking?"

Heather nodded. "Yes...well, no, he told me the truth eventually. I don't blame your mom. I'd drink too if I got diagnosed with something like that. It's not her fault. She was a good mom and she was trying to cope."

"My mom didn't drink. Not heavily. And she didn't commit suicide either."

"I know, sweetie! Those are just rumors. People are going to say awful things."

"He's the one who said the awful things. He started those rumors. He wanted people to think that she was drinking too much and that she was suicidal."

"No, that's—" Heather began but Owen waved her off.

"Mom wasn't that like that," Owen said. "It was him..."

"Him what?" Olivia asked.

"All those rumors about maybe she did it on purpose or was drunk—it's all lies Dad invented," Owen said.

"Tom wouldn't do that," Heather said.

Owen took Heather's hand. "I was there," he said.

"When?"

"I blocked it out with my wall. A big wall. The biggest. And I guess the Valium helped too," Owen said.

"What happened, Owen?" Olivia asked.

"It's still not completely clear, but it's coming back...I was supposed to be at gym. But I hate gym and I got a nurse's note to be excused and I just went home. It's only a five-minute walk from the school."

"You were there?" Olivia said, stunned.

Owen nodded. "I think so. No, I *know* so. I was there. Mom and Dad weren't home when I got back and it wasn't Maria's day, so no one knew I was there. I was in my room playing Mario Kart when I heard Dad and Mom come in. I didn't want Dad to know I was skipping gym and school, so I hid in my room."

Olivia was shaking her head.

"It's true!" Owen insisted. "Dad and Mom were arguing about something. She came up the stairs. It took her ages to get up the stairs. She was crying. I was going to go out and hug her but Dad came up after her. He was the one that was drinking. It was his whiskey glass they found at the bottom of the stairs."

"What happened, Owen?" Olivia asked.

"Mom had found out about some woman Dad was seeing. They were arguing. She was so angry. She told him that this time, she was serious. This new girl was the final straw. When they divorced, he wouldn't get a penny. She would ruin him. She would tell Granddad, and Granddad would fix him . . ."

Heather put her arms around Owen as he began to sob. Olivia held both his hands.

"What happened, Owen?" Olivia asked.

"I think Mom said that Dad would have to pay back the money Granddad had given him for medical school. Dad was laughing at her. I was peeking through a door. She went to hit him and she lost her balance and she fell down the stairs. I saw everything."

"Oh my God," Olivia said.

Heather was shaking her head. "Tom wasn't home—"

"He was! And he's a doctor, he could have saved her, I think, but he didn't even try. He stood there looking at her. He didn't help. And I didn't either. I hid there. I didn't help Mom. I didn't say anything. I hid there and I built my wall. And Dad said he found her like that when he got home, and that wasn't true. And then the ambulance came. And Olivia came home. And I was able to pretend I had just come home too. And Dad called Grandma. And she came. And they took Mom away. And I hid behind my wall. And everything got blurry. And I was able to pretend it had never happened."

Heather was crying now.

She believed Owen.

Tom wasn't guilty of murder. He probably wasn't even guilty of manslaughter. Perhaps he could have done something to save her; they would never know. From his hiding place in his room, Owen couldn't possibly have seen what Tom did when he eventually went down the stairs. Maybe she'd been killed instantly. Maybe all Tom had done wrong, really, was lie about what happened.

But the lie was enough and the inaction was enough.

His first reaction must have been shock but then a different emotion might have set in. If Judith was dead, it would solve so many of his problems.

There was another Tom underneath the Tom she wanted to believe in. There was the Tom who wouldn't let her talk too much to his friends at dinner parties in case she embarrassed him. The Tom who would sometimes be rude to waiters. The Tom of the odd, inexplicable, incandescent rage. The Tom who made sure that Heather medicated Owen early in the morning so the boy wouldn't hassle him as he dressed for work.

Carolyn had warned her that all surgeons were assholes. But it was more than that, wasn't it? Owen's story had shocked her but not, in truth, surprised her.

"I think I've hated him for a year. I'll hate him forever," Owen said in a faraway voice.

She nodded and understood something that had been bothering her.

This deal he said he'd arranged with the O'Neills didn't make any sense. Not after all that had happened. The Tom she thought she knew would have seen that. But the Tom of Owen's story would perhaps grab at any lifeline at any cost.

Even in that initial deal he'd made, he'd wanted to take Olivia with him and leave Heather with Owen. Olivia was his favorite. If things had gone wrong, at least he would have had her. Is that what he'd been thinking? What dad would think a thing like that?

Tom would.

She knew that now.

All three of them were crying.

Heather hugged Owen as hard as she could. And Olivia

hugged him too. They sat there in the grass for fifteen minutes, hugging and crying.

They had a conversation without saying anything.

Heather knew what she had to do.

She wiped their tears and held their hands. She asked them if they were sure.

They were just kids, but they were sure.

They didn't trust him. They did trust her.

"Go back to the cave. I don't like any of this," Heather said.

She sent them off and when they were gone, she crawled through the long grass until she was near the place where the bushfire had burned itself out. A great scorched area of the land, and in the middle of it a charcoal-black snow gum tree. A tree that had evolved with the fire over millions of years and that looked dead but whose slow patient heart was beating still.

She lifted the binoculars to her eyes and saw Tom sitting in a wicker chair underneath a branch in the shade. There was an IV in his arm connected to a bag of saline hanging on a jerry-rigged IV pole.

He had a walkie-talkie in his hand.

But there was something not quite...

He was pale and looked dead, but when she studied him through the binoculars, she saw that he was blinking.

He was alive. It was really him. No *Weekend at Bernie's* trickery from the O'Neill clan.

But something *was* wrong.

She scanned the horizon. All around the tree, the vegetation had been torched, leaving only red dirt. There didn't seem to be anywhere for the O'Neills to hide, but still, she approached cautiously, on all fours, sniffing the air like a lioness as she reached the edge of the grass.

Heather picked up her walkie-talkie. "Tom, are you there alone?" she whispered.

All she heard back was static.

She crawled closer and tried again. "Tom?"

She tried all the channels and looked again through the binoculars. He was breathing. And those eyes seemed alert enough.

It was just a hundred yards of burned grass from here to Tom.

The O'Neills had kept their word. They were nowhere to be seen.

She had one bullet left.

She quietly loaded a .303 round into the rifle and picked up the walkie-talkie again. "Tom?"

Ssssssssssssssssssssssssssssssssssssssssss.

"Tom?"

Ssssssssssssssssssssssssssssssssssssssssss.

She tried again and again but all she got was that long, doleful whisper of static that had been hissing in the background for thirteen billion years.

Ssssssssssssssssssssss and then, out of the void, Matt's sudden, startlingly clear voice: "Heather, where are you, mate? We're waiting for you and the kids. Tom hasn't given us the all-clear yet. Come on, don't blow this..."

She turned down the volume on the walkie-talkie and crawled right to the last blades of spinifex.

Tom was still in his chair in the shade of the dead tree, a silhouette in the setting sun. He was wearing a hospital robe and a straw hat. That bag of saline going into his arm.

He was doing something.

He was fidgeting with the walkie-talkie.

Heather prepared to get up and walk to him.

She did a final scan of the terrain with the binoculars.

Was there anything odd?

Nah, all was—

Wait.

What was that?

A glint of light on the burned ground. On the burned ground, where there should be no light.

Sun on gunmetal? Sun on shotgun barrel? Would they have had time to dig themselves foxholes in the burned land, Matt, Ivan, some of the others?

But why hadn't Tom warned her?

Tom would know it was a trap, he would—

Because his walkie-talkie had no batteries!

Heather backed into the grass.

She let out a breath.

Oh, Tom. I wanted to talk to you. I needed to tell you that the deal was off. To tell you that the kids had made a choice. And they chose me. They trust me to put them first and protect them and keep them safe. They still love you, of course they do, but they don't trust you. Because of Judith. Because of what happened on the stairs. And what happened with us here on the island.

But I wanted to talk to you. I wanted to hear your side of it. I wanted you to talk to me in that Tom voice. I wanted you to convince me that Owen had gotten it wrong. Heather, are you crazy? Owen is mistaken. I found Judith like that. Kids' brains work differently. You know Owen. He doesn't see things straight. He doesn't know what happened. *Tell me I'm wrong; tell me I was blind too, Tom.*

I fell for your whole act. You came to see me for the first time on February 14. Valentine's Day. I'd forgotten that until a couple of days ago. We'd had three massage-therapy sessions by the time Judith died. You met me while Judith was still alive. After our third session,

*we went out for a drink. Remember? I told you I couldn't possibly
see a client outside of work and you were so funny and cool and you
insisted. "Just a quick drink next door." Then you didn't come in
until late May.*

*Judith's accident was March 3. Was I the woman you and Judith
were fighting about? Or was there someone else too? I hope it wasn't
me but I think maybe it was. Judith was smart. She sensed it. She
knew it was happening again. If we hadn't met, maybe Judith would
still be alive.*

*I know you, Tom. You'll deny it and you'll talk about how people
remember things differently and you'll mention that* Rashomon *movie
I still haven't seen and maybe you'll tell me I'm too young to know
the way the world works.*

*Or maybe not. Maybe you'll come clean about everything . . . and I'll
explain I have to leave you here and you'll understand. I'll tell you that
I know that Matt's a liar and there will be no deal and the only way to
save the kids is to leave you.*

Tears again.

Tears dripping down her cheeks onto the stock of the Lee-
Enfield.

She thought about Tom and then she thought about her dad.
She would get by without either of them. She would be by
herself. And it would be OK.

Because that was the price she had to pay. To keep the kids
safe, she had to abandon Tom.

The sky to the west was crimson.

Night was coming.

All this time, Tom had been getting more and more agitated.
He had finally worked out that they had given him a dud
walkie-talkie.

He got it now.

He'd thought the O'Neills were really going to let them go, but when they'd taken him out here, whatever he'd seen had made him realize it was a trap.

Heather watched through the binoculars as he struggled and failed to get to his feet.

"They're here! Run, Heather! Take the kids and keep running!" he yelled from broken lungs and collapsed back into the chair.

Two of the men hiding in the dirt immediately got up with their shotguns. Two others stayed put but moved enough so that she clocked them.

There were four of them dug into the ground around the tree; they'd been waiting for her in prepared foxholes.

Clever. Matt's idea, no doubt.

Heather didn't run.

Didn't move a muscle.

"Thank you, Tom," she whispered.

She lay down next to the rifle.

The O'Neills were waiting to spring a trap.

She could wait too.

Patience was her weapon.

She turned off the walkie-talkie and lay there.

Finally, big Ivan climbed out of his foxhole and waved to the others.

"I'm calling this, lads," he said.

There were four of them, just as she'd thought: Matt, Kate, Danny, Ivan.

Kate took the opportunity to throw up. Matt leaned over and dry-heaved. "Bloody bitch!" Kate said. They all looked sick. The water *had* poisoned them, and Heather was glad they'd had to lie there so long feeling terrible.

Ivan walked over to Tom. He was carrying something in his hand.

His plan B.

It was a jerrican of gasoline.

"This is your last chance to do something, Heather!" he yelled into the spinifex. "Whatever your plan is, Heather, it's not going to work. We're bringing more dogs tomorrow. We will find you."

"No cops have come looking for you, Heather! No one has any idea you're here! We'll bloody get you," Kate said.

"This is petrol, Heather. You really want me to do this, or do you want to give up? Last chance!"

Heather swallowed hard.

"All right, then, watch this!" Ivan said as he poured the gasoline over Tom. They were going to burn him alive in the chair.

She had only one round left. She couldn't kill all four of them.

She knew what she had to do.

It was terrible, but there was no other choice.

Could she do it? She ripped off her T-shirt, wrapped it around the barrel, and tied it over the muzzle. She took aim.

The T-shirt would do nothing about the noise but it would help conceal the muzzle flash.

"For real this time, Danny," Ivan said.

Danny lit a cigarette, took a puff, and threw the cigarette at Tom. There was a vast yellow fireball, but before Tom could even cry out, Heather shot him in the heart.

The shot echoed around the clearing.

"Where?" Ivan yelled.

"Anyone see?" Matt asked.

No one had seen.

Matt threw a blanket over the body to smother the fire.

The Toyota Hilux came with its bullet-cracked windshield and its leaking transmission. They threw Tom into the back.

"What's your plan, Heather?" Ivan yelled. "We're bringing more dogs! No cops have been round looking for you! No one's looking for you here! You're never getting off this island. Never!"

"That's right!" Kate said and they got in the Toyota and they left.

Still she waited until it was fully dark.

"You nearly got me," she whispered as she put Petra's singed, ripped T-shirt back on. She slid backward through the grass. It was her and them now. She'd get off the island or die trying. When she was half a mile away from the cave, she turned south to gather more shearwater eggs. The tide was very low. Her sneakers sank softly into the wet sand.

Was that the moon? A brand-new moon after the dark of the moon?

Yes.

A sliver of beautiful white sickle moon defiantly upside down.

She got the eggs and headed home.

When she reached the burned plateau she took a last look at the one-tree hill.

"Goodbye, Tom," she said.

44

The land had become dark.

A deep, dark ticktocking in time to the rotating stars. Olivia sat under the foliage of the eucalyptus trees. Dusty, dry, kind of ugly leaves, but each one a miracle engine that had spent the day converting light into food.

Birds in a V formation.

Starlight on the water.

She thought about Heather. Worried about her. She'd been wrong about her.

She sat on a root and cried. She cried about herself and her mom. She cried about her dad.

He was her dad, after all.

But Heather would get her and Owen out, not him. She knew that. She had to look after her little brother.

In the cave she could hear Owen cooking the snake by the fire. There wasn't going to be much meat, he'd said. It was all bony and gross. But that was OK.

Olivia stood and peered into the darkness and waited for Heather.

Either Heather would come back or her dad and Matt and the others would come. She missed her dad. She loved her dad. But she wanted it to be Heather. Her mom would have wanted it to be Heather too.

She went inside the cave mouth. If you looked very hard you could see faint drawings on the walls. Stick men and women dancing with spears. In the light of Owen's fire, they danced still.

The men and women with spears were attacking or fleeing from a monster with six legs.

After a while, Heather appeared in the cave mouth.

Olivia hugged her.

Olivia asked her a question without saying anything.

Heather nodded.

Heather put her arms around her and explained what had happened.

Olivia cried and Heather cried and they held each other for a long time.

"Look what I found," Olivia said, sniffing and showing her the cave drawings. "Some of these images are thousands of years old but some must have been done in the last hundred and fifty years. That's a man on a horse, isn't it?"

"I think so."

"They made a record of the black line, of the massacre."

"What are you guys doing up there?" Owen yelled. "I've cooked this, come down!"

They went down.

It tasted like chicken, or maybe wildfowl. It was good. It went well with the eggs.

Owen and Heather talked about TV shows and movies and music to distract themselves.

Heather didn't say anything more about Tom. Owen already knew.

They talked and ate and drank. Owen told them everything about all the videos on the Primitive Technology channel on YouTube. Heather talked about how low the tide was at the shearwater nests, and Owen explained that it was probably because of the new moon. Olivia and Owen talked about his astronomy worksheet. Everything seemed so much clearer now. Owen recited the planets and got them right this time. They did all they could not to talk about Tom.

Later, Heather sang them all the songs on *Sgt. Pepper's Lonely Hearts Club Band*.

They were tired and they settled down to sleep next to one another by the fire.

Heather picked up the rifle and slid on the safety and slept with one hand on the stock.

"That was weird, looking in the mirror yesterday," Olivia said. "I'd forgotten what I looked like."

"You know," Heather said, "when you look *really* closely, all mirrors look like eyeballs."

Olivia thought about that one and smiled.

"Guys, I'm going to try to get some sleep, all right?" Heather said.

Olivia nodded and lay there and thought about the moon.

She closed her eyes.

She began to drift into sleep.

Zodiac, moon, mother.

She sat bolt upright.

"Owen! Your homework. The new moon and the full moon. Isn't that when the lowest of the low tides are?" Olivia asked.

"Yeah. I think that's right. The spring tide. Twice a month..."
Owen's face lit up. He saw what Olivia was driving at. He
shook Heather.

"What is it? Is everything OK?" she asked.

"We know a way to get out of here," Owen said.

45

Back up in the backcountry. In the shadow of Slemish.

Aye, take it back. Somewhere in those high hills, the monster.

Escape it. Escape the poverty and the rain. Go with your ticket on the big boat. Make a new life in another land across the sea. *Good luck, love,* they said. *Good luck, love,* and that was it.

This new land. This empty land. This land of luck.

The monster following after.

I don't need this at my age. It finds you. From under the shadow of the black mountain, it comes.

I know all about her. I know the meaning of her. Morrigan the crow knows her too.

These good-for-nothing layabouts. I didn't get sick. Water? I wouldn't touch the stuff. These eejits. These larrikins. Me with my bad legs. I could do a better job. She will destroy everything I've built if I don't fix this.

"Matty! Matty, get up here! I have a plan. Matthew, where are you? Get up here!"

Him the only one not soiled by the blood.

"What is it, Ma?"

"Get up here! Your plan didn't work, but I have a plan to catch the bitch."

"What plan?" Matt said, opening the door.

"Go to the dresser. Give me that grog. My knees. My bloody knees. Who is she? How did she wreak all this havoc, Matthew?"

"I don't know, Ma. Tom said she was his massage therapist before he married her."

"She's not one of these university types?"

"No, Ma."

"Then what? What does she have? She looks like a stiff breeze would knock her over."

"Yes. I sort of thought the same thing."

"Is she lucky or is she smart?"

"I don't know."

Ma swallowed her grog with satisfaction. It was the good stuff. Well over twenty years old, but smooth. And the seaweed under the still reminded her of Bushmills. "Sit next to me on the bed, that's it. Drink?"

"I'm OK, Ma."

"I sometimes wonder if we're made of shit or if we're made of light—what do you think, Matthew?"

"Um, I don't know, Ma."

"You don't know. You don't know much, do you, Matty? But I know. I know more than you think. I know you and Terry and Kate talked about setting up some kind of tourist hotel here, Matthew."

"An eco-lodge, Ma. Terry's idea. It's all the rage these days. It would have worked. We could have brought a lot of money in. Rebranded. Secured our future. The trust fund's running out. We need to think about things like that."

"I know that! But you know why I didn't think that was a good idea? You know why I don't like strangers coming to the island?"

"Why's that, Ma?" Matt asked.

She patted his leg and smiled and gave a little cackle. "'Cause I knew she was coming. Deep in my bones. Her...someone like her. We have a good thing going here. Open the window for me, will you?"

Matt got up and opened the window. The bush smelled acrid, weary, as exhausted as her. The night's song coiled around her. The bush was indifferent. It didn't care what happened to any of them.

"We have to go forward, Matthew. Forward. Forward into the past when everything was prey. It can be as it was—for a little while, anyway. You see?"

"Not really, Ma."

"Just us, living simple. No eco-lodge, no strangers. I knew she would come and bloody ruin everything. Her, or someone like her. You know what she is, Matthew? She's the monster. The bunyip. She'll destroy us unless we destroy her. We got to get her."

"But how?" Matt asked.

"When I first came out here to the island as a wee girl, I got lost. And you know how Terry found me?"

"No."

"Sit down and I'll tell you."

46

Matt rode out of the farm on Pikey well before dawn. He was glad to get away. They had no water. No power. No one had a clue what to do except for him and Ma.

Heather was out there somewhere.

He would find her without dogs.

He had his trusty .22 small-game hunting rifle that he'd had for years. Maybe not the most deadly gun on the island, but it had low kick and high velocity, and he had never missed with it, not once.

He'd find her. He had to.

She was that thing outside that threatened their whole way of life.

He rode Pikey southeast over the kangaroo grass toward the prison.

He called in on Rory. His guts were rumbling and he threw up in Rory's outdoor toilet.

Rory hadn't seen her. The generator was down so the pump was down, so now he had no electricity or water. "If you see her, shoot her," Matt said and he rode on to the far eastern shore, where the tide was low.

The sunrise on this side of the island was always a beautiful, un-feasible vermilion. But he had no time to wait for the sun today.

"Heather?" he tried on the walkie-talkie.

Static.

He rode down to the far south where the shearwaters nested. "Heather?" he tried as he walked along the beach.

Static.

West to the ferry terminal, but Kate, who was guarding the dock, had seen no sign of her.

"Heather?"

Static.

He rode northwest up the mangrove beach.

"Heather?"

Nothing.

He rode north over the grassland where the country became hilly.

"Heather?"

Static and then a voice: "Matt?"

Ah . . . so that's where she was hiding. "Heather, why did you do all that to us? We have no power, no fuel, no water."

"Sounds like you'll have to bring the ferry over to get re-supplied."

"We'll be guarding that ferry like it's a barge out of Fort Knox."

"You almost fooled me, Matt. You're smart but I don't think you're as smart as you think you are."

"It's a pity, Heather. We could have made a deal. I know a lot of us wanted it."

"You wouldn't have kept to any deal."

"Maybe, maybe not. You didn't get to see the best of us. We were moving into the future. My brothers and I were planning an eco-tourism thing for a few years from now."

"That's a shame."

"It's a shame about Tom."

"And Hans and Petra."

"And Hans and Petra."

"So what now?" Heather asked.

"What indeed?"

"Maybe we'll stay. We like it here, me and the kids. We have water. We have food. You'll all be dead in a week, but we'll be fine," Heather said.

"Bullshit."

"It's not bullshit. Olivia was pulling up some daisies this morning, and you know what she found?"

"What?"

"The daisies are really yam flowers," Heather said. "We found yams. Growing wild. They're all over the island. Did you even know that?"

"No."

"It's so rich in food, this place. You just need to know where to look. Hundreds of Aboriginal people used to live here."

"I doubt that."

"Doubt away. We'll be fine out here in the bush while you roast and die in your wooden coffins."

"All this was your fault," Matt said bitterly.

"Oh, Matt, we're so past *fault* now. We can stay or go. We can fly across the water if we want to. The crows will carry us."

"Sounds like you're hallucinating from lack of water."

"Stay or go. Stay, I think. We have a mission. The crows will help there too."

"What are you talking about, Heather? What mission?" Matt asked.

"Deep assignments run throughout all our lives. I was given

meteor iron. It came with instructions. The past two days were just the start. Killing the dogs. Destroying your fuel. Poisoning the well. Blowing up your generator. I'll be back every night. You'll never find me. I was sent here, Matthew. I was sent here to form another line to erase your line. To erase you. Down to zero. Do you understand?"

"You wouldn't dare."

"Get all the kids over there out if you can because I'm going to cleanse this island of the O'Neills' presence."

"Have you gone mad? Did you drink seawater?"

"We're fine. We have fresh water. Plenty of it. This is our island now. We can live anywhere here, but you're trapped. Trapped on an island that's a tinderbox with a woman whose dad was a sniper and who trained her to be a sniper too."

"Bullshit!"

"Oh, he was conflicted about it, sure, but he told me it was the only thing he was ever good at. I can strip and aim and shoot any firearm ever made. I can take out a sewer rat on the beach at dusk. I can knock the scut off a rabbit at a thousand yards. You're all dead, Matt. You just don't know it yet."

Heather's signal was coming in very clear now on the walkie-talkie. She had to be within a quarter mile of where Matt was riding. There was a clump of eucalyptus trees up on a hill to the west. He'd noticed them many times before but it had never occurred to him to wonder where those big old trees drank from.

Plenty of water, she'd said.

"What's your point, Heather?"

"The point, Matt, is that time is running out for you and Ma and the others. The police are going to be here very soon and they will be looking for us and they'll find us, and the lot of you will be up on murder charges. Every one of you. I will make your life hell until then."

"Are you suggesting a deal?"

"Leave us the ferry. Everyone stay on the farm until we're off the island."

"What's in it for us, Heather?"

"I'll tell the cops Jacko killed Tom and Petra and Hans. And I killed him in self-defense."

"And what about Danny?"

"We won't mention Danny."

Matt nudged Pikey down from a canter to a trot. He was approaching the eucalyptus trees now. The sun had finally risen on another scorching day. He took his rifle out of its leather holster.

"Easy, girl," he said to Pikey. He dismounted and tied the horse to a tree.

He was feeling bad again. He dry-heaved and then pulled himself together. He pressed Talk on the walkie-talkie. "I'll have to run this past Ma," he told Heather.

"Do that."

"I will."

He walked through the trees and there in front of a cave mouth he had never seen before was the little girl. Digging for yams, like Heather said.

47

Heather looked at the radio and waited for Matt's response. Maybe there was a way out of this without more bloodshed. Without putting the kids' lives at risk by trying Olivia and Owen's plan.

Matt was the cleverest and possibly the most reasonable one of the family.

"Matt?" she said into the walkie-talkie. She'd been standing guard with the Lee-Enfield and hadn't noticed anything wrong. But the silence now was worrying.

What—

"Come out, come out, wherever you are!" Matt said, not through the walkie-talkie but from somewhere really close by.

Heather shrank behind the tree trunk.

Oh my God. He was here.

"Come out, Heather! I've got your little girl. I've got a gun pointed at her. Come out!"

How had he found—

"It's so boring, isn't it? To count down from three? But that's what I'm going to do, Heather. Three, two, one..."

Heather stepped out from behind the eucalyptus tree.

"I'm here," she said.

Matt was holding Olivia by the scruff of her neck with his left hand. He had a rifle in his right hand that he was pointing at her.

"Drop your gun or I blow this one to kingdom come," Matt said.

"Matt, no! We can make a deal."

"You Yanks and your bloody deals. Drop it now or she's dead!"

Heather dropped the Lee-Enfield.

"Very wise," said Matt. "Now put your hands up high."

She put them up.

"If you want something done right, you do it yourself," Matt said with a grin.

"How did you find us?"

"Your dad was in the army and he never taught you about radio silence? Triangulation?"

Her face fell. Triangulation. Yes. "I've been trying to remember all the things he said."

"Oh, mate, you should see your face. You look gutted. Come over here, *slowly*."

She walked toward him.

When she was twenty feet away he said, "That's enough."

"Here?"

"Hands high in the air, please. I don't want any last-minute heroics."

Heather put her hands up.

"Where's the boy? Don't lie to me."

"He's still sleeping, in the cave. We found a cave."

"He's in for a rude awakening. Hands higher, please. And farther apart."

She did as she was told. "You're not going to take me in, are you?" she asked.

Matt shook his head. "You know what? You're so much trouble, I think this is the best way for all of us. Ma says you're the bunyip."

"I keep hearing that word. What does it mean?"

"A monster from Aboriginal mythology. Hundreds of years ago, the bunyips were represented as a kind of emu, but gradually, as Europeans and their totems entered the Dreaming, the devil, the bunyip, came to be seen as white men on horses."

"Yes. I understand. The monster is us."

"The monster, indeed, is us. You've learned, Heather. There's nothing more the island can teach you. Close your eyes."

Letting Olivia go, he took aim at Heather. He braced the rifle against his shoulder and looked down the sight.

And then he shot her.

48

All she could do was fall.

It was so easy to fall.

People did it every day. The planet didn't want them up there walking around. It wanted them closer. It wanted them to become part of it.

Under the gum tree, she fell.

And in the falling, she saw the sky and the crow and she heard the rifle crack.

A sledgehammer hit her shoulder. Right where the shotgun-pellet wound had been starting to heal.

The back of her neck hit a tree root.

The pain knocked the breath out of her.

Matt hadn't killed her with his first shot, but it didn't matter.

He'd put her down.

She was down and her gun was gone and he was walking toward her with a rifle.

Olivia tried to grab his leg but he kicked her off, hard, and she doubled over in agony.

Heather looked at her shoulder. The rifle shot seemed to have gone straight through. Only a .22-caliber round but, oh Jesus, it hurt. But at least she could still feel something, which meant that she was still alive.

"Well, well, well," Matt said. "You led us a chase, didn't you? Shook things up around here."

"I tried to...what will you do now?" she said.

"I'll finish you, I think, and I'll bring in the little ones," Matt said.

"I know you, Matt. You're not like this. Do you think this is the right thing to do?"

"To defend my family against interlopers who have wreaked havoc on us? Yeah, mate, it's the right thing to do."

But he should have been shooting instead of talking. You need to focus when you're killing something, be it a rabbit, a deer, or a human being. Heather's dad had told her that. He had killed eleven men in Iraq. He had laid down a deep, multitrack memory of every one of them. He'd never spoken to her about the individual kills. But sometimes she'd hear him talking in his sleep or on the phone...

You need to blot out the world. You need to focus. Matt didn't. He checked to see where Olivia was, and he looked up as Owen came out of the cave.

It cost him two seconds.

She let gravity take her and she slid down the big shiny eucalypt root into the grass. She scrambled to her feet and began limping toward the old school bus.

Matt was unconcerned as he followed. He too wasn't in the best shape, but he was certainly faster than her. "Where do you think you're going, Heather? You think you're going to get that bus in gear and drive out of here?"

He laughed at his own joke.

Heather hobbled to the back of the school bus and collapsed into the dirt.

This was as far as she could go.

Matt grinned.

The kids were trailing him. He pointed the rifle at them. "That's far enough, you two!"

They looked terrified.

Heather managed to catch Olivia's eye. *It's going to be OK. No. Really. I wouldn't lie to you.*

Heather crawled to her left.

Matt would want to make sure with his kill shot.

He would come close.

He would come direct.

The air this morning was thick, sweet, honeyed.

There were butterflies. An egret. An old crow.

Time had slowed.

She smiled at him.

"What are you grinning for?" he said and walked straight into the dingo trap.

He screamed and dropped his rifle as the jaws snapped shut on his ankle.

That would have been it for Matt but for the fact that the trap was very old and the spring rusted. It hadn't broken his leg or severed an artery.

He stood there groaning and then with an almighty roar he managed to pry apart the mechanism.

"Shit!" he yelled and stepped out of the trap.

Blood was pouring from his ankle.

Heather hadn't stopped to look at him. She was crawling for the rifle.

"No, you don't!" Matt said and lunged at her.

The bluffing and the pleading and the reasoning were over. The game was different now. Now it was the oldest game ever invented.

Kill or be killed.

She punched him in the kidneys. He winced and headbutted her in the nose and broke it. The headbutt was almost as painful as the .22 bullet.

Blood poured into her mouth.

Matt was on top of her. He put his big meaty paws around her throat and squeezed. He was squeezing from the wrists. That was good, she thought, her massage-therapist brain kicking in inappropriately; he could kill her without straining his back. The kids were moving in fearlessly. They were going to try to attack Matt with their bare hands. They were too far away to help. *Run, just run!* she wanted to say. But they weren't runners anymore.

"Should have done this on day one," Matt snarled as he choked her.

The world tunneled.

She couldn't breathe.

Couldn't think.

How could she have thought water was so important when the only thing important was air?

The last thing she would ever see was Matt's furious red face.

Even that was fading.

Dissolving into whiteness.

Grayness.

Nothingness.

But there was one hope.

She had to remember that she was the messenger.

The messenger with the meteor iron.

Yes.

Yes . . .

Do you hear it, Matt?

The message cometh.

Matt screamed as Heather stabbed the penknife into his thigh.

She kicked him off and crawled to where the .22 rifle had come to rest.

It wasn't there.

Where?

Where on . . .

Owen was pointing it at Matt's head.

Matt was crawling toward her.

"That's enough," Owen said.

"You think you know how to use that thing?" Matt grunted.

"Heather showed us."

"We know exactly what to do," Olivia said, pointing the Lee-Enfield at him.

There was no way for Matt to know that the Enfield was empty and that Owen had probably not loaded another round in the .22.

Matt looked at the rifles and put his hands in the air. "Relax, kiddies. I'm not bloody going anywhere. How can I? She stabbed me, and look at me ankle," he said.

"If he so much as farts in my direction, shoot him the way I showed you. I'm getting my damn penknife back."

Heather pulled the knife out of the meaty part of Matt's thigh and put it in her pocket. His ankle was a bloody mess and his thigh wound was surprisingly deep, but he would live.

She examined the wound in her shoulder. It hurt like hell but it was a small-caliber round and she wasn't bleeding badly—she would live too.

"What are you going to do now, kill me?" Matt asked.

"Well, Matt," Heather replied, "you've found our hiding place, so I guess the smart thing to do would be to kill you. But that would be murder. And that's not our style. We're going to get a vehicle and get off Dutch Island and then we're going to call the cops."

"And then we're going to leave you a *really* horrible rating on Tripadvisor," Owen said.

49

They tied his hands behind his back with his belt and shoved him in the cave mouth. They took his .22 rifle and made their way to the farm.

They crawled through the grass until they were five hundred yards out.

Olivia and Owen's plan had been to do this at night. But they could do it during the day's low tide too. It would just be more dangerous.

They would need a distraction.

The wind was blowing steadily from the west.

Heather pulled up ten little bundles of the kangaroo grass and spaced them each a yard apart. She took out Jacko's lighter and set fire to every mound. The conditions were perfect. New growth after the rain; dry fuel; steady wind.

The fire caught fast and ran east the way it was supposed to do.

Fire wasn't scary. If you stood on the windward side of the fire, you could watch it work.

For two thousand generations the Indigenous people had used fire as a tool for managing this terrain. Fire became an enemy only if you couldn't move.

If, for example, you had to defend a house.

"Come on, kids," Heather said and they cut south up a small hill.

It was only an hour past dawn and the sun was low in the sky but there was plenty of light for them to see the fire tear through the undergrowth toward the O'Neill farmstead.

Someone started yelling, and men and women and children began heading to the west of the compound. They must have had an emergency generator stored away somewhere because a firehose was produced and it started pumping water from the well.

She wasn't too disappointed by that. It would give them something to do other than just abandon ship.

"Let's move," she said.

They kept low until they were a few hundred yards away and then they got on their bellies and crawled.

They had become good at this.

They crawled to within fifty feet of the farmyard.

Are you sure this is going to work, kids? Heather was tempted to ask but did not. What choice did they have?

They made it to the farmyard and hid behind the big barn. Everyone was out fighting the fire. And there were no dogs sounding the alarm.

"What do we do if it's locked?" Owen asked.

Heather bit her lip. No other car would do. It had to be the hideous Porsche Cayenne with its big, ugly-beautiful snorkel.

She tried the handle.

The door opened. This particular vehicle had a key and a push-button start. It was a Wi-Fi proximity key. As long as the key was somewhere in the car, all you needed to do was put your foot on the brake and press the start button.

The kids climbed inside. She put her foot on the brake and pressed the start button.

Nothing happened. She pressed it again. Nothing. A third time—nothing. She searched the car but there was no sign of the key.

"The key must be inside the house. Wait here, stay low, keep the doors closed, I'll be back in a second," Heather said. She handed Olivia Matt's .22 rifle. "I think there's two rounds left in this thing. Stay in the car. If anyone tries to drag you out, shoot them."

Olivia nodded. "I will," she said.

Heather closed the driver's-side door and took the empty Lee-Enfield rifle and ran to the house. Everyone was outside attending to the fire. Where would they keep a key? She looked for hooks on the wall or a little dish by the front door. Nothing like that. If she didn't find that key, they were lost. You couldn't hot-wire a modern car the way you could an older model. The proximity key needed to be in the god-damn car.

She remembered the stairs up to Ma's room.

She took them three at a time.

At the top of the steps there was a very long hall with half a dozen doors.

"Shit."

The first door she opened was a man's bedroom with a pair of jeans lying on the floor.

The second room was a bathroom.

She was running out of time.

"What are you looking for?" a voice said.

It was a very little girl with big brown eyes.

"I'm looking for my car keys and my phone," Heather said.

"Did you set the grass on fire?" the girl asked.

"Yes. I'm sorry about that. I probably shouldn't have done that. I thought everyone would go and fight the fire and we could escape."

"It's OK. It goes like that every year in the summer. We're used to it. I'm Niamh, by the way," the girl said, offering her hand.

Heather shook the hand. "Heather," she said solemnly.

"Your phone and the keys will be in Ma's room. At the end there."

"Thank you, Niamh," Heather said.

She walked to the end of the hallway. The door opened onto a hot, dusty, stuffy room with a massive four-poster bed, a tallboy, and other ancient pieces of wooden furniture. The walls were covered with faded black-and-white photographs of men with elaborate beards and women with elaborate dresses. There was a framed ship's ticket from Liverpool to Sydney and next to it a photo of a pretty, ridiculously young girl with a suitcase trying to look like a grown-up.

"Jesus! What do you think you're bloody doing!" a voice said.

Heather turned. It was Ma with a little blond-haired boy she was leaning on for support.

"It's time for us to go," Heather said.

"I don't give you permission to go," Ma said.

"You're not in a position to give permission," Heather said.

"It's my island!"

"It's not your island and it never was. Where's the key to the Porsche?" Heather asked, pointing the rifle at Ma's head.

"You won't shoot."

"Ask Jacko if I won't shoot. I'll shoot you and your grandson."

"You're an animal!"

"Where's the key!" Heather screamed, pointing the empty rifle at the little boy's head.

"Nightstand. Right next to the bed," Ma said.

Heather saw the key in a little dish beside the bed on top of all their phones. She shoved the key and the phones in her pockets.

"What's all that yelling, Ma?" a dazed-looking Danny asked, wandering in from the hall. Heather pointed the empty Lee-Enfield at him.

"Hands behind head, kneel on the ground! Now!"

Danny got down on his knees and put his hands behind his neck. "This isn't fair," he wailed.

Heather walked behind him. "I'm sorry about Ellen. I really am," she said and hit him in the back of the head with the heavy rifle stock. Danny fell face-first onto the ancient floorboards.

"As soon as they see you coming, they'll back the ferry offshore. You're screwed," Ma said with a cackle.

"We would be screwed if this *was* an island," Heather replied.

A cold lick of hatred in Ma's eyes. She fortune-told. She could see what this young woman would do to all she had built here if she was allowed to live.

It was also a look of recognition. A mirror. She'd come here as a young woman and mixed things up and married in and destroyed things and built things all those years ago.

Ma lashed weakly at her with her cane. "I'll have you, you bitch!" she said furiously.

"Well, you'd better move fast."

Heather ran down the hall. She waved goodbye to little Niamh and bolted down the stairs. She darted across the farmyard to the Porsche.

"It's me," she said as she opened the driver's-side door. Olivia, in the front passenger seat, grinned and relaxed her grip on the rifle. Heather placed her foot on the brake and pushed the start button, and the Porsche roared into life.

She drove around the farmhouse, checked where the sun was, and headed east.

In the rearview mirror, she saw Matt on horseback galloping into the farmyard.

"Matt!" Olivia said.

"On a horse!" Owen added.

"I see him! Damn it. Keep an eye out behind us, Owen, they'll be after us soon," Heather said after a minute.

"I think they already are!"

"No way!"

She looked in the mirror.

A bunch of them had piled into the Toyota Hilux and were getting it going.

She looked ahead.

Red sun.

Lens flare.

In her head, music from the Pixies, "Gouge Away"—a little on the nose, but so be it.

She drove over the boggy heath, the Porsche bumping over the land. Not *their* land. Never was.

She hoped the kids were right. She hoped the pamphlet from the prison was correct. Two days a month, on the low tide with the full moon and the low tide with the new moon, Dutch Island became a peninsula.

"Look out!" Owen said and she swerved around the wreck of a VW Beetle, beautiful in its red rust, sitting in the grass like an ankylosaurus.

If they crash, they get another car. If we crash, we're dead, Heather thought.

A bullet smashed into the rear window.

Olivia screamed.

"Everyone OK?" Heather asked.

"I'm OK," Owen said.

"Should I fire back?" Olivia asked, holding Matt's rifle.

"Just keep your head down, honey! Both of you!"

She drove around a tree stump and went straight toward a channel that might have been an old drainage canal or a river made wider by the rains.

The hood of the car dived nose-first into the canal and three things happened at once: something heavy ground against the axle, the car veered sideways, and a sheet of mud and brown water sloshed onto the windshield.

"Incoming!" Owen yelled as they slewed toward the wall of the far bank of the channel. They hit it sideways; the car stalled and then stopped.

She hit the wipers and the water-spray button. Nothing came out of the water spray and one of the wipers seemed to be broken.

The other worked and cleared a narrow arc in front of her face.

Visibility zero on the passenger side.

If they were impaled here against the side of the bank, it would be the end of them.

She looked in the rearview.

They were still on her ass.

She shifted down to low gear mode and pushed the start button. "Brace yourselves, kids!"

The car shuddered.

She pushed on the gas pedal until it was nearly on the floor. "Come on!" she said.

The engine growled and the Porsche seemed to understand what she wanted. Its front wheels struggled for purchase in the trench, churning mud and then slowly getting a grip. When she had sufficient momentum, she aimed for the far wall, and the Porsche began to climb over.

It climbed at a thirty-degree angle and she wondered if they were going to flip onto the roof.

Another bullet hit the back of the car with a clang and a terrifying ricochet through the side window. Glass splinters struck her on the right cheek.

"Come on, baby, you can do this, you ugly piece of shit!" she said, and thus encouraged, the Porsche crawled up over the trench and onto the heath again.

She switched back to drive mode and glanced in the rear-view. She watched the Toyota disappear into the trench and held her breath for three seconds until she saw it struggle out again.

"Shit."

Only a quarter of a mile clear run to the ocean now.

The ground was boggy but the Porsche didn't mind. She heard it ascend through the gears. Third gear. Fourth.

Another bullet dinged inside the cab and punched a hole through the windshield. This time, the entire windshield cracked.

She couldn't see anything.

She tried hitting the glass out with the flat of her hand. It didn't move.

"I can't see!"

Olivia smashed it with the butt of the rifle, and the windshield collapsed, spraying them with glass.

The walkie-talkie fizzed to life. "Give it up, Heather! You're

going to get yourself and the kids killed! Nobody wants that!"
Matt said.

Olivia looked at her. "Do you want to answer?"

"Don't worry about that. You just keep your head down."

"I can answer him from down here."

"There's nothing to say."

"Heather, please, pull over before anyone else gets hurt.
We can talk this over. Ma agrees with me that this has gone
on long enough. We can go back to the original plan," Matt
said.

She drove through the boggy grass and stole a look at the
Hilux. The Toyota had much higher wheel arches and was
making easier progress across the terrain.

But it was not so far to the sea now.

Another bullet sang past the car. She flinched after the bullet
had already missed. Olivia sat up. Heather pushed her head
down again.

Heather grabbed the walkie-talkie. "If we're going to negotiate here, Matt, I suggest you stop shooting at us."

There was a pause before Matt came back on. "We'll stop
shooting if you pull over," Matt said.

"You stop shooting first and then we'll talk."

"Where are you going, Heather? This is pointless. There's
nowhere to go."

"How much gas you got, Matthew? How's that transmission?"

"We're doing fine."

Maybe they had enough gas for one car but not enough for
the rest of the family to follow.

She looked in the rearview again. The Toyota was five car
lengths behind them now.

She was hitting fifty miles an hour. A ridiculous speed on this terrain.

She hadn't heard from Owen in thirty seconds. "Owen, are you OK back there?"

"Yeah."

They hit something; the whole car shook and went up on two wheels for a second and then came down with a heavy thud.

Rearview.

Kate driving, Matt riding shotgun. With an actual shotgun. Ivan squeezed in there too. Ash from the bushfire they'd started falling now like snow.

Matt leaned out the truck's window.

"Everyone down!" Heather said.

Birdshot tore through the Porsche.

Olivia was thrown forward into the dashboard.

"Kids!"

"I'm OK," Owen said from the floor of the car.

"Olivia? Olivia? Olivia?"

Olivia wasn't saying anything.

"Owen, get up here and take the wheel!"

"What?"

"Take the wheel!"

Owen grabbed the wheel as Heather bent over Olivia.

"What do I do?" Owen asked.

"Straight for the beach. It's on cruise control. Just steer."

Olivia was a rag doll.

Heather examined her. No gunshot wounds, but she'd hit her head.

"Uhh," she said.

"Are you OK, sweetie?"

"I'm OK."

"Heather, this is crazy! What's your plan?" Matt asked through the walkie.

Wouldn't you like to know? She looked through the smashed rear window and aimed the .22 rifle at Kate driving the Toyota. She squeezed the trigger; the Porsche hit a bump and she missed. She loaded another round and aimed at the engine block. That was a bigger target. She shot into the Hilux's engine, and she definitely hit something.

Damn it. That was the last of the .22 rounds.

"Keep your heads down, kids! I'm taking over, Owen," she said.

But before she could get both hands on the wheel, the heath ended and they were on the beach.

The Porsche went into a spin and the Toyota was on top of them.

Kate rammed them and the Porsche went up onto its side again. If they flipped, there would be no mercy. Logic demanded it. Ma demanded it.

Kate would slam on the brakes. Matt and Ivan would get out, drag them out of the car, and execute them one by one.

Heather wasn't going to allow that to happen.

She slid her legs back into the seat and fought to bring the Porsche level.

The car landed with a heavy clump.

Her foot found the gas pedal.

The Porsche began to accelerate. Kate was still behind her but the Toyota's windshield was cracking.

"Gotta smash that glass somehow," Heather muttered.

"What about this?" Olivia asked, lifting *The Complete Stories and Plays of Anton Chekhov* from the floor.

"Go for it!" Heather said. Olivia switched the book to her left softball-pitching arm, took aim, and tossed the heavy hardback Tom had lugged all the way from Seattle.

It curved across the excited air like a tiercel on its killing parabola and hit the corner of the windshield, shattering it.

"Yes!" Olivia said.

The Toyota veered chaotically as Kate punched out the frozen glass.

Heather slowed and drove them along the beach, looking for the causeway they'd read about. The causeway that appeared only at the lowest of low tides, with the new moon and the full moon.

Where was it?

Where was it?

Where—

There. A little line under the water that went from Dutch Island to the mainland.

She accelerated the Porsche into the sea and pulled the lever that activated the snorkel.

She reached the causeway no one knew about except the two kids.

"We're in the sea!" Owen said.

The causeway was about a foot underwater.

She wasn't sure what to expect and was alarmed when the Porsche began filling with seawater.

Water sloshed around their feet.

The Toyota was still following them.

Olivia and Owen got off the floor as the water got deeper.

The whole car was swimming. She checked the mirror.

They were halfway across.

The Porsche's snorkel was working well.

The current lifted them and began to carry them.

The current set them down again.

"Shit!"

The wheels lost their grip and gained their grip.

The Toyota was still in pursuit.

They were two-thirds of the way across.

"Shark!" Olivia said, sitting up.

Heather opened up the penknife and held it in her mouth. She pitied the goddamn shark that was going to mess with her now.

Come on. Come on.

Water.

Land.

Water.

Come on. We're flying! Under the crow's wing. Under the sickle moon. We're swimming. With the fishes and the—

No . . . we're driving. The wheels were turning; they had hit sand.

"Do you feel that, kids?"

She drove through surf.

Something solid under all four tires. They were on the beach. The mainland!

She looked in the rearview.

The Toyota was just behind them, coming close for a last-ditch ram—

Nope.

The Toyota lost its grip, hit a wave, and flipped.

Heather turned on her iPhone. She had no idea that in Seattle, Carolyn *had* called Jenny, the conference rep, and the Victoria police had been looking for them where the Porsche's GPS had last pinged. If she could get a signal on the phone, they would be rescued in minutes.

The phone came on.

The battery was at 3 percent.

She drove up the dunes onto a deserted beach road and discovered she had a full bar of bandwidth signal. There was a text from Carolyn about *Star Trek: Voyager*.

"Is the phone working?" Olivia asked.

"Yes!" she said and dialed 000.

50

It *was* a dream. It could not possibly have happened.

Tom had dreamed them to the far side of the world.

And she had dreamed them home again.

It was dark out. The kids were sleeping.

She put the hot chocolate mug back on the coffee table next to a Dunkin' Donuts box, a *Seattle Times,* a meteor-iron penknife, and a long letter from Carolyn with song lyrics inside.

She got up and peeked through the curtains. No TV van there today. Yesterday KIRO 7 and before that CBS.

The TV was on as a candle against the dark. The Home Shopping Network, which was always upbeat even at three in the morning. Especially at three in the morning.

She had work to do at this hour. Forms to sign. The Victoria police and the Australian government could not have been more kind. After she'd been discharged from the hospital, they had let her go. They believed her when she said she would come back for any possible trial.

She didn't really know if she *would* come back. The kids

shouldn't have to go through all of that. Now, safe in their house in far-off America, they were sleeping. And the therapists and Dr. Havercamp said they were doing well, considering. They were both off their meds, and that was something, anyway.

Heather sat back on the couch and flipped through the channels.

Five hundred channels but in the wee hours, nothing as cheery as HSN.

She was thinking about phoning them to buy a duster on a long piece of plastic when there was a noise at the top of the stairs.

"Are you down there?" Owen asked.

"I'm here, honey."

"I heard something."

"It was me, I'm awake down here, watching TV. Stay there. I'll come up."

She checked in on Olivia, who was sleeping soundly. She tucked Owen back into bed and kissed him on the forehead.

"Can we go see Grandma and Grandpa on Goose Island this weekend?" Owen asked.

"Of course we can, but Grandma might want to paint you. And I know you hate that."

"It'll be OK," Owen said.

"Sure, honey. Try to go back to sleep."

"I will. I was thinking about something. Olivia's right about something."

"What?"

"She says your singing is OK."

"She said that?"

"Yes. You should sing somewhere. Like at a coffee shop or something. We'd come to see you."

"Maybe I will. Good night, Owen."

"Good night..."

"You don't have to say it."

"I'm gonna say it."

"You don't have to," Heather insisted.

"I want to."

"Kid, I don't even need it."

"Good night, M...o...m," he said, giggling and whispering the letters like they were a spell.

She slipped back downstairs.

She thought about the O'Neills. She'd read only yesterday that there was a proposal to remove the entire family from Dutch Island while Victorian government officials investigated their title deeds; it was said that they were considering giving the land back to its native owners, the Boon Wurrung people.

Maybe that would be something good that would come from all of this?

Maybe.

She opened the front door, opened the screen door, sat on the stoop, and lit a cigarette.

West Seattle was quiet. The Sound was calm.

The moon was up and so bright you could see the snowy mountains of Olympic National Park. There was a crow on the telegraph wire in front of Starbucks.

She knew it wasn't the same crow. Only the shearwaters made that journey from Australia to here. Not crows.

Still, it was looking at her like it knew her. And saying hello cost nothing.

"Hi," she said.

She finished the cigarette and found herself locking the door, pocketing the key, and crossing the empty street to a deserted Alki Beach.

She could see her breath in the moonlight.

The beach was pristine; summer was coming and they raked it every night.

She kicked off her old Converse slip-ons and stood on one of the rake's curves, her toes in the cool sand.

She lifted one leg and let the Earth rotate slowly beneath her feet.

She breathed in and out.

In and out.

She let the tension ease from her shoulders. Her left shoulder in particular, which still ached.

She remembered the Makah word for "water" that her grandmother had taught her: *wa'ak*.

Her grandmother was gone and the last native Makah speaker had died years ago. She thought of that other magic word that she was still extremely skeptical about.

"Mom," she said and smiled. It was all still true. She was too young. She'd never even been an aunt or a babysitter. But sometimes you're given a mission and sometimes you're good at that mission.

She rolled her sweatpants to her knees and stepped into the opaque water.

It was cold.

Very cold.

The beach was kind of eerie.

She was alone here in the dark, but really, there was nothing to be afraid of. She could look after herself and her family. And this was her place. Her home.

A breeze rippled the stillness.

She hugged herself and found that she was crying.

Tears pouring down her cheeks into the crescent moon reflected on Puget Sound.

She looked east toward the rest of the continent.

It was well before sunrise.

But all you had to do was wait.

Patience was a weapon.

If you waited long enough, the dawn would come.

ACKNOWLEDGMENTS

I should say at the outset here that although Dutch Island is a real place (with a different name) the people who live there are unlike the inhabitants in *The Island*. The geography has not been fictionalized very much but the island's residents have. I lived in Melbourne from 2008 to 2019 and I can assure you that Victoria is the friendliest state in Australia.

This book could not have been written without the help of my agent and buddy Shane Salerno. On the phone one day Shane and I were arguing about movies as per usual and I was recounting a *Deliverance* moment I once had in real life: While I was driving in rural Australia on a very isolated island inhabited by one large extended family, a woman wearing a hearing aid pulled out of a blind road on her bicycle and I swerved to miss her. I half jokingly told my wife, Leah, that if—God forbid—we had hit her we wouldn't have gotten off that island alive. When I told Shane this story, he said, "No, you *did* hit her; that's your next book." Shane shepherded this novel through several drafts, during Covid lockdown, when the last thing I wanted to do was write. If you're lucky enough to have Shane Salerno in your corner you're fortunate indeed.

At Little, Brown I want to thank Michael Pietsch and Bruce Nichols, who are great champions for their authors and lovely people. Little, Brown has always put a premium on art and artists and the whole team there has been nothing but a fount of encouragement. Craig Young in particular has been a friend and protector right from the beginning and also a force of nature, captaining the ship through the storm when I'm sure I wasn't the only author who was having trouble dealing with the pandemic. I want to thank my editor, Helen O'Hare, for all her brilliant suggestions, humor, and astute comments. I also want to praise my wonderful copyeditor, Tracy Roe, with whom I dueled and dialogued in the margins of *The Island*.

I need to thank my entire family in Ireland for being such cheerleaders of my writing, particularly my mum, Jean McKinty; my sisters and brothers, Diane, Lorna, Rod, and Gareth; my auntie, Catherine, and all my wee nephews and nieces over there.

I've been fortunate to make a lot of mates in the crime fiction and broader writing community and I want to pay tribute to Don Winslow, Steve Hamilton, Steve Cavanagh, Diana Gabaldon, Stu Neville, Daniel Woodrell, Brian McGilloway, Liz Nugent, Gerard Brennan, Ian Rankin, Val McDermid, Abir Mukherjee, Jason Steger, and many others whom space constraints preclude but who know I love them.

Huge thanks to Jeff Glor and the entire team at CBS News for making me look good on national television (skillful editing and special effects must have been employed there). Thank you too to all my American friends and family and particularly my mother-in-law, Susan Vladeck.

I want to say a quick thank you to Salman Rushdie and James

Ellroy, whom I interviewed just before the Covid crisis and to whom I cheekily pitched the idea for *The Island* to get their take. Both of them came up with ideas that made it into the book.

This novel was written in lockdown with my family in a tiny New York City apartment. My two rescue cats, Miffy and Jet, should get a mention because they were there with me at three a.m., when everyone else was asleep. I want to thank my amazing daughters, Arwynn and Sophie, for making me smile, giving the best hugs, and keeping me sane. Finally I want to thank my beautiful wife, Leah, for being part of this sanity anchor thing, as well as for all the years of love and encouragement and for laughing at my—admittedly hilarious—jokes.

ABOUT THE AUTHOR

Adrian McKinty was born and grew up in Belfast, Northern Ireland. He studied philosophy at Oxford University before moving to New York in the mid-1990s. His debut novel, *Dead I Well May Be,* was published in 2003 and was shortlisted for the Dagger Award and the Edgar Award. In 2011, after moving to Australia with his wife and children, McKinty began publication of the critically acclaimed Sean Duffy series. In 2019, after becoming an Uber driver and nearly quitting writing, he published the award-winning and #1 international bestseller *The Chain,* a stand-alone crime novel that appeared on over twenty-five major "best book of the year" lists, including that of *Time.* McKinty's books have been translated into over thirty languages and he has won the Edgar Award, the International Thriller Writers Award, the Ned Kelly Award (three times), the Anthony Award, the Barry Award, the Macavity Award, and the Theakston Old Peculier Crime Novel of the Year Award.

Also by Adrian McKinty

THE CHAIN

Winner of the International Thriller Writers Award Best Novel of the Year

"This nightmarish story is incredibly propulsive and original. You won't shake it for a long time." —Stephen King

"This is more than nail-biting; think cuticle-shredding." —Bethanne Patrick, *Washington Post*

"Sharply observant, intelligent, and shot through with black humor." —Tana French

"A chilling, diabolical page-turner you'll want to savor." —*People*

"Thrillers don't get much more psychologically rich than *The Chain*." —David Canfield, *Entertainment Weekly*

"McKinty is so good, I'm really starting to hate him." —Lee Child

"*The Chain* is that rare thriller that ends up being highly personal... A satisfying and deeply rewarding read." —Tod Goldberg, *USA Today*

MULHOLLAND BOOKS
Available wherever paperbacks are sold